ADVANCE PRAISE FOR
DISASTER'S CHILDREN

"Emma Sloley has created a lush dystopian novel that is a mesmerizing read as only the magnetic pulls of love and catastrophe can be in the hands of a deft writer. Parallels between Marlo's world of the near future and our own present time raise complex questions about how far we're willing to go for each other in the face of climate emergency. This was an adventure that kept me guessing and hoping for an outcome that would have an answer for us as much as it did for Marlo and her community."

—Jimin Han, author of *A Small Revolution*

"In *Disaster's Children*, Emma Sloley does that wonderful thing that so few postapocalyptic books can do: she builds a convincing and terrible new world but fills it with the kind of warm, brave, remarkable people you're sorry to leave. I wanted a better world for them, too, and I (reluctantly) closed the book, hoping they'll get it."

—Amber Sparks, author of *The Unfinished World: And Other Stories*

"*Disaster's Children* is the kind of book I love, a great story that lets me live out a fantasy alongside a relatable heroine. Marlo has grown up on a beautiful ranch in a communal life. That sounds ideal to me, so I was riveted as Marlo began to question the premise of the lifestyle her parents and others had created. There's a great big story here but also many small moments I savored and reread as I went along. Emma Sloley is a terrific new talent, and I am her fan."

—Alice Elliott Dark, author of *In the Gloaming*

DISASTER'S
CHILDREN

DISASTER'S CHILDREN

EMMA SLOLEY

Text copyright © 2019 by Emma Nicole Sloley
All rights reserved.

Published by Little A, New York

www.apub.com

Amazon, the Amazon logo, and Little A are trademarks of Amazon.com, Inc., or its affiliates.

ISBN-13: 9781542004060 (hardcover)
ISBN-10: 1542004063 (hardcover)
ISBN-13: 9781542004077 (paperback)
ISBN-10: 1542004071 (paperback)

Cover design by Kimberly Glyder

Printed in the United States of America

First edition

For Adam

1

Marlo finished checking the perimeter. As usual, there was nothing out of the ordinary to report, nothing you could put into words, anyway. She kicked at a bald patch of earth with her scuffed sneaker: scrutinizing the shoe's frayed edges and the dirt-rimmed grommets that stared sightlessly at her like rows of gummed-up eyes, she realized it was high time to buy a new pair. It was hard to care about new clothes when you lived out here, though. Who would they be for, exactly?

As she skirted the edge of an aspen grove, the late sun strobed through the leaves and stippled her hair. She kicked off her shoes and swung them by the laces as she stalked barefoot through the field. There was a primal thrill to this naked contact with the earth—nothing but a buzz cut of grass between her soles and the membrane of the planet. The sky, veined with wispy clouds, was turning from blue to lavender at the edges. The smooth pale rocks that she'd always thought looked like humped-over men praying gleamed silver under the sun's final attentions. A scoop of moon just visible, lurking. She loved this liminal time of the evening, a held breath before darkness devoured the light. Hungry and impatient, like her.

Some of the others preferred to take a companion along on these perimeter checks. It took several hours to trace the entire property and it could get lonely and boring. But it was one of Marlo's favorite chores, and she always opted to travel solo when it was her turn. A kind of jealousy drove her toward solitude, an urge to defend her alone time even in the face of loneliness. *Communal living isn't for everyone* was the go-to phrase Marlo's parents pulled out on the very rare occasion when a rancher would decide to fly the coop, but Marlo guessed they didn't include their daughter in this subset. It wouldn't have occurred to them. Though she was well beyond the usual stage at which offspring seek independence from their guardians—her twenty-fifth birthday had come and gone with little fanfare—her parents assumed she loved the place as much as they did, and most of the time that was true. On nights like this, though, the old chafing started up again, the absence of her friends, Alex and Ben, who'd recently departed the ranch, like an abscessed tooth she couldn't stop worrying with her tongue. There were no fences, apart from the one sealing the ranch off from the main road at the southern edge, but she didn't need posts and wire to know its delineation. Like anyone who had grown up there, she kept a map of the ranch and its invisible borders in her head.

She paused in the shadow of a pine forest, inhaling. In her throat the sharp tug of turpentine, the sweet stink of resin. She hummed under her breath as she plunged inside, some terrible pop song dredged up from the ether, but there was no one around to hear her. She was in the southwestern corner of the ranch now, and most of the homes were north of here, closer to the lake or in the high country—what a Realtor might call the prime locations. The ranch's sprawling contours took the form of a misshapen heart, bisected by the river and the main road that traced the water's edge. The homes were all clustered in the lush upper quadrant of the heart's left ventricle; across the river, in the right ventricle, were the sheds, greenhouse, and farmlands where they grew the crops and grazed the animals. The first lights from the nearest prime homesteads already glowed yellow through the trees, but from this lonely vantage point they looked impossibly far away, dim constellations at the ragged edge of the galaxy.

She emerged from the gloom of the forest into a clearing; beyond that was the ridgeline, falling gently away into a shallow canyon. She strode toward it, glancing once instinctively over her shoulder. In one of those arcane accidents of land distribution when the boundaries had first been drawn up, a small arrowhead-shaped sliver of land on the canyon floor—a notch out of the bottom of the heart—ended up belonging to their neighbors. Officially she was supposed to skirt the canyon, travel north along the edge of the ridge and then back down the other side, in order to stay within the ranch's boundaries. But she couldn't resist the illicit charge that came from stepping over the invisible border and onto their land. She scrambled over the lip of the ridge and careened down the slope and into the canyon, black hair flying behind her like a silk flag.

Now she was officially trespassing. The owners of this foreign land were farmers and cattle ranchers, and they had established an informal agreement with their neighbors on either side to keep the land between them unfenced so the cattle could range freely, moving from the valley floor up the slope to the ranch's rich pastures if they chose. The residents from Marlo's ranch were offered a nominal yearly grazing fee, which they had accepted not for the financial reward but because they were keen to be amenable and gain acceptance into the wider community. That was at the beginning, though. Now they mostly kept to themselves.

But the borders remained porous: in this great wide land what use were fences? Unlike the cows, which couldn't be expected to understand or respect arbitrary boundaries, the human inhabitants largely stayed off one another's land. Sometimes the newer arrivals had to be indoctrinated into these unspoken codes of country etiquette, especially if they had formerly been city dwellers.

She lingered for a few minutes alone, without even the cattle for company—they must have been ruminating elsewhere—before heading back up the slope to her own territory, weighed down a little by the anticlimax of it all. As she was ambling back to the vehicle, something exploded out of one of the nearby chokecherry trees. She jumped as a shape grazed the top of the tree. It was a huge owl, the feathers of its underside glowing like pale fire as it flapped slowly away. Her heart skittered, breath coming quickly out of her nostrils like a high-strung horse. She felt hotly ashamed. Not like her to be so jumpy. Perhaps the argument she'd had with her father earlier had predisposed her to being spooked, a conversation that had started in the usual way, with him urging her to take one of the guns on her rounds.

"A lot of us do it, honey," he had said. "It's just common sense. The day might come when you'll need it, and I want you to be prepared. Your mother and I would just feel better knowing you were protected."

"Dad, I have no intention of ever using a gun," she had replied. "It would just be a hindrance. Haven't you read all those statistics, about how gun owners always end up shooting themselves or their families?" It was wicked of her to conjure up this horror, but she knew it would give him pause.

It was funny how comfortable they had become with firearms since moving to the ranch. Marlo knew that in the time before, when they still lived in the city, her parents had exercised the same healthy distrust of guns as all the rest of their elite liberal friends. They were so touchy these days, so convinced that inanimate objects—for instance, the shiny row of rifles lined up in a locked mahogany cabinet in the main house—possessed some kind of innate protection, like magical talismans warding against harm. It bordered on religious, which she found ironic.

Marlo had won the argument this time, mostly by offering him a compromise—"I'll wear a helmet on the ATV, OK?"—to address another of the hazards that worried her parents. At least the horror of an ATV flipping and crushing her was a concern marginally grounded in reality, unlike the other amorphous dangers that worried at them. It galled her to be coddled like this, as if years on the ranch didn't work in the same way as they did in the outside world. Like she was still ten years old. As soon as she was out of sight of the house, she took the helmet off and fastened it to the rear rack, where it bounced around like a disembodied head.

The sky was shot through with streaks of silver and pink by the time she got to the chickens. She herded them from the straw-covered yard into their coop and watched them troop single file up the little wooden catwalk and into their barn, modeled after a miniature Tudor farmhouse. She pulled the ramp up after them, bolted it into place, and locked them in. Across the wooden bridge that spanned the river on the southern boundary of the ranch, she stopped to talk to the goats in their pen. Someone had already put them inside for the night; not that they were in much danger from predators, the hardened old warriors, but it was safer to keep them fenced in so they didn't roam and wreak carnage on anything edible. They were not altogether trustworthy, with their vertical pupils and their sly tendency to butt their heads against you when you turned your back to them, but she loved their resiliency. The way they seemed to always have something they wanted to tell you. Once, years ago, the ranchers had tried making goat milk soap, but it made everyone's skin smell like curdled milk.

She drove to a neat cluster of glinting tin sheds, emptied a container of food scraps onto the compost heap, wrinkling her nose at the rich vegetal stench of decay, and skirted the cedar boxes that contained the beehives. The bees were someone else's purview, and she had always been a little wary of them, with their protectiveness and sudden rages. She peered into the giant geodesic greenhouse but didn't go inside. It glowed in the day's last light like an idling spaceship, like something alive but in stasis. The greenhouse was one of her favorite things, this structure that was both futuristic and a relic from some other, more proper time. She could conjure Victorian ladies in crinolines wandering the narrow walkways, tending to their orchids, but also scientists in white hazmat suits conducting sinister grafting experiments. It had been inspired by the Biosphere 2 experiment in Oracle, Arizona. Strange to have been inspired by a failed experiment, but as one of her teachers had once explained, the biodome had only been a failure because it was ahead of its time.

They didn't use it for living in, as the scientists had, but for growing plants year-round, a feat that would have been otherwise impossible through a frigid Oregon winter. It was an ingenious geothermal system: a series of pipes conveyed the winter air from outside to forty feet underground, capturing the thermal heat and transporting it back into the greenhouse, which was fitted with a state-of-the-art irrigation system and solar panels. There was the pleasure of tomatoes in June; the soft, fuzzy bloom of peaches as part of a cheese plate on a wintry night; avocados year-round, when the only ones in the supermarkets were as rock hard and unyielding as golf balls.

She got back on the ATV, inserted earbuds, and cranked the music and began to make her way home. She was traveling along the paved main road, approaching the big lake, when a flash of white caught her eye. There was something about it that felt out of place. She slowed down, reversed to where she thought she had spotted it, and peered out into the dusky gloom. It was that time of the evening when ordinary objects began to haze and distort, to insist on morphing into other things. But there it was again. In a small clearing beyond a stand of old-growth pines, something white glowed from the ground. It might have been a stray plastic bag, except they didn't use those. And it looked bulky, like a package. Marlo jumped down from the ATV, pushed tugging, sharp branches aside as she entered the grove, and looked over her shoulder a couple of times. No matter how acclimatized she was to walking alone in the woods, there was still something uncanny about the sound of her own footsteps on the carpet of pine needles and dead leaves, the momentary delay of the crackle of shoe meeting leaf that made it sound as though someone were following. It was easy to freak herself out. But there was no one in sight.

Even before she reached the shape, she could tell it was a carcass. But what kind? It was too small to be a deer or coyote. Perhaps one of the chickens, dragged here by a fox and abandoned when it heard her engine. It had the dimensions of a bird. Closer still, and she saw a snowy head and tail feathers like it had been dipped in white paint at both ends. Then she knew. She had never seen one in real life before, but its contours were unmistakable. The eagle lay in the grass with its haughty head in profile, yellow crescent beak and wings outstretched as though it were still suspended in flight, one eye pressed to the ground like it was busy scrutinizing something below the earth.

She knelt down, expecting to see blood. But the feathers were completely pristine, the yellowed claws folded as though in the act of gripping a branch. She found a robust twig nearby, turned the bird over gently, but there were no visible wounds on the other side either. The body was heavier than she expected, disconcertingly fleshy and soft. The eagle's eyes gazed off sightlessly, not yet fully clouded by death. She knew that ascribing to the bird qualities like dignity and strength was nothing more than anthropomorphizing—something they tried to avoid doing—but it was impossible to shake those associations.

She glanced around the clearing, making sure there weren't any predators waiting in the shadows to reclaim their kill, then sat up on her haunches and pulled her phone from the pocket of her hoodie. The signal wasn't great out here in the woods, and she could have just driven to one of the homes instead, but she felt suddenly alone and craved even this sterile reminder that civilization and its various discontents were close by. As soon as she heard her mother's anxious voice she regretted it. It was as though her parents were perpetually waiting for the phone call informing them that their tireless efforts to protect their daughter from all the world's dangers had failed. Now a minor crisis would be set in motion, with Marlo as a central actor. She could have just buried the eagle, not told anyone about it. What could any of them do about it now? Perhaps it had died of natural causes.

A single white feather from the head lay a few inches away from the body. It was perfect, unblemished, a miracle of aerodynamic design.

She picked it up, held it to the dying light for a moment, moved that something so solid could also be so ephemeral, then slipped it into her pocket. As she waited cross-legged in the clearing for the others to arrive, she looked around and was reminded that spring had arrived late this year. There had been something strange about the turning of the season, something out of kilter. It remained unspoken, but it had infected everyone on the ranch as winter moods stretched into April and May. She wondered if the melancholy she had been feeling these last few weeks, a melancholy that bore down as she sat waiting in the lonely clearing with the felled eagle, was communally felt or her own invention. Her life was a clean, blank notebook, waiting to be filled in. There were days when it felt as though she would never grow, never work a conventional job, never get married or even entangled. Never learn anything new. Never leave.

She stroked the feather in her pocket, feeling its strange springy, oily resistance, both drawn and repulsed by it. Was that why birds had never really taken off as our companion animals, the foreignness of their feathers? Not like cats and dogs, with their tactile coats and expressive eyes and humanlike smells. Birds were so resolutely alien.

Three cars pulled up in succession. Her parents emerged from the first one, her mother, Maya, radiating nervous energy, and her father, Carlton, moving more laboriously and with slow deliberation, gripping the edge of the car door for support in hoisting himself out. Then there was the welcome sight of her dapper middle-aged friends, Neil and Jay, in the second car, and someone else emerging from the third. She craned her neck to see. Simon. The sight of him jolted her; she hadn't expected him to show up for something like this. It wasn't so much that he was an ex-boyfriend—the limited dating landscape of the ranch meant there was a lot of unavoidable sexual cross-pollination, and their split years ago had been amicable—but that he'd turned strange over the last year, angry and withdrawn ever since he had married the quiet twenty-year-old daughter of some recent recruits from Alabama. Julia.

That was it. Marlo had to strain to even remember her name. Simon rarely got involved in ranch matters anymore, and while she'd always considered him a strange bird, these days his company tended to verge on the creepy. He seemed aggrieved all the time, simmering with rage. Marlo walked toward the new arrivals, hooked her arm through her father's, and guided him toward the clearing.

The six of them formed a loose circle around the dead bald eagle, as if preparing to enact some kind of death rite. Everyone but Carlton dropped to the earth, kneeling or up on one knee, in order to better examine the bird.

"Be careful," said Jay. "We don't know if it's safe. It might be infected with something."

"He's right. Hold on," said Neil. He returned from the car with a box of latex surgical gloves, which he handed around. They each snapped the gloves on, and the sound ringing in the clearing lent the scene a forensic cast.

"We should do a search of the property. Anywhere that Marlo might not already have inspected today. Let's work out what happened here before we call this in to the authorities."

Marlo explained which areas she hadn't yet gotten to or hadn't looked at closely, and they prepared to disperse to various parts of the property.

"I think you should stay here, honey," said her mother. "You've had enough excitement for the night. And, Carlton, you stay as well. You look tired."

Marlo's father gave a quick nod. He did look tired, or maybe it was partly distress. He was a man who hated to swat a fly, who could be undone by the death of a favorite hen. Marlo was itching to join the others, but she knew how much her dad relished her company. He often implied that he had little time left with her, a habit of his she hated. He had his health problems—he was hobbled by rheumatoid arthritis, plagued by heart plaque, and afflicted with a stiff knee from a patellar tendon rupture acquired during his tennis days—but his insistent hinting at imminent death felt ghoulish and even cruelly manipulative in a way she didn't like to associate with him.

The two of them watched the lights of the cars recede down the main road. Marlo sighed and leaned her back against a tree trunk, its rough skin sharp against her spine. She maneuvered slightly, rubbed against the trunk to relieve an itchy spot, aware that she probably looked like one of the cows trying to get at a patch too far back on her rump to reach. Her father rested against the hood of the car, rubbing his thighs and wincing slightly.

"You OK, Dad?"

He smiled wanly. "I'm fine, honey, just the old arthritis flaring up." He inclined his head toward the clearing. "I'm in better shape than that poor critter."

She glanced over at the bald eagle. It looked so lifelike, as though it were just resting before a long flight. She half expected it to shake itself and take wing. "I wonder what happened to it."

Carlton jutted his bottom teeth out and pulled his top lip under, a gesture that signaled he was uneasy about something. "My first thought would be hunters. But haven't heard any around here lately. And there are no gunshot wounds or signs of trauma."

"It could have just been sick?" She said this more to test out the theory than because she believed it.

You didn't grow up in a community whose members referred to the world outside their utopian ranch as "the Disaster" and not jump to the most negative conclusion when birds suddenly started dropping out of the sky. "Hey, have you noticed anything odd about spring this year? Does it seem particularly late to you? I mean, the trees have only just started budding."

"Maybe, love. But the seasons have been out of whack for years. We're getting closer to the flash point, you see."

She didn't need to ask him which flash point. She had grown up under the shadow of what was coming, and the necessity of preparing for it, but it was still depressing to be reminded all the time and in such a calm, dispassionate way, as if it were all just an academic matter and not a question of life or death. Sometimes she wondered whether it was healthy, to grow up with such a heightened awareness of the end of things. Like her future was being stolen piece by piece. Her father, ever keen to any shifts in his daughter's moods, straightened up with a sudden bright smile and gestured at a clump of nearby bushes with his mother-of-pearl-handled cane, a new accessory he liked to say he carried to make himself look more distinguished.

"I'm sure it's nothing to worry about. I see a whole lot of buds over there!"

Marlo's phone buzzed. She looked at it, read the message, looked up at her father, eyes widened.

"There are more."

"Christ."

His face fell back into its melancholy lines as he pulled his own phone out and read the same message. He inhaled deeply, put his hand to his chest. Shortly afterward the two cars pulled up. The others approached, grim faced.

"We've found four already. There might be more. All the same as this one. No wounds, no signs of trauma. Completely intact, like they just dropped out of the sky."

"This is it," said Simon with quiet intensity. Marlo glanced at him; a current of excitement had run through his voice, but his face was as somber as anyone's in the crepuscular light. She noticed something glint inside the V of his shirt, stared blankly at his hairless upper chest for a moment. Without even looking in her direction, he casually fastened the shirt's top button but not before she understood what she had seen swinging there—a tiny gold crucifix. She was sure she was the only one who had noticed. It piqued her curiosity, and if he were anyone

11

else she might have asked about it. Perhaps he was wearing it ironically, or just because he liked the design, or because it was an heirloom with sentimental value. She was so unused to seeing religious symbols. Although there were no specific rules against faith-based belief systems, religious worship definitely wasn't encouraged. There had never been any trouble from that quarter: the ranch tended to be self-selecting in that way. People either embraced the idea of a society founded on rationalism, scientific principles, and open-mindedness, or they didn't. Religion was considered antithetical to a harmonious society. Look what it had wrought out in the Disaster, where for centuries people had been busy killing each other because they couldn't agree on which deity to worship.

For a few moments no one moved or spoke. They just stood there together in the thickening darkness, as if drawing collective strength for what lay ahead. Finally Jay said, "Neil and I will go back to the house, find some sacks, gather up the bodies so they don't get taken by predators overnight. And in the morning we'll report it to the Wildlife Service. They can take things from there."

"Right," said Carlton, standing up straighter, the hunched arthritic man of a few moments ago replaced by a more potent self, retrieved from some earlier time. He had always been a natural leader, galvanized by anything resembling a crisis. "Then we should all convene at the Commons. To discuss things."

Marlo moved toward the ATV. "Oh, but first, Marlo, you need to take a shower, a thorough one, you hear me? Your mother will come along with you. You had first contact. We need to make sure you wash away any possible contamination."

Marlo hesitated. It was on the tip of her tongue to point out that everyone there had made the same contact she had with the eagles, if not more, and her parents weren't insisting they all have decontamination showers, but then she looked at her parents' faces and saw the concern etched deep there, the old worry for her—their only child, their miracle, the unalloyed light of their lives—and with a sigh she acquiesced.

12

2

Some things were so beautiful you never got used to them. That's how Marlo felt about the main house. The Commons, as they all called it. Familiarity failed to dull its perfect proportions, the curvilinear purity of its form—the sight generated a shiver of pleasure in her every time. The structure rested on the ridgeline of a gentle hill, following the contours of the land like an organic form lately sprouted from the earth. While many of the ranch's homes had been designed by their owners, they'd called in the big guns for this, the future fulcrum of their community. A hotshot architect from LA who had won the Pritzker was enlisted. The building was modernist in design, low-slung and made from rammed earth and steel and concrete, its facade almost entirely constructed of massive panes of tempered glass. Two separate wings were attached to the main house via covered wooden catwalks. At night, lit from within, it glowed like secular salvation.

There was a somber feeling in the air as the six of them convened there that night. The five dead eagles had been locked inside one of the sheds until the ranchers could get Wildlife in to take a look. There wasn't much to celebrate, but someone opened a bottle of wine anyway. By the time Marlo arrived—after a long, this-side-of-scalding shower, during which her mother had hovered anxiously outside the bathroom door, urging different kinds of cleansers, scrubbing agents, and unguents on her until Marlo had shooed her away—a fire was blazing in the floor-to-ceiling stone fireplace, John Coltrane was jazzing away from hidden speakers, and someone had assembled a giant cheese plate to compensate for everyone missing dinner. It had all the hallmarks of a pleasant night in, but there was a nervousness in the air, a silent shared acknowledgement of what the dead eagles might mean. Could they be a harbinger as Simon had implied, the first sign of what they had all been dreading and waiting for? The question hovered like an uninvited guest.

Marlo curled up on one of the sofas—custom built to fit snugly into the wall and heaped with cream tasseled cushions and cashmere throw rugs—nursing a glass of wine and shoveling Brie and crackers into her mouth. She was suddenly ravenous. Doing the rounds always made her hungry. While she ate she discreetly searched the faces of the others, looking for clues, a sign of how seriously she should be taking the situation. That's how her relationship had always been with the elders in the community, a holdover from growing up among them and relying on them to provide assurances or warnings commensurate with the moment. Some habits persisted through the years.

This wasn't an official meeting: those happened on Thursday nights after the communal potluck dinner, a tradition that had been in place since the ranch's founding at the turn of the twenty-first century. In the two decades since, the meetings had morphed from a town hall–style free-for-all, during which residents took turns speaking about various concerns, to a more formal affair headed by one speaker. These days that was Neil, whose formerly freewheeling role in the community had shrunk down to this one obligation. Thinking back, Marlo could never quite pinpoint when it had been decided that everyone in the community would restrict their internet access, cease the daily burrowing down the digital rabbit hole. Everyone but Neil, who had been designated as the sole news gatherer. His job was to digest the news, sift it down so that only the most relevant parts remained, and then deliver it to everyone else in palatable, easy-to-understand bites.

Like so many of the structures in place on the ranch, this recent move to internet-free living wasn't so much a rule as a guideline. They just all happened to agree at the same time that life would be less stressful without constantly being plugged into the internet. No one policed the thing—that would have been too gauche. They didn't disconnect from the satellite or shut down their accounts. If someone lapsed and went browsing online, there was no one to chastise them. But hardly anyone did lapse, at least as far as Marlo knew. They all just kind of happily drifted away, untethered at last from their digital umbilical cords.

Their gathering tonight lacked the formal feeling of those Thursday news-delivery meetings, which were always held in the mess hall—some people called it the dining room—the only space large enough to hold all the ranchers, who these days numbered around a hundred. Those meetings tended to go one of two ways: they were mildly entertaining, if someone decided to share a funny anecdote from the week, or one of the ranchers went on a full-tilt rant about some personal grievance (the price of diesel fuel; boots left too long in the mudroom; the immorality of failing to clean the nozzle of the espresso machine properly), and the rest of the room would listen while trying to suppress laughter; or else they were fatally boring, a mind-numbing rundown of statistics or reports on ranch matters. Only occasionally, when Neil got up to read the weekly report on the Disaster and something grim had happened in the outside world, some catastrophe or violent incident like a terrorist attack, did the meetings feel full of import, connected to a wider world.

In spite of the dead eagles, Neil appeared more relaxed than usual, the burden of being the sole bearer of bad news shifted for a short time from his slender shoulders. He was fifty but could have passed for thirty, with his sandy, cowlick-prone hair, marathon runner's frame, and a soft complexion to which blushing came easily. Marlo remembered, looking at him, that he had been a publisher in his previous life. She had forgotten until now. That's how they talked about it, their previous lives. As in *I was an engineer in my previous life.* Or *I used to love playing squash in my previous life.* Marlo, who had been brought here when she was five years old, had no previous life.

15

His publishing background explained why he had been tasked with this role, a kind of contemporary town crier sharing the bad-news newsreel that summed up life out in the Disaster. It was possible he even enjoyed it, this filament of connection to his old life. But she could see it also weighed heavily on him. With so many catastrophes cascading through the world, he must have sensed that someday he would be the messenger carrying word of something truly unspeakable. And everyone knew what happened to the messengers.

Jay, Neil's husband, came over and sat down next to Marlo, stole a piece of her cheese, and chewed it with thoughtful intensity, as if he might be tested on its discrete flavors.

"Hi Jay-Jay," said Marlo, flinging her arm over his knee. That had been her pet name for him since she was a kid; he had always been one of her favorite ranchers. He secretly reminded her of his namesake bird, a blue jay specifically, alert and social and garrulous, but brimming with generosity.

"Hey, doll. Can you even believe it?"

"I know. I was shocked when I found the first one. It's terrible."

Neil wandered over as well, sat down next to Jay, and rested his head on Jay's shoulder. Jay was one of those tactile people to whom other people gravitated with arms out, seeking reassurance or comfort. As if by osmosis, the rest started moving toward their little corner as well, pulling up chairs and ottomans in a half circle facing the couches. Already the setup felt conspiratorial, their loosely affiliated party suddenly burdened with finding a solution to a problem no one else even knew about yet.

"So," began Marlo's father, in his impressive stentorian voice, which had never needed a microphone, even in the largest room. "Obviously this is an unpleasant situation that brings us all here. Such a shocking, well, *massacre* for lack of a better word."

"You think someone slaughtered them?" asked Simon. His blandly handsome face registered disgust. He was just the kind of person, Marlo realized for the first time, who would say *slaughtered* when he could have said *killed*. She remembered in a flash that he had always been unusually squeamish about anything connected with the body. Fluids, smells, illness. Once, after they had been making out for what felt like hours in one of the haylofts—had they ever been so young and hickish?—Marlo had decided to gift him with a blow job, not least because they'd been seeing one another for weeks now without venturing beyond protracted kissing sessions and she was getting bored, but as soon as she disengaged from his mouth, unzipped him, and bent her head into his lap, he had shied away like one of the jittery horses.

"What are you doing?" he'd asked in a scandalized tone that nothing in Marlo's short sexual history had prepared her for, especially when freely offering fellatio.

"Don't you want it?" she'd asked, genuinely mystified as she discreetly wiped a strand of saliva from her chafed chin.

"Of course," he had said, scrambling to fix his clothes, the rubber soles of his shoes squeaking on the hay. "Just not until we're married."

She hadn't known which part to tell Alex and Ben about first when they met for a confab afterward, to discuss the doomed relationship—the refusal of sexual favors or the unsolicited marriage suggestion.

"How is it possible that someone could be that fucking square?" Alex had marveled. Marlo had broken up with him shortly afterward, but she couldn't help feeling slightly offended when it was obvious how relieved Simon was. It wasn't as though he seemed any happier now that he was married; some people were just born dissatisfied.

As if sensing she was thinking about him, Simon turned his cold eyes toward Marlo. Perhaps he suspected her of having been behind the slaughter. Rattled, she switched her gaze to her father, who was shaking his head slowly. "Hard to say whether they were killed, but I don't think it's likely. Poison, maybe, but it's not as though bald eagles are a threat to farmers or anything like that. And most know what kind of fine they'd be facing for deliberately killing one. No, I suspect something environmental."

"Pesticides? Chemical runoff?"

"How far away do you think the eagles were when it happened, whatever happened? Could it be something in the local area?"

This was the unspoken fear, finally uttered aloud: that the environmental catastrophes hitting the Disaster on a regular basis these days could finally be encroaching on the sanctity of the ranch. Marlo looked around at the faces, at the caliber of fear she saw there that signified concern beyond just the pile of corpses locked in the shed.

"Let's hope not," said Marlo's mother, smiling around the circle. "There's no need to panic at this stage. But we have discussed this briefly, Carlton and me. And we have a proposal we wanted to float. Given that we've just had our meeting two days ago and Neil isn't due to research his report until next week, we wondered if it might be worth breaking protocol this once and checking online to see whether we can find out more about this horror."

There was a low murmur of conversation after this suggestion, but it didn't take long for them all to agree to the idea. *It wasn't like it was some immutable rule,* they reassured one another. This is the kind of exception they'd always had in mind. Marlo turned to glance across at Neil, assuming he would say a few words given that the task would naturally fall to him as newsman. She was surprised to see his face twisted in pain. She couldn't tell at first if the source was physical or psychological. Jay placed a hand on his husband's knee, and they exchanged a brief nod.

"I'm only saying this," Jay began, "because Neil and I have discussed it, and he's fine with me filling you all in. Neil has been having some issues with anxiety lately, related to but not entirely to do with his duties as newsman, and we'd both be so appreciative if he could be relieved of this extra duty. We're handling the situation just fine," he went on, holding up a placating hand as other ranchers jumped in to express concern and condolences. "A few days of cognitive therapy and some adjustment in the meds, and we'll be right as rain."

Without even stopping to think it through, Marlo blurted out: "I'll do it!" like a gifted student eager to provide the right answer before any of her classmates.

"Bless you, Marlo," said Jay, smiling and kissing the side of her face.

"I don't know . . . ," her dad said, frowning at their little trio as though he suspected them of being in cahoots. He also disapproved of blessings, even ironic ones.

"There are a lot of distressing things happening lately," cautioned her mother.

"Don't worry, I'll be fine," said Marlo. "I want to do this."

She smiled, assuring them all that it was just a casual thing, but her pulse had quickened at the thought of this unexpected contact with the Disaster. It felt like ages since she had been off the ranch, so the chance to go online offered at least a secondhand connection to the outside world. She took a quick, eager sip of wine. Her father pushed himself to a standing position, wincing slightly. He announced that he was going to bed because his rheumatoid arthritis was playing up and he was tired, but Marlo knew that was just code for him being disappointed in her. She chided herself for showing too much enthusiasm about the job. Just like everything else contained within the ranch's borders, guilt was never very far away.

3

She took her time making coffee. There was barely anyone in the Commons at this hour anyway, but she wanted to give the impression that she was approaching the task of online research as a dutiful, even painful, matter of necessity. It would have seemed disrespectful somehow to those dead eagles to enjoy this break with protocol. Impossible to shake the memory of their limp necks and unseeing eyes, the formality of their pose as they lay neatly on the floor in a row like a graven image. Marlo fiddled with the key in her pocket. Neil had given it to her the night before, had made a quip about the solemnity of passing the torch to the next generation as he pressed it into her palm.

She filled the coffee maker with water, opened and closed a few cabinets in search of the biodegradable brown-paper filters, and carefully measured out the ground beans. Just as she finished pouring, her mother arrived. Perhaps a coincidence, perhaps not. Marlo gave her a hug and a kiss on the cheek, rubbed her mother's shoulder through an oversized cream ribbed cardigan whose bulk seemed designed to disguise any intimation of delicacy. Yet it was there beneath. Marlo's fingers brushed against a jutting clavicle, and she was reminded unpleasantly of the dead eagle, reduced in the end to a feathered bone-bag. This was her mother's modus operandi, to smother her lean frame underneath androgynous clothing several sizes too big for her—loose denim jeans rolled at the ankle; men's cashmere sweaters that constantly slipped down off one shoulder or the other; billowy white dress shirts that she would cinch at the waist with a ropelike belt. She had that effortless chic so often accorded European women, with her geometric cheekbones and sharply bobbed shoulder-length hair that had morphed over the years from the color of straw to a silvery blonde. Perhaps it had something to do with her Danish ancestry, this insouciant ability to convey style while appearing utterly oblivious to it. At least that's how Marlo thought of her, with admiration and occasional irritation, because sometimes it was a mild burden to have a mother whose odd beauty drew stares and raised eyebrows whenever they were off the ranch. Of course, the stares often encompassed Marlo. It was hard to ignore the fact that they made a striking pair: the tall, tanned she-Viking in the men's clothes, and her daughter, some four inches shorter, with glossy, dead-straight black hair. She was used to the looks in town, but still. When she was younger she had dreamed of moving to a big city, where she imagined these differences could be more easily absorbed into the great churn of urban life.

"So, find anything interesting, honey?"

"You mean online? I'm just heading in now."

"Ah." Maya poured coffee, winced a little at the heat. "Darling, are you sure you want to do this?"

"Of course, Mama. I wouldn't do it otherwise. It'll be fine. I'm sure there hasn't been any big catastrophe."

Maya raised an elegantly sculpted eyebrow. Perhaps she didn't trust her daughter to recognize a catastrophe when she saw one.

"Well, I'm going to head in now."

Her mother smiled and nodded from the couch, where she'd retreated with her coffee and a book, and Marlo realized with a small heart-sink that she fully intended to stay out there until Marlo had finished. The office was tucked in the western wing of the Commons, in an alcove with floor-to-ceiling windows that overlooked a manicured garden filled with rows of beleaguered roses. Like the British explorers who would drag mahogany desks and porcelain tea sets to the colonies, the ranchers sometimes stubbornly resisted adapting to their surroundings.

There were four pristine white desktop computers set up along a blond wood bench, each with an ergonomic swivel chair, and a bank of other gadgets: printers, fax machines (like trinkets from a lost civilization), burners, and a couple of satellite phones in case they ever got cut off. The computer workspaces were separated by little leather panels for privacy, which made sitting there feel like being inside a voting booth.

Since the internet-free guideline had been introduced, the room had barely been used. Everyone had come to think of it as Neil's room. It had the air of a transient place, an airport or a doctor's waiting room, with only the antiseptic hum of machines to break the quiet. Yet Marlo loved it for its very unfamiliarity. Even during her homeschool years, this hadn't been somewhere she'd spent time; she had her own computer, of course, and the internet hadn't been a rationed commodity back then. But now, years later, this ersatz office environment reminded her in a thrilling, lives-of-others way of how people lived out in the Disaster. A job in an office was as exotic to her as the life of a Maasai tribesman would be to a bond trader. She knew cubicle dwelling was nothing to aspire to, but that didn't stop her from sometimes daydreaming about it: dressing in a pencil skirt and pumps to commute to a soulless office in some dank, fluorescent-lit building in Seattle or San Francisco. Why not? Other people did it. People less fortunate than herself.

She opened the browser to the *New York Times*, a habit from the old days. A small jolt when she remembered that it was an election year. Thinking back, she had seen a few scattered yard signs around on recent trips into town, but the impressions never lasted much beyond getting back in the car to return to the ranch. Some of the ranchers were still political, urging Neil to gather intel on his weekly missions, engaging in good-natured arguments over fireside tumblers of whiskey—a nostalgic habit, driven by sentimentality, Marlo could see that—but for most of them the political machinations of the Disaster were a distant distraction. Things had gone too far for any partisan solutions to make a difference. That was one of the key planks of the speeches her parents gave when they were on recruitment drives.

She skimmed the political news, then took a tour of the arts pages, devouring the reviews of all the plays she wouldn't see and exhibitions she wouldn't visit. She fell prey to this kind of maudlin thinking more often these days. Her fingers itched to sign in to her mail account—it must have been months since she'd last surreptitiously checked in—but she chided herself, knowing that there would be time for that at the end, once she had completed her assigned task. A kind of reward. She took a sip of coffee, dutifully clicked on the environmental news page.

"Unrest as Ecuador's Vital Banana Crop Fails for Second Year," one article's headline read. Marlo realized she hadn't seen any bananas in the ranch's storerooms for a while, and with a start she remembered an essay she had once written for school about the Sigatoka complex, a disease wreaking havoc on the world's banana supply. At the time, she'd liked it because it sounded like a Japanese disaster movie. It had all seemed so distant to her back then. She closed that tab and clicked on another article, and then another. She read with a growing sense of horror about the rapid deforestation of the Amazon rain forest, and about how energy companies had just been granted the right to begin oil exploration in the American Arctic.

It was a nightmare. And yet she knew if she went and read the political news at least one of the candidates would be a climate change denier. What a joke. She felt sorry for the people out there, forced to live with the craven decisions of power brokers who assumed that when the great reckoning finally came they'd have a big enough life raft on which to float away.

She made a few more desultory notes for Neil, in case any of this was useful for his presentation next week. Then she searched for any clues as to what had killed the eagles. There was nothing, at least not recently. A few years back, there had been reports of mysterious die-offs of bald eagles in both Emory, Texas, and the Rocky Mountains in

Utah, but she couldn't find any follow-up or official explanations as to what had happened. After half an hour of searching, she gave up. She jotted down the details of Wildlife Service people; someone would need to call them so that they could come and collect the eagles, take them away to be examined. She would probably have to give a statement: the birds were protected, after all. Officious people in uniforms would come snooping around, perhaps implying the ranchers themselves had had something to do with the deaths.

Duty done, she moved on to her inbox. There was the usual garbage, hundreds and hundreds of emails forming their own digital dead zone. There weren't many people she expected to hear from. Everyone she dealt with on a daily basis lived on the ranch, a text or stroll or at most a short drive away. But there were certain names she searched for on these rare occasions, and there they were, in two messages that she saw were miraculously time-stamped only a few days ago. Well, just one name, Alex, but she knew they spoke as one, she and her boyfriend, Ben. She grinned, touched a finger to the screen as if in this way she might be able to make a connection with her old friend.

Hey chica, what's up? Sorry it's been so long between drinks. Ben and I have been to hell and back since we last spoke. Well, not literally but pretty fucking close. We did a stint for a few months at an "eco-resort" in Costa Rica. That was a joke. One of those hotels that thinks green means guilting the guests into hanging their towels up instead of getting them replaced. Then we hit Seattle for a while, lived in a share house with a bunch of gross hippies from the co-op. Remember how we always romanticized going to college, living in a dorm? Well, here to tell you that shit is messed up!! Ugh. So we split from there and hitchhiked up the coast to Alaska. Man, such a gorgeous state, but I'd be happy never to set foot there again. Pity, considering it's going to be the best place to be once the rest of the planet melts down! Oh well. Remind me to tell you about it when we next see you.

After that we decided to head back to Washington. When we were in Seattle we met these cool chefs, a guy and a girl, who had worked on Sea Shepherd. They're based there, out of San Juan Island. Said it was life-changing, going out with them, real honest to god kick-ass eco-warrior shit. Intercepting whaling ships, stealth operations to expose oil companies drilling illegally, that kind of thing. So we decided to sign up. And they accepted us! We're due to sail in two weeks' time, so we're just hanging around the island til then, trying to go out on boats whenever we can scam our way onto one, trying to get our sea legs. CANNOT WAIT. We talked to one of the veteran Sea Shepherd activists, he's been on something like fifty journeys, and his worldview was pretty scary. Marlo, he claims we're maybe ten years away from a total collapse of ocean eco-systems. TEN YEARS. Ben and me, we both feel like this is our last chance to be part of the solution before this whole thing goes completely to shit. If you ever change your mind about leaving the ranch you know you've always got a place with us. They need us out here, people like us. Don't you want to feel as though you at least tried?

Anyway, better fly. Just wanted to fill you in with all things Alex and Ben before we go off to become bad-ass pirates! Hope life is good on the ranch. When are you leaving that place anyway? Ben says hi and to send his love. Say hi to that buncha cultists back home, won't you? ;)

You are missed.
Alex
xxxooooooxxxoooo

Marlo opened the second message. It was much shorter:

Wait, are you still banned from using the internet? I'd totally forgotten about that fantastic totalitarian move, haha. Maybe you won't even get these messages. Sadface.
xoxoxo

There it was again, the irresistible tug of the messy and infinite world. She and Alex and Ben, the once-inseparable trio who had grown up together, running free and semiferal through the meadows and forests before heading to the schoolroom to sit straight-backed at designer desks for lessons in French and biology. She tried to imagine their vagabond lives now, cut loose from the rural-bourgeois trappings of the ranch, but imagination failed her. Did they sometimes sleep out in the open under the canopy of stars, like they all had as kids? Did they ever go hungry, or despair, or long to come back to the fold? It hadn't sounded like it from Alex's message, which hummed with exhilaration. Marlo pictured them both, tanned and beautiful and defiant on board the *Sea Shepherd*, risking prison or worse. Envy coursed in like the tide.

She glanced over each shoulder once, quickly, to make sure no one had entered the room, then began typing a response. There had been no limit put on her time in here, and yet she was conscious of an invisible clock ticking down the minutes. Her mother waiting outside, drinking her fourth cup of coffee and reading the same paragraph over and over. Marlo's fingers flew over the keyboard, an activity she was pleased to find the body recalled instinctively, like riding a bike. In contrast with Alex and Ben's adventures, her own life sounded morbidly tame, but she dutifully filled them in on the happenings around the ranch, including the discovery of the dead bald eagles. She knew they'd be interested in those. Then reluctantly she signed off, urging them to stay safe and keep her apprised of their movements via text message, a form of communication the ranchers thankfully still considered both necessary and harmless to mental health.

When she emerged back into the main house, clutching her small sheaf of printouts, she expected to find her mother waiting, but she was nowhere to be seen. Perhaps she had gotten bored or been called away. Perhaps it hadn't been protectiveness after all but a coincidence that had brought her to the main house on this particular day; Marlo rarely spent time there in the mornings, so it may well have been part of her mom's regular routine. Why not? You could have been inside a cathedral, the way the light tilted through the windows at this time of day. Marlo washed out her mug and left the printouts in Neil's pigeonhole with a note, then at the last minute scribbled another note—"Sorry I missed you this morning . . . love you!"—and slid it into the pigeonhole marked with their family name, Ketterman.

❦

She got back on the bike she'd left propped up outside the main house and rode back home. She'd designed the house herself when she turned eighteen, a gift her parents had promised her without perhaps thinking through its potential impact on their own happiness. She smiled, remembering the tragic enthusiasm they'd expressed every time they visited the building site, watching workers erect the barrier of scaffolding that would separate them from their cherished child. Seven years on, she felt she might have changed a few details—like the twee porthole windows and the sod roof, whose slope you could roll down should

you so desire. "Like, what, *Lord of the Rings*?" one of the dubious build-
ers had asked, and she had beamed at being finally understood. What
could she say? At eighteen she had been heavily into fantasy worlds and
video games, as if believing that her rarely-cut-since-childhood hair and
the black-rimmed glasses she wore to correct her slight amblyopia had
doomed her to such a life. Ben often teased her that she was just making
herself hotter to a certain type of nerd he knew about from spending
so many misbegotten hours in certain dank chat rooms—"Nerds like
you, you mean?" Alex would retort, flicking him on the cheek and then
darting away before he could retaliate—and Marlo would blush to her
middle part. Through her late teenage years, both she and Alex had
nurtured a crush on Ben, and he knew it too. But it became glaringly
obvious after a while that those two were made for each other, so Marlo
made a point of snubbing Ben's attempts at flirtation.

Her two best friends loved her house, which in all other respects
conformed to the tasteful modernist aesthetic that was the prevailing
look on the ranch. Alex and Ben were jealous, given that neither of
their sets of parents would ever have dreamed of letting their delinquent
children design their own house. Marlo's parents, though. Her friends
loved to tease her about how devoted they were to her happiness. Like
all effective teasing it got at a fundamental truth. Other parents on the
ranch loved their kids too, of course, but none with the fanatical deter-
mination of hers. As a child she had been solemn but easily delighted,
and she sensed from a very early age that even her smallest expression
of joy was a treasure they were desperate to collect, like tiny jewels
hoarded for a dowry.

4

She inhaled the day into her body: the sweet sharpness of cut grass, the fertile promise of clean churned earth. The fragrances had trouble slicing through the domineering stench of the cow manure heaped in the wheelbarrow she was pushing along, but she could still detect their subtle threads, invisible gossamer on the breeze. She'd always had this overactive sense of smell, this dubious gift. Andy, a stylish rancher in her sixties who had once worked at a fashion house in Paris, claimed proudly that Marlo could have gotten a job as a "nose," those hypersensitive sniffers whose job it was to develop the next fragrance so irresistible that women from Dubai to Barcelona wouldn't hesitate to fork over two hundred dollars an ounce. Marlo liked the idea, could see herself in a white lab coat, spending her day lining up tiny paper swatches soaked with pure notes.

These were the times when she wondered about her secret lineage, the genes that had bent her into the shape of herself. Did one or both of her birth parents share this oversensitivity to scent? Did her birth mother suffer from migraines as Marlo sometimes did, crushing black episodes that left her weak and shaken and gloomy? From whom had she inherited her tiny earlobes, too small to be pierced? There was a loneliness inherent in these unanswerable questions, but also a sense of liberation—she was free to invent herself without falling prey to the comparison charts used among biological families. (Remarks like *You have your father's ears* had always seemed to her a kind of socially acceptable insult, with implications that the child was somehow a diluted copy of the original.)

She saw Kenneth in the distance with his head down, engrossed, but when she was still several hundred feet away he must have spotted her, or maybe sensed her: he straightened, leaned on his shovel, wiped his forehead with his cap, and watched her approach. He was working in the kitchen garden. He was always working somewhere. His extreme industriousness, often performed with a vigor verging on aggressive, was a kind of guarded joke around the ranch. No one ever made fun of him to his face, though: he was so earnest in his embrace of the community's principles that it would have seemed mean-spirited, for a start. Then there was the fact that he was the single most generous benefactor they had ever had. That gained him a certain amount of respect, although Marlo suspected it also rankled some residents. There was something sanctimonious about how he made sure everyone knew.

Historically, new recruits put forward the minimum contribution (currently set at the distinctly high-roller floor of a quarter million dollars), maybe a few thousand more, but Kenneth had insisted on investing his entire fortune when he joined—a not-inconsiderable sum, given that in his previous life he had been a Big Ag executive who ran a corporation responsible for growing roughly a third of the country's food. To hear him tell it—and Marlo had been his audience for this particular diatribe many times—he had finally become so disillusioned with the industry's malfeasance, blatant abuses, and cover-ups, and outraged over its willful destruction of the artesian basin, local rivers, forests, and lives human, bestial, and insect, that he had thrown it all away, just quit his job and walked away, without even the golden parachute he was entitled to. The uncomfortable truth was never broached aloud, that Kenneth had been such a successful CEO in his time there that the stock price had soared. That was why the ranch had appealed to him, she supposed: it was not just a chance to live in a purer way, but a chance to make amends.

She watched him watching her. It was always interesting to be given permission to study someone without feeling like a creep. He had straightened up to his full six feet two inches but even so he gave the appearance of hunching, a function of the way he was built—bulky across the shoulders and a neck that jutted forward like a buzzard's. His dark ginger hair, released from the confines of the cap, was glued down in patches and stuck up in others. He grinned at her, ran a hand over the scruffy beard that never seemed to either grow or diminish. To dismantle him in this way was to suggest an unpleasant-looking man. Marlo personally found him not unhandsome, yet there was a sourness to him that repelled people.

"How's your day?" he asked once she was within earshot. The puppy-like eagerness that only she evoked in him was almost painful to witness.

"Just shoveling shit," she said, grinning back. Important to hit on the right balance of warmth in the smile: not too cold nor too hot. Kenneth had once tried to kiss Marlo behind the compost shed, back when she was twenty-two and he was forty. She had turned away so quickly that he had grazed the tip of her ear with his mouth. She'd told him she couldn't but made the excuse that it was because she wasn't ready. Why had she left him that sliver of hope? She chastised herself for weeks afterward. But it was simple. She hadn't wanted to hurt his feelings. She had wanted him to keep liking her. It was a decision she still regretted three years later, because she knew that although she had since very firmly made it clear that there would be no relationship between them, he chose to believe her earlier words, the ones that best accorded with his own hopes.

Kenneth laughed, took the wheelbarrow from her, and dumped the glossy cowpats near a row of beets, but when he turned back his face was somber. He crouched down and grabbed something from the ground and threw it on the scarred worktable. He leaned forward, the pale blue eyes he'd inherited from his long-suffering Irish ancestors fixed on her own light hazel ones. (Impossible to know who she'd inherited those from.) She'd rarely seen him so agitated. Marlo looked at what lay on the table: a pile of moldy seeds and a pair of tiny, shriveled carrots.

"Is everything OK?"

He grimaced, but she could see there wasn't a yes or no answer, and that scared her. Kenneth was usually so decisive, his declarations absent of nuance. That even he could be unsure about what was happening felt like a bad omen. He licked his dry lips. She watched him trying to work out how much to tell her and in what manner the news should be delivered, and it irritated her, as it always did these days, that so many of them still treated her like a child.

"Kenneth. Just spit it out."

He threw her a wounded glance. The thick hide he normally presented to the world so perilously thin when it came to her.

"It's probably nothing. But the seeds aren't doing so well this year, as you can see. They should be shooting and thriving by now."

"Hmm," said Marlo, unsure what to say.

Kenneth tossed his head in irritation, like a horse besieged by flies.

"You don't get it. Yeah, there are annual fluctuations with these things, but this is like nothing I've seen. You remember we had that unseasonably warm February, and then when the snows melted and everything started to blossom that huge frost came along in April and wiped everything out?"

"Sure."

"And that's not all. We haven't had the usual rains yet, and the soil's just too dry." His tone was almost pleading now. It was obvious he was trying to enlist her help, get her on his side for something, but she was at a loss to imagine what.

"That does sound bad," she said cautiously. "But I don't know . . . Can't we just make up the shortfall with the greenhouse and produce we buy in town?"

He stared at her, then shook his head in disbelief. A few droplets of sweat zinged off into the ether.

"Wow. I expect a certain amount of magical thinking from the others, but I thought you were different, Marlo. I thought you understood what we're trying to do here."

He began angrily brushing soil off the table. It would have been unthinkably rude to laugh, but he looked so much like an overgrown child taking petulant vengeance out on his toys. She turned her head to the side, coughed her smile away.

"What magical thinking are you talking about?"

"This." He waved a belligerent hand around. "This whole ranch as some kind of bourgeois experiment! The jolly little trips to the supermarket, the wine evenings, that ridiculous golf course idea I had to shut down. It's like everyone here thinks they're at a fun summer camp that never ends. They don't see how bad things are getting out there." He tilted his head in an easterly direction, presumably to indicate the Disaster. "No one but me is preparing in any serious way for when things really go to shit."

"I don't think that's true but OK."

"We need to become self-sufficient, and fast. Do you think when a wave of catastrophes strikes out there that we'll have time to install all the infrastructure we'll need, to get the systems working that we'll need?"

"You're kind of scaring me now. Things aren't that bad." She was aware that saying this only played into his theory of magical thinking. "Unless you know something I don't."

He shook his head again, looking away from her, but all the thunder had gone.

"No, of course not," he said with quiet weariness. "You're probably right, I'm overreacting. We have our insurance, after all. But still. I just think we should begin an irrigation program. Something to get the plants started." He looked back at her, seeking her approval, though god knows why it was valuable to him. She was one of the youngest ranch members; any authority she had was a secondhand investment passed down from her parents as two of the original founders. "I don't know if you remember, but we drilled those three wells a few years ago? I think we should start using them."

"That's a good idea. Why don't you bring it up at the next meeting? I'm sure everyone will be cool with it. And I'll totally have your back if anyone says it's foolish to use them already."

"Thanks, Marl. I'd appreciate that."

"Of course." She reached over to squeeze his hand. "What are friends for?"

"I want to show you something else."

"Oh, god." She put her hands to her face, judging it a suitable time to make a little fun of him. "Is it a mushroom cloud on the horizon? The Four Horsemen? *The seventh seal broken open?*"

She dodged deftly out of the way of his arm as it swung in an arc to cuff her shoulder. He was laughing, though. She felt it course through her, the shameful thrill of being the feudal lord over another person's emotional terrain.

"Come on. We'll need to drive there."

They walked together to Kenneth's truck, Marlo humming and swinging her arms and occasionally reaching out to push his shoulder so that he listed slightly off-balance. In spite of Kenneth's grim prognostications, the balmy weather had wormed its way under her skin and into her mood. She felt wild with savage glee. Kenneth glanced at her, half-smiling, half-frowning.

They drove in silence to a part of the property she rarely ventured to. None of the ranchers had built out here; the land was uneven, dry and rocky, the scrubby trees sparse, and none of the water sources were nearby. They were on the far side now of the ranch's tallest hill. It was strange to look around and not see any of the homes. There were no signs of life at all. Nothing stirred, not a bird or lizard or even a leaf. The air was still, as if the world were holding its breath. They might have been in the wilderness, instead of a mile away from a cellar full of Veuve Clicquot and half a million dollars' worth of luxury cars. Marlo glanced at Kenneth as he cut the engine. She hoped for some reassurance about their mission, but he seemed nervous and fidgety. He swung out of the vehicle and trotted around to her side to open the door. She was already half out of the truck, but she let him shut the door behind her, as if this act of gallantry might set the day back to rights.

She followed as he strode toward a grouping of rocks in front of a steep slope. He walked behind the rocks and disappeared. A trick? Kenneth didn't really seem the kind. She shivered. She had always hated hide-and-seek, the sudden terrifying aloneness: one moment surrounded by people; the next on her own, as if they had all vanished out of the world. When Marlo got closer she saw that the rocks concealed the mouth of a small cave. Kenneth was waiting, crouched in the sandy dirt.

"I've never noticed this before," she said. "How can I not have known there was a cave here?"

Kenneth raised an eyebrow. "Well, I doubt you've explored every inch of the ranch."

"You'd be surprised. I've been here since I was five years old, Kenneth."

He nodded, conceding the point.

"Maybe it was carved out by our little resident doomsday prepper."

Marlo stared at him. He moved aside so she could crouch in the low entrance too, then he turned on the flashlight. Marlo half expected bats to fly out, but there was nothing, just the stale mustiness of spaces deprived of sunlight. Kenneth played the light around the cave. It was small, barely large enough for a grown person to sit cross-legged on the floor, but it looked to have been inhabited, or at least used as some sort of storeroom. She saw a plaid blanket on the ground and niches either natural or gouged into the walls at intervals, deep enough to hold several books. The spines of the books looked ragged, as if something had been nibbling at them.

Kenneth shot a grim look at her, then lifted the corner of the blanket. Beneath it, in a shallow trench unpleasantly reminiscent of a grave, was a stash of weapons. She couldn't tell what kind right away; she had never taken much interest in weapons. Rifles, they looked like, with long wooden barrels. There were boxes of ammunition too and some hunting knives in leather holsters.

Marlo crawled further into the cave while Kenneth shone the flashlight to illuminate the walls. She pulled down a Bible from its niche, flicked through it with a lump of dread in her stomach. It smelled pungently stale. The margins of the book were full of scrawled notes she couldn't make out. They looked like the rantings of a lunatic. There were other books too, crudely bound, paranoid self-published cries for help with titles like *Preparations for the Rapture* and *Surviving the Global Armageddon*. Marlo put them back in place carefully, sat back on her heels, and blew a strand of hair off her cheek.

"It's been here awhile," said Kenneth.

"Do you know who it is? The person all this belongs to?"

"I've got my suspicions."

"Who? Tell me."

Kenneth tossed the blanket back over the weapons cache, sending a shimmering army of motes up into the artificial light.

"Let's get out of here." They walked back out into the fresh air, straightening up from stooping with grateful intakes of breath. "You know what I think?" He switched the flashlight off, threw it with an angry grimace into the truck. "I think there might be a faction of the community who *are* doomsday preppers . . . like hardcore ones."

"You mean our community?" She was shocked to hear him say it, but what else could he mean? "You think this is one of *us*?"

He turned to look at her, but when she met his eye he looked away, as if embarrassed. He shrugged. "Who else?"

"Someone else could have found this place, some loner, or, I don't know, fugitive." She realized before she'd even finished how childish that sounded. How unlikely. "Shit, Kenneth. We should tell someone."

They got back in the vehicle. Kenneth put the keys in the ignition, but he didn't turn the engine on, just put his rough laborer's hands on his knees. Marlo looked at them, at their reddened knuckles and their fretwork of sun spots. It was calming somehow, to look at those hands and imagine the acts they could be put in service to, both tender and violent. He shook his head.

"I don't know, Marl. I've thought about it. Who would we tell, and what would be the objective exactly? It's a free world. We all agreed that weapons were necessary, as a precaution. We've got a whole cache in the house. You probably walk past them every day."

"Yeah, but they're all registered and locked up! This . . . this feels like an accident waiting to happen."

Kenneth turned to look at her with a grin that was almost mischievous. He put his hand slowly into the pocket of his huge Canada Goose coat, pulled out a handful of ammunition.

"Not without these," he said. He smiled, and in the suddenly avuncular smile, she saw him remembering his role as her elder, her protector. His desire to shield her from harm overriding even his fierce desire to confide in someone. "There's nothing to worry about."

She smiled weakly back at him and nodded as if she was reassured, but all the way back to the greenhouse she was thinking about the fact that she recognized the handwriting in the Bible.

❦

At the next meeting, Neil delivered the news about the mysteriously deceased eagles to the community at large. He mentioned Marlo's investigation and stressed that while there had been some other similar incidents, nothing had been uncovered to explain the disaster. Were they poisoned or harmed in some other way by humans, or did they die of natural causes? She had found no definitive answers. He assured everyone that he'd keep tabs on the situation, set a Google alert for anything in a similar vein that might help explain the deaths. There were some murmurings of distress and the usual theories were floated, but no one suggested any kind of decisive action, as Marlo had imagined they might. Now that she thought about it, though, what would they have suggested? But it was still disappointing somehow.

Next Kenneth took the floor to speak in his dour, defensive way about his fears for the new crops and to request permission to draw from the water table. When the vote was tallied later, he was given permission, unanimously. He and Marlo hadn't spoken since the discovery of the cave. For a fleeting moment when he got up to speak she wondered whether he might mention it, but of course he didn't. It was their little secret, but that was hardly a reassurance. If anything, it felt hazardous to hold this thing between them, like a bomb no one knew how to defuse. She caught his eye as he stepped offstage, and she felt the new combustible charge of their complicity and silence. She couldn't be sure, but she thought he gave a brief shrug as he passed her, as though disavowing responsibility.

Afterward she lingered around the main house as she often did after the Thursday meetings. Some of the ranchers melted back into the night, but many others chose to stay around as well, talking and arguing and socializing, or just taking advantage of the opportunity to drink somewhere that wasn't their own homes. She enjoyed these convivial times, even on occasions like this one in which she held herself apart from the revelry and rhetoric heating up over by the grand stone fireplace. When she went into the kitchen to get herself a glass, she saw there was a new note up on the cork noticeboard, usually given over to minor community matters, flyers for social events, or sign-up sheets for trips into town. This note stood out right away. At first she thought it was poetry, but when she leaned in closer a cold hand closed over her heart. It was a printed-out Bible verse. First Corinthians 10:13. The one about temptation and endurance. She might have dismissed it as an odd prank, or something one of the little kids had posted for religious studies class, or some kind of subversive atheist's jibe about eating too many cookies or something—except that this wasn't the first one she'd seen. There had been others over the last few days: one slipped beneath a pot in the greenhouse, another in the second bathroom of the Commons. She couldn't have said why the verses bothered her, except that there was something nefarious about their anonymity. She tore the slip of paper down, crumpled it into her pocket.

When she returned to the lounge room and installed herself back in her seat, she could feel Kenneth's gaze boring into her every time she glanced over that way. She frowned at her open computer screen (internet disabled like a good citizen), willing him to get the message that she didn't want to talk, and while as always he respected her wishes, that didn't stop her feeling irritated. Why did he rub her the wrong way? His behavior toward her was always kind, respectful of her autonomy and personal space, to the point of being deferential. That was part of the problem, though: she didn't want to be deferred to. She wanted . . . what, exactly? To be understood.

As she stared at her screen, she saw her mother reflected wonkily in the liquid crystal, approaching with arms outstretched.

"Marlo, darling. There you are."

"Hi, Mom. How's Dad? Is everything fine?"

Her mother's mouth twisted as if she detected something sour in the air.

"I think we're in for a rough few days, darling."

This is how they often spoke of him, reporting on his condition as if he were the weather. *It's looking fine at the moment; All clear today; We're approaching a bad patch.*

Her father's health was one of the chief anxieties of Marlo's existence. She harbored an almost pathological fear of losing her parents. In her young life she had never really experienced loss or grief, apart from the initial loss of her birth parents, a loss so profound she wondered sometimes whether it shaped her terror of losing her adoptive parents as well. The fact that she had never processed the first grief—not just that; had been a baby when it happened and therefore had barely even *experienced* it—made her nervous that it was all building up beneath the crust of her happy life, like the hydrothermal pressure building beneath the Yellowstone supervolcano.

"That's no good. I'll come see him in the morning."

"Oh, he'll be fine. Just feeling the change of weather in his bones, he says. Nothing to worry about. He's still excited about the trip to New York. He wouldn't miss that for the world."

"Me too," said Marlo, smiling and pushing her laptop aside. Her mother sat beside her, stroking Marlo's silky black ponytail. She made her usual comment about what beautiful hair her daughter had, and Marlo made her usual amused reply: "You always say that, Mom. It's just hair."

"I know that. But I'm allowed to think it's beautiful. So, what are you working on?"

"The History," Marlo answered quickly, turning the screen away with a subtle gesture. This answer appeared to satisfy her mother, who approved of *The History*. A few years back, Marlo had, in a fit of frustrated boredom, declared she was going to write a history of the ranch, charting its ups and downs and chronicling the characters who had played significant roles in its development. Being two of the original founders, her parents were naturally among these characters, but that wasn't why they were so devoted to the idea. It wasn't narcissism that stoked their enthusiasm but a desire to see their daughter so involved in a worthy project. If there were darker, more complicated currents that ran beneath this pure desire, then both they and Marlo studiously chose to ignore them. It was as though they had all signed a pact never to

mention the other possibilities that life might present a young woman beyond living on a ranch with her parents.

Never mind that Marlo had produced nothing more than a flurry of notes and a chapter outline in the first year of the project and then had left *The History* to lie fallow. Her parents treated the undertaking with a hushed reverence that verged on comical. She didn't have the heart to tell them she'd abandoned it. Her mother stayed long enough to finish her cup of tea and then kissed Marlo goodnight.

"I'll drop by tomorrow to see you guys. Tell Dad *love you.*"

"Love you, sweetheart. Good night."

She waited patiently, eyes averted, until she knew her mother had left the lounge room and even then there was a certain stealth in pulling the letter out of her bag, painstakingly unfolding it and smoothing out the page, creased in a grid from being folded and refolded. She'd been carrying it around since she received it, along with a measure of guilt at how much the contents might alarm her parents. The letter—a printed-out email, really—was from the office of Scott Emmerich, director of the National Parks Service office in San Jose. She'd seen the email for the first time while researching the bald eagles. Baffling at first, then quickly connected to a promise long forgotten, months ago when Marlo had been texting with Alex and had idly mentioned how she regretted not ever having had a real job. In a head-spinningly short space of time, Alex had compiled a shortlist of organizations out in the Disaster to which Marlo could apply.

"You'll need to be prepared to go in on the ground floor," her friend had cautioned. "With no experience and not even an accredited degree to speak of you'll have to prove yourself in other ways. Interning, most likely. Unpaid, almost certainly. But you're whip smart, and you don't need the money because your parents are loaded and you care about this doomed planet. You'll kill it."

The list that landed shortly after in Marlo's inbox was alarming. The organizations all sounded important and hard-core, even militant in some cases. She knew Alex and Ben had worked with some of them—Greenpeace, Sea Shepherd, the Earth Liberation Front—and that getting assaulted or arrested, or worse, wasn't entirely out of the question when you worked with activists. At least a national park office radiated a benign, soothing conservatism, although she knew from Alex that even the peaceful national parks people had turned tougher since the federal government had announced they were commencing drilling and energy exploration in the parks. Still, their tactics were mostly lawful—sit-ins, online petitions, and legal action, mainly.

Alex had promised to talk with Scott on Marlo's behalf. Apparently he was always looking for "smart, motivated" people, and Alex had talked up Marlo's dedication to environmental causes. For a few days Marlo had been buoyed by the prospect of this potential escape hatch from the ranch, but the weeks had stretched on, and she hadn't heard back from Alex about it. She'd been relieved in a way. But now here was an email from Scott, expressing his desire to meet with Marlo. She had printed out the message with a pounding heart and a flurry of over-the-shoulder glances at the door, folded it into a tiny origami square, and hidden it in her bag. The process was straightforward, Scott explained: his office just required her to submit a short paper explaining why she wanted to work with the parks service and what she thought she could bring to the organization.

He must have written to her without going through Alex first because Alex hadn't mentioned it. Marlo was dismayed to see that the message was time-stamped three weeks ago. How disinterested he must have thought her! She wondered if it was too late to apply. Even thinking about the possibility of taking the position lit up her frontal lobe, and if the photo of Scott Emmerich aided in the escape fantasy somewhat then that wasn't her fault. No one expected a nature nerd to look quite so much like a Hollywood swashbuckler, with a sexy, scruffy beard and shoulders that seemed to strain at the confines of his sensible khaki shirt. She read the message from Scott one more time, savoring the promise contained in the words *Hope to welcome you to the team this summer!* before folding the paper back into a blank wad. She had texted Alex to ask her advice, and of course Alex had guessed at her reluctance, urging her to reply to Scott right away or lose the chance.

Just imagine, her signoff read. *You might even decide to take him up on the offer while there are still parks to protect! :)*

Alex had a clear-eyed way of cutting through the bullshit to expose the fear beneath. It was part of what Marlo admired about her old friend. She'd always had a wild animal's ability to sniff out weakness.

5

She didn't want to be the sort of person who was dazzled by New York, and yet here she was. Despite having lived briefly in Manhattan, whenever she looked back on it from a distance of two decades and three thousand miles, the city never felt wholly real. Her brain retained scattered fragments of privileged toddler scenes: a hazy memory of pressing her nose to the department store Christmas windows on Fifth Avenue; tumbling sessions in an echoing warehouse on the Lower East Side; the Loeb Boathouse in Central Park; a particular deli where her dad would buy them egg-and-cheese everything bagels swaddled in paper wrappers that went limp with steam. But these could have been anyone's memories. They had lived on the Upper East Side from the time her parents came to pick her up in China and she became their daughter—a second birth into a new world at fourteen months old. Then, abruptly, or so it seemed to her, they had packed up their gilded lives and moved to Oregon to become ranchers. That was where her life began to take on solidity: instead of snatches of scenes that insisted on shape-shifting, her experiences began to coalesce into a coherent whole, days following one another as milestones came and went.

Her parents may not always have been rich, but for Marlo's entire life they had been. Their good fortune felt as unchangeable as the nineteenth-century townhouse in which they lived. Of course she understood in principle that riches came and went—hadn't most American fortunes evaporated by the second generation? And even her parents admitted that luck and timing had played a major part in the founding of their hedge fund, at a time when the city was awash in money and optimism. But she couldn't imagine a life in which money didn't smooth every one of life's rough edges, and this failure of imagination filled her with shame. To be wealthy in a place like Manhattan was to inhabit an elite stratum of existence all the more jarring for its dissimilarity from the level on which the masses lived their lives. Those masses surged on and off the island like a disaffected tide each day: Marlo's parents told her that she would always insist on stopping and watching at subway entrances, fascinated by the people pouring forth from the gaping black mouth of the subway, which they assured her was too dirty and dangerous for children.

The relatively low-key lifestyle of the ranch rendered the rare visits back to the city even more thrilling. As an expatriate she could revel in the glamour and lunches at expense-account restaurants with a clear conscience. She could scarcely believe her parents had sanctioned this trip. Over the last few years they'd become increasingly twitchy about her accompanying them on recruitment drives. Ironically, it had been easier when she was a child. Back then the trips had been used as an inducement, a treat or a reward for good behavior. And her parents, whether it had been both of them (common in the early days) or just her mother (increasingly the case since the decline in her father's health), seemed to enjoy the jaunts as much as she had. Now she could see they considered it a chore, a necessary evil to shore up the future health of the community.

She was even more surprised when her father had insisted on being the one to lead this particular trip to New York. She'd been sure he would bow out, citing ill health, let his wife or one of the other more eloquent ranchers take his place. But not only did he insist on traveling, he insisted that Marlo accompany him.

"We're going to have fun," he said, reaching over the armrest to pat her knee as they prepared for takeoff. He always insisted she take the window seat. As the pilot dipped the plane into its final descent, Marlo pressed her nose to the window and stared in wonder at the city spread out below. Endless rivers of lights, orange and white. A tremor of joy coursed through her.

After they landed and had settled into their hotel—lofty rooms on the same floor overlooking Columbus Circle—he proposed taking her for oysters at Grand Central, a tradition he insisted she must remember from her short time in New York. Of course she didn't remember, couldn't imagine she would have appreciated oysters as a toddler, but that didn't dampen his enthusiasm for the outing.

Marlo insisted on taking the subway there, though it was only a few stops, not just to alight in the chaotic cathedral of Grand Central Station but also for the novelty of the train itself. She loved the way the stations would materialize out of the grimy black tunnels like salvation, at first just a dim glow glimpsed out the window and then an island of light and movement bobbing in the darkness. She even loved gripping the dull, slightly greasy pole that had been touched by millions of hands before her. She pictured it teeming with the bacteria of hordes of people she would never meet, and the thought gave her a perverse thrill. The train car she and her father got in was populated mostly by tired-looking commuters who didn't even look up when new people entered but huddled inside puffy black jackets with chins tucked into their necks and braced their bodies against the rocking of the train even in sleep. Such thick jackets for the warm weather, as if these people lived their entire lives underground, cursed to go around and around and never emerge into the light.

There seemed to be more energy in her father's gait than usual as they made their way through the subterranean crowds to the Oyster Bar. They sat on low stools at the counter, skin burnished by the warm glow of the vaulted tiled ceiling. Her dad explained that only tourists ate in the restaurant proper and that in spite of their years away from this town, he refused to act like a tourist. Looking around, Marlo was surprised to see that the other diners in their section were just regular-looking people in jeans and rumpled shirts, not starched and polished like at the restaurants her parents usually frequented.

"This is nice," she said, meaning it, and her father glowed with pleasure at her approval. Their waitress came over and dropped off a basket of blindingly white bread and butter.

"Hey there, folks," she said with a little extra smile for Carlton, as if she recognized him from somewhere, which was how strangers often greeted him. He could easily have been an aging movie star. Marlo devoured several pieces of the springy soft bread (white flour wasn't generally used on the ranch, so it, like pretty much everything else she was experiencing, pulsed with the high frequency of novelty), while her father deliberated over literally dozens of types of oyster as though the choice carried weighty consequences. She teased him about his indecision, but really it warmed her to see him so engaged in the moment, taking careful measure of the ingredients of this memory and at pains to get each moment absolutely right. She dutifully leaned into his shoulder and frowned at the menu as though the choice were just as important to her, although in truth she could take or leave oysters, with their off-putting sliminess. "Bluepoints from Long Island might be a good, if safe, choice," he mused, "or we could wade into brinier waters with a dozen Weskeag from Maine?" Marlo, mouth twisted in concentration, pretended to consider the merits of each. "Nothing from the West Coast," he declared, although she knew the oysters from Washington and British Columbia tended to be sweeter: it seemed important to him that the bivalves have a geographical connection to their current location. Perhaps he sensed the power of the unfamiliar on his daughter, the liberation of being sprung loose from the ranch, and wanted to immerse her in the thrill of strangeness. Eventually, with some prompting from Marlo, he decided on some mild Rhode Island oysters—"to start." Their waitress smiled at him again, stealing a discreet glance at Marlo as well before she strode away. This also was not unusual on the rare occasions they went out in public together: the familiar tableau of an attractive young Asian woman and a much older white man seemed not to surprise or shock people so much as satisfy some deeply held assumption as to how the world worked. It rankled, but it wasn't as though you could seize a stranger by the shoulder, show your ID, demonstrate that your relationship was innocent and familial. Luckily her father appeared completely oblivious to such assumptions. She would have wanted to die on the spot if anyone had vocally mistaken them for a couple.

Once the oysters arrived there were further solemn ceremonies to be enacted. Her father carefully spread his red-and-white checked napkin over his lap and waved each shell beneath his nostrils, breathing in its aroma for a moment like a sommelier testing a cork. He held each oyster briefly in his mouth, not swallowing or chewing, just holding it in his mouth with his eyes closed for a few seconds as if meditating. Marlo looked around quickly, embarrassed, but the other diners were either similarly engrossed in their food or talking animatedly to one another. For her part she plucked the oysters out of their shells with the tiny fork, popped them into her mouth, and swallowed in one swift movement so as not to dwell on their disconcerting viscosity.

After the first dozen shells had been dispatched, her father dabbed his mouth with his napkin, carefully replaced it across his lap, and turned to face her.

"Are you having a good time?"

"Of course." She patted his knee. "Thanks for letting me tag along this time. Feels like ages since I've left the ranch."

He flinched a little, as though these words hurt him. She hadn't meant it to sound like a recrimination. He cleared his throat in the way he did when he was about to address an audience.

"Sweetheart, there was a reason your mother and I decided to ask you to join me this time. Of course we're going to give you time to think about it, but the fact of the matter is that we want you to take over all this someday."

"All what?"

"This." He performed a vague gesture.

"Running the Oyster Bar?" She grinned, trying to lighten the mood. He smiled faintly, but there was a sadness in it she remembered from her school days, when she would flunk a test because she hadn't bothered studying or willfully refused to understand a particular principle being explained to her. It was an expression that said she wasn't taking things seriously.

"You know what I mean. The recruitment. Making sure the ranch has a future."

"Oh."

"I'm not saying you have to decide now. But your mother and I have discussed it at length, and you're the only person we really trust with this. As you know, some of the community's vital members . . . doctors, teachers, scientists, etcetera . . . are getting, ahem, old, and we need to think about recruiting eventual replacements. We need an infusion of both funds and new blood. And an old dinosaur like me—or even your beautiful mother, youthful as she is—we're not likely to be an effective recruitment tool forever. We need a new, fresh, smart face."

"But what about Neil? Or Liz? They're so much better at public speaking than I am. Seriously, I basically screw up ordering at restaurants. I'm definitely not the right person for this, Dad."

His mouth twitched at the edges. "You don't have to decide now," he repeated. "Besides, we could teach you everything you need to know to take over."

Marlo shook her head.

"Why all this talk of taking over? You and Mom aren't going anywhere. I don't like to hear you talking like that."

But even talking about it had brought a cool change gusting over the afternoon. She felt the familiar weight bearing down on her, the pressure to be everything to them.

"It's just a matter of planning." He looked down at his legs, began to fold the napkin into halves, then quarters, then eighths. "We all have to think of the future. Look around you."

She obeyed, looked around the room. It looked like a room full of people involved in various degrees of gustatory enjoyment.

"What am I supposed to be looking at exactly?"

He sighed. "Things are coming apart, love. The systems are starting to fail. These people . . . I don't mean just the people in this restaurant, everyone in this city and other cities . . . They're so unhappy. They're victims of the system, but most of them can't articulate or even necessarily see how they're trapped. They just know things are going bad fast."

Marlo narrowed her eyes, did another visual sweep around the restaurant. She tried to consider the diners and waiters through a different prism, as unwitting victims of a vast global meltdown that was all the more alarming for how much it lacked any central organizing principle. Her parents and the other elders on the ranch scoffed at conspiracy theorists: she had often heard them expound on the fact that there was no vast global conspiracy to ruin the planet, no shadowy cabal of evildoers intent on destruction. Rather, there was a vast global disinterest in the difficult actions necessary to reverse course. That's what differentiated their community, in the end, from the other whackjobs and paranoids who'd set up similar communities in places like Oregon. The ranchers were governed by rationality, not emotion.

"Let's talk about it some other time," she said, pulling his bulky shoulder toward her for an awkward sidelong embrace. "I want to enjoy this trip with you!"

"Of course, sweetheart." His face softened. It was obvious he was satisfied that the seed had been planted and felt confident in leaving it to germinate for a while. "What do you want to do after this?"

Pushing through the revolving doors, borne on a stale puff of over-breathed air back out on East 42nd Street, she indulged in a little skip. Her father laughed at this, delighted as ever in her delight.

"Just like when you were little and I'd bring you on trips," he commented approvingly. They had concocted vague plans to visit The Met and Guggenheim after lunch, but her father begged off, saying he needed to lie down for a while back at the hotel, gather his strength for the next day's seminar. If it felt to Marlo like a ploy to ensure she didn't feel dragged down by his presence, she didn't acknowledge this any further than to ask, "Are you sure?" before agreeing to meet him back at the hotel later.

She spent the rest of the afternoon in heavily perfumed environments, drifting through a kind of delirious fugue state as she stocked up on pharmacy items, beauty products, non-small-town clothes. She bought a Stella McCartney clingy black dress at Bergdorf Goodman, handing over the credit card with a certain furtive excitement. God knows where she thought she would ever wear such a thing in the wilds of Oregon, but it made her feel effortlessly beautiful and sophisticated like the other women she saw on the street. It took a while after landing in a city to shrug off the paranoia about looking provincial. She experienced a momentary pang of guilt at the sheer waste of money, but she was proficient by now at managing the cognitive dissonance associated with life on the ranch—with its general rejection of late-stage capitalism—and the sheer extravagance these acts of consumerism entailed. She knew that even if she told her father how much she'd spent on the dress, he wouldn't have any problem with it. In fact she could imagine him applauding this single act of frivolity as a welcome antidote to her relatively monastic life back home. He was probably purchasing rare cigars and having a new suit made in the same spirit. They were all good at it. Spreading the gospel of self-sufficiency sometimes required transcontinental flights, expensive hotel rooms, and lavish dinners—that was a given. None of them saw any hypocrisy in this, no meaningful ethical gulf between what the ranch represented and the level of expense required to keep it in good health.

In the spirit of this sentiment, she also got her hair trimmed and worked out at a midtown gym to which she'd purchased a day pass. Even the steamy locker room and the sweaty reek of the weight room were exhilarating to her. Other people's odors, secret lives, unguessed at.

In the morning she helped him go over his speech. He wasn't nervous; he never was. His actual nerves—not to mention his joints, ligaments, bones—may have been sources of pain and discomfort at other times, but not when he was addressing an audience. This was his wheelhouse. She admired his cool ability to command a room, to speak to people in that natural, heartfelt way of an orator. Her mother had the same gift, a kind of warmth that the best politicians possess: that magical ability to convey the impression that the person at the lectern is talking directly to *you*. Once again she marveled at her parents' belief that she would want to inherit—or even be capable of inheriting—this aspect of their lives.

"Ready?" she asked, dusting some lint off his jacket. She had dressed in jeans and a white button-down shirt and black kitten heels, with a small, discreet gold pendant around her neck: the uniform of an assistant rather than a lead player. Her self-appointed job was to hand out brochures and flash drives, steer guests toward the coffee, hors d'oeuvres, and flutes of Bollinger, and generally act as a friendly ambassador for the ranch's "brand."

They walked together the three blocks to the hotel conference room where the seminar was being held. They had received sixty-five RSVPs to the event, no doubt the usual mix of curious casual observers, venture capitalists, and investors with a genuine interest in the ranch project. It was easy for prospective residents to research the ranch: there was a website, of course, and in earlier days the founders had given several interviews to prominent magazines and newspapers, although the enthusiasm for doing that had waned after they had been plagued with busloads of gawkers driving up to their gate, demanding to be shown around "the cult." The residents often laughed about that, the pervading idea that any organized community must be built on a foundation of unhinged religiosity and unorthodox sex. God forbid a group of people should simply try together to carve out a safe and functional society. Not that God had anything to do with it, of course.

Walking down the street together on the way from one hotel to the other, several times she found herself getting jostled or withering under irritated looks from other pedestrians, and it took her a moment to realize that it was because the two of them were dawdling, weaving along without any respect for sidewalk etiquette, and in doing so identifying themselves as out-of-town hicks as surely as if they'd been chewing straw. *This isn't personal,* the looks seemed to say, *but I'm a New Yorker and I need you to get the fuck out of my way.* Her dad noticed as well.

"We've gotten rusty from living on the ranch," he laughed. "I swear I used to know how to properly navigate a sidewalk. I was one of those people giving tourists dirty looks."

"How the mighty have fallen."

"Indeed."

To Marlo it was all intoxicating, even the dirty looks; how rich it all seemed to her, the sights and smells and *Sturm und Drang* of the outside world. She couldn't get over how loud it was, like the soundtrack of life had been turned up to its highest volume, and how saturated in color this world was compared to the gentle chiaroscuro of her rural existence. It didn't seem like such a disaster when you were immersed in it. It just seemed like normal life. Where was the dark pandemonium the ranchers always talked about? She was pretty sure the people who made up the crowds churning around her weren't occupied with the end-times but with the minutiae of their quotidian concerns: paying the rent or mortgage, getting that promotion, saving for a vacation, looking for a new job or boyfriend. She felt a pang of—not envy exactly, but wistfulness, that she might never experience any of that. She wanted to stop random people and interrogate them. What were their dreams, their secret despairs? Did some of them dream of getting away from it all, the rat race, and living off the land? She'd read articles about that. Funny to be living the life that others dreamed about, to possess unearned privilege that some people would have killed for.

💐

The room was silent but for his voice.

"Look. The world we live in today is the anomaly. Ancient Rome and pre-Revolution France and feudal England and the Mayan civilization and slavery weren't the anomalies. Those systems in which a tiny elite grabbed everything for themselves while the masses lived appalling and brutally short lives, they're the norm and have been the norm throughout the history of humanity. That is on its way back. Our Western-style late capitalist democracy is a mere pinprick on the timeline of human history; these ideas of freedom and equality and a fair playing field that we cherish are the relics of a disappearing world."

Marlo held her breath. Her father was a pro, but she still got nervous when he started speaking because she wanted the audience to love him like she did. A quick look around the room showed that all eyes were on him; so far, so good.

"It's already happening. Power has already been consolidated. Our system has a life of its own now: no movement or party or leader is going to alter in any meaningful way the trajectory this society is on. Corporations will accumulate even more power as more of our institutions fall prey to their influence. Sooner or later there will be no part of our society's food production that isn't under the control of Big Agriculture and the agrochemical industry. Very soon they're coming for the remaining regulatory bodies that have historically kept chaos in check, and then all bets are off. Soon the poisoning of our rivers and oceans and air and the corruption of our food systems will be complete, and when that happens things are going to get really bad, really fast."

It was like watching the prologue to a disaster movie, that same thrill you felt knowing you were about to witness the destruction of the world from the comfort of your armchair.

"Some of us once believed in grassroots activism," Carlton said, as the listeners strained to imagine this patrician, impeccably tailored old man as a long-haired hippie. "In the idea that the will of the people, if properly harnessed, could change the direction in which things were going."

A few people shifted in their seats; a few coughs were muffled into sleeves. This is when he shifted into regretful mode, like a father trying to explain death to a child. Which was, now that Marlo thought about it, an apt metaphor to describe growing up among survivalists: adults continually explaining death to children.

"That chance—if it ever really legitimately existed—is long behind us now. It's too late to take evasive action. We used to talk about putting on the brakes. That was back when this train still *had* brakes. The only rational action left to us is preparation, and we intend to prepare as thoroughly as we can for the coming crisis."

Now came the part that had so scared her when she'd overheard her parents rehearsing it one night when she was a kid.

"There's nothing radical to the ideas we're proposing. To be clear, we're not offering a solution. Large-scale population collapse across every species on earth, including humans, is inevitable. We advance no cure or salvation. Instead we are providing the chance for a small group on the margins of this dying world to survive the coming collapse and form a new society from scratch. Let me repeat that: a *chance*. There's no guarantee that our little group will be capable of surviving a large-scale apocalypse—for instance, a nuclear strike—or that there won't be incredible hardships in store for any who do survive what is to come.

Our sole interest is in creating a microsociety in which the remains of the human race can have a fighting chance at starting again."

The mood in the room had turned now. Marlo saw disapproving glances being exchanged. *I mean, this is apocalyptic shit,* she imagined them thinking with growing distaste. Did the guy have to be so grim? Couldn't he just let them enjoy the plush surrounds and the prospect of free drinks and snacks afterward? *Don't worry,* she wanted to tell them, *the reassuring part is almost here. The part where you get to be saved.* Carlton lifted a placating hand.

"While our group is unanimous in its belief that the lust for money and power are major contributing factors in the ravaging of our planet, I want to be clear that we have no current objections to wealth accumulation." There was a burst of laughter. "In fact, you're actively encouraged to amass as much wealth as you can in the time that is left. We require a minimum investment from each new member, adults and children alike, with no cap on how much you may invest. Note the term *invest-ment.* This money isn't a gift, or a donation, or a scam, it literally is an investment in the only viable future left to us. These funds are used to purchase equipment, infrastructure, medicine, lab supplies, vehicles, and a whole host of other necessities on which our society will depend."

Marlo reached into her bag for her tube of lip gloss, reapplied it in a kind of trance, like a boxer psyching herself up to enter the ring. He was wrapping things up now, and her moment to be useful was nearly here.

"The second phase of our new community is well underway. Feel free to peruse the plans on the illuminated displays behind you." He gestured toward the back of the room. Necks craned to look, and Marlo waved. "There are application forms available, and you'll also see a call-out for new members who excel in specific disciplines—agriculture, biology, construction—along with a list of items we're hoping to acquire over the next year. So if anyone happens to have a spare fleet of heli-copters lying around, we'd welcome your input!" A few people laughed. "No, really, we actually do need helicopters. Several members of the community are currently training to fly them. Anyway. We encourage you to visit the website to gain more insight and to offer any suggestions or comments on the community board. Thank you for listening today. Help yourselves to caviar and champagne."

She hadn't heard the speech in a long time, and it churned up the usual feelings. Discomfort. Despair. Pride. She wasn't a big fan of the speech's evangelical overtones, its fire-and-brimstone quality. There was also something of the stump speech about it, a rote spiel whose main objective was to shore up support with the party faithful rather than win over new converts. There was the hypocrisy in its clarion call—"Escape with us from the ruins we helped create!"—that caused a prickling sensation in her armpits. But she also thrilled to his voice and the conviction she knew lay behind the words.

They had a glass of champagne together after everyone had left. Marlo plumped down in a folding chair, stretched her legs out in front of her, and tore the crusts off a sandwich, eating it with slow steadfastness. Her father watched her with a look of indulgent affection.

"You know, you've always been a good eater."

She laughed, covered her mouth quickly to avoid spraying crumbs. "What does that mean . . . A good eater?"

He smiled. "I mean you always approached food with this deliberation. Never fussy, never wolfing it down. Just this almost dainty concentration."

"OK." She laughed.

"When we first picked you up in Zhengzhou, you wouldn't stop crying." Marlo put the sandwich down on a small china plate, balanced it on her lap. She always both dreaded and longed for stories about her adoption. "That was normal, the ladies from the orphanage told us. The kids were naturally scared when their new parents came to take them away. They were quite, uh, un-PC about it, you might say. 'The little girl is scared of your white skin and round eyes,' they told your mother and me. 'They've never seen people with those before.' Either way, you were inconsolable for that first day. It broke our hearts. We took you back to the hotel room, where you proceeded to cry for the next eight hours. And you know what finally calmed you down?"

"I'm guessing, from the way this conversation started, some kind of food?"

He laughed as if she were fiendishly clever to guess it. "Yes! We bought some fruit yogurt and offered it to you. At first you kept crying but we could see you gradually taking note of the yogurt. Considering it. You kept looking from the container to our faces and back, like you were making this internal calculation."

Marlo winced. It was excruciating to have your own origin story, which you couldn't even remember, recounted out loud.

"And gradually you stopped crying, until you were just sniffling a bit and hiccuping. Your little angelic tear-stained face. Ah, I'll never forget it." He chuckled, lost in the memory. "Anyway, you put your tiny hand out, and you pulled the yogurt toward you. We peeled off the lid and started feeding it to you with a spoon, and as you took each spoonful and slowly swallowed it you didn't take your eyes off our faces. It was like you'd understood that we were your caretakers now and had given us your seal of approval. It was one of the best moments of my life."

"Dad, I was probably just hungry."

"That's the whole point, honey. You entrusted us to feed you."

What choice had she had, that tiny helpless, abandoned child, but to entrust them to feed her? But Marlo refrained from pointing this out. She had never been interested in hurting his feelings, not even as a teenager. And to be fair, all children made such calculations, entrusting their well-being to adults who may or may not prove worthy of their trust.

"Speaking of food, what do you want to do for dinner tonight?"

"Would you mind horribly if your old papa stays in his room tonight? Thinking of ordering room service and taking an Advil. Today was pretty exhausting, and I've still got tomorrow to get through."

She fussed over him for a while, which she knew he liked in spite of himself, brought him a pot of tea, and arranged for the butler to have a bath filled for his return to his room. Assured him that she would be perfectly fine, would get room service herself and catch up on TV, a white lie she justified as allowing him not to worry about her. Then she was free, sprung loose for an entire night.

She had dinner at a sushi bar in midtown, near MoMA, chose to sit at the bar while chefs worked their knife magic from behind a glass partition, slicing through the pale, glossy flesh as though it were butter. She felt like a child in an aquarium. The chefs bent and straightened behind the glass, sea creatures moving through the water. The restaurant wasn't particularly busy or particularly good, although she appreciated that she could see her food being transformed from lifeless flesh to art. (Fish itself was a novelty, a rare treat on the ranch, thanks to its distance from the coast and the prevailing idea that it was faintly immoral to add to the world's severe overfishing problem.) She ordered a carafe of sake and sat there for a few hours, savoring it all, the quiet, stoic talents of the chefs performing their silent opera, the soothing fire of the sake in her throat, the book, the hushed hum of life being lived around her. The utter pleasure of being surrounded by strangers. When she couldn't draw the sake or the book out any further she reluctantly called for the check and walked back to the hotel room, a full participant now in the city's arcane rules. (Keep to the right, jaywalk with confidence, don't make sudden stops, just keep moving.)

❦

He approached her on the second day of the recruitment conference. His name tag read "James Salter." *Like the writer,* she thought, through a kind of mental fog. She had tuned out her father's speech and the following Q&A session, had handed out brochures with a friendly but not altogether present smile. Her feet hurt, and she was dreaming about spending her last evening ordering room service and devouring the internet while it was available to her guilt-free.

"Hi there . . ." He glanced down at her name tag, and his gaze brazenly brushed her breasts on the way back up to her face. "Marlo."

"Hi."

She looked down and shuffled the brochures, trying not to blush. It had been a long time since she'd been so thoroughly eye-fucked. He looked to be around Kenneth's age, perhaps a few years older, but this man was far more confident and suave, aware of his own magnetism. He had a full head of dark, close-cropped hair going gray at the sideburns, and a suit so perfectly snug it could only have been custom made for his frame.

"So what's your story?"

"My story?" Her hackles instantly rose. She shot him an icy look. It had been so long since she'd been in a big city, but every time she'd left home as an adult she had encountered some version of this. Occasionally outright racism or fetish chasing, but somehow more offensive when it was subtle, as now.

"Yeah. Like, how are you connected with this fantastic enterprise." He half turned, gesturing toward the screen on which a slideshow of idealized images of the ranch looped. A gold ring glinted on his left hand.

"Oh. Carlton is my dad."

The man raised an eyebrow.

"Ah. So you live in this little Oregonian utopia as well?"

"That's right. So before we get to know each other too well, let me just preempt the question you're about to ask me. Let's see. 'What are you?'"

"'What *are* you?' What kind of question is that?"

She shrugged.

"The usual question people ask. That, or something more polite like, 'What race are you?' or 'What's your ethnic background?' or just 'How come you're so exotic?' Stuff like that."

"Wow. Those are pretty rude questions."

"Yeah."

"Well, I definitely wasn't going to ask any of those."

She let her mouth form a stiff smile. "That's a good start, then."

"But wait. Who are these people asking you these questions? Don't you, uh, already know all the people on the ranch from, like, way back?"

She laughed.

"I guess you think I never leave the place, that we're all prisoners there or something?"

"Well, not exact—"

"I leave quite a lot, actually," she said brusquely, then realized how prissy she sounded. Also it wasn't really true, these days. "Mostly when one of my parents is giving a talk like this. I've been to lots of the major cities, Los Angeles, San Francisco, Chicago . . . Anywhere people are rich and scared, basically."

He laughed. "I see. So, any interest in having a drink with a rich scared guy tonight?"

The trick was coming up with an excuse to tell her father. If she didn't tell him she was going out, he was likely to call her room for a chat or even offer to watch TV together in his suite. So she told him she felt like going to a real-life movie theater to see a movie. She was confident he wouldn't offer to accompany her: he'd been complaining all day about his arthritis, and she could tell he was counting down the moments until he could take a painkiller, mix a gin and tonic from the minibar, and lie down. She experienced a twinge of guilt when he smiled broadly and hugged her, expressing his gladness that she was continuing the tradition of seeing films on the big screen at a theater, because that had been one of her greatest joys as a child, a reliable way to make her day.

She took the subway down to the Village, where James lived, because he claimed that's where all the best restaurants were, and she obviously wasn't in any position to suggest alternatives. She wore her new black dress and more dramatic makeup than usual, but she refused to think of it as a date. He had arrived before her, and she tried to feel offended rather than gratified by the obvious and carnal pleasure he took in watching her walk in, this younger woman who had agreed to meet a married man she didn't know for dinner.

"Wow," he said, taking her coat. "You look great."

She didn't appreciate the way he rested his hand with such surety in the hollow of her lower back, as if he had already claimed her, so she said with a certain acerbic coyness, "Oh, you didn't bring your wife? I was hoping to meet her."

He laughed, wagging his ring finger at her. "So perceptive. Maybe we're separated?"

"I actually don't really care. Presumably you have some kind of arrangement."

"You're kind of cynical for a twenty-five-year-old, aren't you?"

"Maybe. There's a lot to be cynical about."

He gave a mock frown. "Wait, but I thought you lived in paradise?"

She sat down next to him on the banquette, picked up the wine list, and started perusing it.

"Hmm. I don't remember ever calling it that." She couldn't help feeling stung by his perceptive teasing. Wasn't that exactly what they were selling, after all? "The ranch has its problems, just like anywhere else."

"To be honest, it looked like some kind of heaven to me, but maybe that's just the overworked capitalist in me talking. What do you feel like drinking, Marlo?"

They ordered wine and salad and bowls of pasta, and Marlo relaxed a little into the convivial beauty of the candlelit restaurant, which was styled in that ersatz, particularly Manhattan way after a highly specific type of Parisian neighborhood bistro. After they had clinked glasses, James studied her face in the candlelight with a small smile on his handsome face. She was so sure he was about to make some flattering remark and so ready to graciously receive it, perhaps even reciprocate, that she was legitimately taken aback when he said instead, "I genuinely, no bullshit at all, admire your dad. But I don't know. I mean, from what I can tell, it's a bunch of survivalists with great taste in architecture and fat bank accounts, right? All that paranoia about the coming apocalypse."

"So you don't believe the human race is on a path to disaster?"

He shrugged. "No more so than at any other time in human history. I'm not scared."

"If you're not scared, it's only because you're not paying attention." That was a line the ranchers liked to use. She was aware of how prim, how insufferably smug, it sounded.

He laughed. "What flavor is the Kool-Aid at your ranch, anyway?"

"You don't need to insult me. Being a climate change denier isn't exactly the way into my pants."

That sobered him up. "Sorry. Look, for argument's sake, let's say that the earth really is on a collision course with disaster. You really think your little corner of Oregon is going to survive it?"

"Maybe. It's worth a try."

His arrogance irritated her, but she was also pulsing with the exhilaration of talking with someone whose entire history she didn't know intimately. The giddy newness of defending her position on the inevitability of societal collapse was a luxury not available to her at home, where everyone agreed with one another. She hadn't realized how much contrarianism had been missing from her life. It was kind of a turn-on.

Perhaps this same contrarianism drove her to take a car back to her hotel with James, then whisk him into the elevator before the concierge could recognize her smuggling a strange man into her room, then fuck him senseless, then fall asleep, then wake up in the soft-focus dawn and rouse him so she could be on top this time, her thighs straddling his body and her hair dangling to his chest, knowing how good she must look to him from this angle. It was easy enough to justify: when might she have the opportunity for casual sex again? It wasn't the first time she had used one of these trips as a pretext to get discreetly laid. She wondered if it would always feel this detached from intimacy, though. It always felt as though she were floating a few inches out of her body, waiting calmly for it to be finished.

They lay there for a few moments on top of the sheets, weak limbed and out of breath, returning slowly to their own private selves. Then he kissed her neck appreciatively and joked that he really needed to find more end-timer babes, before jumping up to shower. She used the bathroom after him, and they put their respective armor back on. She didn't turn away as she dressed, and she could tell from the hungry way he watched her that he liked that. Seeing him disappear into his beautifully tailored suit gave her a pang of something like nostalgia, imagining how she would dream about this encounter in lonelier times to come. He had agreed to them leaving the room separately but told her he wanted to grab a coffee from the dining room before he went to the office.

"I promise to pretend I don't know you," he said, flashing a charming smile, hand over heart. He slipped his business card into her back pocket, patted her ass playfully. "If the end of the world doesn't end up happening, I'd love to see you again."

She smiled, kissed him on the mouth, and left the room.

🌿

In the restaurant she took a seat at a two-top by the window overlooking Columbus Circle, assuming her father would probably join her. She looked around but didn't see him. The newspaper had been laid beside the coffee cup, but she was too distracted to actually read it. The words swam like ants across the page, gibberish. She felt something touch her neck and looked up with a start to see James's back as he strode away from her. Marlo watched him order a coffee with the waitress. He bantered in a flirty way that opened a tiny pit of jealousy in her stomach. She looked back at her paper, flustered, and the next time she looked up, her father was standing beside the table.

"Oh, hi, Daddy, how are you feeling?" she said, neglecting to look closely at his face. "Come join me."

She pulled out the other chair, folded the paper up, and finally noticed that he was failing to sit down. He was leaning on his cane, and she realized he must have had a bad night.

"Marlo, who was that man?"

Her heart skittered. "Which man?"

"The man who touched you just then. It looked like you knew each other."

The way he was looking at her, the disappointment in his eyes. She withered beneath it.

"Oh, him? That was one of the investors who came to the seminar yesterday."

"That doesn't really explain why he, a presumed stranger, felt entitled to touch your neck."

Marlo took a deep breath, prickly-hot with embarrassment. "We went out for a drink last night. That's all."

Her father sat finally, but more in physical defeat than to keep her company. He looked years older, pale and worn.

"Marlo, he has to be twenty years older than you."

"Not that much," she mumbled, but even to her own ears it sounded like a paltry defense.

"Regardless. What were you thinking, hanging around with a man like that?"

She looked down at her coffee going cold, a repulsive skin of milk forming on its surface.

"Dad, please. I'm not a child."

That was just it though, she thought. She was still a child to them, always would be that adorable little girl who overcame her fear of them because she needed to be looked after. There had been an incident, back when she had first entered puberty and could finally, miraculously, fill out a bra, albeit a modestly sized one, when Alex had returned from a European trip with her parents. Alex had always enjoyed greater freedom to explore the world, and this had sometimes been used against her parents after she and Ben broke free—that they had been altogether too liberal with their enthusiasm to expose her to travel. Alex had brought Marlo back some saucy lingerie from her trip to Paris. Among the haul was a deep-blue lacy bustier whose pneumatic uplift caused Marlo's young breasts to levitate. It was a faintly absurd garment, even she could see that, like something a bawdy wench in a Western might wear, but it made her feel impossibly sophisticated, and the next day she wore it, went down to breakfast as usual with it peeping out from beneath her shirt. Her parents had gone nuts, one of the few times in her life they had ever raised their voices at her, had forbidden her to take the scheduled trip into town. The shame and humiliation could still be summoned and prodded years later, like a phantom limb.

"You don't even know that man," her father said, pulling her back into the equally uncomfortable present. "He could be . . . anyone!"

"He is anyone. I mean, he's a person. Just a guy, a normal guy."

"You know what I mean. You could have put yourself in danger. You don't know what men are like."

"How am I supposed to ever find out what men are like on the ranch?" She hadn't meant to bring it up, but she was pissed off now. "Everyone's either your age or a teenager! There's no one for me there."

Her father looked chastened. "I know, honey. But this isn't the way."

"That's not really your decision, though, Dad. I'm not sorry for doing it, but I'm sorry that you're upset."

She hadn't calculated how the phrase *doing it* was going to act on him. He blanched further, shrank away from her, and looked like he was going to throw up. She had confirmed a deep-buried dread that his daughter had not only gone out with this man, this vile, predatory older stranger, not only allowed him to touch her on the neck as he passed her in the restaurant, as though she were a piece of newly acquired art he was caressing, but had possibly let him touch her in other intimate ways. Ways that he refused even to consider.

"I guess we'll just leave it at that, then," he said stiffly. He hated confrontation, especially with his beloved daughter, and Marlo felt the lonesome guilt of the only child descend.

"Yes, let's. Where's our waiter? I'll order some tea for you."

He nodded, his mouth set in a grim line, but she could already see him cataloging the hurt away, locking it up in some inner vault where it would do less harm. The hurt was receding because it had to in order for him to survive. She was reminded of the story about herself as a baby, how even her tiny still-forming brain had understood the absolute necessity of accepting love when it came from the only people who promised to look after you forever and never hurt you.

6

There were two signals that carried the tragedy to her on the breeze. The first was the echoing report of a single gunshot, followed by a long, ringing silence. The second was the sound of a man's scream, just once, short and high-pitched and never to be forgotten. Marlo stood straight up, and the book she had been reading slipped off her lap, splaying pages-down on the floor. Even outside goose- or duck-shooting season, occasionally hunters could be heard in the far hills beyond the property. But she knew the shot hadn't been a hunter. She ran to the door, opened it a crack, and looked out, half shielding herself, like a suspicious tenant peeking out of their apartment door in a bad neighborhood. She'd seen the police shows, had always thought it ludicrous, the idea that civilians would be so reluctant to get involved when their neighbors were in danger, but she understood now, could see the impulse was deeply embedded in the risk-aversion functions of the brain. For a while nothing more happened, and she tried to take comfort in this. Already she doubted her own memory of the sounds. The only other house she could see from here was Neil and Jay's, a beautiful ranch home overhung by maple trees, and beyond that the ugly terra-cotta roof of the house Simon and Julia had built. There was no movement from either building. She considered calling Jay to see whether he had heard anything, but that seemed ludicrous, an overreaction.

The temptation to step back inside, to close the door on whatever might be unfolding, was overwhelming. She obeyed the impulse, returned to her Marlo-shaped depression in the sofa, and went back to reading her book. But someone must have replaced the words with hieroglyphics from some dead language, because her brain refused to comprehend them. After a while, though, her heartbeat resumed its normal rhythm, and the marks on the paper reverted to words again.

She looked up at the sound of engines, in time to see two cars scream past on the main road. No one ever drove fast here. She ran to the window, tried to identify the vehicles, but it was hard to tell. It was one of those strange things—somehow, out of all the vehicle makes and colors available, almost every rancher drove a shiny black, late-model sedan or SUV. Close on their tail followed two more cars, and then she saw the people on foot, coming across the fields and hills, running . . . toward what?

Without a plan, she threw open the door and started running too, and as she ran, Kenneth's pickup truck passed her. He slowed down briefly when he saw her and through the driver's window he gestured and said something, but she couldn't hear him, and he soon passed by. The blood pounded in her head, filling her ears and blocking out any other sound. When she was close to Neil and Jay's home, she tripped on a knot of dead tree root, went flying toward the ground. She thrust out her hands to break the fall, but her chin still made second contact with the recently thawed earth. The blow shuddered through her. She tasted blood: she had bitten the inside of her lip. (Later a blood blister would rise there, and she would worry it with her tongue, and as the blister grew smaller she would become panicked because she had come to associate the wound with the person she would lose that day, as if once it were gone there would be nothing left to remind her anymore. But that was later.) She rose unsteadily, brushing off her clothes. There were two dirty patches on the knees of her jeans. Even the pain felt like a dream, at a remove, like being on gas at the dentist.

When she arrived outside Neil and Jay's house, there were clutches of people gathered on the front lawn, faces grim and scared.

"What?" she asked no one in particular. A few people looked at her, then away. Where was Kenneth? What were they waiting for? Lacking any idea of what else to do, she dropped to her knees and sat on the lawn, staring around as if seeing her friends' home for the first time. Her gaze landed on a pair of twigs, roughly lashed together with twine to form a crude cross shape, staked into the ground just to the left side of the jaunty red door. The sight put her in mind of a story her father had once told about his travels in South America, how the workers on building sites always fashioned makeshift crosses to protect the construction site, created from whatever was free and plentiful—barbed wire or scrap timber or rebar torqued into shape. How she had been fascinated by this superstition, but had also felt sorry for those workers, who placed all their faith in something so irrational.

As she was staring at the twigs, Kenneth emerged from the house, head bowed. That's when she knew for sure. A few of the other ranchers followed him out the front door, gripping one another by the arm or waist. Strangers all, their familiar faces distorted in grief.

"Who's in there with him?" someone asked, and there came an answer Marlo couldn't hear.

"Well, we need to get him out of there," the first person said, voice rising.

"Someone call the police and an ambulance," said Kenneth, his gaze aimed at a patch of lawn. "Tell them there's been an accident. Tell them there's a body."

A collective moan rose up from the waiting crowd. Marlo hid her eyes behind her upraised knees as the dizzying nausea came lurching up. She felt someone crouching in front of her, then a large hand reaching out to rest on her shoulder. She detected Kenneth's loamy scent, acrid with sweat and something else.

"Let's get you out of here," he said in a soft, private voice, like he didn't want anyone to notice he was playing favorites. He half rose, called out to unseen people: "Let's get everyone cleared out of here! To the Commons."

He gently propelled Marlo to her feet, walked her over to his truck while she clung to his shirt like a child. Only once they were inside the cabin of the truck and shielded a little more from public view did he lower his grizzled head, resting it on the pocked leather of the steering wheel. He tapped the crown of his head several times on the wheel.

"This is bad, Marl."

"Who is it?" Marlo didn't even recognize her own voice. "I don't know anything! Is it Jay?"

He shook his head. For once he seemed lost for words, overwhelmed with an emotion too large to wrestle into submission. Marlo covered her face with her hands, as if that might keep the truth at bay for a little longer.

❦

It wasn't the first death inside the ranch. There had been Mr. Pearson, back in 2012, the best landscape architect they'd ever had, who'd suffered a heart attack while pruning his lemon tree. His wife didn't hear a peep, only discovered him a little while later spread-eagled on the lawn with the shears still gripped in his hand, so polite even in the act of dying that he hadn't wanted to disturb her. That had been sad, but the sorrow was grounded in a comforting reality. He had been eighty-four years old, after all, had led a long, happy, and productive life. Those were the kinds of things they said to one another afterward, smiling gently when they'd recall little anecdotes from his life that definitively proved it to have been worthwhile. There were no such comforts available this time around. How to make sense of something so patently senseless? The obscene waste of life. The fact that there hadn't been any signs of whatever had been going on in Neil's head that led him to kill himself. The fact that his husband, Jay, had been in the house, had been the first to find him.

The police arrived, grim faced and interrogating, their low staccato questioning going on into the night. Finally, when they had pulled as much information as they could get out of a succession of shocked, disbelieving faces, two somber-looking strangers arrived at the main house and after a brief consultation with one of the elders, loaded Neil's body onto a stretcher and into a long white van. Marlo, staring out the window, was struck by how small the bag was, how the modest lump beneath the rubbery black skin of fabric seemed only marginally to suggest a human life. Jay had been sedated, was sleeping at Marlo's parents' house.

Her mother called Marlo the day after to say that Jay had asked for her, and so she went to see him. She found him sitting on the platform that jutted out over the stream running beneath her parents' house, a mug of tea in hand. He looked the same at first, perhaps just a little paler, but when he released her from a long, rib-crushing hug, she saw that something had gone out of him, some essential light snuffed out.

"Jay-Jay, I'm so sorry." She had resolved to be strong, not to try to snatch any of his grief for herself, but on the last word her mouth began to quiver. Jay pressed his hand to her bottom lip.

"I know, honey."

She took his hand, gripped it in her lap. They sat and looked out at the indifferent stream, burbling away.

"Did you know he was a pastor when I met him?"

Marlo turned to look at him, astounded. "Neil? No. Seriously?"

"Oh, yeah. He was super into it. And here was I, a San Francisco party boy who'd never been in a church in his entire sinful life. I always figured it was some repressed gay man thing. Like his self-loathing had driven him to religion. But I don't know." He stopped talking for a long time, so long that Marlo thought that was all he was going to say. But then his shoulders twitched as though he'd been jolted out of his reverie by some unseen, insistent prompter. "I think differently now. I think he really found comfort in it. In his faith. He left the church once we got together, then he started working for the alt-weekly paper, and we never really talked about religion again . . ." He trailed off. "I thought that was the last of it. But the last year or so, he, well, something terrible happened to him. Having to research all that bad news, it was like a toxic chemical, the kind that's harmless in small doses but builds up over time when you're exposed to it for too long. Do you know what I mean?" His voice was pleading. Marlo could tell he had been burning to say all this, and through the veil of grief she was touched that he had chosen her.

"Of course," she said softly. "Of course. Poor Neil."

"He started acting really weird. He'd go into these depressions, and he'd disappear for hours at a time, sometimes even overnight. I never knew where he went. And in the last few months he started talking about God again. In this really . . . aggressive way. Like he was testing me or something."

"I'm so sorry," she said, squeezing his knuckles even tighter. How inadequate words were.

Jay sighed and leaned his head on Marlo's shoulder. "Hon, will you help me with something?"

"Of course. Anything."

"Clearing out the house. I just can't bear to face it on my own."

"Clearing out? You're leaving?"

"What do you think?" He gave a grim laugh. "You think I want to stay here after what happened? I've lost everything I ever cared about."

"No. Of course not. I understand." But the bitter, selfish thought arrived that she would be losing something too.

"I'm going to demolish the house as well."

"I understand." It seemed to be all she could say.

"You were always my favorite, Marls."

"You were always mine too, Jay."

Below them, swallows swooped just above the skin of the stream, plucking insects on the wing.

The wake was winding down. There had only been one truly terrible moment, when Simon had come forward and demanded to say a prayer for Neil. A hush had fallen over the room: people glanced at one another, subtle grimaces rippling from face to face. Marlo's chin had jerked up at his words. So that crucifix she'd seen under her old boyfriend's shirt hadn't been for decoration, after all; she wondered if Simon had known all along about Neil's past, had encouraged him in his religious reawakening. The thought made her feel sick and unbalanced, like teetering on the edge of a cliff. Jay had walked over to Simon, who stood straight-backed, hands clasped piously at his breastbone, and had said very quietly, "I think we've had quite enough of your fucking religion for now, thanks."

Simon and Julia had left the wake shortly afterward, his head held high, hers drooping, defeated, on her long neck. Marlo retreated to the kitchen of the Commons, where she began to mechanically wash mugs and plates. Kenneth found her there—it was obvious he had been looking for her—and came up beside her, so close that she knew he wanted to say something that no one else could hear. She didn't want to look at him. Before he could say anything, she blurted it out, the thing that had been haunting her. "Do you think that stash we found . . . Do you think it was Neil's?"

Kenneth swallowed, nodding slowly. He picked up a cloth, began drying the dishes, reaching over her head to replace them on their shelves.

"Should we say something? To the police?"

"No. Hell no. What good would that do, Marl?"

"I don't know," she said miserably. "Do you think that maybe we could have, I don't know, prevented this somehow? I thought for a while it was Simon. I thought it was his writing in the books."

Kenneth put the cloth down, pulled her around to face him.

"Ow, you're hurting me."

"Sorry." He relaxed the vise of his grip. Spoke in a hissed whisper that surely would raise more suspicion than a regular tone. "Don't even think that! This is one person's responsibility. *One person.* Neil. He chose to take his life. It's terrible and it's tragic, but there was something not right with his brain."

"But maybe we could have headed it off somehow." She didn't believe this, but there was a chilly kind of comfort in being reassured. "We could have done . . . an intervention?"

Kenneth shook his head. "He was determined, see, I've seen it in the Army. He would have found a way even if we had warned everyone. Some people are a bomb waiting to go off."

Marlo nodded, but the tears finally fell. Kenneth was harder. He had been out in the real world, and even though she knew certain things academically, he knew them from a more painful lived experience. For instance, that you couldn't save people from their own destructive impulses.

"Religion is poison," he said quietly, looking around to make sure no one was listening. "And some poisons will just seep out of the earth, no matter how far down they're buried."

Marlo sniffed. She tried on a weak smile. "I like how even your metaphors are agricultural."

He laughed gruffly then, gave her a playful hit with the cloth, but almost immediately he sobered up again, as if being recalled to his real duty there.

"Listen, we'll keep that cache we found a secret between us, alright?"

"Sure. But what if the police find it? Won't it look bad? I don't know. Like, prove their theory that we're all survivalist lunatics?"

"That's why I'm going to get rid of it."

Marlo opened her mouth to speak, and Kenneth laid a warning finger across her lips.

"Leave it to me. Please. That's the safest way."

Marlo looked at him, swallowed further questions. "OK. But be careful."

"Always."

Then he spun around and walked out of the room without another word, leaving Marlo feeling strangely abandoned. Only later did she wonder why Kenneth, too, had connected Neil to religion. She thought she was the only one who knew.

The police returned to finish their report. There was no reason to believe they had any suspicions about the death. Suicides were a tragic reality in these rural areas, nothing out of the ordinary. "It's just bureaucracy," the ranchers assured each other. "Just paperwork." But having police around felt like yet another egregious tainting of their world. The ranchers had little choice but to let them through the gates and inside. One of the detectives requested a tour of the property. When he said, "Anyone is free to join us," it sounded like a threat.

Marlo and several of the other ranchers tagged along as the detective performed a leisurely, thorough tour of the ranch, sitting stiff and upright in the back of one of the golf carts, looking around with curiosity as though he were a tourist being shown around a resort. When they came to the mausoleum, he tapped the driver of the cart on the shoulder, indicating he'd like to stop. The flotilla of carts all drew to a halt, and people piled out of them to stand around, arms hanging, determined to bear witness to whatever was going on.

"What's this for?" He glanced with distaste at the huge marble urn placed outside the locked entrance to the mausoleum. Then his eyes roamed over the imposing white stone edifice itself, its entrance a black steel door flanked by twin Doric columns. Three mossy stone steps led up to the door, and he gingerly mounted them and tried the door, which of course didn't open, as they had all known it wouldn't.

"It's where we honor our dead," said Carlton stiffly.

"Hold on. You're telling me there are human remains? Here?" He made as if to pull something from his shirt pocket, perhaps a notepad. "That's unsanitary and illegal."

Carlton laughed. "Of course not, Officer. We know the law. Several of us are environmental lawyers. This is just a place for remembering. Like a shrine."

He nodded slowly twice in the way of someone unconvinced, but for all his bluster he seemed intimidated by the ranchers. Especially Marlo's dad.

"This is private land," said Carlton pleasantly.

"I'm aware of that."

When their little convoy got close to the cave where Neil, or whoever it had been, had stashed the weapons, Marlo's heart galloped. But she should have known to trust Kenneth. The detective walked around the area, peering behind rocks and occasionally lifting a tumbleweed or kicking away a stone, but Marlo saw at a glance that the cave was empty, nothing but a black hole. As the detective drove away, taking the ranch's meticulously paved roads painfully slowly, Marlo's father put his arm around her shoulder, squeezed her arm.

"Hopefully we can all move on now."

She smiled up at him.

"Hopefully we can all begin to move on now," he repeated, much louder this time, for the benefit of the group. There were murmurs of what sounded like assent or relief, as if everyone had just been waiting for permission to put things behind them.

In the weeks that followed, a pall fell over the ranch. It turned out not to be so easy to put the past behind them. It caught up, insisted on dogging their heels. People took to avoiding one another's eyes, as if they shared a shameful secret. Communal gatherings ceased. Despair dragged Marlo through the days. She often found herself staring at objects until they blurred at the edges, unable to start or finish anything of substance. Her stomach ached so she more or less stopped feeding it, apart from the scraped-together leftovers or pieces of toast she would choke down whenever her hunger pangs became too demanding. Often at the end of the day she would contemplate the dishes and mugs scattered around the kitchen, still crusted with remnants of old food and caked-up liquids, and she would be overcome by a ballooning, inexplicable rage. That they should still be there, these inanimate objects, taunting her with their squalor, seemed an additional, unjust outrage.

She helped Jay pack up his belongings, endured a bitter farewell as he piled up the car and drove away from the ranch, and kept watch over the next few days while workers demolished the house where he and Neil had lived. Amazing how long a house took to build and how quickly it could be torn down. Within hours there was nothing but a wooden skeleton silhouetted against the white sky. The plants in her garden drooped, reproaching her every time she stepped outside, but it felt like too much trouble to water them so she turned her head away.

Then, even worse, other people started recovering. Joy returned in small portions and was snatched up greedily. Marlo began to resent the ability of the other ranchers to move on while she still felt as though she had been flayed, her raw skin left exposed to the elements. She missed Neil, but she missed Jay even more. It was as though they had both been disappeared by some repressive regime, and everyone had to pretend they had never existed.

One night she went to her childhood home and made dinner for her parents. It was time to let them know what she'd decided. When the meal had been cleared away and she'd refilled their glasses of wine and there existed no further feasible way to delay it, she told them her news, that she had decided to accept an internship with the National Parks Service and would be moving away soon. They didn't even try to hide how stricken they were. Marlo rushed into the aghast silence to assure them it wouldn't be forever.

"I wasn't sure I wanted to leave, but it's just this terrible thing with Neil . . . I just need to get out for a while. But I'll be back, of course, I'll be back as soon as the internship's over and they don't need me anymore. And for vacations."

"I guess we'd been expecting this," her mother said quietly. "But, honey, we can't pretend it's not devastating. We hoped we'd have you for a few more years."

"If it's just a case of wanting continuing education, well, there are some wonderful correspondence degrees now . . ."

Maya laid a hand on her husband's knee, shot him a look that might have been a warning.

"Now, Carlton, you know that's not what Marlo wants."

"Surely we should ask her that."

Marlo sighed. "Daddy, that's not what I want. Mom's right. I just need to clear my head for a while, get out there and see some of the world before I settle down here for good."

This sly move worked. Her parents squeezed each other's hands as if they had just been told the happy results of a test they'd been dreading.

"Of course it's your decision, darling. We'll support you in whatever you decide."

"Thanks, guys. I appreciate that. I love you."

She felt light-headed all of a sudden, breathless. The realization that she could actually leave had momentarily wrenched all the air out of her lungs. She didn't know whether it was fear or happiness: in that moment there seemed no functional difference between them.

7

There was an oppressive sameness to the days. The internship was only a month away from starting, but it felt unbearably distant. With the site of Neil and Jay's house razed, cleared, and planted with a memorial tree, the time for healing should have arrived. But instead fractiousness became a hallmark of communal gatherings. Passive-aggressive notes materialized around the Commons:

COMPOSTING IS A FAVOR FOR THE PLANET!
PLEASE REMOVE SHOES BEFORE ENTERING—PRETEND
YOU'RE IN JAPAN!
PLEASE ENSURE FRIDGE DOORS CLOSE COMPLETELY . . .
NO ONE LOVES MELTED ICE CREAM ;)

And a text went around one day after the weekly meeting suggesting that in the future, people wanting to continue socializing after the meeting should retire to one of the private homes so that those who cherished the peace of the Commons could continue to do so.

This new low-level social toxicity only served to convince Marlo that she had made the right decision in applying for the internship, but she could tell from the exaggeratedly supportive attitudes of her parents and friends like Kenneth that they considered her desire to break away a kind of madness. They treated her with gentle caution now, like a beloved family dog that had shown symptoms of rabies.

She wondered how she would explain her life on the ranch to outsiders. There weren't too many ways to explain it that didn't make it sound like a cult, or a survivalist enclave. She decided eventually that she'd tell people she lived in a gated community. That at least sounded neutral.

Some days she worried that the internship would prove a disappointment. Throughout her childhood, her father had written her letters, even though they lived in the same house. He was very formal about it, would seal them in envelopes and slip the letters beneath her bedroom door. Often they were little life lessons, homilies he perhaps would have felt uncomfortable articulating face-to-face. One time a solar eclipse was predicted. She was around eleven at the time and pretty into everything astronomical, and she and her friends had eagerly anticipated the moment. The adults had entered into the spirit as well, had planned a picnic with special eyewear and long-focus lenses, and the whole lot of them had decamped to one of the open fields to view the phenomenon. But at the last minute a storm had blown up, clouds scuttling across a charcoal sky. A sheet of blankness pulled down over the world, blotting out any sight of the sun and moon in their cosmic coupling. Marlo had been bitterly disappointed, had retired to her bedroom in a storm of tears. She had felt the eclipse's loss deeply, as if it had signified some last chance. The next morning one of her father's letters was there, a provocative white corner peeking out from beneath her door. *Dearest daughter,* it began as always. The general theme had been consoling her, naturally, but part of the letter had struck a different note. She had never forgotten it.

Everything you ever look forward to will disappoint you. The greatest and most beautiful things that will ever happen to you will take you unawares.

She kept the letter in a small mother-of-pearl box. She had kept all his letters.

Everything was out of whack, including the circadian rhythms that governed her sleep. No longer was she the person who slipped effortlessly into slumber like it was a warm bath. A great sleeper! That was another of the qualities her parents liked to embarrassingly praise, as if it were some hard-won personal achievement and not a fluke of biology. This new person lay staring at the ceiling for hours after she had put her book down for the night. When she closed her eyes she saw Neil and Jay's house crumpling into nothingness, heard the life-ending retort of the gun. So she was wide awake on the night her mother called. The phone lit up on her nightstand, and Marlo's heart cratered. Who else but disaster called at 2:00 a.m.? She knew the call would concern an emergency to do with her father: it was a call she had been waiting for and vividly dreading most of her life. Immediately she began making bargains with the deity she didn't believe in: *I'll give up the internship if he needs me. Just let him still be alive and we can go from there.*

"Mom, is everything OK? How is Dad?"

"Yes, darling, we're fine. We're both fine." The relief was so potent it left Marlo nauseated as it ebbed away. "It's, well, it's a bit hard to explain on the phone, but we have a visitor." Her mother paused as if checking with someone else on how to proceed.

"Um, what kind of visitor? It's two o'clock in the morning."

"I know. Listen, darling, it's a bit difficult to explain on the phone as I said. Why don't you just come here to the Commons?"

"Mom, you're kind of scaring me. Is it a person . . . An animal? An alien? Something bad?"

Her mother laughed, but it was the clipped, artificial, nervous laugh she reserved for parties.

"Nothing bad, nothing to be scared about. It might even be good, I don't know. Your father and I would just like you to be involved in . . . this."

Marlo would have been annoyed by this obfuscation if she hadn't still been experiencing the heady dopamine aftershocks of relief. Now that she knew neither of her parents was dead or dying she felt she could face whatever it was.

"OK, fine. Just give me a few minutes to get dressed and drive over there."

"Thanks, darling. I'll put some tea on."

"Right. Bye." Marlo stared at the phone for a few seconds, as if it might have some insight to share. It stayed silent and blank. She switched on the overhead light, got out of bed, and started pulling on clothes. The floorboards were cold under her feet, and she shivered, balancing on each foot alternately as she dragged the other sock on. She was so bleary, her brain so unaccustomed to being required to perform tasks at this hour, that it took until she opened the front door to realize it was raining. A gust of wind snatched the door from her grasp, and rain whipped her cheek like a slap.

"Jesus Christ," she complained to nobody, running back inside for an extra outer layer. It was June, and they were besieged by November weather. She put her hood up, ran to the car. The rain angled down in sharp, spiteful sheets. She started the wipers, swiped at the fogged-up windshield with her jacket sleeve. "Fuck."

With the moon and stars temporarily extinguished, her headlights were the only illumination. It was a relief to finally see the lights of the Commons wavering at the crest of the hill, a comforting yellow gleam coming gauzily through the downpour. She parked next to her parents' BMW and ran, slipping and sliding through the mud, to the front door. She lowered her hood and the water trapped at the sides cascaded down her neck. She shivered like a wet dog, pulled her damp hair back, and tied it in a messy bun, then went to find her parents.

She found them in the main lounge, facing the fireplace, their backs to her. Their old friends Sven and Amber were there too, talking quietly over by the bookshelf. There was an impressive fire going, but she also noticed that someone had dragged a clunky electric fan heater in. It emitted a musty electrical smell that singed the air. Her nose twitched. At the sound of her footsteps they all turned, and her parents stood, ushered her over with exaggerated gestures indicating she should approach quietly. Marlo almost laughed: the whole thing felt like bad theater. She approached the sofa, expecting to be confronted with a dead or dying animal, or perhaps a tiny baby swaddled in a blanket, a foundling child left at their doorstep. Instead she saw a fully grown man, his lanky body slumped across two cushions of the couch, heavy-lidded eyes closed. Her heart lurched. She slapped a hand to her mouth, adding her own bit of pathos to the drama.

"Oh, my god. Is he dead?"

"No, no." Her father limped over, leaning heavily on his cane. "He's fine, we think. Just sleeping."

"What happened to him? Who is he? How did he get here?"

Questions bubbled up on her tongue. Her mother shook her head and glanced over at Sven, who moved closer to explain.

"I found him just inside the gate. A couple of hours ago. We woke up because we could hear something rattling out there. It was this guy, climbing the gate. He got pretty torn up, doing that or something else. We're not sure."

Marlo nodded numbly. Sven and Amber's house was positioned the closest to the front gates, and perhaps because of their military backgrounds or perhaps because they were just community-minded, they had long ago agreed to act as a kind of first defense for the ranch, guardians of the gate. It made sense that they would have been the first to detect an intruder, and yet it made no sense at all that this stranger was here. The ranch was miles from the nearest town and an arduous walk from the highway, particularly in the middle of a storm.

Marlo looked around at the gathered faces. Their bright-eyed expressions suggested some heightened awareness that reminded her of the alert caution of nocturnal creatures caught on infrared. She looked back at the stranger, could see now that he was breathing very softly. She was ashamed to have assumed he was dead, as if Neil's suicide had forever altered her radar for tragedy. As she was studying him, he woke with a spastic little shiver, stared straight at her with eyes as dark and haunted as a crow's. She couldn't help it: she jumped. The movement caused a ripple of reaction among the others. There were little gasps and exclamations, a communal surging toward the man on the couch. Everyone started speaking at once. The stranger looked at them blankly, neck swiveling to examine each face in turn. Then he closed his eyes again.

"Honey." Her mother was at Marlo's elbow, steering her toward the kitchen. "Help me fix him some more tea. I think he may have come down with something, a cold at least, maybe even pneumonia. His chest sounds a bit worrisome."

Marlo followed, glancing once over her shoulder at the little group clustered around the patient. Her mother prattled as she moved around in the kitchen searching for herbal tea bags and perhaps some small thing to eat, and after a while Marlo could no longer stand it.

"Mom. Who the hell is that out there?" She gestured dramatically out toward the main lounge. "What is he *doing* here?"

Her mother's eyes widened.

"Darling, I have no idea. He just turned up."

"Shouldn't we . . . I don't know. Call the police?"

She laughed. "Oh, honey, what good do you think that would do? Haven't we had enough of the local law enforcement sticking their noses in here? We can handle this ourselves."

Handle what exactly? Marlo wanted to ask. But she was suddenly weary, her stomach hollow and queasy from being awake at this unexpected hour. She accepted a cup of steaming tea and stood at the window blowing the steam away, looking out at the howling rain while her mother fussed over a tray.

"It's like *Wuthering Heights* or something," Marlo muttered.

"What is?"

"This. A stranger arriving in a storm. Kind of Gothic?" Her mother smiled indulgently. "What are we . . . Well, what are *you* planning to do with him?"

Maya shrugged. "We haven't discussed that. For now, we're just concerned with keeping him warm and dry. As soon as he's up to it we'll question him."

"With the whole group?"

"Of course."

Her mother picked up the tray, instructed Marlo to bring the little lemon and sesame seed cookies.

Marlo wasn't satisfied. While her parents went to fetch more firewood, she went and sat beside Sven.

"So. Where do you think he came from?"

"We don't know." Sven covered a yawn. "Sorry. I'm pretty wrecked. Not used to being a night owl. He hasn't told us anything. He just . . . appeared. But he's obviously in trouble. So we're taking him in until we can find out more."

"The thing is, we don't just take people in. Right?"

"Well, not usually."

"How did he arrive? By car?"

"No. We don't think so." He ran a hand through already-tousled hair. Marlo noticed for the first time that he still had on his pajama top under his sweater. "Look, the whole situation isn't ideal, believe me. After what happened with Neil, we could have done with a little less drama of this kind."

"What if he's dangerous?"

Sven shook his head unhappily, but it was unclear whether he was agreeing with her or trying to convey that the stranger wasn't, in fact, dangerous. But really, how could he know either way?

"OK." Marlo patted his knee. "No worries. We'll get through it."

Her mother returned with a small stack of wood, threw it to the side of the fireplace, and bent over with hands on hips, exhaling a melodramatic sigh. There was something strangely performative about her moves, like she was playing a long-rehearsed part.

"My goodness, that was strenuous." She reached a hand toward Marlo. "I'm so glad you're here, honey."

Marlo gave her a little hug. "Of course." She lowered her voice. "But, Mom, just wondering why you wanted *me* to see him?"

"I just thought you might be able to talk to him, sweetheart. He looks about your age."

She couldn't help but laugh. "Seriously? That's not . . . how things work."

"Oh, you know what I mean. I feel like you'd have more luck getting something out of him. Look, he's awake now! Why don't you go over there?"

Marlo sighed in resignation. She was fully awake now. The night no longer unfolded with the fuzzy logic of a dream. Everything looked sharp and indisputably real now, which made the renewed sight of the strange man hunched on the sofa even more bizarre. She had some experience with drugs, almost certainly more than her parents did, and both the pallor and hollowness of the stranger's face suggested to her a noncasual relationship with pharmaceuticals. This didn't exactly endear her to her task. She knew junkies could be paranoid, defensive, even violent, so she approached him gingerly. She sat down beside him on the sofa, but far enough away to respect his personal space. He blinked, so slowly that for one startling second his entire pale eyelid was on display. There was something distinctly reptilian about the languor of his movements. She half expected a narrow tongue to shoot out, flickering. When he opened his eyes again, he fixed them on her with a look of puzzlement. His wet hair was black and dense in the dim light, slicked back like an otter's pelt. She realized he was shivering. Without thinking

Emma Sloley

Marlo picked up one of his hands and rubbed it between her own hands to warm it.

Her mother watched from the sidelines. She moved away, then returned with a tray bearing another cup, a little jar of honey, and a steaming fresh pot of tea.

"Thanks," said Marlo, looking up. Maya poured the tea, and Marlo took the mug with her free hand, blew on it to cool it down. Once she deemed it sufficiently drinkable, Marlo tried to gently curl the stranger's fingers around the mug, but he pushed it away and grabbed hold of her hand again with such force that she yelped in surprise. She glanced at her mother, put the tea down on the table, and resumed rubbing his hands, taking care to avoid the raw scratches gouged around his knuckles. She sniffed discreetly, searching for the telltale metallic chemical scent of drugs leaching from pores, but he smelled oddly neutral, of nothing more sinister than the world outside—trees, soil, rain.

Over the next hour more ranchers arrived, trickling in from the wet and windy night to stare from a distance at the stranger, then retreat to huddle in corners, conferring. Whenever anyone approached the sofa where she sat with the stranger, Marlo would shoo them away or give orders to collect more wood, stoke the fire, fetch her a glass of water. Finally the stranger's hands ceased their tense shivering, and she saw that he'd fallen asleep. As if she'd just been waiting for this moment, Marlo's mom came over with a blanket to cover him. Marlo disengaged herself from his grasp, shook out her hands, cramping now with the effort of rubbing. Her eyes felt raw. She walked like a zombie over to a big leather chesterfield chair and dropped into it. As she slept, someone laid a blanket over her.

❦

She woke to the hum and clamor of morning. The comfortingly domestic aroma of coffee and toast made her stomach growl. She yawned and

88

sat up, throwing off the blanket. The fire was still blazing, or perhaps it had been newly lit, and a lot more ranchers were present than there had been the night before. It was practically a party. She padded to a window, peered out. The rain had stopped, and the trees surrounding the house were looped around with glittering veils of raindrops. She checked her phone: it was 11:00 a.m. The stranger wasn't anywhere to be seen. Part of her hoped he had just disappeared back into the woods.

But a few seconds later, he emerged from the bathroom, showered and shaved and looking, to her relief, less like a feral animal or an apparition and more like a regular human, albeit a tired, disheveled one. She took the chance to observe him before he noticed her, found it curious the way he stared around the Commons in a kind of—not wonder, exactly—but surprise, as though it were somehow different from what he had expected. But what was he expecting? How had he even known where to find them? Finally catching sight of her, he flapped his hand in a funny, bashful wave and walked over.

"Hey. You're Marlo, right?"

She nodded but didn't smile, just started pulling her hair into two braids. He stuck out a hand and she shook it, but the touch of his flesh reminded her too starkly of the intimacy of the night before, and she quickly dropped her hand, pretending to concentrate on her hair.

"I'm Wolf. Your mom, that's your mom Maya over there, right? I think I recognize her from the photos. She told me you stayed with me all night."

Marlo gaped at him, confused. What photos was he talking about? Then she remembered the dictate to be nice to strangers and flashed him a smile.

"Um, yeah. I was here. Along with a lot of others. Mom called me when you arrived. She was worried about you." This didn't sound like an entirely honest reckoning of events, even to her own ears. "How are you feeling, anyway?"

He shrugged. "OK, I guess. Considering."

"Right. Considering."

He looked down at his hands and then back at her.

"Sorry. I know I owe you all an explanation of why I'm here."

Before Wolf could explain anything, Kenneth appeared, looming like a burly bodyguard at Marlo's side.

"Just thought I should introduce myself. I'm Kenneth."

He thrust a rough hand into the space between Marlo's and Wolf's bodies. The freckled, golden-hair-stippled skin was nicked all over with small wounds and weathered by the elements, and half-moons of dirt were embedded under his nails, an impression that suggested more a creature's grizzled paw than a hand, and Marlo felt a quick, hot shame flare up. An old shame, one she carried with her always but only remembered at times like this, when it occurred to her how the ranchers must look to outsiders. Like savages. Scratching away in the dirt, creating a false world. Wolf hesitated for a moment, looking at the proffered appendage as if seeking more information as to what should be done with it. But then he grinned and grasped Kenneth's hand in his own, shaking it with the enthusiasm of someone being introduced to an unmet but long-cherished relative, and Marlo breathed again, knowing she had misattributed his hesitation, ashamed now of her own shame.

"Nice to meet you, Kenneth."

Kenneth shot the newcomer a dour look, as if he personally doubted this.

"What kind of a name is Wolf?"

"Ha, um. The kind my parents gave me? I don't know."

"Huh. Your daddy called Wolf too?"

"No. Why?" Wolf was still smiling, eager to get the joke, to be a good sport.

"Just wondering if you were raised by wolves."

Kenneth smirked, in a fittingly lupine way, at his own wit.

"You're a real funny guy, Kenneth."

When Kenneth walked away, Wolf scowled at his retreating back. "I take it Kenneth is the resident jerk."

"He's not so bad. He just really hates strangers. He takes a while to thaw out. Sorry."

"Don't worry about it, it's not your fault. But I am curious. Are all the guys here in love with you or just him?"

"What?" Her heart thumped with mortification. Heat rose to her ears. "No, of course not. I mean, that's not true."

"Are you kidding? The way he looks at you. Jesus."

Wolf laughed but in a fake, defensive way, like he was trying to prove Kenneth's unwelcoming words hadn't stung. Marlo was about to say something to smooth the fractious mood when Sven came over and placed a friendly hand on Wolf's shoulder.

"Sorry to interrupt, guys. Just needed to let Marlo know that there's a meeting starting in half an hour, in the hall."

It was obvious to everyone that the meeting concerned their new arrival. Sven seemed to realize the awkwardness of it all because he quickly followed up with, "Hey, Wolf, isn't it? We've got a place all fixed up for you to stay for a few days, until we . . . Well, anyway, if you come with me I'll drive you up there. It's about a mile up the road there."

"Sounds good. Thanks, man, really appreciate it. Let me just grab my stuff."

He shot Marlo a quick look, as if he wanted to say something more, but then he turned away and followed Sven out of the house. Marlo, watching them go, drew her spine up straight, achieving the haughtiness she'd failed to project when it was needed. Better late than never. *It's not my job to save you,* she thought, *whoever you are.* It felt good to say these words, even if only to herself.

After Wolf left, everyone started to move into the mess hall. Marlo wandered into the kitchen, where two pots of coffee were brewing. She poured herself some, yawning, mumbling hellos to various people and apologizing for her newly awakened, bed-headed state. She wanted nothing more than to return home, shower, and change clothes, but she knew she didn't have enough time before the meeting started. She went in and found a seat toward the back of the hall, balanced her coffee on the chair to reserve it, then went to the bathroom to pee, splash water on her face, and rub a finger futilely over her fuzzy teeth.

When she returned she saw that someone had dragged the lectern over and that her parents had arrived. They were both dressed neatly and semiformally: her father even had a tie on. She should have guessed they'd be the ones to chair the meeting. But it gave her a strange, displaced feeling to see them there, ready to address the room. Their body language radiated nervousness—her father kept tugging at his left earlobe, and her mother wiped her hands compulsively down the sides of her voluminous white linen pants, as if trying to rid herself of something slightly unsavory. These were familiar tics, but she'd only ever seen them in private. In public, on stage, they always presented a preternatural calm.

The two of them moved to the low platform at the front of the room and scanned the crowd, perhaps looking for their daughter. Marlo couldn't have said what spirit moved her to avoid their searching, but instinctively she slumped down in her chair like a teenager, making sure her head was in line with but slightly lower than the man sitting in front of her so that she effectively disappeared behind him. The searchlight of her parents' gaze passed over her row and moved on without identifying her. It made her feel naughty, like she was playing truant. She sipped her coffee, her eyes darting from side to side to see who was here. *Everyone who's anyone,* she said under her breath, then laughed for no earthly reason, delirious from interrupted sleep.

"OK, everyone." Carlton's voice did its commanding work on the room. Chatter died down, and eyes swiveled forward expectantly. "Maya and I just wanted to get out in front of this situation. Our new arrival. We've talked to him this morning and found out a little bit more about the circumstances of his arrival, so we wanted to fill you all in. His name is Wolf, and it turns out that he knows, or at least knows *of*, several of us here. I don't know how many people remember Danny and Michelle?" There was a hum of responses, of ranchers turning to partners and friends, a scattering of nods. "Back when we were young, a group of us had the idea to set up a kind of commune. Nothing on this scale. More like a small ashram, really, somewhere in California or upstate New York. The idea never went anywhere, but Danny and Michelle were part of that original plan. And this Wolf, turns out he's their son."

Little murmurs of interest rippled around the hall.

"We'd all lost contact over the years, so we didn't even realize Danny and Michelle had a son. The sad news is that Danny died recently. In a car accident. Very tragic. And Michelle lives—where did Wolf say, love? Brazil. That's right, Brazil. With her new husband. So bottom line, this kid is all alone in the world. And he decided to make his way here. That's about all we know for now. He's resting at the moment. But we just wanted to fill everyone in on the situation. Questions?"

Kenneth, a few rows in front of Marlo, stood up, pushing his chair back with a clatter. The buzz of conversation died down.

"Yeah, I have a question. When does he leave?"

There was some low shocked laughter at this. Marlo tried to stifle a smile. Kenneth was known for his frankness, but it wasn't a quality that many people admired. Marlo's father held up a hand.

"OK, thanks, Kenneth. Fair enough question. We know some of you are concerned about Wolf's ability to contribute financially. Perhaps more pertinent, though, is discussing what we can do for him, as a son of once-dear friends, to help him recover from his ordeal and return to, uh, society."

"What ordeal?" Kenneth had remained standing. "Kind of interested in what ordeal you think this kid has been through. As I understand it he's barely said two words, apart from letting you know he's related to some old friends."

Maya stepped forward on the stage with a wide smile.

"We'll take a vote of course, but I think most of us will agree that the compassionate thing to do is to at least wait until Wolf is feeling better before we throw him back out onto the streets."

Kenneth snorted disdainfully. Marlo knew he hated emotional language, considered it cheating.

"I think we should definitely vote on what to do about letting him stay," Amber called out, and Sven nodded beside her.

"What we should do? It's simple," retorted Kenneth. "Send him on his way like we always have with people who've tried to muscle their way in here."

"I kind of agree." A rancher called Nick stood up, swiveled around to try to make eye contact with as many people as possible. Marlo rolled her eyes inwardly: Nick was a one-time actor who had gone on to found a successful self-improvement seminar business, and she couldn't help harboring the mean-spirited suspicion that he just liked the idea of holding the room's attention. She also knew—because unlike many other ranchers, she was occasionally privy to the vetting process for new recruits thanks to her parents' high status—that he had only barely scraped into the ranch financially. As was sometimes the case with recently arrived immigrants to a new land, he and Kenneth were usually the most vehemently opposed to admitting any further new arrivals.

"We don't know anything about this guy," he protested, warming to the thrill of the public gaze. "He could be a spy, or I don't know, someone sent by the police to sabotage us." There was some laughter at this, but not all of it was comfortable—Marlo noticed a few ranchers exchanging worried glances. "I don't know, it just seems unwise to let him stay any longer than he needs to get on his feet again. Unless he goes through the proper channels, like everyone else. That's my two cents." He sat down again abruptly, and Kenneth, his arms crossed, nodded.

"Yeah, I'm with Nick," Kenneth said. "Let's take a vote. I'll respect whatever the majority decides. But I don't trust this guy, like I don't trust anyone who just turns up here in the dead of night, sneaking in with no explanation."

After the vote was taken and the result read out—the majority were in favor of allowing Wolf to stay for a few days, enough time to recuperate before returning to wherever he came from—Marlo went and sought out her parents. Their faces brightened with relief when they saw her, as if they had been afraid that Wolf had somehow taken Marlo's place, their daughter whisked away from them like some dark fairy tale. Did they think because she hadn't sprung from their own bodies that she could more easily be taken away from them? It chilled her that they might consider the familial bonds so fragile.

"Wild stuff," she said when she had extricated herself from their crushing hugs.

"Very unexpected," her father agreed, rubbing his neck and wincing.

"So you knew him already, this Wolf guy?"

The quick glance that vibrated between her parents confirmed her suspicion that they were hiding something from her, or at least withholding information. No doubt for her own good. Wasn't that what parents always did?

"Well, no," her mother said. "Knew his parents."

"How come you never mentioned them? Sounds like you were pretty close back in the day."

"When you get to be our age, sweetheart," said Carlton, "you forget a lot more people than you remember." They both laughed. "It just never occurred to us to mention Danny and Michelle. They haven't been part of our lives for decades."

"Did you have some kind of falling out?" She was just casting around now, a blind pig trying to snuffle out an acorn. But she saw with a little tremor of triumph that she'd struck the truth. *A* truth, at least. Her father blinked heavily, with great weariness.

"Something like that. All a bit regrettable. But ancient history now."

She could tell from his tone, and the way he tapped his cane twice softly on the ground—a subconscious signal—that the discussion was over. She understood that she'd simply caught them unawares, but that from now on the gates to this particular line of inquiry would be closed. Not that she was really that interested in the details of some decades-old feud. Her parents loathed confrontation, anything that could have been described as a scene. She wasn't surprised about their disinclination to rehash it, but it made her wonder about Wolf, about why he would be so keen to visit people he'd never met. People to whom his parents no longer spoke.

It was only after a surprise second meeting was called three days later, at which it was decided that Wolf could actually stay on at the ranch on a probationary basis—thanks in large part to a speech by Carlton in which he made an eloquent and persuasive case for Wolf joining the community and offered to personally cover the entry fee on the newcomer's behalf—that Marlo recognized how prescient Kenneth had been. He must have known that if it came up for a vote the other ranchers would want the newcomer to stay. And once that happened, the die would be cast. It was all a little puzzling, though. Her parents had never before volunteered to cover the initiation fee for any other would-be ranchers.

When Marlo questioned them afterward, her parents claimed their decision had been based partly on emotion—they felt a certain loyalty to Wolf's parents—and partly on practicality. There was an urgent need for young new residents, especially after the recent tragic events. New blood might be just the thing to help the community recover from the recent losses, they explained, as if Wolf were a new toy to comfort a grieving child.

8

It was time she went to him. Past time, really. It had been almost a week since Wolf had arrived at the ranch and Marlo had barely seen him in that time, except at a distance. She knew via her mother that so far no one had conducted the usual orientation for new arrivals. It was obvious from the eager looks and pointed silences whenever his name was raised that this task had been reserved for her. But the stubbornness that sometimes ruffled her composure surfaced. She pretended not to hear the hints, feigned obliviousness to the subtext. But she couldn't maintain the stance forever. The welcome celebration had already been planned, and it was considered poor etiquette to let someone attend their own party without having even been shown around the place. When she finally gave in, she made sure to frame it as her own idea.

She dressed a little more carefully than usual. Washed and blow-dried her hair and put on a summery dress in a shade of red that flattered her skin tone, then thought better of it and changed back into jeans and a light sweater. She applied blush and pink lipstick, then frowned at her reflection and smeared it all off with a tissue. She knew he'd grown up in Los Angeles and even if she hadn't known, there had been something about him that spoke of urbanity, a certain unconscious cosmopolitanism that she knew from experience was impossible to fake. Why did she care if he thought of her as a country hick? She hated that she'd already bound herself in the knot she always did with strangers, by trying to present herself as someone different so they'd like her.

Every night since her New York trip she'd fallen asleep thinking about her encounter with James Salter. The way he had looked into her face with a little smile when he came, as if they were sharing a secret. How appreciative he seemed, not in a pathetic older-man way, but more like he was a connoisseur who understood her value. The same excitement surfaced now when she thought of this stranger, Wolf. Hope cast up flares, searching for a friendly shore. It was wrong to think of him in this way, as if he were a ship steaming to her rescue, but it had been so long since she had been able to dream of a new prospect.

The object of her fledgling fantasies was living in one of the workers' cottages that had been hastily constructed after Kenneth had instituted his permaculture-based crop system. The rotational system demanded a lot of work, harder and dirtier labor than any of the ranchers were willing and able to do. That's what Kenneth had claimed at the time, anyway, calculating in his sly way that he'd be given carte blanche to employ as many temporary workers as he needed. These laborers arrived every season, the men and women alike dressed in denim jeans or overalls and baseball caps and bandannas and coming and going with so little fanfare that it was easy to forget they were even living and working there until you encountered one of them on the road or in a field (always with a swift deferential swiping-off of a hat or a chin-down shy smile). They were like industrious ghosts. The ten identical houses had been constructed on-site of raw pine, with tin roofs and cheap aluminum window frames. An eyesore by anyone's lights, but Kenneth had the sense to plonk them down on the escarpment east of the river, out of sight of the main homesteads and close to swampy marshlands that thrummed with bugs. Perhaps the other ranchers considered this dud real estate, a part of the ranch to which they'd never bother to venture, but Marlo found a wild beauty in its loneliness and would often pause to sit here on her rounds, although only when she knew there were no workers in residence—she wouldn't have wanted to infringe on their privacy. She had never been inside one of the houses.

Wolf took a while to answer her knock. His thick dark hair ran off in several contrary directions, and his expression was glazed, opaque, as if she'd just woken him up. He blinked a few times, trying to clear his vision, then ran a lazy hand through his hair, pushing it off his face. A strand fell back immediately over one eye. Marlo beamed. She felt as fresh and scrubbed and bright as first light striking dew on the grass. The sunshine was not reciprocated: Wolf frowned, like he was trying to recollect who she was. Hip cocked and an elbow propped on the doorframe. The subtle earthiness of unshowered flesh emanating from his shirt. Not off-putting, though, not to her.

"Oh, hi there. What's up?"

She hadn't rehearsed anything, had assumed the conversation would flow organically. Assumed her presence at his door would be welcomed as an unlooked-for but appreciated gift. Instead there was this stilted reception, just shy of hostility. The instinct was to turn on her heel and flee, but she hadn't been brought up to do that. She had been brought up to stand her ground, even as humiliation stained her cheeks more efficiently than the blush she had so recently wiped off.

"Hey. Just thought I'd, you know, see how everything was. How you're settling in."

Wolf nodded as if grudgingly accepting this explanation. He stepped aside, ushering her in. *If a gesture could be sarcastic . . . ,* she thought.

"Fine so far. It's all a bit surreal, though, I guess."

She stepped inside, looking with interest around the cabin. Discomfort dissolving into curiosity.

The cabin consisted of three small rooms. The main room was simply furnished, with a 1950s sofa that might have been salvaged from a thrift store, a tiny fold-down wooden table with two Thonet café chairs and a few tribal print rugs. In one corner, a cast-iron potbellied woodstove squatted. The door to what she assumed was his bedroom was open a slit. She glanced quickly at it, then away.

"Cozy."

"Better than what I'm used to, that's for sure." She looked at him, and he scraped his hand over the dark scruff on his chin. Maybe embarrassed at having revealed something of himself. "Anyway. Can I get you anything?"

In spite of the invitation, he didn't move to fetch anything, just stood with a kind of stubborn resolve in the center of the room, in his sagging jeans and a white shirt that he'd buttoned wrongly in two places. One side dipped to his crotch and the other rode up, grazing his ribs. These intimate spaces. She wanted to lean over and adjust him, brush her fingers over that patch of smooth taut belly.

"Oh, speaking of which," she said a little too loudly. "I brought you some muffins. I've been on a bit of a baking binge lately."

This sounded so trite, so hopelessly bound to some anachronistic notion of domestic female servitude, that she laughed nervously, more of a horse's snicker than anything related to humor. She pulled the backpack off her shoulder and thrust it toward him, a little angrily. *Take it off my hands,* she pleaded silently, but instead he turned away with a little smirk and opened a cupboard, stood aside like one of the sequined presenters on a game show to reveal its contents. Inside were stacked baskets and container after container of Tupperware, layered with pastries, fruit, crackers, donuts. So she hadn't been his first visitor.

"Uh, thanks. But I think this should see me through, oh, I don't know, the Rapture."

He grinned. Was he trying to be charming now? The happiness she'd felt on the way over, the jumpy, hollow excitement, curdled into disappointment. A quiet rage kindled in her—to be rebuffed by this stranger, this person who had shown up on their doorstep like some sodden waif, who had every reason to be grateful for their unprecedented hospitality. But almost immediately the rage snuffed itself out. The giddy excitement she'd felt on the way over had receded, and she was glad to see it go. She didn't need rescuing, and if she did it certainly wouldn't be by this sullen stranger, with his narrow, sloping shoulders and his unruly hair and his bad manners. Already she wished she had never come. She flashed him her best fuck-you smile, shrugged, and slung her backpack over her shoulder again and turned back toward the door and her lonely freedom.

"Hey, listen. But can I get you something to drink? I have tea, I think, and coffee."

She glanced back over her shoulder. "Nah, I'm fine."

He looked at her pleadingly now, wanting so hard to make amends but clearly lacking in the necessary experience to initiate such a gesture. *How does this end?* She was suddenly tired of it all. Her desire to get out, not just out of the cottage, but out of this life, returned like an unbearable itch. She would leave, soon, leave them all to it.

Wolf hurried to the table, pulled out the two chairs, and gestured for her to sit down. "Do you think we could kind of start again? Please?"

She stared him down with arms crossed, lips pulled into a thin line, willing him to understand how crushing it was to be humiliated by someone to whom you had offered gifts. He seemed to understand because he smiled for the first time, a bashful starting-over kind of smile, and she saw that he had nice teeth, straight and white. He also had a tiny scar above his upper lip on the left-hand side, a little notch she hadn't noticed before, and she realized he hadn't been smirking previously, that this was just how his face looked, the tiny scoop of flesh pulled upward like it was caught in a fishhook. Always on the verge of sneering. *Unfortunate,* she thought, *the kind of thing that could get you into trouble.*

Relenting, she sat down opposite him; the table and chairs were so small it felt like they were children playing house. He poured her coffee and then pushed the mug across to her.

"So they sent you here to see me, huh?"

Marlo frowned down at the lip of her mug, blew a little plume of steam away. "No. Why would you think that? I always come to see new arrivals. It's the neighborly thing to do."

101

He looked chastened. "Sorry, no offense intended. It was nice of you, that's all."

"It's OK. I'm kidding. They did all want me to come see you. There were some things that came up in the meeting, and I guess I'm supposed to be the spokesperson if no one else is going to do it." She was thawing now, even against her will, yearning to be accepted. It took extraordinary control to refrain from beaming at him again.

"Things about me?"

"Yeah. Just, you know, housekeeping. Nothing major. I feel like I got nominated to talk to you, because apparently we're sort of the same age?" She rolled her eyes. "I don't even know if that's true, although I suppose you're so much younger than most people here, so . . ."

"I'm twenty-nine," he said quickly, as if wanting to establish that he wasn't interested in keeping secrets. "Almost old. How about you? If that's not rude to ask."

"Twenty-five."

"You look even younger. I mean, not that you don't look grown up." When she raised her eyebrows, he groaned, dropping his head into his hands and then eyeballing her through scissored fingers. "Sorry. As you can probably tell I don't get out much. I can't remember the last time I properly talked with a chick. I mean a girl. A lady. Fuck."

She burst out laughing, leaned across the table to lay a placating hand on his wrist.

"Seriously, Wolf. It's fine. I know I look young. It's an Asian thing." Just to get it out of the way, what he was likely already thinking. Her words seemed to fluster him even more so she quickly followed up with, "Listen, back to the ranch rules or whatever you want to call them. Not sure if you realize, but what's happening? It's really, *really* unorthodox. It normally takes about five interviews with prospective residents, and lots of background checks and all that stuff before the ranchers will even *consider* voting on a new resident. So because your acceptance was kind of fast-tracked, mostly thanks to my parents, everyone voted that you staying had to be on a probationary basis."

Wolf nodded, gnawing the inside of his cheek with a vigor that must have been painful.

"You're kind of on trial for the next six months. But of course it's a two-way street. If you decide you don't want to stay then that's totally fine too. You can leave whenever you want. You might not even like it here."

"I get it. Still trying to work out where I'm going next. This is just temporary, of course."

"Well. The other thing is that you'll be expected to contribute to the community. Not just during the trial period, of course. If you stay there'll be chores, regular things we're all expected to do. It takes a lot to keep a place like this running."

"Of course. I'm up for it." The sour note had returned to his voice, as if he were used to defending himself against charges of lacking enthusiasm. "Anything and everything. I'm not afraid of hard work. I've worked in kitchens, on oil rigs, on film sets. And film sets, man, they sound fun, but they're fucking brutal."

"OK, cool. As it happens, the community has already chosen a role for you."

His eager smile melted away, and he threw her a mock grimace.

"Oh, god, what is it, emptying the septic tanks or something? Skinning live cattle? Did that Kenneth guy suggest it?"

She laughed in spite of herself. "Bees."

"Bees."

"Yeah, you know those little fuzzy things that fly around and make honey?"

Her fingers waved patterns in front of his face. He wrinkled his forehead as if trying to place them. Marlo didn't tell him that Neil had been the previous beekeeper, that the hives had been suffering since he left, under the half-hearted attentions of a series of unenthused or timid would-be beekeepers. The bees were a little like horses, Neil had once explained to her. They could sense when a person was scared or uncomfortable with them, and they could make your life hell. Thinking of him gave her a little pang. It still haunted her that she might have heard his cry for help and turned away from it. A shiver coursed up her spine. Her companion across the table didn't seem to notice, though: he was locked away, perhaps envisioning a shining future in which he and the bees coexisted in some blissfully symbiotic sylvan state. Marlo knew better. The bees were hard work, which was why it was a typical job for newcomers. She wasn't about to burst his bubble, though.

"Great," Wolf said, exposing those excellent teeth again. "Looking forward to it. I mean, I don't know anything about beekeeping, obviously, but there must be a ton online about it."

"Oh, that reminds me. I meant to tell you about the internet rule. Not sure if anyone else explained, but we have certain times that we use the internet. And it's usually just one person who spends a few hours online, and then kind of aggregates the news for everyone else." In saying these words aloud she realized how bizarre and draconian it sounded. It made them seem like crazy people. And of course since Neil's death the newsgathering had been suspended. The community seemed to be waiting for another volunteer to come forward, but Marlo couldn't exactly see people clamoring to fill those shoes. Even she, after the initial excitement of getting to research the dead bald eagles, had felt an uneasiness about the task. It had newly struck her what a grave burden it had been for Neil, to carry bad news to people he loved. "I mean, obviously it's not, like something you get punished for or anything. And you can put in requests, like with this beekeeping research there wouldn't be any issue at all . . ."

To Wolf's credit he made an effort not to look too incredulous, but one of his eyebrows rose seemingly of its own accord. He cleared his throat.

"Fair enough. I respect that. Sure, I can work around it." He looked down at the table, swept a few crumbs off it while he considered things.

"Can't people just connect on their phones, though, even outside of the allotted times? The satellite still works for other devices, right?"

"Yes," Marlo answered with as much hauteur as she could muster. "But we choose not to."

"But how do you enforce that?"

"We don't enforce it. Everyone just respects it."

"Ah."

She was about to match his ironic *ah* with something snitty, but it suddenly felt like too much work.

"Look, I realize it's kind of a dumb rule. But you know, everyone just got so sick of the bad news, just the constant, relentless onslaught of bad news from the Disaster, that we just all decided it was a good idea. And you'd be surprised, it really does make your life less stressful."

"The disaster?"

She shifted on her narrow wooden seat. Had Kenneth swiped them from a schoolhouse, or a circus?

"Oh, yeah. That's just our nickname for the outside world."

"Huh." She was grateful that he didn't laugh or make a patronizing face as other people outside the ranch had whenever she'd been stupid enough to share that. He just nodded approvingly. "Yeah, that's pretty fitting. Certainly felt like a disaster on my end."

"Anyway, so if you're cool with the beekeeping then that will be your main duty. But of course you'll be expected to chip in with a ton of things."

She outlined the general tasks, which operated on a rotating basis: taking turns checking the perimeter, clearing brush, chopping wood, cooking, washing up. Keeping the grass down with the ride-on mower. Inventorying. Jarring and pickling for the winter months. Repairing the common buildings. It sounded exhausting when you had to recite it out loud.

"Anything else you're particularly good or bad at?"

"Anything but driving," he said quietly. Marlo bit her lip.

"Right. Sorry." She had forgotten about his dad dying in the car accident. The idea of that as a way to die, the idea of anyone she loved dying that way, was too abominable to contemplate. She stood up from the table, started clearing the dishes.

"I should give you an orientation of the ranch as well. I've got the golf cart here." She didn't want to sound too eager. "Or we can do it some other time."

"No, now is great. If it works for you?"

As they drove around the ranch, Marlo pointed out various landmarks and buildings and explained the purpose each served. He was particularly awed by the biodome: his wide-set eyes seemed to take up even more of the real estate on his face as he craned his neck to take it all in. They strolled the raised catwalks of the greenhouse, Marlo stopping occasionally to examine a plant or pinch off deadheads.

"Holy fuck. How long have you had this?"

"It was all Kenneth really," she confessed. "Before he arrived, to be honest, we'd all kind of fallen into a lifestyle that was almost completely dependent on the outside world. We barely grew anything, we had only a few token animals, and we just got everything we needed on trips into town."

"When did he get here?"

Marlo closed her eyes, thinking. "I think it was about ten years ago. It seems like forever. I was a teenager. He convinced everyone to go back to the original ideals of the movement, try to become something close to self-sufficient. So all the solar, the successful crops, this"—she waved a hand around to indicate the biodome—"was all him. He brought in the right kind of animals to help with his crop rotation. Oh, and he was the one who suggested the nightly patrolling of the perimeter."

Wolf looked surprised. "I didn't know about that. Sounds kind of . . . militant."

Marlo laughed. "Yep, that's our Kenneth. He was in the Army once."

"So how does the perimeter checking work? Whose job is that?"

She snapped off a strand of chives, rubbed the slender green shoot between her thumb and finger. It emitted a sweetly pungent smell that perfumed the air.

"Now it's mostly me and Kenneth and a few of the others, and we don't do it every day anymore. More like once a week?" She shot him a sly smile. "I'm sure Kenneth would appreciate you volunteering if you're interested."

Wolf contemplated this. "Hmm, depends what it entails. Do I have to shoot anyone?"

"Not *usually*, no. He says it's mostly about knowing what's happening on your land. 'The integrity of the ranch. Good practices.' Some talk like that. Anyway, we test the soil and water pretty regularly. Along with the river, which comes from that mountain range over there, there's a stream up on the western border. And it's just a chance to see what's changed, if there's any broken equipment, hurt animals, stuff like that."

She stopped just short of telling him about Kenneth's other reasons, the times he had hinted darkly at more nefarious things, like the weapons cache or the monopoly-minded company hiring people to spread seeds on private property so that they can later accuse the farmers of using the company's proprietary seeds without buying them. (Kenneth knew these things because, as he was fond of reminding her, he'd been on the Inside.)

"The thing was, after a while of adopting Kenneth's practices, we all noticed that we were making far fewer trips into town. I mean, we're nowhere near self-sufficiency but we're much closer than we were before."

"And that's an unmitigated good thing, right?" Wolf asked with a gently ribbing smile. She was a little taken aback at his ability to correctly guess at her thoughts.

"Actually, you're right. I do kind of miss going into town so much. It was kind of a novelty getting to see different faces, shop at supermarkets, get stuck in traffic, that kind of thing."

"You're not missing much."

"I know. But still. The grass is always greener and all that."

"Speaking of which, why is the grass so green just here?" They had emerged from the greenhouse and in wandering around behind it had come to her favorite meadow.

"I don't know. It's always been like this. After the snows every year it's always the first thing to get green again. Not sure what kind of grass it even is. Kenneth would know."

"Kenneth doesn't really seem like my biggest fan."

"He'll come around. Come on, take off your shoes!"

"What?"

"Take them off. I always do here. It feels incredible on your bare feet."

"Are you sure?"

"What are you scared of, city boy?" she said, teasing him. "There aren't any syringes hiding in the grass."

After a moment of hesitation and watching her first toss her sneakers, he took off his shoes, wrinkling his nose as he walked, pretending to be disgusted about the feeling of grass underfoot. She laughed, ran off like a child hoping to be chased.

As she was running she felt her phone vibrate in her pocket. She stopped, pulled it out, and saw there was a message from her mother asking if she was planning to join her parents for their usual Sunday night supper. Marlo quickly tapped out a response. Wolf wandered over, cast a curious glance at her texting.

"I thought you weren't supposed to use those."

Marlo laughed. "That's just the internet. We still use them for texting or calling each other." He looked confused. She'd forgotten what it was like trying to explain the ranch to outsiders. "The whole idea was that we didn't want to know too much about the Disaster, only what was absolutely necessary. I know it sounds weird and creepy. But I swear, in most other ways we live just like everyone else. We get together to watch big games. We have barbecues. We celebrate birthdays and certain holidays, like Christmas and New Year's."

"Christmas, huh? Kind of unusual for atheists." She didn't like his brand of teasing. There was something mean-spirited about it, like he was probing to find the most hurtful way to expose the ranch's faults.

"I suppose," she said, trying not to bristle. "But everyone agreed back in the early days that they wanted to have nondenominational feast days as a way to, I guess, bond the community, and rather than come up with another date it was just kept as December twenty-fifth. We hang wreathes and everything."

They got back in the golf cart, and she continued the tour, strangely pleased when he expressed surprise that the fields where they grew the crops weren't in neat, furrowed rows as he'd expected, but haphazard (at least to the uninitiated), tangled with benign weeds and wildflowers. She explained that this was the noninterventionist method, that beneath the surface teemed whole universes of beneficial insects and bacteria, and that creatures of all kinds toiled here, living out their symbiotic dance.

She was so engrossed in talking to him, this new person, a person whose entire history lay shrouded, ready to be uncovered and picked through—it was as exciting as having a critically-acclaimed new book to read—that she didn't realize she had driven them close to the site of Neil and Jay's house. She cut the engine, grief twisting in her gut. Wolf glanced at her, but he stayed sitting in the passenger seat as if waiting for a sign from her indicating what should happen next. She got out of the cart slowly, reluctantly, and he followed.

The earth was still bare in parts, with bright tufts of new grass struggling through here and there. It had seemed a nice idea at the time, to plant the Japanese maple as a living memorial to Neil, but it was so tiny and its striving so heartbreakingly futile in the ugly sea of naked earth once containing a house that Marlo had to look away, blinking. Wolf stretched out a hand as if to lay it on her arm, then withdrew. She didn't know if anyone had told him yet what happened here, and she wasn't in the mood to be the one.

"Do you ever think about leaving?" he asked quietly. "The ranch, I mean?"

"Of course." She turned away from the site quickly, glad to talk about something else. They began to walk, not going anywhere in particular, just away, their strides quickly syncing up. "I applied to a liberal arts college in California about five years ago. It was a long shot. I mean, I don't even have a formal education, but anyway before I even heard about whether I was accepted or not my dad got really sick with pneumonia, and I decided to withdraw my application so I could stay here with him." She laughed roughly. "Part of it was being a good daughter, and part was making sure I could never be disappointed. This way I can convince myself I would have gotten in."

"I'm sure you would have," he said gallantly. "And let me tell you, being saddled with literally hundreds of thousands of dollars of student debt isn't exactly something to aspire to. Hope you don't mind me saying, but I'm blown away with how good your homeschooling was. I mean, everyone here is much smarter than anyone I went to school with. I'd always had this negative perception of it, I guess, that it was for, like, Mormon kids and shut-ins."

She laughed. "Funny, I've never thought of it as homeschooling, really. Our teachers were always real teachers, professors some of them, who had education degrees from the real world. So it never felt like this subpar thing. In fact, because there have never been many kids here, the classes were really small, and the teachers could give us all a lot of attention."

"Yeah, I'd kind of noticed the demographics here don't exactly skew youthful."

"Well, there used to be more of us, more young people. But they all just gradually left, to go study or get normal jobs in the Disaster, or in the case of my friends Alex and Ben . . ." She realized she hadn't thought about them in a few days.

"What happened to them?"

"They left under, um, not great circumstances. Had huge fights with their parents, told them they were just big cowards, hiding here on the ranch. Then they ran away to become eco-warriors. Attacking whaling ships and all that stuff."

"No kidding?"

"Yeah. I miss them. We used to be inseparable. The Terrible Triumvirate, my dad used to call us. When we were little we'd run around like lunatics without clothes on, or find hideouts and spend the night away from home, freaking all our parents out. And then when we got to be teenagers, doing more, well, teenage stuff, like smoking the weed Ben grew behind the greenhouse."

She was thrown back in an instant to those restless, twitchy years, when the volcanic excitement and discontent of adolescence had been amplified by the isolation in which they lived. And then when she did get out, to the town or on trips with her parents, noticing how the ways in which men looked at her had changed. No longer was she cloaked in the sanctity of childhood, those innocent years when strangers had either barely noticed her or doted condescendingly. Once she hit puberty it was as though her body began to emit a signal that only men could hear. The brazen ones studied her and Alex on their trips to town, observed the girls with searing eyes as if cataloging them for a secret project. Or they refused to look at her at all, as though she might be contagious. After a while she and Alex would dress deliberately for the trips into town, in cut-off shorts and halter tops, their lips glossed to a plastic shine. They rubbed lotion on their summer-tanned legs to make them gleam. Marlo's skin tinted a pretty shade of dark-gold in the summer, while Alex's, so ethereal-pale in winter, freckled into constellations that laced her calves and chest and arms. "Let's give those pervs something to look at," wicked Alex would say. The electrifying shock of realizing that this is what had been inside men all along.

Marlo decided to show Wolf her own house last, so she skirted the meadow and brought him to a low wooden pavilion with a wide veranda, obviously abandoned.

"What was this?"

"Ha. Get this. That was going to be the clubhouse for the golf course."

"Seriously?"

"Yep. It was around 2009 I guess, and a few of the ranchers were really eager to put a golf course in. Like, nothing huge, just nine holes, to putt around on. Some of them were serious golfers when they lived out in the Disaster, but no one wanted to have to join a club outside the ranch."

"Doesn't really jibe with the whole hippie back-to-the-land thing."

"Exactly. But you know, by that time the original principles of the ranch were kind of . . . flexible. It had been a decade by then. I think especially the original ranchers were kind of bored, or at least thought maybe they'd overreacted with shutting ourselves away in here. Anyway, there were those kinds of rumblings. Making the ranch a bit more in line with what they knew from the outside world. But then Kenneth arrived. And, well, you've met him. He's not exactly Mr. Tactful. Heard about the plans for the golf course and nearly had a fit. Said he hadn't given up everything to join this community so he could be surrounded with country club assholes who were just as busy fucking up the environment as anyone on the outside. Accused them all of going soft. Lectured them about how environmentally irresponsible golf courses were, diverting precious water resources so a bunch of rich jerks could have a nice green carpet to hit little balls around on."

Wolf laughed. "Go, Kenneth."

"Yeah, it definitely shamed them. Funnily enough the golf course was never spoken of again. Although I've always had my suspicions that a few of them sneak off and play a few rounds when it's their turn to do a provisions run. Anyway, after that things kind of got back on the original track, with aiming for self-sufficiency, growing our own food, and all that stuff."

They wandered further on, skirting one of the solar fields, with its neat rows of silvery panels, toward a small clearing marked with a large concrete circle next to a metal shed.

"Talking of rich people things, is that a helipad?" asked Wolf, as they approached. He shook his head slowly, as if refusing to believe it. "A motherfucking helipad," he added, in a whisper. She doubted he even knew he was saying it out loud.

"Yeah. I mean, it's not like a golf course, though. It's supposed to be a safeguard, for when . . . if things go to hell in the Disaster, so that we can get in and out easily."

"So have you been up in one?"

"A helicopter? Of course. It's in that shed there. We sometimes go to meetings in it, if the city my parents are talking in is close enough."

Wolf flashed her a caustic smile and shook his head.

"What?"

"Nothing. Just, your life has been . . . very different from most kids I know. Lucky you."

By that time there was nothing left to show but her own house. As they approached, she felt it surface again: that quick, hot bubble of jealousy he had trouble keeping submerged. She performed a rushed tour, pretended to be ashamed of the mess although the place was spotless, and soon hurried him back out the door. They crossed an open grassed area to the golf cart. Marlo spotted a ragged figure in the distance and waved.

"Who's that?"

"That's Izzy. She was a vet in her former life, so she spends a lot of time with the animals. You'll probably meet her later on. She's kind of gruff and seems angry all the time, but she's got a heart of gold."

113

They each raised a hand to their forehead, making shade canopies for their eyes as they looked out across the landscape. Izzy appeared to be chastising one of the goats, which was running in short, manic bursts around her legs. Marlo laughed, her heart suddenly light. For the first time she had a pang of regret about leaving to take up her internship. It might have been fun to stay for the summer, perhaps show Wolf around some more. She shook the thought away before it could properly embed itself.

"Come on, I'll take you home," she said. "That's about all there is to show."

As she drove, Wolf leaned his head out of the cart, inhaling deeply. He half closed his eyes as if slipping into a little reverie.

"You OK there?" Marlo asked, swerving slightly as she turned to look at him. His eyes sprang open. He turned to look at her.

"I don't understand why you'd ever want to leave this place."

"Who said I wanted to leave?"

He smiled genially.

"You did, remember? The college in California? But anyway, I just assumed being young and all that you'd want to get out eventually, go join the, what do you call it? Disaster."

"Maybe I will one day." This would have been the perfect moment to mention that she was planning on leaving for real this time. But for some reason she hesitated. Instead she found herself saying, "I'm happy here for now. And hopefully you'll like it here too."

"It's the most incredible place I've ever seen," he said, and she was startled at the intensity in his voice. "I didn't understand what it would be like."

She walked him in a heavy silence to his front door, her attention turning inward again now that the tour was over. When they arrived at the threshold of his temporary home she stammered out, "So, anyway, welcome," tossing her keys in the air and only just catching them.

"Guess I'll see you Saturday for the barbecue? The welcome parties are always fun."

"Can't wait. Listen, thanks so much for coming to see me, and for showing me around."

He stepped closer, and she wondered if he was going to kiss or hug her. But instead he held out his hand palm-down, whether deliberately or through some awkward misplacement, and she, unsure, slid her palm under his and just sort of held it there. They stayed that way—for a microsecond or a week, it was hard to say afterward—until her hand started to prickle with sweat and she dropped it to her side. He stood in the doorway, leaning his shoulder into the doorjamb and watching her as she climbed into her golf cart.

"I hope I end up being worth the trouble," he called out as she turned the key in the ignition. Which Marlo thought was an odd thing to say.

9

The sky was a bright clear bowl of blue upturned over the world. Birds exploded out of trees, scolding each other as they scattered, then re-alighting fussily onto branches. The first thing she noticed when she stepped outside was the fat bees humming like industrious hovercraft around the lavender bush in her front yard. They were busy in other plants as well, more than she had seen in a long time. Their appearance felt auspicious on Wolf's big day of being officially welcomed into the fold, as if the bees were paying homage to their new keeper. She was all springy excitement, full of anticipation for the barbecue. The day that new residents were welcomed had always been a source of deep pleasure for her. Like a festival and birthday and Christmas rolled into one. The sharing of food and stories and later, as an adult, too much wine and joints or pills that she sneaked behind a shed with her friends. Even if the newcomers weren't people you felt particularly passionate about, there was something solemn and sacred about the welcome party, this ceremonial rite, like being initiated into a gang or made a citizen of a new country. In a way the ranch *was* its own country.

She hummed as she fumbled for her keys, balancing the bowl of potato salad on one hip. Her German friend, Greta, had taught her the recipe: the trick was to drench the warm boiled potatoes in vinaigrette right after cooking, leave them to cool, then add the mayonnaise, chopped pickles, and herbs. It was her star dish, a perennial hit at parties, and from the beginning Greta had been gracious enough to let Marlo take full credit for it. Everyone now knew it as Marlo's

Potato Salad. Greta and her husband, Marco, were in their seventies now; both their parents had fled Germany during the war, and they had been among the first settlers on the ranch. They knew something about new beginnings.

The long pine tables had been set up beneath the cherry trees, and someone had gathered great bunches of wildflowers and grasses and laid them artfully end to end down the middle of the tables. Observing the scene sent a bolt of pleasure up her spine, the chance to see her own world fresh through the newcomer's eyes. It reminded her how negligent she had been lately in attending to the beauty all around her.

On her second trip to the Commons, ferrying plates and dishes and glasses, she bumped into her parents.

"Where's our guest of honor? Has he turned up yet?" chirped her mother after kissing Marlo on the cheek.

"I have no idea, Mom," she said, amused that she was already considered some kind of expert on his whereabouts. "I'm going to help Kenneth with the ice. See you over there!"

She skipped over to Kenneth, who was at the midway point between lugging bags of ice from the deep freeze to his truck. His expression was about the same as usual, which was to say he looked like a man trying to calculate the cost of something he needs but can't afford.

"Hi, K." She beamed, trying to coax a smile out of him. "Let me help."

"Sure thing. Grab as many as you can carry."

She liked that he didn't baby her or insist on some kind of fake gallantry. For all his puppy-eyed devotion to her, he had always treated her like an equal when it came to anything physical. She ran to the room behind the kitchen that held the chest freezers, leaned in, and hauled out two heavy bags of ice, then carried them out to the car, her arms hanging so low with the weight that the bags dragged every now and then on the floor, leaving long steaks of water on the boards. When she'd dumped the ice into the bed of his truck, she returned to the house to mop up so no one would slip on the melted ice. Kenneth waited for her in the car, and then they drove over to the picnic spot.

Later, when she had finished her chores and the party was in full swing, she sat down between her parents and Greta and Marco, poured herself a glass of rosé, and took a deep happy breath.

"What a day."

Greta nodded, stroked Marlo's knee affectionately. They clinked glasses just as a tiny white butterfly sailed past, and Greta declared it a good omen.

"They're everywhere," she said, and when Marlo looked around she saw that Greta was right. Clouds of them flitted among the trees and occasionally alighted on the rim of a glass or plate. "I'm a little worried about the monarchs though," she said, reaching across Marlo for a slice of bruschetta. "Remember how we had so many come through here the last couple of years? Was hoping they'd started their northern migration by now. All that milkweed we planted usually gets 'em going. But so far I haven't seen so much as one of the little suckers. You, Kenneth?"

Kenneth, who was sitting opposite them, having gravitated as usual to the margins of Marlo's orbit, looked up at his name.

"What's that?"

"Seen any monarch butterflies yet this year?"

He shook his head.

"To the monarchs," said Marlo, raising her glass with mock solemnity in a toast. She wasn't in the mood for apocalyptic doom and gloom today. It seemed impolite on a day like this, with the earth engaged in its full flush of seasonal rebirth, to dwell on its extinction. "May they get off their little fuzzy asses."

A few people laughed, but Kenneth frowned down at his plate, attacking his potato salad with aggrieved gusto. Marlo hadn't seen him this grim for a while. She didn't have long to wonder at the cause of the dark cloud over his mood, because at just that moment the dark cloud came over, bent down to say hello to her—they had only waved at one another from a distance before now—and Marlo caught the furious look Kenneth flung across the table. She still didn't understand why he hated Wolf so much. They chatted for a while, and when Wolf walked away to rejoin one of the other tables, Marlo's mother looked after him approvingly.

"It's so nice to have a new face in the community," Maya said, white teeth gleaming in her deeply tanned face. "Don't you all think? Especially after the Terrible Tragedy. A kind of healing."

Marlo hated that Neil's death had been consigned to euphemism. The Terrible Tragedy. Our Awful Loss. The Tragic Events. His and Jay's names were never uttered aloud anymore. Now that she thought about it, this process was common whenever anyone left the ranch, as if the leavers ceased to exist once they closed the gates behind them for the last time. It made her uncomfortable, this erasure.

"Wolf's arrival was a boon, in many ways," added Carlton, and this uncontroversial assertion was met with knowing nods and murmurs of agreement.

"Quite a coincidence too."

Heads swiveled to look at Kenneth. He was clenching his butter knife as if considering driving it clean through the table.

"Not sure what you mean?" Carlton answered pleasantly. "Coincidence how?"

"Well just that he happened to turn up, out of the blue, at the precise moment when we were in need of new residents, new youthful blood. Just curious, that's all."

His words roused plenty of disapproving looks, and Marlo suddenly felt terribly sorry for him. She knew that Kenneth was respected far more than he was liked in the community, and it occurred to her that she had always undervalued the noble steadfastness of his friendship. He had always acted as her champion and protector, while still regarding her as an equal in a way that virtually no one else did, all without ever expecting her to reciprocate or stand up for him. Perhaps that was what drove her to his defense now. She glanced around to make sure Wolf was well out of earshot.

"Yeah, I kind of agree with Kenneth that there was something weird about Wolf arriving just out of nowhere. And we still don't really know the full story of how he got here, or why. I'm definitely curious." The look Kenneth shot her was so full of raw, throbbing gratitude that she had to pretend not to have intercepted it. "I mean, I'd just love to hear his story," she added quickly, popping a cherry tomato in her mouth to prevent it from spouting any further words. She felt miserable at having both betrayed Wolf and foolishly aligned herself with Kenneth's unpopular stance.

"I'm sure we all will, in time," said Maya, beaming around the group with her best water-smoothing hostess smile. "As soon as he's had a chance to settle in."

The subject was changed to less incendiary topics, and everyone soon resumed eating and drinking and teasing one another, but Marlo drifted into silence. She felt the deflation in her buoyant mood like a pinprick. Once she had finished her food she excused herself and went over to where Wolf was sitting listening earnestly to Izzy hold forth about de-worming cattle.

"Hey there," she said. "Scooch over."

She squeezed into the space he made on the bench next to him. She pointedly didn't look over at the other table, but she could well imagine the laser-like hatred Kenneth was no doubt directing their way. It pained her to have to choose between loyalty to her old friend and the desire to get to know Wolf better, but in the end she feared losing her new friend more. Kenneth would always be there, wouldn't he?

"How's it all going, party boy?"

"Great." He grinned, clinked glasses with her. Then under his breath: "To be honest, it's kind of overwhelming. Do you really do this for every new arrival?"

"Are you kidding? You think we'd miss an excuse to gorge on cake and drink copious amounts of alcohol? It's been a couple of years since anyone new has joined. So we're all really grateful you gave us a chance to break the drought."

She winked at him, her exuberant mood returning like those monarch butterflies from their long difficult journey. It was nice to just sit there with him, their thighs brushing in the innocent intimacy of the crowded table. It had been too long since she'd talked with someone of her own generation. She often feared she had aged before her time, calcifying into an older person's shape. It struck her how much she missed the easy camaraderie she'd had with Alex and Ben. Her people. Maybe Wolf could be one of her people too. That was her earnest hope as she sat with him that balmy spring afternoon. As the day drew on, the feeling grew more and more intense—a fertile sense of promise as darkly exciting as ripe figs nodding on a stem, ready to fall.

10

Their courtship was largely conducted in the kitchen. She was amazed to discover that he had barely ever cooked, that his family had always subsisted on takeout and Frankenfood out of boxes. Cooking had always been the lingua franca of her family, a means of communication and social bonding that was its own form of nourishment. She was secretly scandalized at his illiteracy in the kitchen. He had never made risotto before, never tasted couscous or baked a pie. But Wolf was eager to learn, and he was a quick study: after seeing her prepare something once or twice he could faithfully reproduce the dish. The business of pot stirring, finger licking, measuring ingredients, and faces meeting over steaming pans proved to be a fairly effective aphrodisiac.

It started with an agreement to institute a weekly get-together, Monday Margarita Madness, in homage to a bar Wolf used to frequent in West Hollywood. *Booze is my wheelhouse,* Wolf had proudly declared on their inaugural meeting, insisting on taking charge of the libations. He was determined to show off his mixing skills, carefully writing his order on the Commons whiteboard for a bottle of the best tequila he knew of, and measuring the Cointreau and lime juice as if the future of humanity depended on getting the formula right. By the time their second Monday together came around, he was confident he had gotten it just so. She couldn't keep her eyes off him. He was a knee shaker, a fidgeter, a nail biter, a lip chewer. He gave off a kinetic energy that could be exhausting to watch. But she found him beautiful too. His charcoal eyelashes like insect wings. The sharply defined bones of his face. She had never considered a man beautiful before.

"This is actually pretty good," she said through salty lips, as if she'd been dubious he could pull off the feat again. His answering smile was so wide, so bursting with gratitude, it made her wonder if he had ever experienced praise as a child. "I'm making tacos al pastor. Or a vegetarian version of them. Izzy makes the tortillas herself."

"What I want to know is, how do you know about things like tacos al pastor, anyway? Have you ever been to Mexico, or even Los Angeles?"

She blushed. "No. I mean, yes, I've been to LA, once when I was a kid."

"Did you eat at any food trucks? Or just at your five-star hotels?"

His tone was gentle and teasing, but the words still stung.

"This may be a news flash, Wolf, but you can actually know about things without having directly experienced them."

He held up a peacemaking hand. "Of course. I'm impressed, that's all. You haven't missed out on anything."

"As I'm sure you've noticed by now, this isn't some crazy cult or whatever. It's just like any other place, really."

She blushed. His very presence seemed to refute her words—the thoughtless style implicit in the way he dressed, because unlike her, he wasn't hopelessly behind the times; the music he played for her from his phone that was all by bands she'd never heard of; his firsthand observations of art and architecture she had never had a chance to see. She could tell he knew certain things by osmosis, like the right sneakers to wear and how much to tip doormen. She might as well have grown up in a real cult for all she knew of the world. Wolf sipped his cocktail, then held the glass out in front of him and stared at it critically. As if reading her mind he said, "The funny thing is, before I got here I was fully prepared for this to be some kind of end-times cult. I'd heard all about the pre-apocalyptic paranoia from my folks. I mean, not that they used those words, but that was the message I got."

She came over and sat down next to him on the sofa. They stared together into the empty fireplace. A single gray feather lay curled on the hearth, sucked out of the sky by some errant breeze.

"I didn't realize your parents knew that much about the ranch. I mean, the end-times cult. So what do you think now?"

He turned to face her, shrugged, and put on a sly grin.

"Jury's still out, I'm afraid."

She punched him on the arm and pretended to pout. "Creep."

"But seriously. Even though I love this place I'm not going to say I agree with everything it stands for. I feel like some of the ranchers are kind of . . . over-the-top evangelical with the whole 'coming catastrophe' disaster-movie rhetoric. And that internet rule, that's just nonsense. But you know, I don't follow the rules, man. Check it out, I'm going to connect to that sweet, sweet internet. And you can't stop me!"

He pulled his phone out of his pocket, opened the browser, and held it out of her reach tauntingly. She put her drink down and lunged at him, tackled him horizontal trying to get at the phone. He laughed, trying to both hold the phone and fend her off.

"No need to fight me, Marlo. Join me on the dark side. We can Google things together."

She got to her feet, laughing. "You're just jealous. You're a slave to that thing, and we're freeeeeeeeeeee!" She went twirling and pirouetting around the room until she collided with the sideboard. She bent down, groaning and rubbing her leg. "Fuck. That hurt."

"Are you OK?" He approached her, dropped to his knees on the rug and kissed her naked calf.

"Get off me, you perv!"

She beat him with a cushion. Later, over their second cocktail, the tortillas had all been devoured, and darkness was pressing at the windows, and she dared to ask him what had been on her mind since the moment they had first met.

"How *did* you end up here, anyway? I'm kind of curious."

He shifted slightly beside her and looked down into his drink. They both watched the ice cubes clink together and melt. It felt like a long time before he answered.

"Well, like I said, I'd always known about the ranch. At least, for a long time. My parents used to talk about it a lot."

"Why were they so interested?"

He glanced at her. His brown eyes read as black in the granular light, the iris subsuming the pupil or the other way around. She recalled the night they first met, how she had fancied in him an alien presence. Some kind of resistance to being read.

"Because they had this dream of coming here. Seriously, it was their life's dream. Like, some people dream of taking a cruise to Antarctica or, I don't know, running for president. My folks had this."

"So why didn't they just come here?"

"Well, in the early days they tried, but they didn't have enough money. They were just public schoolteachers, and my mom hadn't even been working full-time because she was raising me. I remember them arguing about money all the time. It caused this really bitter rift between them. My family has always had a talent for being poor." He went back to scrutinizing his ice, swirling the glass around as if it might give up its secrets. "I hated the idea of this place for a long time. It just seemed so mean-spirited, you know, these people living like hippies but acting like elitist assholes. I couldn't understand why my parents were so fixated. It sounded like my idea of hell."

"So why did you come here, then?"

He didn't answer, got up, and fetched the cocktail shaker, topped off their glasses.

"*That* is a very good question." That nasty streak she'd seen a few times before flared again in his voice, and she could tell he was about to say something that he'd been rehearsing. "Have you ever considered that when these catastrophes really do arrive, if they do, the catastrophes that you're all so convinced are 'round the corner, that the rich are as

125

usual going to be able to insulate themselves while all the poor fuckers drown? Or burn up in a wildfire, or starve to death?"

Marlo shrank from his voice. "I don't really see what that has to with anything."

"Don't you?" His smile was shifty, almost menacing, casting malign light.

"So because you hate rich people you decided to come and join a bunch of them on a ranch in the middle of Oregon. Makes sense, I guess."

He sighed, and his whole body seemed to sag. The dark circles like bruises under his eyes.

"Listen, I'm sorry. That really wasn't fair. I know it's not your fault, that you grew up with all this . . ." He waved to encompass the room and everything that lay beyond it, all her unexamined birthright. "It's just my parents would have given anything to be part of this brave new world, and they never got the chance."

She placed a tentative hand on his knee, and he looked down at it as if unsure where such a thing could have come from. It freaked her out, this habit of his, of looking like he had momentarily dropped out of the world and upon reentry was having to rediscover sensation.

"I'm sorry," she said, resting her head on his shoulder. She could feel his tensed muscles against her scalp. "I'm sorry they couldn't join. It must suck to want something that badly and not be able to get it."

"Yeah, well, that's just the human condition, isn't it?"

"I suppose."

"Hey, I wanted to tell you something." She had no idea she was going to say these words before they tumbled out. She had just been wanting to change the subject, but now she had no choice but to forge on, to open that door.

"What's that?"

"Um. Well, I got offered a job, an internship with the National Parks Service in San Jose. And I've decided to take it. It starts soon."

A rogue muscle twitched at his temple.

"Oh, wow. So cool."

"You don't think so really."

He laughed ruefully. "How can you tell?"

"Your face. You have tells."

"You got me." He made a wry gesture of surrender. "I don't get it, though. Why do you want to get a job? Especially one so far away."

"I don't know. Experience. Fun. To earn my own money for once. To get away from here for a while."

He scraped a hand over his jaw, eyebrows dented in a kind of confusion.

"It's just . . . Aren't you happy here? What else could you want?"

"What do you think? To see the world. To live outside of this gated community."

"Believe me, there's nothing out there worth seeing."

"Well, thanks, Dad. Guess that settles it."

"I'm serious. The Disaster, as you guys call it, really is that. A disaster. Everything is so fucked up."

"I'm not sure that's a good enough reason not to go."

"What better reason do you want?"

"I don't know. Give me one."

"Because I'd miss you." She started to laugh but stifled it when she saw that he was in earnest. "I mean it."

"Come on, Wolf. You don't even know me very well."

"So? I'm a good judge of character."

"I don't know. Anyway, I'm still deciding."

She had been looking forward to the internship ever since they had accepted her. It had been like a bright silver string these last few months, tugging her out of the ranch and into the glare of the world. But now the string tugged in the other direction, snaring her in a sweet bind.

11

It hadn't been any one thing. That's what she explained when he wanted
to know how the ranch came into being. There wasn't a single defining
catalyst that drove her parents and the other founders to set the place
up, but rather a steady, ominous dripping. *You know, choking pollution,
shrinking ice caps, swelling oceans? Cities drowned in poisonous fog, refugees
spilling across borders in an unstoppable tide of misery?* He knew. Marlo's
parents and four other couples—the original founders, the *Elders*, if
you wanted to get all religious-y about it—had settled on the land,
completed construction of their homes, and moved in, a few years after
the September 11 attacks had happened, an era when retreating from
the world's horrors felt like the only sane thing to do. He nodded along,
thirsty for details. Already the edges of his cynicism were softening.

I used to drive around LA, picking out houses I wished I could live in.

She remembered how bitterly he'd said those words the week after
he had arrived, when she had been showing him around the ranch. She
knew he had said it to make her feel bad, or at least pique her sympathy, and it had succeeded. He no longer said things like that. Perhaps
he was just grateful that he had inherited his parents' dream, had come
into the fantasy family legacy at last. It was easy to be seduced by the
pure, uncomplicated beauty of the ranch's landscape, Marlo knew, and
to marvel at how smoothly egalitarianism had been implemented. The
darker undercurrents weren't yet visible to him. Not that Marlo wanted
him to see that side of the ranch. She put off telling him certain things,
the whole story about Neil, on whose unready shoulders they had placed

the sole burden of knowledge. Or the cave filled with weapons, or how no one ever talked about how both Neil and Simon had been ruined, in part, because they hadn't felt permitted to follow their faith. It had driven Simon and Julia away—they had left the ranch shortly after Neil's death to join a devout Christian community in Washington—and Neil to obliteration. But she didn't have the language yet to tell him these things. And even if she had, she had begun to love his enthusiasm for her home, and the avid hunger with which he devoured her stories.

❦

OK, she told herself sternly as she walked across the field to see Wolf one late summer day, *this is what's going on.* They hadn't been in one another's orbit for very long, and yet there was already an inevitability to their coupling. But the knowing didn't diminish the thrill; if anything, it added a piquancy to the waiting. What was happening to her had happened before, and there were plenty of rational explanations for the symptoms. She couldn't remember any male on the ranch roughly her own age about whom she hadn't nurtured at least a moment of infatuation. Even some of the older men—teachers and parents of her friends—although of course those unorthodox passions needed to be buried far out of sight.

With Wolf, there were all the details yet to be discovered, the excitement of the unknown circumstances that would precipitate their coming together. The precise location and physical details. The weather conditions. How quickly it would happen, and how widely the repercussions would ripple out to affect their lives. That their affair had been accelerated by the pressure-cooker environment of the ranch only made it feel sweeter to her.

The problem was mostly neurological. The ventral tegmental area of her brain was lit up like a Christmas tree, merrily generating dopamine. The reaction was almost identical, biologically, to that experienced by addicts upon getting their fix. Love was literally a drug, but unlike the harmful effects of substances like nicotine, alcohol, or opioids, it wore off. That's how she consoled herself as she made her way toward the object of her affection, who was moving among the beehives, a sinister figure in a bulky white suit, his face obscured by the netted headgear, his moon-booted feet treading ponderously across the earth. He could have been an alien, harvesting organs. Which, to be fair, was probably exactly how he appeared to the bees when he came to rob them.

The macabre figure Wolf cut was enhanced by the backdrop: in the meadow behind the hives was the ranch's largest solar field, which blazed eerily as the panels—blank metallic faces lifted to the sun—caught the light. She was only a few feet away when he finally heard her footfalls and looked up, pulled off his long gloves, and unzipped the veil like a bride to reveal his face, flushed and glowing with perspiration. Her heart performed a little flip as if it had been flicked with an invisible forefinger. He smiled, wiping his face with his forearm.

"Hi," she said shyly, not knowing what to say. "I see you found the protection suit?"

His face screwed up, and he flung the headgear aside with a sulky élan.

"Ugh, I kind of hate it. It's so cumbersome. Thinking of experimenting with not wearing it. The bees haven't turned on me yet, so."

"Is that a good idea?" Then she realized she sounded matronly in her concern and shrugged to counteract the effect. "I'm sure they'll learn to love you."

He grinned in a rueful kind of way, then stripped off the suit entirely, letting it puddle at his feet, which she noticed were encased in wheat-colored Carhartt boots conspicuous in their newness.

"Everything OK?" she asked, the teeniest bit offended that he didn't seem as pleased to see her as in the fantasy she'd concocted on the way over.

"Oh, sure. Just a bit distracted by some bad news."

Assuming he meant something personal, she took a step toward him with her hand already outstretched to offer succor. He looked up and seemed surprised to see her there so close to him, as though they'd been playing hide-and-seek but he'd somehow forgotten. "Oh, I mean, nothing bad to do with me. More to do with the Disaster. And because I assume no one else knows about it yet, it kind of has me preoccupied."

"How bad is it?"

He hesitated. "Should I even tell you? I mean, the whole no-internet . . ."

"Jesus, just tell me, Wolf."

He seemed relieved then, as if he'd been bursting to tell someone.

"So you know about the melting ice caps and glaciers disappearing in the Arctic and all that." She didn't even grace him with an answer to that, let her eyebrows respond instead. "Right, no shit. But so I was just reading this news story"—he took a deep, grim breath, but there was an odd excitement in his voice too—"that said this tiny village on the tundra in Siberia, where you know the permafrost has been melting over the last few years, had this mysterious outbreak of disease that killed a few people. And the other villagers have isolated the bodies, bricked them up in a house or something, because, get this, they think the people might have died of smallpox. Motherfucking *smallpox*, can you believe it? All those things scientists were warning about years ago, that the ice might contain weird ancient spores or whatever, they were true."

Marlo eased down into the grass, and Wolf followed. They sat close together but not touching, tearing slender stalks of grass out of the ground as if engaged in some banal but useful task. Every fifth or sixth blade Marlo would slice down the center with a fingernail. She could hear the low hum of the bees at their back. Were they content? It was tempting to anthropomorphize the buzzing, to invest its tenor with some meaning. They certainly seemed calm enough. She might have preferred them agitated, aware through some sixth sense of the peril of their world. She'd seen them agitated before, when Neil used to tend them, and there was something biblical about their angry swarming and buzzing. In that mood they'd attack anything that came within their reach, Neil had explained: the wooden brush he used to disperse them when collecting honey; a human; a fellow bee. Even the smoke sometimes failed to calm them down. It was as though Wolf was following her train of thought.

"You know, when I got given the job as beekeeper, I expected there would be those white wooden boxes you see, those ugly stacked things that the hipsters in Silver Lake have in their urban gardens? I was surprised they looked like this instead."

"Top bar hives."

"Yeah. I found out."

"We used to use the white ones. But Kenneth said the top bar hives were more sustainable, that the mechanisms disturbed the bees less. So, like most things Kenneth thinks are a good idea, it came to pass." She grinned, stuck a grass stalk in her mouth, and flinched at its sharp chlorophyll taste on her tongue. "The next big thing he's trying to push is bringing back the slaughterhouse."

She said this mainly to get a reaction and was rewarded by Wolf's face twisting in disgust.

"Ah, what now?"

"Yeah, we had a mobile slaughterhouse for a while. Why do you think I'm mostly vegetarian?"

"What happened? How did it work?" He gave an exaggerated shudder.

"The idea was to have a closed-loop food system or something. But no one really knew anything about slaughtering cattle. I wasn't there of course. My parents refused to let me go anywhere near the shed, but I heard things. It was gruesome. Took five or six hours for the poor cow to die."

"Jesus."

"I know. Let's not talk about it anymore. I can barely stand to go near the field where it used to be. After that we just all quietly went back to buying meat from the supermarket again."

"But there's a herd of cows on the ranch again, isn't there?"

She nodded. "We send them off to slaughter, to some place supposedly known for its humane killing practices. But I know Kenneth's really keen to bring back the mobile slaughterhouse idea, though. He brought it up at a meeting just before you got here."

"And do you think enough people will go for it after what happened?"

"Maybe. He's pretty persuasive when it comes to this stuff. And he's actually had experience, so it wouldn't be like before. At least, that's what everyone's hoping."

"I guess it's a reasonable idea," Wolf said grudgingly. "If he can really pull it off."

They sat in silence for a while, as pollen-laden bees went about their industrious work. Wolf seemed sunk once again into gloom. Marlo wondered whether it was the smallpox news or something else. The last few weeks had seen him striving, as far as she could tell, to ingratiate himself into the fabric of the community. Contrary to Kenneth's dark prognostications, Wolf had proven a worthy worker around the ranch, tireless whether it was mending fences, chopping wood, chasing chickens into their coop, or cooking a casserole. He was always the first to volunteer for dishwashing duty after the potlucks. On an impulse that immediately propelled her back to the night they had first met, Marlo took Wolf's hand in hers.

"Hey, I want to tell you something."

"What's up?"

"Well, you know that internship I told you about?"

"Yes?" She had his attention now, nascent hope shimmering in his eyes.

"I've decided to postpone it."

"No kidding. How come?"

What to tell him? That since his arrival her world had shifted on its axis, that leaving no longer seemed an antidote to what plagued her?

"It just didn't seem like the right time, that's all. Mom and Dad are getting old, and Dad is pretty sick. I would have felt bad leaving them. And Scott, the director, says the position will be there for me whenever I want to start."

That last part wasn't true. Scott had expressed his disappointment, but it was clear to her that she was infinitely replaceable, and that in doing this she had shut a door unlikely to be opened so wide for her again.

"Wow."

"I don't know. Do you think it was the right decision?"

"Me?" He looked genuinely surprised to be consulted. "I think you're a smart woman who's capable of making reasonable decisions about your own life, if that's what you're asking."

Marlo scowled and looked down at her knees unhappily. She didn't know exactly what she was asking. She became aware of the fact that they were still holding hands. Wolf squeezed her hand, as if he too had only just noticed.

"If it helps, I'm selfishly glad that you're staying."

She grinned, looked at him sideways through her eyelashes.

"Really?"

"Dude, yes. Of course. You're my only friend here."

She hated that she craved his validation. It seemed to her a chronic personality fault, this desire to win approval for even her most minor decisions.

Naturally, her parents were delighted with the news that she was staying. Perhaps they had known all along she'd make this decision. She was sure Kenneth would also be relieved, as would most of the ranchers with whom she was close, but after that there were diminishing returns—not least when it came to letting Alex and Ben know. That was the moment she really dreaded. There were several unanswered messages from them on her phone already. They knew the starting date for the internship was approaching, had been sending encouraging messages of support for weeks. They had been talking about flying to San Jose to meet up with her, help her settle into life out in the Disaster, now that they were veterans of the outside world. She was finally getting out, and they continually expressed how proud they were of her. What would they say when she told them that she was staying after all? It would feel like a betrayal. When she finally summoned the courage to tell them, four excruciating days after she first told Wolf, the reaction was even worse than she imagined. The responding message came rapidly, like a sudden cold front.

Did someone put you up to this?

Of course not, she responded. *It was my own decision.* She explained that it wasn't a permanent rejection of the position, just a postponement, but the words sounded hollow and delusional even to herself. She didn't mention Wolf. The last message her friends sent was short and curt, a warning:

Marlo, these people don't have your best interests at heart.

She didn't answer.

12

Lightning cleaved the sky. The sharp tang of ozone hummed in her nostrils. Marlo shivered, but in anticipation rather than fear: she had always loved storms. The plan had been to take the golf cart, swing by Wolf's place and then on to her parents' house, but as the sheets of rain came angling down, the sky tainted with a gray-green cast, that idea of taking the golf cart went out the window. She had been going to her parents' house for Sunday dinner for as long as she had been living out of their home, but this was the first time she'd ever taken a guest, the first time her parents had ever suggested such a deviation to the routine.

"Oh, and feel free to invite Wolf if you'd like."

A casual addendum to the weekly message from her mom. Without warning, the Sunday ritual—sacred and inviolable—had been broken open. She wasn't sure what to make of this. At the time she'd made no promises, saying only that she'd ask him. There was a whiff of collusion about it, as if she'd been excluded from an important family decision and an outsider consulted instead. It didn't occur to her that Wolf would be anything but enthusiastic when she told him about the invitation, so it was something of a surprise when he hesitated.

"Oh, what, you've got other plans that night?" she said, teasing him, then realized with an unpleasant jolt how thoughtlessly one assumed on the ranch that people had no other plans. "I mean, you don't have to come, of course. It's usually just me and them, so."

He rushed to assure her that he'd love to join them, joked that he was flattered to be included in their sacred family ritual, but she wondered afterward about his initial reluctance. She had just assumed he would naturally love and admire her parents, as everyone did. It took her a while to figure out the real reason, that he must feel uncomfortable about the fact that Marlo's parents had covered his investment to join the ranch. Sometimes it was easy to forget the tortured relationship other people had to money, even easier to take for granted the luxury of never having to think about it. She felt guilty that she hadn't been more sensitive and vowed to pay more attention, to learn something about the burden of financial obligation for when she finally made it out into the Disaster. After all, she wouldn't always have her parents' wealth as an emotional and material buffer zone. The thought wasn't an entirely happy one.

They parked the car in the driveway of her parents' house and ran together through the rain to the front door. Maya greeted them at the threshold, scolding them for forgetting umbrellas. Wolf shook his head like a dog, spraying droplets and making Marlo screech.

"Darling, you sound like a banshee," Maya remarked, beaming indulgently at them.

As they followed her down the hallway, Marlo leaned in to Wolf and said, "The house is actually modeled on Fallingwater."

Wolf laughed. "Naturally. I mean, we all grew up in replicas of mid-century modern icons."

"Shut up. It is kind of cool, though, isn't it? They were the original founders of the ranch so they got the pick of the best sites. You'll see when we come out into the lounge room, the compression and release." She knew she was showing off, but she didn't care; it was so fun to introduce someone new to the quotidian wonders of ranch life. His face was all sweet reverence, his gaze caressing the surfaces like he was taking mental notes at a museum.

Carlton greeted Wolf as warmly as his wife had, with a bear hug and a flurry of *welcomes*. Maya smiled so much the fretwork of tiny lines around her eyes radiated out to her ears. Marlo considered her mother a great beauty, but it could be alarming seeing age trace ever deeper runnels into her tanned skin. As with everyone young, Marlo could recognize aging in other people while not quite believing in it for herself. The decay of the body was something that happened to other, more careless people.

"What a boon to have you here, Wolf," Carlton boomed, clapping Wolf on the shoulder with a gnarled hand. "We've been looking for an extra player for cards for ages." This was news to Marlo.

Wolf seemed shy, even sullen, in their presence, and for the first little while Marlo had to do all the conversational heavy lifting, uncomfortably aware of how they all knew but pretended not to remember the debt her new friend owed his hosts. His mortification seemed to permeate the air, to create an unwholesome atmosphere like a dank cave. But at some point during the house tour, in which Wolf was invited to admire each ingeniously designed corner—the open-riser staircases that had always looked strangely naked to Marlo; cantilevered lounging spaces; the bathing platform suspended over the creek running beneath the property—he began to thaw a little, smiling and asking questions at various junctures, stroking their egos in a way that made her suspect with a pang that this was one of his gifts, flattering the parents of girls in whom he took a sexual interest.

When the tour was over, Carlton and Maya retreated to the kitchen on an important mise en place mission, while Marlo and Wolf were relegated to the lounge room to mix drinks. Wolf's eyes lit up when he spotted the dedicated cocktail-mixing station that loomed gaudily out of the corner like some kind of louche 1950s-era fever dream. There was a coppery vintage trolley and a fully stocked bar complete with a mirrored backsplash and a tufted velvet front panel in lurid scarlet. It was the house's one nod toward kitsch, and Wolf declared he loved it more than anything he had ever seen. He ran over, kneeled in front of the velvet front and spread his arms out, hugging it with his cheek laid reverently against its plush. Marlo laughed and shook her head.

She shucked ice cubes out of the tray while Wolf carefully measured out the liquors into a chrome cocktail shaker. Once satisfied with the formula, Wolf sealed the mirrored vessel and began to shake it expertly with one hand, the ice rattling and ricocheting inside. He wandered around the room as he shook, perusing the bookshelves and whistling softly. She watched him scrutinizing the family photos. There was an embarrassing number of her, at every age, except for the first year before she belonged to them. (Although even that was represented in a single blurry snapshot of her at perhaps six months old, dressed in a little Mao-collared shirt and staring, solemn and wide-eyed, into the camera.) He hesitated at a particular photo of her as a toddler, grinning tooth-lessly, velvety cheeks round as a chipmunk's. She was clutching a limp, soft doll, pushing it toward the camera like an offering. At first she assumed he was studying the photo intently, but then he leaned down and retrieved another, smaller snapshot out of a frame that had fallen behind the others. Marlo felt a tug of recognition, something half-forgotten resurfacing. She came to Wolf's side, and they both looked down at the image, faded and grainy like stubbled skin, of a shyly grin-ning little dark-skinned boy dressed in a button-down white shirt and black tie and trousers too big for him. He might have been a miniature missionary.

"Who's this little guy?"

Marlo took the photo from his hand, ran her thumb over the sur-face. Even now, years later, it still radiated a musty sense of loss.

"That was going to be my brother. Jeremiah."

"Oh, shit, I'm so sorry."

"Don't worry. I don't mind talking about it. Although they . . ." She gestured with cocked head toward the kitchen and pulled a warn-ing face.

"Anyway, they were on track to adopt him, from Somalia, in the late nineties, a few years after they got me, but the adoption fell through. It was kind of a big scandal. The adoption agency turned out to be shady, had talked all these families into giving up their kids by pretending they were being sent away to boarding school. This kid actually had lost his parents, to the war, but his grandparents were still alive, so when the truth came out, they came to the orphanage to claim him. Which of course was totally legit, and my parents wouldn't have stood in the way even if they had legal standing. But still, they were pretty devastated."

"Ah, Jesus, that sucks."

"Yeah. My parents still send him gifts and things for school. I think they'll always kind of be in mourning. It was weird, losing a family member you'd never met."

Wolf put his arm around her shoulder, then bent down and kissed her cheek. Just a chaste kiss, unless your thoughts were already tending toward lust and its dark promises. Just then her mother walked in, looked flustered, turned away, but Marlo saw the smile on her face as she turned. It all took less than three seconds—the kiss, the intrusion, the turning away—but Marlo felt the molecules change.

❦

Wolf turned out to be both a skillful card player and a shameless parent-flatterer, and over the course of the night Marlo began to feel her own presence as an encumbrance somehow to them all getting to know one another. They laughed a little too hard at Wolf's story about how he had once been semipassionate about Marxism and smashing the capitalist state, which ended with him pulling out of his wallet a laminated card to prove it: "See, I'm a card-carrying member of the Communist Party of America!" Followed by an incredulous grin. "Wow, I've always wanted to make that joke." There was something performative about it that put her in a sulky mood. She drank a little too much, and when they finally left (not before promises were demanded and given over regarding Wolf joining them all next Sunday), Marlo asked Wolf if he would mind driving home.

"I'm tired and kind of drunk," she said, mussing her hair so that it covered her eyes like a feral child. There may have been some exaggeration of intoxication. She held the keys out to him, letting them dangle coquettishly from a finger. He hesitated, and she saw under the ashy light of the lamp on her parents' porch that his mouth had tightened in trepidation.

"Oh, I forgot. You don't like to drive," Marlo said. Where did it come from, this sudden waspish meanness? Why did she suddenly feel the desire to punish him?

"I just . . . OK, fine."

Marlo hummed as she opened the passenger door, then lurched her body inside into a slumped, splayed-leg position that wasn't entirely graceful. It had stopped raining, and the headlights briefly illuminated ghostly, dripping trees, like skinny-dippers caught in the act. Wolf drove slowly through the ranch, white-knuckled, starting any time there was movement at the edges of the road where it melted away into darkness. It felt lonely, realizing how little she knew of him and the places where his fear lived.

"I'm going to pay them back."

"What?"

"Your parents. I'm going to pay them back, you know."

She shrugged. "That's so not necessary. It's not like they need the money."

The intention was to reassure him, but she saw right away what an error she'd made. He looked as wounded as if she'd delivered a gut punch. Like the joy had all been dragged out of him.

"You know, when you say things like that you seem even younger than you are. Like a little girl who's spent her whole life shut in her little golden tower."

Now it was her turn to be offended. She turned her head away just in time so he wouldn't notice the tears that welled, abundant and shameful. But he must have seen because he reached a tentative hand across the console to cover her kneecap, taking his eyes off the road for a few long moments. The car veered a little, tires squealing on the gravel. Wolf snatched his hand back and steered the vehicle back to the center. His breath came out loud and labored, like he'd been running.

"Listen, I'm sorry, Marlo. That was a fucked-up thing to say. It's just tough, feeling indebted to people. To strangers. If I'm going to stay, I want to earn my place here."

"It's OK," she said and sniffed, wiping her nose and looking out into the forlorn darkness. "I'm sorry too. And for the record, it's true. I don't know anything about the real world. That's why I want to leave someday. And also for the record, you're not a stranger. My parents already knew your parents. And they like you."

"I like them too."

"You're like the son they never had."

It was only in hearing herself say the words that it came into focus, that what she had been experiencing all night had been like a form of sibling rivalry. He took his eyes off the road again, stared in his intent way at the side of her face. She put a hand involuntarily up to her cheek.

"Huh, that's flattering I guess. But I'm hoping you don't think of me as a brother."

"Why not?" she asked innocently. "I always wanted a brother."

"I think you know why."

She didn't answer that, just smiled in the darkness and wrapped her arms around her chest like she used to do as a kid when she was happy or needed comfort. The hug of an only child.

13

If it came as a slight surprise to find him in her bed the next morning, then it was a surprise several weeks in the making. She lay there for a while coming to terms with consciousness, stealing tiny glimpses of him before he woke up. His face in repose didn't look that different from his conscious face, but she hadn't known it was possible to frown in one's sleep. She studied the shadows under his eyes, his heavy lashes, and the defined ledge of his cheekbones. It felt like spying on him, and it excited her.

The details were fuzzy, which was disappointing. Had they talked once they were back at her house or tumbled straight into bed? Had they seen each other fully naked or gotten there by degrees under cover of darkness? Moments came back in flashes like a movie scene full of jump cuts: more red wine, sloshing to the top of their glasses; his hot, boozy breath on her neck; the tangling encumbrance of some kind of clothing that had made them giggle; his muttered, almost aggrieved declarations of how much he liked her; the fact that when he came it was in absolute silence, with only a sharp grimace and the flicker of his eyes closing. This last memory provoked a quick, excited spasm in her stomach, like a pebble dropped in a pool. At least it was behind them now, the first time. There was the sense that the world could properly begin now.

She slid out of bed without waking him—although she could see his eyeballs twitching beneath his lids as if some disturbing movie were playing on the other side—and padded to the kitchen to get coffee started. She picked her phone up from where she had dropped it the night before, upside down on the sofa cushion, scrolled through messages, yawning. There was a new one from Alex. Seeing her friend's name sparked the usual flint of pleasure until she remembered they weren't speaking at the moment. She opened the fridge to retrieve milk, read the message:

I figured you might not really care but Ben insisted we tell you. Hey, might give your weekly doom and gloom meeting some extra spice! Miami is underwater. Huge floods, mass evacuations. American refugees with nowhere to go. Crazy shit, huh?

Take care of yourself, Alex xooxo.

Marlo reread it a few times but the discrete words refused to cohere into a distinct message. There had been flooding in Miami plenty of times over the last few years; she knew that several neighborhoods there were basically uninhabitable these days. But for Alex to think it worth informing her about, things must be pretty bad. She stared at her screen a little longer, debating whether and what to reply. She yearned to be back in contact with her friends, but she knew if she made peace then they'd expect her to come and join them. She glanced back toward the bedroom. As if on cue, the sight of Wolf's dark tousled head on her snowy pillows released endorphins into the reward center of her brain. She turned the phone facedown. Clearly this was a situation best tackled postcoffee. Her parched body craved the caffeine, even though water was what it needed. Funny how the body sent counterintuitive messages sometimes, like it didn't always know what was good for it.

The coffee had just finished brewing when Wolf appeared, dressed again in shirt and jeans, although she hadn't heard him having a shower. She suddenly felt exposed in just her T-shirt and underwear. She smiled at him, discreetly tugged the hem of her shirt down.

"Coffee?"

She held a mug out to him with a fully outstretched arm, expertly keeping him at arm's length. You learned a lot about buffer zones living in a contained community. But he sidestepped her defenses, ducking around the arm and nuzzling his face in her neck. She kissed the top of his head experimentally. She liked the way his hair smelled, both clean and earthy. After a while he pulled away from her, accepted the mug, and took a sip of coffee.

"Mmm."

"Miami's underwater," she blurted out. She'd meant to ease into the news, but a kind of panic valve released the words. "Major ocean flooding. Most people have left."

He blinked at her, struggling to process the words, just as she had.

"What? How do you know?"

"My friends, you know the ones who live out in the Disaster. They texted me."

"Fuck."

"I know."

"Jesus Christ."

"I know."

For the first time in a long time she was scared. Perhaps in some tucked-away part of her she had always assumed that the apocalypse could be put off, that it would happen in another time, to other people.

"What should we do?" As if there was something the two of them could do, standing there in a kitchen on a remote ranch all the way across the country.

"Do you want to fuck?" she asked. It felt like an appropriate time to be brazen. He didn't miss a beat, just nodded, put the mug down, and took her hand, and they walked back to the bedroom together without saying another word.

Later, they went up to Marlo's favorite ridgeline to watch the sun set. Usually after sex Marlo liked to retreat for a while to regain her sense of self. But with Wolf she didn't feel the usual postcoital desire for separation. Instead she was oddly superstitious about letting him out of her sight, and he seemed to feel the same. They sat on the ridge with its fresh carpet of grass, watching darkness engulf the curdled sky.

"Hey, I've been wondering," he said, his warm hand resting on her thigh. "What's in that mausoleum, anyway?"

She turned to look at him with an incredulous laugh.

"Where on earth did that come from?"

He shrugged. "I've just been wondering about it. I know it's not for storing ashes or anything. Is it really just a memorial?"

So it had come, earlier than she'd expected or wanted—the necessity to keep information from him. She thought back to the promise she'd made, at that first meeting after Wolf's mysterious arrival. One of the conditions of him staying was that certain ranch matters would be concealed from him. Kenneth had insisted on it. It hadn't seemed that big a deal at the time: the ranchers had always been averse to letting strangers know too much. A simple security precaution, but it didn't feel so simple now.

"It's kind of on a need-to-know basis," she mumbled, fidgeting with the hem of her denim skirt. She pulled an errant thread taut, snapped it off. The thread left behind a little red groove in her flesh.

"And I'm one of the people who doesn't need to know."

"Look, it wasn't my decision."

"I'm sure it wasn't. Don't worry about it."

He let it drop, but she knew it festered, like an untreated wound.

❦

It was the first news meeting without Neil. Marlo had mentioned the Miami flooding to her parents, and they had decided to call a special meeting to inform anyone in the community who didn't already know. After the communal meal was over, Marlo and Wolf trooped into the hall with everyone else and sat close together toward the back of the room. No parts of their bodies made contact, and yet a crackling energy moved between their chairs like a poltergeist. They had agreed before arriving at the Commons to keep a lid on what had developed between them for a while. Wolf remained largely a stranger here, still on probation. It might have looked rash of her to take up so quickly and enthusiastically with someone who had never been properly vetted, as Kenneth was fond of saying.

Like a fairy-tale character who is summoned only when you think about him, Kenneth materialized by her side.

"Hey, Marl." He glanced with naked distaste at Wolf, who answered with a wide, teeth-baring smile of the kind male animals use to disarm their foes. "Haven't seen you in a while."

"No?" She looked up brightly into his frowning face. "Well, I'm around."

He nodded once brusquely but remained standing there, arms hanging by his sides, for several excruciatingly long moments. When it became clear that no new conversation was forthcoming, he reluctantly moved away, his broad back stiff with anger as he strode to the front of the room. Heat rose to Marlo's ears. She glared toward the front of the room, willing the meeting to start. Wolf was kind enough not to comment.

Carlton chaired the meeting in Neil's absence, and everyone tried to pretend it had always been so. There was something creepy, out of whack, about seeing her father up there where Neil used to stand. In a somber voice he went over the events in Miami, summarizing how the unprecedented king tides had decimated whole neighborhoods, briefly describing the evacuations, the massive wave of displaced people radiating out across the state. Once he'd finished reciting the details of the crisis, he looked over the top of his glasses at the room and hazarded a sober smile, adding that he actually had a piece of good news to relate as well.

"I'm not saying the floods aren't a catastrophe, and a really bad omen of what's to come in other coastal communities around the globe, but I thought it was only fair to share a bright spot of news as well." He left a little showman's pause. "There's been a huge increase in uptake of wind power around the world over the last year. US carbon emissions have fallen 20 percent since 2005, and electric vehicles have increased to an impressive 15 percent of the car market. Of course, most of these positive changes are purely economic decisions, but a net good nevertheless, I think you'll agree."

Carlton looked out at the crowd, blinking. Perhaps he'd been expecting smiles, or even high fives and whooping. But the lake of faces displayed nothing more dramatic than mild surprise, maybe even ambivalence. A few people even shrugged.

"Too little, too late," Marlo heard someone a few seats away mutter. Wolf leaned in, aimed his lips toward her ear.

"Why isn't anyone happy about it? I mean, repairing the ozone hole is better than nothing, right? Burning less coal is good?"

Marlo didn't answer. It would have been too hard to explain to him that when you'd spent the better part of your life preparing for Armageddon there was something a little deflating about being told it might be delayed. It almost felt like an anticlimax.

14

Whenever she wanted to find him and couldn't locate him either at home, with the bees, or on any of the scheduled work shifts, she knew she could find him in the library at the Commons. It had become Wolf's new obsession, sitting for hours contorted into bizarre positions in one of the library's mint-green Eero Saarinen womb chairs, working his way through the nonfiction section. The first time they had been there together, Marlo had pointed out the section of dog-eared books and manuals dedicated to off-the-grid lifestyles.

"Think of this as the religion section," she had quipped.

He had taken her literally, had become a devotee of sorts, devouring the mantras espoused in those deeply unfashionable tomes with wholesome faded covers and titles like *Living the Good Life*, *Whole Earth Catalog*, and *The Contrary Farmer*. Marlo had pointed out Kenneth's favorites, the workingman's bibles and clarion calls against Big Agriculture that he used to guide his organization of the ranch's many moving parts toward a totally self-sustaining future.

"He wants us to be totally off the grid and producing everything we need by 2030," Marlo had explained. "I don't think anyone else truly believes we can do that, but we all kind of humor him. As you do when someone works as hard as Kenneth does at making the place you live into utopia. You know how it is."

"Hmm," said Wolf, distracted, his nose buried deep in Masanobu Fukuoka's *The One-Straw Revolution*, which Marlo knew was Kenneth's personal New Testament. She found it amusing that the two men, who openly despised one another and took great pains to avoid ever being in the same room together, should find common ground in their devotion to the alternative farming lifestyle.

She largely left him alone when she found him in the library, apart from ruffling his hair or dropping a furtive kiss on his cheek. He had already lost some of the pallor he'd sported on arrival, his face a shade darker after weeks working in the open air. Was he happier? Well, that was harder to gauge. Although they had sex often and enthusiastically, his emotional landscape remained mostly closed off to her. He would fall into dark moods during which he became close to unresponsive. Often he was gone when she woke up in the morning, and she'd find him sitting outside on a tree root or stretched out flat on the ground, staring at nothing. Sometimes he reminded her of one of the feral cats who hunted in the wake of the harvests: they both yearned for and shunned affection. One moment it would be rubbing against your legs and mewling pitifully, the next taking a swipe at your ankle. The trick was patience. And not minding that it hurt.

The few women's magazines she had read in her life (furtively, at airports or on supermarket runs) had informed her to expect this of men, that while getting into bed with them was easy, navigating their feelings was another thing altogether. Yet her own prior experience had never borne this out. The only men she'd ever slept with could be divided into two distinct camps: one-night-stands—people whose interiority was of no interest to her—and fellow ranchers whom she'd known forever and whose lives and stories were as transparent and accessible as her own.

During the long summer days, Marlo found unexpected delight in small tasks that had once seemed banal: collecting eggs, vacuuming her house, stacking crates in the barn. She had always loved patrolling the perimeter of the property, but now her journeying was no longer solo; Wolf seemed to get even more of a kick out of it than she did.

One evening they sat together on two wooden stools in the balmy purple dusk, shelling peas into a big stainless steel bowl and drinking from icy bottles of beer they had brought with them in a cooler. There was something erotic about the heavy, drooping bright-green pods lying cradled in her palm, warm from the day's intense sun. She relished the uncomplicated physical pleasure of easing the small, perfectly round green spheres out of their pods with a fingernail, the satisfying way they bounced into the bowl. There was a sense of achievement in witnessing the bottom of the enameled bowl be subsumed under the growing pile.

"Confession," said Wolf, expertly unzipping the pod and flicking a cascading chain of peas into the bowl. "It never occurred to me that I'd one day be sitting shelling peas in the great American pastoral. And enjoying it."

"You mean when you were trapped out there in the American berserk?"

He stared at her, then laughed.

"I didn't pick you as a Philip Roth fan."

She brandished a pea pod in his face, glaring.

"Can we dispense with this idea that because I grew up on a ranch I'm somehow this backward country bumpkin who's never picked up a book? I'll have you know that our homeschool curriculum was every bit as rigorous as whichever Ivy League school you attended, thanks, mister."

She was just teasing, but his face clouded over.

"Are you kidding? I couldn't afford a decent college even if I'd had the grades. I went to a crappy CSU in LA. Then I dropped out because I couldn't pay the student loans and ended up working as a bartender. Then a runner on movie sets. Really glamorous tertiary education."

"Sorry." She hadn't realized he'd never finished college. "You're so smart, I just kind of assumed."

He smiled, pushing the rancor back to the sidelines.

"Guess we should both stop assuming things."

"Right." They clinked their bottles together. "Hey, after dinner I want to take you to this place I know you'll really love."

He grinned, slid his hand between her legs, and squeezed ever so gently. She batted him away, laughing.

"Not there, you pervert. Somewhere better."

He threw her a mock frown as if he doubted that possibility.

The tree house had endured, through storms and decay and years of neglect during which there had been no little children on the ranch to claim it. It had been built in the fork of a spreading old tree in a copse near the stream. The boughs dangled strange pods that cracked open in spring and scattered tiny evil-looking red seeds like confetti. Marlo had been ten years old when the tree house had been built; she and Alex and Ben, already inseparable at that age, had watched in wonder as the house took shape under the ministrations of a gang of parents. It was constructed largely of planks left over from the ranchers' own homes, so the materials were expensive and hardy, and someone who knew what they were doing had overseen the construction. There were plenty of prosaic reasons to explain why it had endured. Still, it was tempting to imbue it with some sort of childhood magic, because its silhouette was so endearingly wonky-looking, with its crooked peaked roof and temperamental hinged door. It looked less like it had been built than plonked down into the crotch of the tree in a storm. You had to have played in it for years or watched it being meticulously crafted—Marlo remembered blizzards of nails and solemn measuring of planks—to appreciate the integrity of the thing.

"It's probably full of spiders and bugs," warned Marlo as they stood at the tree's base, fingers laced together, staring up at the underside of the house's floor, but Wolf was completely charmed. He clambered up the ladder and after poking his head inside declared it perfectly intact, apart from a couple of loose boards, but they could easily remedy that.

"Can we sleep out here one night?" he asked, bright-eyed and pleading.

She laughed at his earnest expression. For the first time it was possible to see the boy he had once been.

On the way to one of the sheds to gather materials to fix the house up, Wolf told her about when he was a kid and he'd read about people camping but had never done it.

"I could barely imagine the countryside. We didn't even go to the beach all that often, and we lived within a thirty-minute drive of the ocean."

"How come?"

He didn't seem to hear her.

"I was obsessed with the idea of going camping. *Obsessed.* I don't know why, I think I'd seen it in movies, and it just became this exemplar of everything joyous in the world, or something. So one time I borrowed a tent from this friend from school, Mike Carson, yeah, and I pitched it in the backyard of our house, and I camped out that night. I remember I took an insane amount of time to choose provisions from the kitchen. Ham slices, half a loaf of bread, a cold roasted potato, a bit of salt in a twist of foil. I stayed out there with my book and flashlight, and I kind of rationed out the food, like it might run out and I'd starve before morning light. I felt like such a fucking pioneer." He laughed hoarsely. "I remember being really scared by all the noises of the neighborhood, which I guess were always there, but I never usually heard them safe inside in bed. Anyway, that was my one and only experience of camping."

Marlo put her arm through his and leaned into him, trying to transmit comfort. Like most of Wolf's stories, they started off as casual anecdotes before taking a turn for the melancholic.

"Well, I was always really jealous of kids who lived out in the Disaster, that they got to be Girl Scouts and go to summer camp and all that stuff."

"But you had all this," he said, with the usual incredulity he displayed whenever she brought up even the tiniest example of dissatisfaction with growing up on the ranch. "This place basically *is* summer camp!"

"The shoe hurts the wearer, I suppose." A dredged-up old expression her father liked to use. Wolf didn't say anything to that, but she could tell her attempt to find common ground had failed. It was a false equivalency, in his eyes. What did she have to complain about?

They packed sheets and blankets and cushions and a few dozen of the battery-powered candles the ranchers kept in drawers in case of blackouts. Marlo had prepared a picnic basket, and they each took a backpack with water in thermoses, a change of clothes, and toothbrushes. They packed it all into the golf cart and drove out to the tree to set up camp. On the way they passed the mausoleum, and Marlo noticed Wolf turning his head to look back at it; she knew he'd ask about it again, and sure enough, once they had settled into their cozy, musty den, sprawled on their raft of cushions and blankets, with feet sticking out the tree house's door, which they'd propped open with a rock, he brought it up.

"I'm still really curious about what's in that mausoleum. Are you ever going to tell me?"

She laughed. "For the thousandth time, no. Why don't you ask someone else?"

"I have," he said sulkily. "They won't tell me either. I mean, Frank, Ben's dad, right? He did let slip something vague the other day, like *It's something our future will rely upon,* but after that he clammed up."

"You'd be really disappointed even if you found out. It's just a storage space. Pretty boring, really."

"Storage for what?"

She rolled her eyes then, pulled a blanket up to cover her head. When she emerged, hair crackling with static, he was sitting up hugging his knees and staring at her intently. She groaned. "What?"

"OK, how about this? Why don't I try to guess what's inside, and you tell me if I'm getting close?"

"Are you three years old? Seriously."

He laughed, but a fuse had been lit.

"Is it gold bullion?"

"What? No."

"I knew some survivalists back in LA, libertarian types who listened to too much talk radio. They were obsessed with stockpiling gold."

Next he guessed a cache of weapons, then a nuclear warhead, then a robot army. Marlo alternated between laughing at his guesses and being exasperated. His guesses were all couched as jokes, his tone light, but there was something beneath the interrogation that worried Marlo.

"I'm serious now," she said, taking his hand. "Why do you want to know so badly?"

He gazed out the door at the rectangle of black, the stars like a gleaming net slung across the sky.

"It makes me feel like a little kid being punished. Like when parents withhold information. *It's for your own good.* It always felt kind of despotic to me when my parents would refuse to tell me something because they thought it was bad and I should be sheltered from it. Like, family Freedom of Information Act, you guys."

"It's not like that," she said quietly. "It's not personal."

But was that strictly true? A few recent interactions had rankled, like when two of the older ranchers had approached her during a potluck dinner to voice their concerns about Wolf's mysterious arrival and accelerated admission to the ranch. She could tell Kenneth wasn't the only one who considered Wolf not entirely trustworthy, a usurper, even. It was unfair. Just because he hadn't paid his way in, that didn't mean he should be subject to extra scrutiny. But there was nothing to be gained from adding fuel to his paranoia. With the intent of distracting both of them, she swiveled around on her butt, retrieved the picnic basket from a web-festooned corner, and began to pull items out of it one by one. She placed a white wax paper package on a small checked picnic blanket between them.

"Ham." Then she pulled out a plastic container. "Roasted potatoes." A baguette, broken in two pieces. "Bread." Finally, two twists of aluminum foil. "Salt and pepper."

Then she drew out an insulated bag containing a bottle of Bollinger and two plastic flutes.

"And champagne. A slight deviation from your childhood campout, if you'll forgive it."

She closed the lid of the basket, sat back on her haunches with hands on knees, shyly grinning.

"Wow. I don't know what to say."

He smiled at her and then quickly looked away. He busied himself with rifling through his backpack, and she pretended not to see him dash at his cheek with his sleeve. He turned back to her, brandishing a pile of paper napkins.

"Not very earth friendly, but I didn't have any real ones."

After they had eaten and cleared up and all the champagne had been drunk and they'd made awkward, knee-jarring love, slipping several times off the raft of blankets and onto the splintery boards, they lay close together under the covers. He seemed enraptured by specific parts of her body. Not just the usual parts but less examined ones, like the bottom of her rib cage, the bones at her ankle, and the jut of her hipbones when she was lying down. He stroked the flesh in those places in a kind of reverie. They lay silent, listening to the night sounds: rustling and hooting and the occasional call of a coyote, all the noises that reminded them why humans build walls. After the third bloodcurdling animal sound drifted up to their precarious little aerie, Marlo snuggled in close to Wolf's bare flank. Laughing she asked, "Are you sorry we came out here?"

"Are you kidding? I've literally never been happier in my life. Even if we do get eaten by a fucking grizzly bear or something before dawn."

She kissed him. "Wait 'til the mosquitoes start biting. Then you'll really be singing a different tune."

And sure enough, when the morning light came, both their legs and arms were speckled with tiny red welts. But in spite of the exquisitely nightmarish itching and the angry red marks that persisted for weeks, for Marlo the memory of that night remained the same, poignant and almost unbearably sweet.

15

The ranch was overflowing with sheer abundance, running wild with life. In the midst of all this fecundity it strained the imagination to believe in the terrible things playing out in the Disaster. How could this grove of quaking aspens, for instance, tall and pale and crowned with halos of glossy green leaves, possibly exist in the same dimension as the dust bowl–desiccated wastelands in the parts of Southern California the government had recently declared an emergency zone? The ranch's streams ran quick and clear, silver-bellied fish spangling the surface in an orgy of vitality, yet on the other side of the country, entire coastal cities were at risk of drowning like modern-day Atlantises. At times like this Marlo could understand the deniers: if you blinkered your view of the world, focusing only on the most encouraging signs of continuity, no matter how anomalous, you could pretend for whole stretches of time that nothing bad was happening.

It was on one of these near-identical days of sylvan torpor, the sky blazing and cloudless, that Marlo's mother called to remind her that the appointment for her annual physical was coming up. Her mother kept track of things like that. She was the family's self-appointed record-keeper, obsessive about reminder notes and the syncing up of calendars. The call reminded Marlo that she hadn't actually left the ranch since her trip to New York with her father. Hadn't really thought about it since Wolf had arrived. She thanked her mother for the reminder, jotted down the date and time of her medical appointment.

Their family doctor had been treating Marlo since she was six years old. It had been one of those early compromises on the ranch: they all agreed that obtaining medical care outside the ranch was a necessary evil for which it was worth breaching their self-sufficiency. There were a couple of ranchers with medical degrees who attended to minor injuries and maladies, and an on-property dispensary where you could get hold of most over-the-counter medications. But Marlo's parents were adamant that their daughter receive top-notch preventative medical care, and so from the time she had been young she had trooped into town with them once a year to have blood drawn, receive vaccinations, have her blood pressure checked, and later, once she had started menstruating, have annual pap smears. The visits weren't something Marlo looked forward to exactly, but like any chance to venture outside, they had the flavor of novelty and so became bright spots on her increasingly blank calendar.

Her doctor's name was Betty Duranni, and she had been born in Bangalore, India. She and her family had migrated to Oregon when she was a teen, and she had ended up marrying a rosy-cheeked, affable Baptist minister and settling down into this family practice. Her desk was littered with photos of family—she and the minister and their four children, who had all inherited their mother's coffee-colored skin and black hair, not to mention her sly half smile. Dr. Duranni surely knew something about being an outsider. With her steeply arched eyebrows and permanently wry expression, she always gave the impression of being both amused and astonished at having ended up stranded in this predominantly white, wide-open part of the country. Her manner occupied the typical medical professional territory between kind and gruff, and she had a way of intuiting Marlo's state of mind that occasionally swung her appointments into psychotherapy sessions. She was the only nonrancher who had continually been in Marlo's life since childhood.

"How have things been, my dear?" Dr. Duranni peered at her patient over the top of tortoiseshell wire-rim glasses. Her hair in its low bun was glossy and unmarred by even a thread of gray, though Marlo guessed she must have been at least fifty years old. Marlo tried to imagine her outside the context of this antiseptic office, shopping for groceries at the supermarket or swapping small talk with the hairdresser at the sad salon whose windows were plastered with bleached posters of models with popped collars and desperate fixed stares, but the visions failed to convince.

"Fine. You know."

"How are the folks? Your dad's arthritis?"

"He has his good and bad days. I think he mentioned he has an appointment with you coming up next week. How is your family?"

"Fine." Dr. Duranni smiled. They both knew that no further details would be forthcoming. Her job was to collect knowledge, not offer it. "Alright, then, roll up your sleeve, and I'll check that blood pressure."

After having pronounced Marlo's blood pressure "absolutely perfect" (which made her feel strangely proud, as though she'd won something), listening to her chest, and examining her skin for suspicious moles or freckles, Dr. Duranni signaled it was time for the dreaded pap smear. Marlo changed into the white gown, took her underpants off, and lay on the examination bed, which was sheathed in slippery paper. Marlo gazed up at the ceiling, hands crossed over her chest like a saint on a tomb.

"Roll slightly onto your side, dear. It will be more comfortable that way."

"Oh, sorry." She always forgot the mechanics in the general dread of the act. The metallic cold of the speculum never failed to make her shiver. Or perhaps it was more the unpleasant intimacy of the moment, reminiscent of sex in the most clinical way—legs parted to receive the penetrating instrument—with the extra indignity of the scraping inside her cervix. She closed her eyes and tried to think of something, anything, else. Then it was over and Dr. Duranni was briskly instructing her to get dressed again. There was a lightness to coming down off the bed, the euphoria of a small ordeal passed.

"You know something," said Dr. Duranni from over on the other side of the room, where she was placing the sample in a medical bag and writing instructions on the outside. "A lot of my patients your age are beginning to think about starting a family. Not sure whether that's in the cards for you, but I'd be happy to help arrange a fertility test if you're interested."

Marlo pulled her shirt back on, frowning. A cold sensation rippled over her skin.

"Hmm," she said. "Do you really think it's, well, necessary?"

Dr. Duranni looked up, blinking.

"Not necessary, exactly. Some of my patients just find it reassuring to know more about the state of their fertility. It's a very inexact science, mind you, but there are certain tests that can show problems early, and can predict how many healthy eggs you have and when might be an optimal time to think about trying to get pregnant, if indeed that were on one's agenda."

"I guess I'll think about it. I mean, I'm not even sure I want to have kids."

"A lot of young women say that, but they often change their minds."

Marlo began to dislike the tone of this conversation. She shifted in her seat, unpleasantly aware of the lube Dr. Duranni had used on the speculum drying on her inner thighs.

"I'm not really interested in knowing, to be honest," she said. It came out more curtly than she had intended. "I think I'll take my chances with fate." Not that she believed in fate. She smiled warmly, eager to restore the doctor-patient status quo. *If only you could suggest a cure for my chronic need to be liked,* she thought with some bitterness. But Dr. Duranni didn't seem in the least bit offended to have her suggestion rebuffed; if anything, she seemed relieved.

"Just know the option's always there. Now, any prescriptions I can write for you?"

"Hmm. I think just a refill for the pill," said Marlo innocently, and in this way she got the last word.

But on the way home the exchange started to irritate her. Instead of savoring the joy of less-familiar terrain, reveling in imagining the lives being lived behind all those strangers' doors as she normally did on any excursion off the ranch, she stared straight ahead at the road, replaying the appointment over and over again in her head. Why had Dr. Duranni brought up the question of her fertility, unprovoked? Surely that was nobody's business but hers. She had so little business of her own to protect.

When she arrived back at the ranch, she went straight around to see her parents, as she always did after her physical, just to reassure them in person that everything was fine. Her dad was lying down in the den, a *New Yorker* draped over his eyes. Marlo dropped a kiss on his cheek, insisted he not get up (she noticed with a twinge of worry that he didn't even try to argue, a sure sign he was in one of his health slumps), then went into the kitchen, where her mother was perched on a barstool, leafing through a gardening book. Tendrils of steam floated up from a white porcelain cup. The room was filled with the tropical scent of jasmine tea.

"Oh, hello, darling. Did you look in on your father?"

"Yep. He's fine, just wanted to rest a little."

"How was your appointment today? Everything OK, I hope?"

Marlo nodded, opened the fridge, rummaged inside. She pulled out a block of cheese and a jar of cornichons, got some crackers from the pantry, and assembled a plate. She was ravenous all of a sudden.

"Just the usual checkup," she said, balancing a square of cheddar on a cracker and topping it with a wee pickled hat. "Look, it's too cute to eat. Almost."

She bit down daintily into the cracker, chewed the mouthful slowly as she'd been taught. Funny how these pointless childhood lessons persisted.

"Hey, Mom?"

"Yes, love?" Her mother closed the book and placed it on the counter. As always when she spoke to either of her parents, undivided attention. She tried to imagine what it must be like to suffer parental neglect.

"So Dr. Duranni suggested something kind of weird when I was there. She said I should think about having a fertility test done."

Her mother raised her reading glasses from their lanyard and put them on. Her eyes instantly enlarged like a cartoon cat's.

"Well, you know, perhaps she's right, honey. It couldn't hurt to find out, could it?"

This wasn't the reaction Marlo had been expecting.

"Find out what?"

Her mother raked a hand through her silver-blonde hair, disturbing to a miniscule degree its habitual bobbed perfection. Three discrete strands floated free. "Well, it's just they have ways now of finding out how many eggs you have, that kind of thing. And girls these days don't even have to decide like we did. There's the freezing of embryos, all the technology . . ."

"Are you serious? You really think I should do this? I'm only twenty-five, Mom. I don't know if I even want kids."

"Of course you do. You will. I'd hate you to go through what I, what your father and I, went through. I don't know what I would have done if you hadn't come into our lives."

"Don't worry about it. Let's forget I brought it up." She drew her mother in for a hug, inhaled the nostalgic bergamot-scented aroma of Shalimar embedded in the warp and weft of her clothing. "It just makes me uncomfortable talking about that stuff."

"Sweetheart, I understand," her mother said, stroking the smooth hair falling over Marlo's shoulders. "I'm sorry, I don't want to put pressure on you. But have you thought about talking about it with someone who's not one of your old parents? A friend. Wolf, perhaps?"

"Wolf? Why on earth would I talk to him about it?"

"I don't know." For the first time her mother looked flustered. "I just thought . . ."

"Can we drop it?"

"Of course, honey. Of course."

That night she had her one and only recurring dream. A nightmare, really. In the dream she was tasked with trying to return dozens of stranded goldfish to a tank, over and over. Every time she tried to rescue a fish it would slip out of her hands, until she was standing at the center of a flooded room, surrounded by scaled bodies that writhed and flipped and stared up at her with baleful, dying eyes.

16

They were driving out to see about a downed tree one day when Wolf told her that he had once killed someone. She was behind him on the tandem ATV, her thighs pressed into the small of his back—he had gradually become more confident with getting behind the wheel, even seemed to relish it sometimes, so she always let him drive if he appeared in the mood—and the engine was so loud she thought she'd misheard him. After they stopped at the fallen tree and had jumped off the vehicle, Marlo turned to him and asked him to repeat what he had said.

"I said I think I killed someone."

She was sure he had added the *I think*, but the fact that the killing had been downgraded from a certainty to a possibility didn't offer much solace. When she questioned him further—*Are you serious? When? Who? What the fuck?*—he backpedaled.

"I was just joking," he said. His smiles were like gifts, and she had never turned one down before. But she felt anger flaring.

"What kind of a joke is that?"

"Bad taste. Sorry."

"Were you in the Army or something?" She realized she knew so little of his story. He shook his head, aimed an experimental kick at the tree trunk.

"Babe, seriously. I have a twisted sense of humor." He caressed her neck, and all the tiny hairs on her body stood up at attention. "I used to try it on my shrink all the time, telling him I'd done things I hadn't done. It drove him nuts. But I shouldn't have done it with you. I'm sorry."

She scrutinized his face, puzzled, but he quickly turned to the tree, and they examined it together, agreeing that it looked to have been struck by lightning. She snapped a few photos. That was a relief, at least: Marlo was always fearful that the kind of insect blights that plagued other forests would one day strike the ranch, sweeping away whole forests and ecosystems and leaving the land barren. So far her fears had been unfounded. They climbed back onto the ATV, and when Wolf turned the key the vehicle shuddered into life like a horse beneath them. She hesitated for a moment before putting her arms around his torso. She could feel the life thrumming beneath his skin as well, and it filled her with a savage joy. She didn't like to think there was still so much he hadn't told her, would probably never tell her. This unexpected, unlooked-for friendship, its barbs so much more painful than its longevity warranted.

🌿

"I like how you have more weather here," Wolf said approvingly. They were almost at the end of checking the perimeter, had stopped to clear some branches that had blown across the road leading up to the Commons during the same storm that had toppled the tree. "Not just different weather, but more of it somehow."

Marlo laughed. "I guess it seems like the normal amount to me."

"In LA I barely ever noticed what the weather was like. It was either sunny or smoggy, you know, but there was this sameness to it."

"That doesn't sound too bad to me," she said, still grumpy about his weird fake confession. It made her want to disagree with whatever he said, no matter how inoffensive. "It sucks dealing with rain and snow. You might not be so delighted when winter comes around."

She meant it too, thinking about how by January the sky seemed to collapse, its gray weight crushing and deadening the land.

"Hey, how old were you when your parents adopted you?"

She threw the branch in her hand as far as she could. It gave a satisfying twang as it sailed across the grass. "Why do you ask?"

"I don't know. Just realized I wasn't sure."

"Well, I was fourteen months. I don't remember any of it, though. I mean, there are photographs of course, and stories my parents tell that make me feel as though I remember, but I really don't. It's like this big blank at the beginning of my life."

"If it's any consolation I can't remember anything before about the age of five. And even then, it's like what you said, things my parents told me that came to seem like my own memories."

"It's weird seeing photos of yourself that you don't remember being there for at all. Like retroactive dementia."

"Exactly."

They walked back to the ATV, Wolf's arm slung around her shoulder. She liked how naturally she fit into the crook of his arm, like they were discrete parts of a machine whose function could only be revealed when the two sections were joined.

"Can I ask if you've ever thought about trying to find your birth parents?"

"Of course. I used to want to, a lot. When I was around ten. And my parents were hugely supportive. You know, they promised when I was old enough that we'd travel back to China and see if we could track them down. They didn't tell me, but I found out later how hard that would have been, almost impossible. The orphanages never kept data on birth parents, and in fact most of the time the babies were just left at their doorstep, or at an underground church. No way of finding out. The government had certain rules about the need to post announcements about the child in the papers, in case the family came back to claim the child. But of course no one ever claimed them, not with the one-child policy in place. So it would have been futile going there, but my parents were totally determined to do it. I think they wanted it more than me in the end." She climbed into the driver's seat this time, lost in memory. She hadn't thought about her birth parents in ages. "But then something just happened one day, like a switch was turned off, and I didn't care anymore. I've barely thought about them since."

"You're not even curious?"

She shrugged, flicked the fuel gauge with a fingernail. "Not really. I mean, they couldn't be anything but strangers in the end. I guess I occasionally wonder about my ethnicity, you know, with the strange-colored eyes and the pale skin. Apparently at the orphanage they called kids like me this word, not sure if I'm saying it right . . . *Hun-xue-er*, which means mixed-blood. One of my parents was Chinese and the other was probably white. A foreigner. As a kid I always had in mind that my mother was Chinese and my dad was white, some tourist falling in love with a girl from the village, some romantic crap like that, I don't know."

"So you never intend to try and find out more? I mean, these days with things being more open, maybe the orphanage could help track . . ."

"Seriously, I'm really not that interested. Unless, I guess maybe if I wanted to start a family someday, maybe then I'd consider making more of an effort to fill in the blanks. My parents have always offered to help me get DNA tests if I want, but what's the point? DNA isn't who you are."

"Yeah. Funny, I feel a similar way about my real parents. You're lucky. Your parents are so . . . normal."

There it was again, that little flicker of sibling rivalry. She pushed it away. It was important to remember what he'd suffered, his mother gone and his father dead in a car crash. It made her feel selfish, thinking about how lucky she had been, hoarding good fortune like a kid grabbing too much candy on Halloween.

"I know they like you too, Wolf."

He waited until she had started the ignition and the engine was roaring before he yelled out to her: "Hey, speaking of which, I've been meaning to tell you. I spoke with your parents the other day and they offered to help me build my own place here. Which is obviously, fuck, incredibly generous. But I wanted to see what you thought, if you were OK with it."

She stopped the vehicle again. It groaned like a testy animal.

"So you're staying?" A lump constricted her throat. "I'm so happy for you!"

"Really? Are you sure? Your folks even offered to help me design a place. I mean, I've worked construction, but I have no clue about this stuff when it comes to making it look fancy. I'd love any input you have on the design too. If you have time."

The tentative eagerness in his voice was almost unbearable. At times like this it felt as though their destinies had been swapped, that he was actually the orphan left on the doorstep instead of her, and now he'd finally found his family. When they hugged, Marlo could feel all the muscles in his body tensed, vibrating under her embrace as if he were trying to keep his emotion trapped. But happiness, that flighty escapee, demanded to fly.

17

It might have been a scene plucked from a Manet painting. The trees bawdy with life, sunlight through their heavy canopies weaving mosaics of light and shade on the ground. Swampy air rising from the lake, heat haze shimmering above the grass. Knots of people sprawled on picnic blankets or towels or in the case of the older hippie ranchers, lying right on top of the earth, absorbing its warmth. Marlo wore a white bikini and knew she looked good in it, basking in the fact that Wolf couldn't take his eyes off her even when he was engaged in conversation with someone else, sneaky sideways glances humid with desire.

Someone proposed a game of boules and was greeted with a chorus of groans. But the box was produced anyway, and the ranchers situated closest to the special-purpose sandy court grudgingly shifted further away to allow the game to commence. Marlo rummaged around in her tote bag and retrieved a patterned sarong, tied it over the top of her breasts. She put on a broad-brimmed hat.

"You playing?" she asked Wolf, patting him lightly on the butt. He grinned.

"Sure, I'm game."

The boules set was heavy, old-fashioned, the balls silver orbs that flashed in the sunlight. The game was languid, punctuated by taunting and laughter. Most people had started drinking rosé earlier in the afternoon, a tradition on these high summer days when the chores had been completed and no one felt like being solitary. Kenneth was nowhere to be seen, Marlo noticed, but that wasn't so unusual: even before her and

Wolf's relationship had become common knowledge, he hadn't really been one to enter into the spirit of leisure time. She used to tease him about having a Protestant work ethic mixed with Catholic guilt, and there had been a time when he'd found such teasing charming, coming from her. But he was rarely to be seen these days, apart from a silhouette in some far field or a figure slipping in late to meetings to stand at the back wall, arms crossed. She hadn't seen him at a potluck dinner for weeks, couldn't remember the last conversation the two of them had. She missed him, but any recent overtures to mend their friendship had been politely rebuffed.

Wolf had just rolled a ball that progressed on a drunkenly weaving course then stopped short in the sand, when the crack of gunfire, over and over, came from somewhere close by. They all looked at each other and then around, heads swiveling to try to identify the source of the shots. The people who had been lying down got to their feet.

"It's not hunting season, is it?" someone asked. Marlo shook her head. Dread pulsed in her throat.

"We should go check it out," she said, trying to channel her father's forceful calm, but the same feeling of panic that had engulfed her when she had heard the shot that ended Neil's life returned, and she wondered whether she'd be able to bear another tragedy. Pants were hurriedly pulled on, shirts donned unbuttoned, flapping around sun-mottled chests. Gunshots weren't entirely unusual to hear in this region—Kenneth and a few of the others sometimes brought down a deer or wild turkeys in the farthest-flung woods—but there had been something urgent and panicked about the flurry of shots, as though the shooter had been taken unawares. Besides, it was ranch policy that anyone planning to go hunting needed to send a group text stating their intentions, to avoid accidents. They all had fluorescent orange vests they were supposed to wear when hiking in the woods during the season. There had been no notification today. Whoever was shooting wasn't one of them—at least not in any sanctioned way. No one needed to say what was on all their minds. Wolf put his hand on Marlo's arm.

"Let's wait to see what's happening."

He sounded spooked, so Marlo squeezed his arm back, but she wasn't exactly feeling carefree herself.

"Hey." It was Frank, Ben's dad, one of the original founders. "I just got a message." He looked in alarm at his phone, then back up at the small gathered crowd. "It's Sven. He's in the back meadow, and he needs some backup."

"What's happening?"

Frank shook his head. "He doesn't say. Just says everything's OK, no one's hurt, but that something a bit weird is going on."

Marlo glanced at Wolf. He was staring, transfixed, at Frank. They all were. They watched as Frank received another message, read it out slowly.

"He says that we should all stay where we are."

"Why?"

"Don't know. But I'm going up to the Commons to get weapons. Who's coming with me?"

Without any discussion a small clutch of people broke away, coalesced around Frank, and then jogged together over to the nearest vehicles. Instinctively, the people who were left moved closer together. Marlo felt her phone jerk in her hand. At the same time other phones pinged around the circle, making their various idiosyncratic sounds or vibrations. Everyone scrambled and looked down at the screens as one entity, heads bowed. It was a group text from Sven.

WATCH OUT, IT'S COMING YOUR WAY!

There was a chorus of *fucks* as everyone looked wildly around for a clue as to what was coming. A few people raised their eyes to the sky, as if whatever it was might arrive from above.

"What is it?" hissed Wolf in Marlo's ear, but she couldn't speak. She dug her fingers into his forearm, leaving white marks. "Maybe it's a hoax."

She could tell from his voice that he didn't really believe that. The ranchers weren't exactly pranksters. They stood close together, scanning the area and then further to the distant horizon, but morbid seconds passed, and they couldn't see anything out of the ordinary.

"What's that noise?" asked Wolf. Suddenly they could all hear it, a deep, low rumble that started off like distant thunder, then intensified until Marlo thought she could feel the ground shaking.

"An earthquake!" someone cried, but they had never had an earthquake, and if this was the first time none of them knew what to do. It was almost comical how unprepared they were. A group of rational survivalists without a properly thought-out disaster plan. Marlo suddenly recalled the story she had read about the Cascadia Subduction Zone, the epic continental plate collision off the Pacific Coast that was centuries overdue: when they finally clashed together, earthquakes and tsunamis would follow, wiping out a swath of Pacific Northwest coastline. But reason quickly took over: they were too far inland to be affected by such an event.

Wolf, who was facing the road where it disappeared around a corner, was the first to see it. He shouted out and pointed and they all turned. Careening down the main road was a black-and-white cow, moving in a grotesque fashion, lurching from side to side, and roaring. Its hoofs threw up dust and tiny stones that ricocheted like tiny missiles. Marlo felt one sting her calf. As the creature galloped closer it veered to the side, closer to their circle, where everyone stood as if paralyzed. In the slow-motion unfolding it seemed to Marlo that the cow saw them or sensed them, but she couldn't guess its intent. Did it want to get their help or to attack them? As it ran closer she saw that its eyes were bulging and running with blood. Screams ripped the innocent blue day apart; ranchers scattered like buckshot out of the crazed creature's path.

The cow adjusted its course, moved back to the road, and continued on its way. As it moved out of sight, Sven and Kenneth appeared, barreling down the road in an ATV. Marlo stood and watched, mouth agape, as they passed by in a blur of noise and motion, pursuing the cow. A few seconds later a gunshot rang out. They all jumped, clutched at one another like refugees on a sinking ship.

Sven and Kenneth returned, ashen faced, to explain what had happened. Sven had been slashing grass in one of the far meadows when he noticed a strange movement on the horizon. A shape moving toward the ranch, fast, but moving oddly. When the shape got closer he saw that it was a herd of cows, maybe a dozen, definitely not the ranch's herd, all acting completely bizarrely. Staggering, mooing, in obvious distress. When they got close enough, he saw they were all foaming at the mouth and bleeding from the ears and eyes. Sven called Kenneth, and they were speculating about what to do when the farmer from the adjacent property, who owned the cows, appeared, barreling along on his tractor. He jumped out, gun in hand, and began shooting his cows in the head while weeping.

"One of the surviving cows broke away and ran down the road. That's when I sent you that message." The group of listeners stood around Sven as if in a healing circle, some with hands clapped over mouths, others reaching out to touch him. His voice shook. "I tried to stop him! But it was like he was crazy too. It was horrible, like a murder scene."

He stopped talking then, covered his face with grimy, dirt-streaked hands. The scene's inescapable parallels to the day Neil had died, the same sense of dislocation and nightmarish unreality.

"What the fuck happened to them?" said Wolf.

"Was it mad cow disease or what?" asked someone from behind Marlo.

Kenneth put his hand on Sven's shoulder, took up the story, which he delivered in his rumbling baritone.

"So when we finally got the farmer to calm down and tell us what happened, he talked about a chemical company he suspected of poisoning the stream that runs through his farm. His cows all went crazy and died gruesome deaths. This was the last of his herd."

The feelings shifted in an instant from sympathy for the farmer and his doomed herd to a more local concern: if their neighbor's stream was poisoned, why not theirs? As if reading minds, Kenneth added, "Of course the first thing I thought was that we might be contaminated as well. But I conducted a water test just yesterday, and we're pure." He paused for an ominous beat. "For now."

He didn't rub it in, that his brand of over-the-top environmental paranoia had been vindicated finally. But he didn't have to. He sighed deeply, as if already regretting what he was about to say.

"That's not all, though. He told us that a few of the farmers around here, closer to town, they're all ill with various mysterious diseases and maladies."

As if by silent command they all dispersed soon after that, like the information was too much to digest at once, and they needed to retreat to their own corners. Sven's wife, Amber, led him away to the car. Marlo couldn't stand to look at his retreating back any more than she had been able to stand looking at his face as he recalled the afflicted cows. He had looked so broken.

❦

That night Marlo cried for the first time since Neil had died, the first time since she had known Wolf. They lay in bed together, shivering and chaste in T-shirts and shorts. She laid her head on his chest and wet the front of his T-shirt while he stroked her hair. At first she sobbed with abandon, but the storm subsided quickly, until she was just self-consciously sniffling. When she sat up and caught sight of his face, he looked scared too.

"I'm sorry. I don't know why I'm so upset," she said between sniffles. "It wasn't as though a person died. Just a poor stupid cow."

"Poor cow."

The visceral horror of that creature's demented, blood-streaked face—she knew she would never forget it. Nor would anyone who had been there to witness it.

"Let me show you something." Wolf gently disentangled himself from her, sprang up, and came back with his laptop, which along with most of his other possessions he kept at her house these days. The machine hummed into life, and she sat close to him, looking at their solemn, distorted faces reflected in the screen as it booted up. He went to the browser and then to his bookmarks, opened one of them.

"This story. I don't even know why I bookmarked it. Apart from the fact that it was just so fucking disturbing."

She read the headline: "Chemical Pollution Devastates Virginia Community."

They sat with shoulders and thighs touching as they read it, and occasionally one of them would read a line or phrase aloud.

"In late 2015, farmer Tom Gilbraith noticed his cattle becoming increasingly aggressive, charging, foaming at the mouth, and 'acting crazy.' Eventually the entire herd died, and autopsies showed severely enlarged livers, organ deformities, and lesions associated with chemical poisoning.

"A chemical company headquartered in the region was found to have been illegally dumping toxic waste in landfills and local waterways.

"Residents complained of myriad health issues, from diminished eyesight to miscarriages to cancer.

"The company covered up its internal findings regarding the toxicity of the chemicals . . ."

By the time she had finished reading the ten-page article, daylight had fled the room, and she could barely make out the contours of Wolf's face.

"Holy fuck," she said. "Do you think something similar happened here?"

"I don't know. I really hope not. But let's face it, there's no comforting explanation. I mean, mad cow? That's almost worse."

Marlo threw off the cover, swung her legs out of bed.

"Let's get some light in here." She shivered as her feet touched the floor. The warmth and carefree camaraderie of the afternoon felt less like a lived experience and more like a movie they had watched together—one of those European movies saturated in nostalgic beauty. She went around the room, lighting candles and switching on lamps until the darkness had been banished to the corners and the rafters, then she climbed back into bed. Wolf kissed her cheek.

"What are we going to do?"

His tone was genuinely anguished. She pulled her neck back in order to fully look into his face.

"Whatever happened to your ironic detachment?" she said, teasing him. He grinned, but there was a certain desperation in it.

"Must have detached itself."

"Everything will be OK."

For the first time she understood why children love to hear those words so much, despite how hollow they sound coming out of an adult's mouth.

❦

A few of the ranchers decided to rally and boost morale by organizing a spur-of-the-moment potluck. The message went around, pinging its way through the houses. Marlo replied yes for herself and Wolf, but she felt uneasy all through picking ingredients and preparing a huge salad, showering and dressing for the dinner. Should she and Wolf share the article he had shown her? Or might it send panic through the ranks, to think that the world from which they were running had caught up with them, after all, was in fact right on their doorstep? She discussed it with Wolf as she was drying her hair. He advised caution, as she'd secretly hoped he would.

"We don't even know if this is the same thing," he reasoned. "That shit happened in Virginia, so far from here. There aren't any chemical factories around here, are there?"

"I don't think so. I feel like Kenneth would have sniffed them out by now if so. He's obsessed with this stuff. But maybe."

"We could do some sleuthing. Wait until we know more before we tell everyone."

"Sure. Let's do that." But there was something disagreeable about keeping a secret like this that reminded her all too forcefully of the arms stash she and Kenneth had kept from the other ranchers. Folly upon folly.

She was distracted all through dinner, which was a rollicking affair in spite of what had brought them all together. Ranchers sat wherever they could find room—cross-legged on the floor, on cushions, on each other's laps, and spilling out the French doors onto the lawn. More than the usual number of bottles of wine were polished off. There was a rowdy karaoke session and then games of Jenga in the lounge for those whose fine motor skills were still up to the task. Someone repaired to the cellar and came back with cobwebs in his hair and brandishing the good whiskey, holding it above his head like a trophy. There were drunken cheers. When she and Wolf went to the kitchen to scrape dishes, she gestured at the growing sculptures of discarded bottles in the corner, ready for recycling. They spilled out of boxes and crates.

"Partying like the end of the world," Marlo remarked grimly, but the disapproval was aimed mostly at herself: she couldn't shake the feeling that there was so much more she could have done.

18

Later she found it difficult to recall whose idea it had been. One day the ranchers were discussing how to respond to the deranged cow incident, and the next day, or so it felt, plans for the wall had already been cemented. She couldn't pinpoint any detailed discussions about it, just a percolating idea followed by an uneasy consensus that *something* needed to be done. And from that consensus the wall grew.

They still hadn't elected a new newsman or newswoman to take Neil's place. The meetings, when they happened, were haphazard, spearheaded by no one. Marlo suspected most people felt relief at being spared the grim tidings from the outside world. She hadn't been the only one shaken by the Disaster's sudden encroachment on their little world, but it bothered her that the solution was to become even more isolationist. Wolf didn't see it the same way.

"Well, it just sounds like a precaution," he said. "People are scared. It makes sense to protect the ranch from any local contamination, right?"

Marlo frowned. She had expected him to share her unease.

"But a wall?" she protested. "Why not a fence? It'll be like living in a fortress."

"Probably because cattle can break through a fence pretty easily," he suggested gently. "Even an electric fence, if those poor deranged creatures we saw are anything to go by."

She had to concede he had a point, but it didn't make her feel any better.

"Oh, I meant to tell you. I happened to be in the Commons with my parents and some of the other ranchers yesterday, and they were having a kind of informal meeting. For some reason it was decided that we need to temporarily discontinue Kenneth's visiting workers program. Something about not wanting strangers on the ranch for a while, until we can get to the bottom of the poisoned cow situation. So the wall? The ranchers are going to have to build it themselves. Ourselves. The plan is we're going to take it in shifts over the next few weeks. Anything that can't be done by professionals."

Once again Wolf failed to react in the way she had expected. He looked amused more than anything.

"What did good old Kenneth have to say about that?"

Marlo smiled against her will, recalling Kenneth's stormy face.

"Yeah. He made that expression where he looks like he's about to explode."

"That doesn't exactly narrow it down, to be honest."

Marlo flung herself on the couch.

"I don't know. I just don't like what's happening here lately."

Wolf came over and sat down, lifted her legs up, and draped them across his lap.

"Listen. Everything will be OK. We've known for a while that things are going to shit out there. Maybe the wall will be for the best."

"You sound like my parents."

He grimaced, lifted up her naked foot, and pretended to bite it. She screamed and wriggled around in mock fear, kicking out at him with long bare legs tanned golden from the summer sun, and before too long they had found a way to forget about walls.

In the end, Kenneth got his own way. The scheduled working bee (Kenneth's name for communal work days) was a disaster by the first morning—it turned out to be much more difficult, hot, and backbreaking work than many of the ranchers had anticipated—and there had been a hurried vote to allow the skilled laborers temporary access to the property. The battered pickup trucks with their silent loads of bandanna-wearing laborers sitting knees-up in the cargo beds reappeared the next day, driving slowly down the ranch's roads on their way to the property's outskirts. Marlo was surprised at first that Kenneth didn't also argue to keep his workers for the ongoing planting, harvesting, and maintenance of the ranch. But she found out later—through a third party as Kenneth was still avoiding her—that he was actually pleased the other ranchers were prepared to help him run operations without outside help. That had always been part of his long-term plan.

In the end Marlo had to grudgingly admit that the wall, while morally questionable, had a certain aesthetic appeal. They had decided to build it using pale river stones of various sizes, mortared with white clay. The construction had been shockingly, ruinously expensive but everyone had agreed it was worth the investment. Roaming the property she would come upon sections of the wall and be struck by its simple, rustic beauty. She could see that after a few months of rain and mosses worming their way into cracks it would look as though it had always been there.

"That doesn't mean I have to like it," she declared defiantly to her father over Sunday dinner, a family ritual that now regularly included Wolf.

"We all wish it wasn't necessary, darling," he answered. "Pass those potatoes, would you?"

"Oh, did we tell you?" her mother said. "One of the investors from the last New York trip is thinking about joining."

Marlo's head jerked up from her plate. She swallowed: it couldn't be James Salter, the man she had slept with on the trip, could it? She didn't dare look at her father's face.

"Who is it?" she asked quietly, her heart pounding.

"Now, what were their names? I wrote it down somewhere. Kerry and Jenny, I think their names were. Is that right, Carlton? A lovely lesbian couple from New York City. We think they'll make great additions to the community. After thorough vetting, of course," she added hurriedly.

"That's great," said Marlo, shoving a potato into her mouth. She hoped no one could tell how relieved she was. "New blood."

"Exactly," said her father proudly. "I like to think it was Marlo's influence. She's my lucky charm."

"Dad."

"Well? You are. My beloved New York would have been a wash without my little sidekick."

She was so relieved that he appeared to have forgiven her for the one-night stand, she forgot to be embarrassed about her father's way of talking about her. Wolf, digging into her leg under the table, reminded her. She glared at him, but he just grinned, crossing his eyes and chewing with exaggerated gusto like a witless hick. More and more she understood what it would have been like to have a sibling.

"Oh, by the way, Carlton, I've never really asked, but did you grow up in New York?"

Wolf swiveled toward Marlo's dad, his face morphing expertly from tormenting older brother to attentive dinner guest. She continued to be amused by how suavely her lover had slipped into the polite son-in-law role. The way they basked in the warmth of his attention like cats being scratched under the chin caused Marlo acute daughterly embarrassment. Sometimes she wondered if they were more in love with Wolf than she was.

"No, I didn't actually, Wolf. I grew up in a little town called Meriden, Connecticut. But New York is where everything important happened to me. I met and married this wonderful woman." He stroked his wife's neck. "I started my business. We were blessed with Marlo. My youth came and went there." He rubbed his head ruefully, although he still had most of his hair, and they all laughed.

"What was the business?" asked Wolf, as if he were conducting a friendly interview, the kind with softball questions designed to make the interviewee look good.

"We started a hedge fund in the late nineties," explained Maya. "Ketterman Capital. It was, well, a different time then. There was so much money around, and frankly so little regulation. We did pretty well for ourselves."

This part of the story, the false humility part, always made Marlo cringe. They had done more than pretty well, had built the fund into a global enterprise and had walked away with millions when they sold out to their partner and moved west. That windfall, along with their substantial liquidated assets, had paid for most of the first phase of the community.

The wall wasn't mentioned again. Maybe this was just the new normal, and she would come around to seeing it in the same positive light as everyone else. The thought made her feel intensely alone in a way she'd almost forgotten. Her parents were keenly interested in alternative farming practices, though—at least on an intellectual level—so they found plenty of common ground with Wolf on which to ruminate about heirloom seeds and rotational agriculture and organic pest control, all subjects on which Wolf was increasingly an expert. He seemed genuinely interested in discussing the life cycles of rhizomes and the problematic effects of yellow wasps on orchards. Marlo smiled watching her boyfriend, his hands an animated blur and his eyes shining with cultish enthusiasm.

"I've been reading a lot about these new technologies. Like, for livestock, equipping them with biometric sensors and GPS so we can do real-time monitoring of the animals, their location, their health. I mean, after that cow incident, we can't be too careful, right?" His eyes gleamed with pleasure at finding a receptive audience for his discoveries. "And there are smart sensors now that easily keep track of the plants and their water and nitrogen needs. I know Kenneth has all that stuff in hand, but there are much more efficient ways now . . ." He trailed off, perhaps realizing the heresy of criticizing Kenneth's methods aloud, but Maya and Carlton just nodded as if what he was saying were indisputable.

"So, Wolf, have you had any more thoughts about the house you want to build?" asked Maya, encircling Wolf's wrist with her slender fingers. Wolf shot Marlo a questioning look, and she nodded encouragement.

"Well. Marlo and I have talked a little about it. I really like that kind of mid-century, Californian bungalow-style house. Richard Neutra with a bit of Zaha Hadid thrown in. Kind of like this one, actually."

They both nodded approvingly.

"Well, just let us know when you want to sit down and draw up some plans. Frank was an architect in his previous life. He did the plans for this place too. Great eye. Detail-oriented."

Wolf nodded studiously. "That would be, um, great. I can't thank you both enough. And Marlo, of course."

Her parents both made a show of self-deprecation, waving his gratitude away magnanimously. It was unclear to Marlo what her own role was in this little gratitude theater, so she just expressed small enthusiastic sounds that blended into the general bonhomie.

"Have you picked out a building site yet?" she asked the room at large, given that Wolf's future house appeared now to be a communal endeavor. It turned out that he had, or they had: a flat parcel of land not far from her own home, where there had once been a windmill. The ranchers had decided to tear it down after realizing that the harnessed energy was too little to justify the upkeep and the "eyesore" of its clunky aesthetic. Marlo still remembered Kenneth's wry comment to her afterward, that they were all NIMBYs deep down. She had to go and look the word up.

As they all rose to clear the dishes and repair to the lounge for a card game, Marlo heard her parents talking in low voices behind her. She caught the words *Thank god for the mausoleum*, and she gave Wolf a sharp look to see if he had heard. He hadn't pestered her about it for a while, but she suspected he still thought about it.

In the car on the way home, she chattered away until she noticed Wolf had fallen silent.

"Hey. What's up, comrade?"

Although she could guess.

"Don't you think it's weird that no one will tell me what the deal is with that fucking mausoleum?"

She sighed.

"Wolf."

"To be honest I don't even care what's in there anymore. It could be a nuclear warhead. Whatever. We all have to die somehow. It just makes me feel like a pariah. Like I'm still on the outside, and you're all on the inside."

"Believe me, I wish I could tell you!"

She was on the verge of frustrated tears, and he must have been able to hear it because he snapped instantly out of his sulky reverie.

"Listen. I'm sorry, baby. I know it's not your fault. How about we forget about it? I'm just being childish."

🌿

That should have been the end of it, but as she was learning, Wolf had his tenacious side. One day he turned up on her doorstep, throwing paranoid glances around the vicinity of her front yard before entering, like a fugitive casing a safe house. She stifled a laugh: he looked both ridiculous and genuinely shaken.

"Everything OK?" she asked and kissed his distracted mouth.

"Oh, sure. Just a bit weirded out."

He sat down heavily at the kitchen table. She brought him a cup of coffee, and he stared at it with the same disconcerting sleepwalker's confusion that he had worn the first time she had met him.

"Promise you won't be mad?" His forehead furrowed, eyes pleading. She laughed.

"Was there ever a more emotionally blackmailing question in the history of questions?"

"Fair enough, you don't have to promise. But listen. I kind of . . . well, I decided I was going to investigate the mausoleum for myself."

"OK. How did that go?"

He took a sip of coffee, avoided looking at her directly while he was telling her the rest.

"So I just thought I'd have a little look around. You know, as a new rancher, just exploring the place. But when I got to where the mausoleum is, I noticed there are new security cameras now. Have you seen them?" Marlo shrugged, kept her expression neutral. "Well, anyway, they're there. And they're installed pointed at the entrance, like it's some kind of high-security zone. So as I'm standing there looking at them, trying to work out whether they're operational or not, our old friend Kenneth emerges from behind the compost building, like he'd been waiting for me or something. Scared the shit out of me. He asked me what I wanted. Which frankly is a bit rich. I mean, am I not free to travel around the ranch like everyone else?"

"Of course you are." She stroked his shoulder reassuringly.

"Yeah, well, you wouldn't know it to judge from Kenneth, that asshole. But anyway, here's the thing. As he turned to walk away, I could see he had a weapon inside his coat. A handgun, I think. It kind of glinted as he turned."

"Really?" Marlo frowned. "Well, he sometimes arms himself when he does the rounds. A lot of the ranchers do, unfortunately. Maybe there was a sick animal?"

Wolf raised an eyebrow. "Do you know anyone who puts cattle down with a handgun? Wouldn't he use a rifle or something for that?"

"I guess so." Marlo sat down opposite him. "So what did you do?"

He laughed grimly. "I made an excuse, of course, and fucked off out of there. I may be an idiot, but I'm not about to provoke some nutjob with a gun and a grudge."

"Stop it. You've got Kenneth all wrong."

"Do I?"

"Yes, you do. And you need to stop with this whole mausoleum nonsense. How many times do I have to tell you it's not personal? It's just dumb ranch protocol. Just think of it as classified information that someone decided a long time ago not everyone needed to know about."

"So who else doesn't know then, besides me?"

"Um, lots of people." She wasn't very good at evasion and hoped he'd drop the subject before she had to name names. That seemed to satisfy Wolf, or maybe he was just preoccupied with whatever else was on his mind.

"There was one other weird thing, though, Marl. Kenneth had this black stuff all over his hands. Like, I don't know, soot. Or ink. What was that about?"

"How should I know?"

He looked at her then, full in the eyes, trying to gauge if she was lying. She met his gaze steadily, and after a while he smiled in a bashful way like he was a little ashamed for overreacting or not trusting her. Later, lying in bed next to him in the darkness with her hand resting on his thigh, unable to sleep and listening to the soft thunk of insects throwing themselves against the window, she marveled at her own newly hatched talent for deception.

19

The ranch began to feel smaller and smaller. Whenever Marlo and Wolf emerged from the cocoon of their coupledom, she was jolted to find the community engaged in its own tightening. The subtle distinction between arbitrary, invisible borders and a literal wall had never felt so significant. At twilight the wall glowed with an eldritch luminosity, like a force field made visible. How long before they installed checkpoints and guard towers? Wolf laughed when she complained in this way, but she reminded him he was used to living in a state of perpetually heightened security out in the Disaster. All those Amber Alerts, the security theater at airports, the Orwellian departments the government hastily constructed after any major terrorist attack. The ranch had always felt removed from that particular brand of panic. Theirs was a much calmer fatalism.

"Isn't that precisely the reason to be glad we're in here and not out there?" he argued, persuasively enough.

"I guess."

But she couldn't stay morose for very long. She continued to suffer from an excess of joy that spilled over into even the most banal of things: steeping a tea bag in hot water, the feel of her bare toes slipping into sandals. After Neil died, dread had slowed time down. Now she understood that happiness sped it up. The days seemed to spin by with alarming speed, the moments slippery and prone to fly out of her grasp. If there were constraints on her joy they were all external: the disconcerting solidity of the wall, always hovering at the edge of her vision;

the certainty of events continuing to unspool out in the Disaster. And something else. She finally heard again from Alex. She (and by proxy, Ben) emailed Marlo breezily and without acknowledging the brief chill that had descended on their friendship. The dispatch had been all about their adventures on board the *Sea Shepherd*, a tale so full of swashbuckling near-death clashes with various marine authorities and nefarious rogue government figures that Marlo was half-inclined to doubt it. But Alex and Ben had always had a talent for attracting the kind of danger that never fully tilted into catastrophe. They were, ironically enough, among the few people in her life about whom she didn't really worry.

That had been the first communiqué. The second, sent a week later, lacked the insouciant bravado of the first. It was stated more starkly and without any of the narrative flourishes: that's how Marlo knew what they were telling her was serious.

> *So we went out with Sea Shepherd again. Up to Nova Scotia, where the government recently placed a temporary ban on bluefin tuna fishing. We'd gotten wind that a huge industrial fishing operation out of Massachusetts was going to be defying the ban and fishing for tuna under cover of darkness. So the SS and a Greenpeace ship arranged to go up there and expose them. The main idea was to get footage of them doing this illegal fishing, send it to various media outlets. But of course we were prepared for confrontation if it came down to it.*

> *Marlo, it was fucking crazy. We sailed up there from Boston, and when we arrived at the fishing grounds, sure enough these rogue fleets were there, ready to get their illegal catch. So there's this standoff from the beginning, them firing warning shots into the air to try to scare us off! Ha! Fat chance. But the weirdest thing. There were*

no fish. Like, literally none. The industrial fishing boats had these obnoxious spotlights shining into the water and we were looking overboard, ready to start filming if we saw them start chasing fish. But the water was completely empty. Can you imagine? The Atlantic fucking Ocean. I'm not talking just tuna either. We were staked out there for two days and we literally never saw a fish. One of the richest fishing grounds in the world, and it's empty.

So we sailed back to port and did some investigating. Turns out this is the second season that the fish have been gone. Entire fisheries are going broke. The acid levels off the east coasts of Canada and the US are off the charts. There are algae blooms and explosive growth in certain types of seaweed that have adapted to the acid. But everything else is gone. Whether they've fled to safer waters or actually died off, we don't know yet. But it's sure not looking good. We finally did it: we killed the oceans.

She spent the days after receiving the message worrying about when and how to tell Wolf. He seemed so happy, content for the first time since he had staggered into their world. She dreaded puncturing the fragile membrane of his happiness. Wouldn't he find out on his own anyway, she argued with herself, given that he kept up to speed with happenings out in the Disaster? Surely he would come to her with the news eventually, and then they could figure out how to tackle things together. But the days slipped by, and he didn't mention anything, and neither did any of the other ranchers.

❦

It was stifling in the library. The floor-to-ceiling windows faced south to take best advantage of the building's passive solar design, which made the room one of the best places to sit in winter, when the weak sun hitting the huge panes of glass could still generate pools of warmth. Marlo had spent many happy hours curled up in there like a cat as the wind howled outside and naked branches knocked against the walls like bony hands demanding a hearing. But in warmer months the room's advantages melted into discomfort. There was no escape from the beating sun, which heated every surface. You could burn your hand picking up a brass paperweight. Book pages turned damp with humidity. The back walls were sheathed in panels of cedar wainscoting; when the room heated up, it smelled exactly like a sauna. The windows were designed not to open. The air-conditioning was supposed to regulate things, but Marlo was a conscientious objector when it came to air-conditioning: it was the only form of electricity they used that couldn't be run off solar. It seemed hypocritical to aspire to live an off-the-grid life only to buckle when it came to keeping cool.

So there was a certain defiant, self-sabotaging quality in her decision to spend time there. It was so bright she had to wear sunglasses to even see her screen. Her finely woven dress clung to her thighs. She fidgeted as perspiration trickled down her neck. But she also had the whole library to herself. She could hear some of the others outside, playing some kind of ball game on the newly mown meadow that doubled as a sports field in warm weather. Their voices floated, muffled like sound from a faraway television.

She was talking with Alex. While she hadn't consciously sought out privacy for the communication, she also wasn't expecting someone to enter the room silently and lay their hand on her shoulder, so when it happened she started so violently that she nearly dropped her laptop.

"Jesus." She snapped shut her computer and turned around. "Oh, hey, Wolf honey. You startled me."

"Sorry." He grinned sheepishly.

"I thought you were helping with the planting."

"I finished up early, on a hunch that you might be in here somewhere. Christ, it's like a sauna in here."

"I know." She showed him all her teeth. "I love it."

He shook his head. "Weirdo." He swung his legs over the top of the low-slung sofa, plumped down, and then shuffled the side of his body up against hers. He smelled rich and earthy from the soil. "What are you working on?"

Marlo hesitated. There was no reason not to tell him; she was so used to subterfuge when it came to communicating with Alex and Ben, it had become second nature. She looked over her shoulder to make sure no one else had entered the library.

"I was chatting with Alex and Ben. Remember? My childhood friends who ran off to become eco-warriors?"

Wolf indicated that of course he did, but his expression was slightly pained. Marlo had always suspected he was jealous of Alex and Ben, in that insecure way you feel about the important people in your lover's life whom you've never met.

"Why the cloak and dagger?"

"It's stupid really. It's not like there's a rule or anything, but there are some people who don't exactly approve of Alex and Ben. They're pretty much persona non grata around here these days. Even their parents stopped talking to them."

"What did they do, anyway?"

"It was more just the conditions under which they left. They were kind of scathing about the ranchers by the end, and they essentially called everyone cowards. Disowned their parents. Said they were never coming back."

"Yikes."

"I know. They're very, well, passionate. And they thought everyone else here was just sleepwalking. Or burying their heads in the sand. The metaphors changed a lot."

"No offense, but they sound kind of sanctimonious."

"Hmm. If only I could remember who it was who arrived a while ago, someone who was very vocal about our inability to face reality? Whoever could it have been?"

He grimaced at the memory. "Point taken."

"So what are you and your friends talking about? If it's any of my business."

Marlo put her arm around him, stroked the back of his neck absent-mindedly. She loved the stubbled roughness of the hair there that had been razed by the clippers.

"It's all of our business, actually."

"What do you mean?"

"Here." She reopened her laptop, and it powered back into life, the screen dim under the glare. "Let me show you some things."

She was surprised to see him looking shocked—she hadn't even shown him any of the news stories yet—until she realized the reaction was to her being online. She laughed.

"Oh, that. I finally came around to your position on the dumb internet ban. It was after the sick cow incident. I mean, I try to hide it from the other ranchers. Don't want to start some kind of international incident. But I suspect half of them have broken the ban as well. I doubt we're the only ones."

"Actually, I've mostly stopped checking things online myself. You were right. All of you were right. There's nothing but bad news out there."

"Sure. But what about our right to know what we're facing? Isn't that what you said?"

He shook his head as if disavowing his former self.

"I didn't know what I was talking about."

"Does that mean you don't want to hear about the latest string of catastrophes out in the Disaster?"

Wolf grasped her hands, turned her to face him.

"Yes, that's exactly what it means. Please don't show me! Please don't look at them yourself. Please, please, please." He buried his face in her chest, then raised his head and began to kiss her frantically all over her face: her eyes and nose and mouth. She was half laughing, half trying to respond, but every time she went to say something, he'd press his mouth to hers until she threw up her hands in surrender and wriggled her face out of his reach.

"OK, I submit! I won't show you anything bad."

After she had the chance to explain the other news—that Alex and Ben were coming to town briefly and wanted her to meet up with them, and that she'd decided she would—Wolf had insisted on accompanying her.

"Fine, but you have to keep this a secret. Alex and Ben don't want anyone from the ranch knowing they're back in the area."

"Of course." He looked offended at not being trusted with a secret. "Why are they visiting, anyway? I thought they hated it around here."

"Oh, they do. But they need something." She hesitated for a moment, weighing up how much to tell him. "Something they left at the ranch."

Wolf's eyes gleamed with the excitement of being inducted into a conspiracy.

"What is it?"

"It's an antique diamond ring Alex's mom gave her, back when she'd been hoping Alex and Ben would get married. I think it was supposed to act as this irresistible incentive." Marlo rolled her eyes. "Like some trashy diamond was going to sway her if she didn't want to get married. They thought if they could get the two of them married, settled down, then their dream of the next generation of little ranchers would be closer to being fulfilled. Let's just say that Alex's parents don't know their daughter very well. That was part of the problem."

"So Alex and Ben didn't want to get married?"

"Don't get me wrong, they're madly in love. You'll see. They just don't see the point in getting married. They think it's totally bourgeois. Heteronormative. Another oppressive institution to keep citizens conforming and obedient."

"And what do you think? Do you think marriage and parenthood are bourgeois traps too?"

"I guess." She shrugged. "It doesn't seem to make any difference, as far as I can tell. So anyway, when Alex and Ben told their parents they had no intention of getting married, her parents were disappointed, but they said the ring was hers to keep. When they left for good, Alex left most of her stuff in plastic crates in a storage facility on the ranch. They didn't care about material stuff. They just wanted to go and disrupt the world order."

"And now they want to get the ring back?"

"Exactly. Ben told me they've run out of funds, and they want to hock the ring. Alex had it valued years ago, and it's actually worth a lot of money. Maybe twenty grand?"

There was a silence as he digested this. Perhaps weighing the sum up against other things in his life.

"I suppose they want you to retrieve this ring for them?"

Marlo nodded.

"And I suppose you've agreed to take all the risks while they just breeze into town and cash in?"

"What's your problem with them, anyway?" Her face felt hot. "There aren't any risks. Even if I got caught taking the ring, no one would mind."

"Not even Alex's parents?"

"Can we sort of change the subject? I don't need to justify myself."

Wolf reached out to her, but she shrugged him away.

"Listen, I'm sorry, Marlo. It just rubs me the wrong way that they're taking advantage of your kindness."

"It's not like that." But she wondered whether he was right. She had always felt like a little sister to Alex and Ben, even though they were all the same age. The breezy way they assumed that Marlo would do whatever they instructed. "Anyway, I've agreed to do it. I'm meeting them on Thursday in town."

That's when Wolf suggested coming along for the ride. He said he was dying to meet these friends of hers, and Marlo guessed that his motivation wasn't entirely pure: he wanted to vet them, assess for himself whether they were worthy of Marlo's devotion. That seemed to be a pattern with the people who loved her, this compulsion to save her from dangers only they were qualified to identify.

He also came along when she went to retrieve the ring from the storage shed. He kept lookout while she rummaged around inside, searching for Alex's things. It didn't take long to find. Marlo emerged from the shed, palming the black velvet box so he could see, then slipping it into her pocket with a triumphant grin. Back at her house they opened the box. The ring gleamed with a ferocity both seductive and sinister. Marlo had always reflexively hated diamonds—she knew this was the correct position, but now that she had one in front of her, she couldn't deny the gem's singular beauty, its luminous light.

"Probably a blood diamond," she said, feigning disgust. But Wolf looked transfixed as well, like it was something loathsome that he nevertheless couldn't turn away from. She shut the box abruptly. "I'm glad it will finally go to a good cause."

"Listen. You're not thinking of running away with these dudes, are you?"

"Of course not," she said lightly, getting up to stretch and put coffee on. She wasn't considering running away with them, not really, although they had of course reiterated their desire for her to do so. But still the idea lurked there in the back of her mind, as a wild card, her plan B, the ultimate backup. She busied herself with the coffee for a while, but when they sat back down together, she decided to send up a trial balloon.

"Like I said, I don't plan to run away with them. Not on my own. But would it be so crazy for the two of us to leave the ranch together?"

She hadn't expected him to look so genuinely shocked.

"Yes."

"Yes what?"

"Yes, it would be crazy."

"Oh."

"I mean, is that really what you want? I can't believe it is. We're so happy here. Things are going so well."

Now she couldn't quite believe what she was hearing. She put her mug down. Her fingers vibrated around its handle.

"Wolf. Baby. Things are not going well. I know you didn't want to know about the various crises that are going on out there. But fuck. They need us out there."

"Who does?"

She gesticulated helplessly. "They. Everyone. The devastated communities. You know, people. Our fellow citizens. Human beings."

His face turned sulky then.

"It's not like we have any power to save them."

"You're wrong. Alex and Ben have plans." She realized how lame this sounded even before he raised a skeptical eyebrow in her direction. "There are still things that can be done. It's not too late. That's the kind of defeatist attitude they're fighting against. That's why they left the ranch. We're all sleepwalkers."

Wolf put his hand on her thigh and began to stroke gently.

"You know, sleepwalkers get a bad rap. Being awake is overrated, in my opinion."

"You should definitely open with that line when you meet Alex and Ben," she said, grinning, relieved to have veered away from an argument. There didn't really seem to be much to argue about, anyway. Ever since Wolf had arrived, the idea of leaving the ranch to join her friends' swashbuckling save-the-planet crusade had been growing less attractive. It made her ashamed to wonder if she had just been waiting, all along, for someone to talk her out of it.

🌿

One of the tricky things was coming up with an excuse for driving into town. Marlo's parents hadn't explicitly prohibited her from leaving the ranch, but they had made it clear they didn't encourage it. There were strictly scheduled supply runs these days, mostly carried out by the tougher male ranchers. Unless there was a good reason to venture out, people tended to stay inside the walls. They were planting whole new fields of crops in anticipation of eventually weaning off from the town runs altogether. This seemed wildly impractical to Marlo, not to mention slightly frightening. What about modern necessities like batteries and power tools and tampons? Were they planning to revert to some sort of preindustrial Iron Age life? The thought was unnerving. The ranch had enough supplies and provisions stockpiled to last a decade or so, but that didn't mean life wouldn't be hard, especially when the stores started running low. She'd noticed the older ranchers were more enthusiastic about withdrawing from life on the grid. Funny that: they knew they'd be dead by the time people would have to face real hardship. Sometimes she couldn't prevent these uncharitable thoughts from bubbling to the surface.

Eventually they made up a story about Wolf needing to refill some medication in town that required his signature. She would explain that Wolf wasn't feeling emotionally up to driving, and that's why she needed to accompany him. He claimed not to mind her exploiting his father's death in order to make the story sound convincing. The one thing they hadn't banked on was her own father and his hypochondriac's fascination with all things medical.

"Is everything alright with Wolf's health?" Carlton asked Marlo, his eyes gleaming with avid, morbid concern. "Anything you can tell me about? Perhaps I can suggest some home remedies?"

"It's nothing major," Marlo hastened to assure him, hoping she wouldn't be called upon to invent some malady her father would be sure to know wasn't real. "Just an ongoing condition he needs to attend to."

Her parents looked disappointed when they failed to talk her out of driving him in. They tried to volunteer anyone else—themselves, Sven, Kenneth. But Marlo shot down all their suggestions with the sly response, "Wolf said he only wants it to be me." She knew they approved heartily of their daughter's budding relationship and considered Wolf almost a family member. That swayed them in the end.

❦

The town seemed to her meaner and uglier than before. They drove past several ranch homes with For Sale signs hammered into patchy lawns. Paint peeling in long strips from barns. Shuttered stores on the main street and a scarcity of smiles from passersby. Instead it seemed to her that people regarded her and Wolf with a suspicion she hadn't encountered before. She was used to curiosity, especially from locals who recognized them when they did supply runs into town—the ranchers were all aware of the glamour that clung to them out in public. The ranch was the stuff of local legend, a tale to tell visiting friends and family. The rich eccentrics in their gated community. *They have helicopters and everything!* But it wasn't as though they were the only wealthy landowners around the place, or the only community holding views considered unorthodox. There was a group of Wiccans a few counties over and a John Galt–inspired clan of benign nutjobs eking out a hardscrabble living in a valley a few miles out of town. But this time Marlo thought she felt a certain hostility directed toward their shiny car and their air of elite otherness.

❦

"You look hot," Alex declared, holding Marlo at arm's length and scrutinizing her head to toe.

"Thanks. Same. This is Wolf," she said, thrusting him forward. Alex and Ben set their expressions to pleasant social mode, each shaking Wolf's hand formally. Everyone proclaimed to be delighted to make everyone else's acquaintance. But Marlo could feel the chilliness between her friends old and new. It was only when she hugged them tight—inhaling Alex's buttery caramel scent and Ben's more astringent but not unpleasant tangy odor—that she realized how much she had missed them.

After they had all sat down in the restaurant's cracked red vinyl booth—Marlo and Wolf on one side, Alex and Ben on the other, like they were interviewing one another, which in a way they were—Marlo pulled the little black box out of her bag.

"First things first." She slid the box across the table. "Congrats, you guys. May God bless you with a long and happy marriage." Everyone but Wolf laughed at this.

"Atheist humor," remarked Ben helpfully for Wolf's benefit.

Alex pulled the ring out of the velvet box, held it up critically in front of her nose. Fractals of Technicolor light bounced frantically around the room. She slid the ring onto the correct finger, stretched her arm out theatrically, then turned to Ben, and they pretended to kiss passionately. Then she shook her hair, slipped the ring casually in her shirt pocket, and took a sip of her shake. When the waitress returned they all ordered. Wolf laughed a little nervously when Marlo ordered a veggie burger and fries and onion rings and a side of guacamole and a thick shake all to herself.

"She doesn't get out much," said Alex with a wink. Wolf smiled as if he didn't quite get the joke.

When their food arrived, the plates and wax paper–lined baskets of deep-fried substances spilled across the entire table like a calamity. Marlo and Alex and Ben shoveled the greasy food into their mouths with single-minded, lip-smacking devotion. When it was over the table looked like the aftermath of a battle, scattered from corner to corner with the ravaged ends of fries, curdled-looking globs of milkshake, discarded rings of purple raw onion, and crumpled napkins bloodied with sauce. Wolf gazed upon it all, shell-shocked.

"So Ben is thinking about running for Congress." Alex sat back, took a final deep slurp of her shake, and rattled the cup, a cheeky grin teasing up the corner of her mouth.

"What the actual fuck? Are you kidding me?"

Marlo looked from one to the other of their faces, searching for signs she was being teased. But they both looked more shyly proud than anything. Ben nodded.

"It's true. I sold out, man. But here's the thing. We're going to change things from the inside. There's a bill coming before the state senate in California next year that would make it law that all new construction, both private and commercial, has to install solar panels that make up 90 percent of their energy use. That's *90 percent*. Plus, it would offer huge, incredibly attractive subsidies to anyone who wants to retroactively install solar on existing properties. Imagine it, the third-largest state in the union being weaned off fossil fuels for good!"

"Wow."

"Yeah, other states are watching to see what happens in California, and if it's a success we might see a nationwide rollout. But here's the thing. Looks like the bill might go down in flames unless they get an extra vote. And there's a seat up for grabs this year. I just need more of this behind me." He rubbed his thumb and forefinger together. "Running for office costs a fuck-ton of money. Who knew?"

They all laughed cynically.

"But we've got some pretty cool funding going on. Some Silicon Valley types, you know. And Alex here is a genius when it comes to messaging, fundraising, and all that. I really think we've got a shot."

"Why doesn't Alex run for office too?"

Everyone looked at Wolf. It was the first time he had spoken beyond the initial greetings. Alex actually blushed, gave a mock bashful grin.

"Well, you see, I would. There's just the little matter of my criminal record."

"What?"

"Yeah, these Japanese fuckers we got tangled up with on one of the first *Sea Shepherd* missions. I kind of punched one of them in the face."

"Oh, my god, Alex."

Alex grinned, showing a row of small teeth including her pointed incisors. "Don't worry, he survived. And I only had to spend an afternoon in the lockup. Sweet-talked my way out. But it still goes on my record, alas."

Ben squeezed her arm and gave her a loud kiss on the cheek.

"That's my badass."

"The thing is, people are so shitscared these days, they'd probably waive the rules if they thought someone would come along on a white horse to save their pathetic asses."

"This may be another reason you're not quite suited to politics," suggested Marlo, and they laughed. The waitress came over at that moment, asked if they'd like anything else.

"Four shots of tequila, please," said Alex without even consulting anyone. The waitress nodded morosely and spun on her heel to go shout the order to the guy behind the counter. After she brought them over on a tin tray and deposited one shot glass in front of each of them, Alex raised hers and asked what they should drink to. Before anyone could answer, though, she came up with her own toast:

"To the deep-pocketed motherfuckers we're going to sucker into funding Ben's campaign for Congress!"

Ben cringe-laughed. "Don't you know everyone records everything on their phones these days? There'll be a video on YouTube tomorrow of you saying that!"

Alex looked with exaggerated concern around the empty diner, chin resting in hand.

"Hmm. Given it's just you and me, babe, plus these two hayseeds, I think we should be good. But on a serious note, Marls, if you ever run out of things to spend that fat trust fund of yours on, I have just the cause for you."

Marlo felt her face getting hot. She had never told Wolf about the inheritance sitting in her bank account. It wasn't even the kind of inheritance that gets held in a trust, but was available anytime she wanted to draw from it. In truth she wasn't hoarding it; there had never been anything she'd considered spending it on before, apart from the occasional clothing purchase or an upgraded car. It just squatted there in her mind, like a slightly embarrassing relative.

"I'll definitely consider it," Marlo said, and she meant it. What else did she have to spend money on, after all, especially now that she was staying on the ranch? She didn't relish telling her parents what she would use it for, though. You didn't need to be a fortune-teller to predict their reaction if she used her inheritance to fund her friend's long-shot political career.

"I was just kidding," said Alex breezily. "Shall we get the check? We'd better get out of here."

The whole time they talked, Marlo noticed Wolf staring at Alex. He would dart a glance at her, then look away immediately, but then his gaze would be drawn again as though an invisible cable between their faces had drawn his attention back. Marlo wasn't jealous. If anything it made her happy to see any kind of connection between them.

"She's beautiful, isn't she? Alex?" Marlo gushed in the car on the way home. "Doesn't she remind you of a young Catherine Deneuve?"

There was an uncomfortable beat of silence.

"She reminds me more of the *Titanic* setting out from Southampton."

Marlo took her eyes off the road to glance at him. He was slumped down in his seat as though crushed by the delayed weight of the encounter.

"What's that supposed to mean, you goof?"

He sighed. "I don't know. It's just, their plans. It's a doomed enterprise."

"What is?"

He threw up his hands, exasperated at her inability to understand him.

"Everything. Blowing up oil wells. Changing the system from within. All of it."

"They don't blow up oil wells," she chided.

"You know what I mean."

❦

They stopped for gas at the last gas station on the way out of town. A sign informed them that customers could pump their own gas at this time, so Wolf, perhaps keen to make amends for his earlier crankiness, volunteered to fill the tank, leaping out before she could even get her door open. He mugged and made rude gestures at her when he grabbed the pump, and she shook her head, laughing. Theirs was the only car in the place, apart from a police car at the opposite pump. The light on top of the car flashed lazily, a hypnotic red and blue. Wolf came around sheepishly to her window, and patted his pockets.

"It won't start until I pay and I don't have any money. Sorry."

Of course he didn't. It only just occurred to her that they had never been in a situation together that required payment before now. Alex and Ben had insisted on settling the check at the restaurant. She handed him her card, and he went and paid at the machine, then filled the tank. When he returned she threw him a coquettish smile.

"Ready to hit the road, Jack?"

But his face had changed. He looked scared. He quickly got back in the car, slid down in his seat, and urged her to start driving.

"What is it?"

"You see that police car? Don't look now!"

"Yes. What about it?"

"I think he recognized me."

"Recognized you from where?"

"Please just drive," he said through his teeth, and she dutifully started the engine and pulled out of the station, glancing once in the rearview mirror at the police car. She was startled to see that the policeman was in fact staring at them. Marlo could see something in his hand that might have been a radio. He wasn't pumping gas or doing anything but just sitting there. It gave her a creepy feeling, like waiting and watching for a door to open when you don't know who's behind it. She half expected the car to follow them, but as she indicated, then pulled slowly out onto the highway, she was relieved to see the car remained there, its lights still flashing in nonurgent mode. When the gas station was out of sight, Wolf sat up straight again.

"I don't know that exact cop. But when I was filling up I saw him staring at me. Like, real hard, and kind of hostile. As though he recognized my face."

"Why would he recognize you? Is this the part where you confess that you're an escaped felon or something?"

She said it aloud mainly as a spell to make it not true, but she didn't like how long he took to answer.

"No, nothing like that." His voice was so small now, she could hardly hear it over the engine. "I'm sure I'm just being paranoid. I've never trusted cops, that's all. I've got too many friends who've had, shall we say, less-than-ideal encounters."

She knew this explanation was supposed to satisfy her, because he deftly changed the subject after that. His light tone and laughter did half the job of convincing her it was just a case of overblown suspicion of authority. It wasn't as if there weren't ranchers who avoided law enforcement. But even as they pulled up to the gates of the ranch, a little voice in her head insisted that something about the encounter at the gas station didn't feel right.

20

In the time before Wolf, she had stepped into each day as a train moves along a rail: the journey through the hours delineated and knowable, tasks and rituals performed unthinkingly. Those times had not been without pleasure, certainly, but they paled in comparison to this. She woke each morning taut with possibility: What delightful mysteries might the day bring? But such expansive joy came with a caveat. Worry for Wolf gnawed at her. Visions of calamity woke her with heart palpitations in the dark; paranoia sparked by incidents like the one at the gas station left her dry throated and queasy. For the first time she understood what parents went through on behalf of their children, how a certain caliber of love could feel indistinguishable from terror. She began to suffer from an itchy, morbid compulsion to check on him whenever he was out of her sight. She didn't, of course, but every time, a knee-weakening relief came whenever he was returned to her, safe and sound.

They had fallen into a routine of sorts: at the end of the working day, after each of their chores around the ranch had been completed, they would come together to eat and talk and watch movies and have sex and sleep. It was unorthodox for her to seek him out during the day, when they were both supposed to be involved in tasks. But three days after the trip to town, she gave in. It was her turn to clean the Commons, and she was trying to lose herself in the pleasantly mundane task. It wasn't working. Her arms—swathed in yellow latex to the elbows—trembled as she wiped down the countertops and nosed the vacuum into corners. She became grotesquely aware of her own breathing, lungs laboring like faulty bellows. In and out, in and out, the sudden horror of awareness. The vague sense of unease she'd been experiencing began to tick over into full-blown panic. She had always been scornful of people who believed in ideas like the sixth sense, fate, destiny, but on this day she was convinced that something terrible had happened to Wolf. The superstition worked its way into her brain, whispering that it would be bad luck to text him, that she needed to lay eyes on him if she wanted a chance of averting the unspeakable. Obeying the voice, she peeled off the gloves, left the Commons, and, jumping onto her bike, pedaled briskly along the road to the beehives, trying to maintain a steady, unhurried pace to convey a confidence of purpose she didn't feel. It felt better to be in the open air, and she drew ragged, grateful breaths.

She tried to make sense of it all. The anxiety had something to do with Wolf's reaction to the policeman who had watched them, as if he really had killed someone and feared being found out at last. But other, smaller signs felt disproportionately ominous too. Just that morning she'd noticed with creeping alarm that the bees that had lately taken to congregating around the flowers in her front garden weren't there. The flowers drooped, as if in a funk without their partners in crime. At least it gave her an excuse for seeing him: she was worried and needed to check on the bees' welfare.

Even from a distance she could see Wolf was there, in a checked shirt rolled up to his elbows, bent over the hives. Euphoric relief flooded in, and in its wake embarrassment at herself for falling prey to such jumpy paranoia. She could have fainted with gratitude that her sixth sense turned out to be fatally flawed.

When she was within shouting distance, she called out to him, and he turned, shading his eyes with his hand. He watched her approaching. She skidded the bike to a stop a few feet away, threw it down on the grass, and leapt nimbly to the side and into his outstretched arms.

"Hey, baby. This is a nice surprise."

"Hey. What's the buzz?"

"Ha ha."

"I was missing some bees from my garden and wondered if you'd stolen them."

"Hmm." He pretended to look concerned. "Can you identify them by sight?"

"Oh, sure, yeah. Not a problem."

He gave her a playful smack on the ass.

"Want to come say hi?"

They walked over to the hives, Marlo staying just behind Wolf's shoulder. She knew that bees were less likely to get agitated around someone with whom they had established a rapport. She was virtually a stranger to them. There were maybe a dozen plump bees flying lazy figure eights near the front of the hive. Their legs were clumped with pollen, like fuzzy, yellow leg warmers.

"I was just about to collect some honeycomb, actually," Wolf explained. "Want to stick around? They seem pretty calm today, but just to be safe you might want to grab one of the suits."

She shook her head, suddenly feeling foolish for checking up on him. The sensation that something bad was bearing down had been so real and visceral the last few days, but now she felt silly and indulgent for having given in to it.

"It's OK. I'll leave you to it. Think I'm going to pick some of the vegetables from my garden for dinner. This will probably be the last for the season."

"That sounds great." He drew her in for a kiss, and she breathed in the already-cherished natural scent of him overlaid with the note of cotton warmed by the sun.

"See you back home, then!"

She picked the bike up, blew him a blizzard of kisses, and rode away, heart lightened. Back at the house she changed into gardening clothes—a tank top and overalls, boots, a spotted scarf tied around her hair, and sunglasses. She grinned at her reflection: Rosie the Riveter, updated for the twenty-first century. In the garden, she gave herself over to the sensuous pleasures of pulling growing things from the earth as soil rained down, plucking plump, sun-drenched tomatoes from drooping vines, and snipping handfuls of herbs, which she tied with rubber bands and placed in the front pocket of her overalls, where their bouquet wafted up to tickle her nose. Kneeling in the dirt, evicting the occasional harried worm or beetle, she felt the last threads of anxiety unwind themselves and float away.

Marlo was alone when she got the message from her mother. As soon as she received the text she dropped the trowel and raced to the car. Her parents and several of the other senior ranchers were at the Commons talking with the police by the time she arrived. Her hands were shaking, and she could barely swallow as she strode past the police car—the sinister crackle of its radio slicing through the air—pushed open the front door, and joined the group. Kenneth was there too, although he took no part in the conversation that was going on but stood off to the side, leaning against the wall and listening intently. His gaze followed Marlo as she approached the meeting. Her mother shot her a warning look: she had urged Marlo to stay at home, assured her that they would take care of it. She had also asked Marlo not to give the police any information about Wolf, as if that needed to be said. It was all more or less over already. The two officers, a man and a woman, were rising out of their seats. The man nodded brusquely to the assembled ranchers. "If it's fine with you we'll just have a little look around the place now. Mr. and Mrs. Ketterman, appreciate it if you could show us the way to the cabin where you mentioned he's been staying."

"Of course," her father answered, smiling widely and with perfect equanimity. Marlo had never been so grateful for his talent at defusing tension. "As we mentioned, he's visiting relatives out of town at the moment, but it's no trouble to show you the place."

Marlo followed behind without saying a word. Kenneth was standing just outside the doorway when she exited the Commons. She went to brush past him, but he detained her with a firm grip on her arm. Marlo tried to shake him off, but her compact, wiry form was no match for his sheer bulk. Glaring felt inadequate; she wanted to hiss at him like a feral cat. But he just took her by the shoulders and asked kindly, "Is there anything I can do?"

They looked into one another's faces for a moment, then she shook her head. He dropped his hands as if her body suddenly burned, took a step back.

"I have to go," she said, gesturing toward her parents waiting in the golf cart. She started walking away but turned back at the last moment, racing up the stairs to grab Kenneth's huge right hand in her own slender one and squeeze it, hoping the pressure might convey everything she wasn't able to say. *Thank you for being an ally. Thank you for not saying I told you so.*

She climbed into the golf cart with her parents, and six of the other ranchers followed in their own carts, like a casual funeral procession. Her mother gave her a somber smile, but that was all the communication they had, or needed to have. They all knew it wasn't safe to talk until the officers had left. When they got to Wolf's cabin, no one but the police were surprised to find that he was gone. Not just him but his backpack and other belongings. The relief of not finding him there caused her stomach to spasm with nausea. She sat down quickly on the front step of the cabin, head on her knees, until the feeling passed. Then she stood up shakily and entered the small room, which felt claustrophobically tight with so many people in it. Marlo hung back toward the entrance and the fresh air. She tried not to think about the time she and Wolf had sat at the tiny table for tea, their love not even seeded yet.

"Well, as you can see, Officers, he's not here. Now can you tell us what this is all about?" Her father's voice was calm and friendly, but Marlo could hear the anger vibrating behind it. The policeman picked up an old newspaper from the sideboard, turned it over slowly and then looked up at her father with a small, tight smile on his bland saucer of a face.

"Mind if we conduct a search of the entire property?"

"To be honest we'd really prefer not. As you know this is private property on which a lot of families live. It would be very disruptive to have police searching the houses of private citizens without cause. And as you won't tell us what you want with Wolf . . ."

"We can get a search warrant."

Her father's nod and smile were as economical as they could be and still convey cooperation. "Very well. Until then. Can we get you some more coffee or anything else before you take off?"

"Just give us a call when he turns up here again, if you don't mind." The woman handed Marlo's father a card, and he glanced at it briefly before tucking it in the inner pocket of his sports coat. "Or tell him to call us. We have some questions for him."

"Of course. I'm sure he'll be eager to help with your investigation."

No, thought Marlo. *That sounded too facetious. Don't bait them, Dad.* But the officers just gave one more passive look around the cabin, strode outside, got in their car, and drove away. Everyone stood and watched their painfully slow retreat down the main road and out of sight.

"What was that about?" said Amber, disgusted. "How insufferable, throwing their weight around."

Her reaction cheered Marlo. On the whole the ranchers fostered a suspicion of authority, and they had always presented a united front when it came to outsiders trying to snoop around. But you could never be sure when that might change, when another outsider might force

211

them into an alliance with the Man. And it occurred to her with an unpleasant jolt that Wolf was still, for all intents and purposes, an outsider. But for now at least they seemed unanimous in their outrage at the visit. Everyone remembered all too well the last time the police had showed up on the ranch, the aggressive way they had all been questioned about Neil's death and about the mausoleum.

"You know what they're like," said Marlo's mom, beaming an indulgent smile around the group. "Probably some unpaid parking fines!" Her soothing voice acted like a balm on everyone's frazzled nerves. You could see it in the way their faces all loosened into their habitual expressions. Yes, that explanation felt plausible, one they could all accept without interrogating it further. Little smiles were passed around the circle like gum. "Darling, would you like a ride home?" This last smile to Marlo, who nodded mutely. She didn't trust herself to speak.

The ranchers all dispersed to resume their respective days, as if nothing had happened. Marlo could see they were all already papering over the situation in their minds. Wolf would pay his "parking fines" and come back from the "vacation to see his relatives," and everything would go back to normal. For the first time Marlo understood how propaganda could be so effective. It was all about reinforcing existing biases. They must all have known he wasn't off-site visiting relatives: at least one or two of them would have encountered Wolf that very day. Yet because the explanation had the thinnest veneer of veracity it was accepted. Like other shifting signs lately, it scared her.

"So where is he?" she asked her parents as soon as they were out of earshot of the group, and she could trust herself to speak. Her mother, in the front seat of the cart, swiveled to face Marlo.

"He's fine, darling. He's safe."

"OK. That wasn't the question, though."

Maya glanced at her husband, who kept looking straight ahead but gave an almost imperceptible nod.

"Your father and I decided it was best we keep his location a secret for now. For his own safety. In case those assholes return over the next day or two." Marlo was surprised at the vehemence in her mother's voice. She rarely cursed, so things must be serious. "I hope you understand, honey. He'll return as soon as we deem it safe."

"But what did he *do*?" She could feel her pitch rising to that of a frightened child. "I don't understand!"

Maya reached over the seat back and grasped Marlo's hand.

"We know, darling. Neither do we. There wasn't time to find out. All the police would say is that Wolf is wanted for questioning with regard to an incident in Los Angeles. An 'incident,' that's what they called it, isn't it, Carlton?" He nodded. "Now I know what you're thinking, but they never said anything about Wolf himself being in trouble. Just that he might know something of interest to their investigation."

Marlo steepled her hands over her nose and mouth and took deep breaths. It was a self-care trick from childhood that made her feel like she had an invisible oxygen mask on, and it had always soothed her. She didn't answer. She was too busy reflecting on the fact that her parents were the ones who were so insistent that Wolf couldn't have done anything wrong, anything criminal. When Marlo herself wouldn't have staked hers or anyone else's life on it.

21

The police didn't return the next day, but neither did Wolf. A few hours into the day she permitted herself to give in to despair. It was clear he wasn't coming back, no matter what her parents said. She was already nostalgic for it, the late spring and summer she had spent with him. Perhaps he *had* done something terrible, but as the hours wore on she became more and more convinced that she would forgive him even if he had done the very worst thing possible—if he had murdered someone. So when he did return, two days later, she was surprised to find her first reaction to the sight of him wasn't relief but rage. He materialized in the middle of the night, just as he had on the night of his first arrival. She heard the furtive knock on the door and knew it was him as soon as her eyes snapped open in the darkness.

"He's back," she whispered into air heavy with her own sleeping breath. And then the anger flooded in. She pulled on a robe, flicked a lamp on, and padded out to the front door. She opened the door silently, held it wide, and stepped to the side so he could enter. He hesitated, perhaps wondering whether to embrace her. Evidently deciding against that, he slid past her into the stifling stillness of the hallway.

She stalked ahead of him into the house, and without really thinking about it led him to the kitchen, where she switched on all the lights and proceeded to angrily pull items out of the fridge—a bowl of eggs, a loaf of bread, butter, fresh herbs—so she could make breakfast for him. Wolf pulled out one of the barstools and slumped his elbows onto the counter, resting his head on his arms and watching her as a chastened dog might watch his master. She glanced at him in between violent shakes of the pan, as the eggs spat and bubbled in the hot oil.

"I'm guessing you haven't even eaten," she said, the words dragged out through her teeth. He looked five years older, drawn and sleepless. "Are those spiderwebs in your hair?"

He put his hand slowly to his head and rubbed his scalp in a kind of trance. He held his hand out in front of his face, then shrugged, as if hoping she'd provide the answers he was unable to.

"I'm so sorry." His voice was raspy, like he hadn't used it for a while.

She finished frying the eggs, then used the hot fat to fry the slices of bread as well, then slid it all onto plates, sprinkled it with herbs, and came to sit next to him at the bar.

"It's"—he looked at his phone—"four in the morning."

This seemed less a statement than a question.

"If you say so."

"Thank you. I don't deserve you. Or any of this."

"Listen." Marlo felt the anger rising up and choking her again. It was an extraordinary sensation, not completely without its self-righteous pleasures. "Spare me the humble stuff, OK? Just tell me what happened." She bit into a piece of toast, its edges curled and brown and flecked with crispy patches of egg white. She closed her eyes, savoring the larded comfort of carbohydrates.

"I was at your parents' place a few hours after I saw you. I promised I'd deliver some honeycomb to them. And Jamal texted them to say the police were here, and they were looking for me. I told you, that cop at the gas station didn't like the look of me for some reason, and he must have called your plates in. I don't think he even knew for sure I'd done anything wrong, just acted on a hunch and got lucky. They wanted to talk to me about . . . some case."

Marlo chewed exaggeratedly until her jaw began to hurt. There was a masochistic pleasure in that as well.

"I pretty much know all that. Then where did you go?" Even before the words were out, she suddenly knew the answer. It had been under their noses—or rather feet—all along. She swallowed the mouthful abruptly. "My parents' basement. The old fallout shelter."

Funny, she had almost forgotten it was there. It seemed such a Cold War relic when they had first put it in. But the last few years had been fucked-up enough out in the Disaster that a lot of the ranchers had followed their lead and installed concrete-reinforced bunkers of their own. Just in case.

"Yes. They thought it was safest. I just want you to know, I didn't want to go down there. To hide. I wanted to turn myself in, go with the police, and explain everything. But they wouldn't let me. They said we could work it all out later, that this was better for the time being until they could sort something out. They told me how upset you'd be if I got whisked off to the police station for questioning. I know it was kind of emotional blackmail on their part, but it worked. I've been there ever since. Me and the spiders."

He smiled so bleakly it would have broken her heart under other circumstances. He didn't attempt to touch her, but she could feel his whole body straining toward her, taut with misery and the desire to be loved again. He was like a child in so many ways.

"You haven't even eaten anything." She could feel the anger ebbing away now, in little pulses that grew ever weaker as the crisis receded. The desire for him that always lay just below the surface. "Please eat something." She picked up his fork and stabbed a piece of toast and egg, brought it close to his face, and held it there like a stern mother waiting on a recalcitrant child. He opened his mouth obediently, took the food, and chewed it slowly, without taking his dark eyes off her face. The rest of the meal was silent and companionable. She laughed at the way he laid waste to his plate, forking the food into his mouth with a ravenous single-mindedness until there was only a bright-yellow smear of yolk left on the dish. When they had both finished, Wolf took the plates to the sink and rinsed them off and then came back to sit with her. They sat facing one another. Wolf ran his hand around her jawline and up over her cheeks, like he was trying to memorize her face with his fingers.

"So I suppose this is the part where you tell me what it is those police officers think you did?"

He smiled and dropped his hand into his lap. "Thanks for asking what they *think* I did rather than what I actually did."

"Of course. But you have to tell me what this is all about. That policeman we saw in town last time, was he something to do with this? Were you involved in something bad back in LA?"

The questions felt inadequate, but she had no other words with which to say, *I love you, but I don't trust you.*

"Yes."

He dropped his head slowly, as if his neck had suddenly gone on strike. Marlo put her hand on his thigh, held it there as he gently but hypnotically kicked his leg out to meet the wall. She thought she felt his clenched muscles trembling. That's when she realized how cold it was in the predawn chill of the kitchen.

"Come on," she said, standing up and extending her hand. "Let's get under the covers at least if we're going to do this." In a way, she was just trying to put it off. She had a feeling that whatever he was going to tell her might draw a line between her old life and new.

The story flowed in a neat, linear way as though he'd rehearsed it, which he may well have, given that he'd spent three days in a basement with no other distractions. Some of it she already knew, like the part about how Wolf's parents had always talked in a dreamy way about wanting to join the ranch someday, if only they could raise the money. But he hadn't talked before about how hard his father took his mother leaving, how her desertion—her betrayal, as he called it—more or less sent him off the rails. After Wolf's mother left to go and live in Brazil, cast away on a remote island called Florianópolis with her new husband, Wolf's dad grew obsessed with the idea of getting to the ranch. He'd drop oblique hints that he was close to having the funds. Wolf knew that was impossible on his public schoolteacher salary.

"I always suspected there was something illicit going on," he said, staring at the ceiling with his hands crossed over his chest. "You know, there were always shady characters around Dad's house. He installed blackout curtains in every room, and he got really twitchy and para-noid. He'd always been a casual pot smoker, but he got even more heavily into it over the last few years, to the point where I hated going around there." Marlo knew Wolf had experimented with drugs, but he professed to hate weed; she supposed this explained why. He sighed deeply, made as if to turn and look at her, then thought better of it and resumed his horizontal ceiling examination. "Surprise! It turned out he was running a hydroponic pot-growing business in his basement. I mean, it started that way, but then he got into other stuff."

"Fuck, Wolf. What did you do when you found out?"

"I swear to you I didn't know anything about the growing. I mean, I knew he was unstable, especially after Mom left, but was he fucking nuts? You don't become a grower, let alone a dealer, without doing things the official way. Not even in California. I knew the police had been cracking down on unlicensed growers, small-scale guys. Typical, the state protecting corporations as usual. So anyway, I went around to his place one night because he'd called me and he sounded really bummed out, really down, so I went and the place was a fucking pigsty. Garbage overflowing, roaches all over the place . . . I mean, both kinds. And he was so clearly high as fuck and paranoid as all hell, getting up to peer out the curtains every two seconds. So I cleaned up and told him I was going to the store to get some groceries so I could make him a proper meal."

He paused for a moment then, like a swimmer catching a breath. Marlo felt dread pool in her stomach. She could tell he was leading up to the part about his father's death. She could see it all unspooling in her mind's eye, like a lurid movie. That his dad must have insisted on getting in the car with Wolf, and that there had been an accident on the way to the store. Not Wolf's fault—she wasn't willing to believe that. But perhaps the police thought it was, and that's why they were looking for Wolf. She couldn't believe he had been living with this, with the guilt of being the driver in the accident that killed his father. Or, she reconsidered with a start, perhaps his father had insisted on driving? That made more sense. Either way, what he must have gone through. She lay on her side, stroked his hair.

"I'm sorry," she whispered. Perhaps there was a way to save him the anguish of telling her, by filling in the gaps herself. "I'm so sorry. That was when your dad died in the car crash, right? Was he at the wheel?"

Wolf turned to look at her, and his eyes reminded her of the night when he first arrived, less human than crow, black and unreadable. His voice, when it came, sounded wrong too.

"No. I was the only one in the car. So when I returned to the house there was crime scene tape, an ambulance, police cars. Neighbors standing around, shocked and crying. I stayed in the car, and I watched as they wheeled my dad's body out of the house on a gurney in a zipped-up body bag. I could tell it was him somehow, by the shape of the body under there. People were shouting."

"Oh, my god." Marlo clapped her hand to her mouth. It felt false, like the kind of gesture someone in a movie would make. "No, Wolf."

The story dried up there. She didn't push for the rest of it, just let him fall asleep curled up against her while she lay awake, waiting for the first cracks of light to invade the room. Over the next few days she coaxed the rest of the story out of him, about how he had panicked and fled the scene of his father's death. No one had noticed him leave, and it was only later, when his aunt called, that he found out about the raid in which his dad had been killed, supposedly resisting arrest. It turned out his dad, his loser public schoolteacher dad, had rigged up an ingenious hydroponic system with lights and automatic watering, the full bit, and the police had been tipped off by the electricity company, who had reported his stupendously high use of power, a suspicious amount for such a modest suburban home. They were trained to recognize such activity, especially when a residence went from using normal amounts of electricity to powering the equivalent of a petroleum refinery. His house had been under surveillance for a couple of months before the raid, cameras monitoring the activity in and out.

His aunt had been hysterical on the phone, barely able to speak coherently, apart from the clarity of her warning that Wolf wasn't to come anywhere near her and her family for the time being, that the police sought him for questioning in connection with the operation. She implied it had been more than just growing plants, that his father had been into other, shadier stuff too. She had warned Wolf that he was likely on tape entering and leaving his dad's house. She advised him to lie low until she let him know it was safe to return to LA.

So he had missed his dad's funeral, had hightailed it to San Francisco, where a friend had taken him in, and he had embarked on a creatively self-destructive spiral that had frayed the friend's patience and hospitality, after which he was out on his own in a city in which he knew no one, in a state where he was being sought for questioning by the police who had killed his father. At his lowest point he had remembered the ranch, and how his dad had always yearned to go there. Addled on painkillers, he had made his way north, with only the vaguest idea as to where the ranch even was and zero plan for gaining entry.

He had kept downing drugs on the road—anxiety meds, antidepressants, Adderall—and by the time he arrived in Oregon he was in a kind of fugue state. In a roadside motel he had succumbed to paranoia and decided to ditch the car in case the police were hunting him. He sold it to a salvage yard for a hundred and fifty bucks and then hitchhiked and walked the rest of the way to the ranch.

By the time the story was finished, they were both exhausted, empty, and enervated, like they were coming down from a binge. She could tell she was the first person he had ever told.

"Baby, I'm so sorry that happened to you. It wasn't your fault about your dad."

"No," he said, hollow and distant.

"Just because he made bad decisions, that's not on you."

"You know the funny thing? The irony? My dad was really good at the hydroponics. Like, he really loved that stuff. He would have been great on the ranch. He and Kenneth would have been great buddies."

"We have to tell the police what you just told me."

"You really think they'll believe me? I heard from one of the ranchers that the police have been jonesing for a scapegoat to blame the local heroin epidemic on. I'm sure they'd love to nail a drug dealer's son. It would look real good on their end-of-year reports."

"But they can't do that. You're innocent."

He turned to look at her, a small smile crinkling the edge of his mouth as he cradled her cheek in his hand.

"You really have led a sheltered life, haven't you?"

"Stop it. You have to tell them."

Now that she knew the truth—a truth of course terrible and sad, but at least it didn't reflect badly on the man she was just beginning to love—her focus instantly pivoted to proving Wolf's innocence to the police. Once he did that, everything would be OK. That was the story she told herself.

22

What to do with the tomatoes?

They were too soft for a salad, close to overripe. She had picked a whole basketful the week before and then forgotten them in the chaos of Wolf's disappearance. They wrinkled in protest when she pressed her finger into their flesh, leaving behind little divots. She worried over them like an anxious mother until the solution presented itself—she would pulverize them into a sauce and invite her parents over for dinner. Wolf, their liberated fugitive, would be the guest of honor. Once she had decided on this course of action, the anxiety receded or at least was redirected into the culinary project.

She spent most of an afternoon blanching the tomatoes and peeling the spent skins away, then harvesting onions, tiny heads of young purple garlic, and basil. She decided to make the pasta from scratch, which necessitated rooting around in a spare cupboard filled with the ghosts of passions past to find the pasta machine. She eventually located it behind the badminton rackets and a dusty loom. A loom! Had she once imagined herself pioneer womaning her days away, spinning thread into heirlooms for her nonexistent heirs? She pushed it back with a shudder. After chopping the mountain of tomatoes, she tossed them into a pot almost as big as she was, threw in lavish palmfuls of salt, pepper, fresh herbs, and chili flakes and several quarts of water, then left the sauce on the stove to simmer for hours. Every now and then she'd return to stir the pot, and each time the high tide line would have receded, leaving behind a viscous rim, dark red like clotted blood. The sight made her throat close up. What if Wolf failed to turn up again, instead disappearing for good this time? She wasn't sure she could stand it.

But Wolf appeared at her door that night at the appointed time, with a bouquet of ragged wildflowers gripped in his fist and a crooked smile that seemed to seek forgiveness before he'd even had a chance to trespass. She hugged him a little too tightly, and he laughed as they pulled apart, clutching his ribs and pretending she'd choked the life out of him.

"Happy to see you too, beauty."

But the jollity receded once they were sitting together on the front lawn with gin and tonics and she put forward her proposal, the one she'd been thinking about all day. He shot a look of dark distrust her way, as if wondering whether she was really on his side.

"An easy suggestion to make when you're not the one who stands to end up in jail if it doesn't go well."

"But you're innocent!" She could feel tears sprouting. "If you go to the police first, they'll have to see that. They'll let you go, I'm sure of it."

He started to contradict her, then shut his mouth with a little click of his jaw and took a contemplative, birdlike sip of his drink instead.

"It'll be OK, baby," he said after a while. "I'll work something out, I promise."

"Kenneth is livid, you know."

Wolf gave her a look that was mostly skeptical eyebrow. "No shit."

She laughed. "I know. Who'd have guessed it? But for real, he wants you out of here. That's another reason we need to clear your name. To prove to him . . ." She trailed off. Prove what exactly?

"I don't give a flying fuck about Kenneth. He's always hated me. But what about the others? Do you think they feel the same?"

For the first time anxiety replaced defensiveness in his voice.

"Of course not," she rushed to assure him. "Everyone else loves you."

"Right, Marlo. They're dying to make me their new king."

It was true that she'd overstated the case. Her parents felt a deep affection for Wolf, that was indisputable, but the other ranchers? She couldn't be sure. Marlo had been around long enough to understand that it didn't make sense to get too attached to someone who might not go the distance. Would-be ranchers hadn't worked out in the past for various reasons. After the probation period they sometimes melted away, back into the more familiar terrain of the Disaster.

"That's Mom and Dad," Marlo said, smoothing her hair and extricating her limbs from where they'd become tangled with his. Wolf looked up, puzzled, and she explained, "I recognize the sound of their car."

Her ears were finely attuned to the slightly hiccupy purr of their BMW engine, and, sure enough, within a few seconds the nose of their car appeared around the bend. Wolf got to his feet, running fingers through his hopeless, physics-defying dark hair, which tended to fall in strange and endearing ways over his forehead. Marlo often had to restrain herself from smoothing it down, because it seemed like such a regressively feminine thing to do.

The two of them waved at the approaching car, although they couldn't see its inhabitants through the tinted windows.

"Oops, we stayed out here longer than I thought. Let's go inside—there are still a few things I need to prep. Wolfie, would you set the table?"

Marlo skipped off to the kitchen to see to things. A formal knock came at the front door a few minutes later—her parents made a religion out of respecting her privacy—and she heard Wolf walk out there and open it, listened with a detached pleasure to the sounds of greeting. Low laughter and the clack of her father's cane on the hardwood floors. Her mother's warm voice foisting good health on Wolf whether it was warranted or not. (*You look so well, Wolf!*) Marlo smiled, blew cool air onto a spoonful of sauce before bringing it to her mouth. It was perfect, better than any sauce she'd made before.

After they sat down at the table to eat, Wolf poured wine for everyone. Carlton raised his glass for a toast.

"To our health," he said, his sonorous voice amplified so close to the rim of the glass. "To *your* health!" He looked pointedly at Marlo and Wolf. "God knows it's too late for mine."

"Dad."

"Well, honey, it's true. You kids are the future of this place. And we're mighty glad you are."

She sipped her drink in pensive silence, mentally preparing to raise her proposal, but the salad course wasn't even over before her father beat her to it. As he laid out his recommendations, his wife nodded her approval of a scheme that they had quite obviously settled on long before dinner began. The plan was this: Marlo's parents would accompany Wolf to the local police station and "help him explain the situation." Marlo cocked an eyebrow.

"How will you do that, exactly?" she inquired, knowing full well that if anyone could convince skeptical police officers that someone was innocent, it was her parents. She'd noticed that blue-collar authoritarian types—local police, security guards, TSA officers—tended to be impressed and a little cowed by them. Marlo had never quite worked out why; perhaps it was because they wore their wealth and whiteness and privilege so lightly. That kind of self-assurance could throw people.

"Leave it to us, honey," her father said smoothly, spearing a piece of lettuce with great gusto.

"Does Wolf get a say in this?" Marlo asked, turning to her boyfriend. She expected him to lodge a token protest to the proposal at least, but she saw in his face a glimmer of hope. *So that's it, then,* she thought. *As usual it's all been decided without me.*

"I can't expect you to do that," he said finally, after Marlo dug her fingernails into his knee. "This is *my* problem. My responsibility."

"Oh, it's nothing, Wolf," her mother assured him briskly. "We've done this kind of thing for other ranchers before. We look out for each other here. And we do have a certain standing in the community."

Wolf looked down at his plate, ears reddening. Marlo could tell how excruciating this was for him, how destabilizing to his sense of self it was to grovel for help. But it was obvious to them all that he had no other options. After a few more intense minutes of discussion, he reluctantly agreed to go with them to the police station, although not as reluctantly as Marlo in agreeing to staying home.

"Why can't I come?" she whined, petulant as her five-year-old self.

"Because this will be a tense enough situation, darling, without extra people in the mix," her mother explained. "We'd just rather you stay here while we sort things out."

After her parents left and they were in bed together, Wolf sounded cautiously optimistic.

"I think I might not need your mom and dad at all," he told Marlo. "You know, I think I can explain it all away. But it's nice to know there are three people who care about what happens to me."

"More than that," said Marlo, though she wasn't even sure what she meant.

❦

But when they returned from town, Wolf was subdued and moody. For the first time in a long time he stayed back at his old worker's cottage instead of with her, and she tried not to feel wounded. She could tell from her parents' upbeat behavior and air of having satisfactorily closed a deal that the trip had gone well, so she was puzzled by Wolf's withdrawal back into his gloomy self. She pried it all out of him over the next few days. The police had questioned him for a few hours at the station. Marlo's parents had insisted on being present, and the policemen had asked what their relationship was to the suspect, and they had answered that they were his counsel, and the policemen had shrugged and acquiesced. Marlo rolled her eyes good-naturedly at this part, urged him to continue. After he had finished explaining what had happened back in LA, that he had simply turned up at his father's home, had seen the aftermath of the raid, and had fled, they had wanted to know if anyone could corroborate his story. Wolf had given them his aunt's phone number. After a lot of time-wasting they had called the aunt and the county police from Wolf's former residence, and the aunt had vouched for him. No one would tell him what the county police had said, but he got the impression things were still serious. The cops were showing no signs of letting him go.

Then Marlo's parents had requested to speak with the police chief, and the three of them had gone off into a room together, leaving Wolf outside, and when they emerged the chief had informed Wolf that they had decided to let him go due to lack of evidence. Not without a typical fucking cop lecture though, about how it was a serious offense to flee the scene of a crime and how his name would remain in their system as having been a person of interest to an investigation and how he had to promise to keep his nose clean from now on.

"Not a fucking word about my dad, of course," Wolf said bitterly. "No apology for murdering him for the crime of growing some measly weed."

"I'm sorry," Marlo said, but she was flooded with a relief so intense she thought she might choke. Later, when she went looking for the missing piece of the story, she discovered that her parents had gifted the town a staggeringly generous cash donation—no one was even going to breathe the word *bribe*—to rebuild the crumbling stadium and finish an important, long-neglected stretch of highway, and that the wheels of justice had been greased in their usual way. She could tell how humiliating it had been for Wolf to accept their benevolence. The way he described the mortifying ride home, during which Carlton and Maya had insisted that the gesture in no way indebted Wolf to them.

All they asked was one tiny concession: that Wolf swear not to tell the other ranchers about the deal they had made. His eyes were so wretched as he told this part of the story that Marlo's heart went out to him, but afterward it was pleasant to bask in the novelty of having someone with whom to share the burden of their goodness. She had been weighed down with it her whole short, charmed life, and now she finally had a comrade in arms who understood the impossible debt of this love. Who could ever hope to pay it back?

23

They were swimming in the smaller of the two lakes, the one closer to the swampy grasslands at the ranch's southern border. They liked that they could swim naked there. It felt like the last chance for the year. The muddy banks may have sucked against the soles of their feet and the tangled reeds harbored a host of potential slimy hazards, but nevertheless this felt like their place. They had begun to lay claim to select secret corners of the ranch, leaving invisible traces of themselves like dogs marking their territory.

They alternated between lazy paddling and floating on their backs as midges swooped and the air shimmered. Water beaded across Marlo's breasts and belly. She felt like a fish gone belly-up. There was a new, autumnal chill in the air, and the exposed parts of her skin prickled with goose bumps. She closed her eyes, allowing her mind to go perfectly blank and raw feeling to take over. After a not-long-enough stretch of time, Wolf's words etched themselves over this blissful blankness:

"Which countries do you think will survive the apocalypse?"

Marlo flipped over and treaded water, squinting at him. He didn't seem to require an answer, his face dreamy and distant.

"I read the other day that the entire Maldives will be completely gone soon. Like, fucking gone. Atlantis style." He demonstrated by curling his fist into a ball and letting it sink, as if she couldn't imagine what an island chain underwater might look like. "Bangladesh too. Most of the Middle East is going to be uninhabitable in a few decades.

And that's not counting Western cities, like, basically the whole Eastern Seaboard of the US."

"Tell me. Did you ever take much notice of all these terrible things happening in the world before you came here? Or has being in here amplified them and made it seem like they've only just started happening?"

He had the decency to look abashed. "Yeah, well. I had my head in the sand at the beginning. Side effect of living in the Disaster for so long. But doing the research, I realized how widespread it is, and it's scary as shit, dude. There's going to be a massive displacement of people over the next decade. It's already starting. Millions and millions of desperate people on the move. It's going to completely disrupt the geopolitical makeup of the world as we know it." After a glance at her expression, he paused his lecture and laughed, and the sound of his laugh sent a thrill of pure sensation through her. Joy, unadulterated. "Sorry. You already know all this. Preaching to the choir. But you get it too: shit is going to get real, really fast. I never used to believe that, but . . ."

"Yeah, this place tends to have that effect on you. Try growing up here."

"I wish I had."

"Really?"

"Are you kidding? Of course. I'd want my kids to grow up somewhere like this. Our kids."

"Excuse me?"

He grinned. "Well. I guess that's one of the possible endgames. Right?"

"I hadn't really thought about it." Although she had, of course. But it had never felt like a legitimate option, just a far-fetched alternate timeline. "Would you really want to bring these fictitious children, these baby Wolves, into this world?"

He paused, staring with somber eyes into the middle distance. "Granted, not *that* one." He tilted his head toward the Disaster out beyond the horizon.

"Are you serious? It's the same world. Whatever happens out there is eventually going to happen in here as well. You must know that."

He closed his eyes and kept them closed for a while as though the conversation were fatally wearying. Then they snapped open again and were interrogating her face.

"Listen, babe. I need to tell you something."

"What?" The nasty little realization returning, that all his dark corners might not yet have been excavated.

"I was talking with some of the guys in the greenhouse the other day . . . Well, not really talking. I was repotting some plants and was just kind of idly eavesdropping. And Jamal and Frank, I heard them talking about the fact that we might be building the wall even higher. Like, making it into some kind of fucking fortress-type shit."

"Seriously? Why wouldn't I know about it?"

His shoulders rose above the surface in a shrug. "Don't know. But like you said, since those regular meetings don't happen anymore, I guess there's no community forum to talk about these things. Anyway, when the guys saw me listening they changed the subject, like it wasn't really something they were supposed to be talking about."

"What the fuck? What is happening around here? That sounds like a crazy overreaction."

"Right? But I got the impression it's really happening. I don't know. Maybe it's for the best."

A cloud scuttled over the sun, and the water instantly became colder. Marlo shivered, hugged her arms around her chest, her legs working furiously beneath the water. She could have moved to a shallower part of the lake, but she feared her feet making contact with the squishy bottom.

"What do you mean?"

"Nothing. Just that we have to start thinking about the future. About keeping the community safe. Maybe this is one of the ways."

"By barricading ourselves inside the ranch? Because that's never ended badly, historically speaking."

They were both irritated now, hostile waves of thwarted understanding flowing back and forth in the air between them.

"I just want to stay in here with you," Wolf said finally. She heard the fear rippling through his voice. Propelling herself toward him through the water, she closed the space between them, pressing her body against his. They paddled for a few minutes twined together beneath the cloud-stained sky, a conjoined, oddly shaped entity working to keep itself afloat.

Kenneth found her with the chickens. He had always had a knack for knowing when she was alone. Now that she and Wolf spent almost every moment together, he must have decided to seize this rare chance. She was in the process of attaching the mobile chicken shed onto the back of the truck when she heard a footfall, lifted her head to see Kenneth striding toward her. She raised a hand in greeting. As he got closer she saw how haggard he looked now, as if he'd been cheating sleep or it had been cheating him. She thought there might be more silver bristles in his scruffy beard than the last time she had seen him.

"Hey," she said, smiling, genuinely happy to see him. He didn't answer her smile, just bent down as if to examine the trailer hitch and make sure the henhouse was properly attached.

"Which field?"

Marlo shrugged. "Not sure. What do you suggest?" This was another aspect of Kenneth's revolutionary farming strategy, this moving of the hens around the property so that they fertilized and turned over the soil in patches each day without depleting it, before moving on to another virgin piece of land. Thanks to his painstakingly plotted-out grazing methods, the ranch now had some of the most fertile and healthy land for hundreds of miles around. "Maybe that clover meadow near the big lake?"

He nodded slowly, scrutinizing the thought. "Sure. I'll graze the cows there next week."

"How are things, anyway, Kenneth?" she asked, yearning to make things right. "Sorry I haven't been around so much."

He ceased ruminating on the henhouse for a moment to shoot her a dark look.

"Not my business."

Marlo's cheeks flushed. She felt guilty whenever she saw him now, then guilty that she hadn't given him any of her time since Wolf had arrived.

"So, uh, what have you been up to?"

He shrugged and plunged his hands into his pockets, rattling the keys inside, refusing to look directly at her. "You know. Just working. Trying to close the loop."

"Close the loop?" It really had been a long time since they had properly conversed, or she might have remembered that this particular jargon was one of his fallback conversational tools. "Remind me what that means again?"

Kenneth sighed, or perhaps that was just the hens, rustling restively in their house, eager to get to work.

"It means making the systems inside the ranch fully autonomous. So we don't have to rely anymore on easily fallible and corruptible public utilities."

"Right." It was all coming back to her. With a start she realized this was the kind of thing Wolf had been talking about a lot lately too. "So, like, more than usual?"

She hated sounding like a dumb schoolkid, but it felt like there was a crucial part of the puzzle of their lives on the ranch to which she was no longer privy.

"Yes." He looked directly at her now, his intense, pale-eyed gaze finally piercing through her little protective bubble of happiness. "Yes, you could say that. You could say we're into the final stage of our long-term preparations."

Now it was Marlo's turn to sigh in exasperation. "Do we always have to speak in code around here? Is there something you're trying to tell me, Kenneth? Just say it. What are we all supposed to be scared of now?"

Color rushed to his face. He twisted his hands in his pockets, working the fists against his thigh, then he dropped his hands to his side, where they dangled, swinging gently as if signaling the cessation of his anger. She had the unpleasant thought that his arms looked like hams hanging in the curing shed.

"There's nothing specific. I just have a feeling."

She hadn't planned to laugh, but it gusted out of her. She put her arm around his slumped shoulders, careful to make the grip hard and sexless, like a male friend would have done. "Kenneth the rationalist just *has a feeling*! Wow."

It took a moment, but his stern face gradually softened, and the lines around his mouth pulled upward in a sheepish smile. They were back in familiar territory now: Marlo teasing, and Kenneth basking in her attention.

"I know. It sounds irrational, but even the biggest yuppies on this ranch are starting to get the message that time is running out. We need to get our house in order, if you know what I mean. If that's not too coded for you."

She shook her head sadly. "I can't believe you still use the word *yuppies*."

It was easier to keep teasing him than to properly acknowledge what he was saying. Kenneth flushed, ruffled her hair, as if by infantilizing her he hoped to dilute her power over him.

"Anyway, can't hurt, getting the place ready."

She nodded and changed the subject so she didn't have to find out what they were getting ready for exactly, instead asking if he'd like to ride along with her to deliver the hens to their new poultry paradise for the day. He agreed to come along, gruffly, as if he were doing her a favor, although they both knew it was the other way around.

It felt like she and Wolf had talked about everything under the sun, and yet somehow they had avoided discussing their romantic pasts. Marlo had nothing to hide and had always been frank with lovers about her admittedly slim sexual history dossier if they asked, but Wolf never brought it up so she didn't either. Then one day out of the blue he asked if she'd ever been in love with anyone at the ranch. She saw no reason to keep her past from him, so she explained about prudish Simon, and her brief crush on Ben, and the few others with whom she'd had casual hookups over the years. She omitted the encounters she'd had with various men on the recruitment trips off the ranch. She could see he was already grappling with jealousy about the childish dalliances she'd described, and there seemed no utility in introducing leering, anonymous older men into his no doubt lurid imaginings.

"Even in the infatuation phase, though, I always knew none of them were keepers."

She teetered on the cusp of telling him that even from a young age her fantasizing about the eventual Big, Important, and Serious Love that surely awaited her had never involved ranchers. She always knew that love, if it came, would be found in exile. But how did Wolf's arrival change that secret conviction? He was both apart from and of the ranch.

"How about you?" she asked, and only as she spoke the words did she understand with a surge of panic what was about to happen. The feeling came roaring in, literally unbalancing her. She swayed a little on her feet. Jealousy was mostly the province of men, Alex had always said, a side effect of the patriarchy and most men's inability to separate love from ownership. The three of them—she, Alex, and Ben—had always congratulated themselves on their open-minded approach to relationships, their rejection of retro, heteronormative ideals when it came to love and sex. That stuff was the vestiges of a failed ideology, the last gasp of the bourgeoisie. They weren't advocating free love or anything lame like that, just the unshackling of love from proprietary feelings. Nothing could be more rational and right-minded.

So waiting for Wolf to read from his own sexual autobiography, she was astonished to arrive at a never-before-imagined truth: jealousy might, after all, have less to do with ownership and more with the amount of equity you had in the relationship. How did anyone stand it? She felt like she was going to be sick. Unacceptable ideas already swirling in nauseating spirals in her head: What if he had been married, had children stashed somewhere, or worse, had loved someone so fiercely that he had never gotten over it? She wanted to block her ears, stagger away.

When he spoke it was in a blessedly offhand way: "Nothing much to speak of. Girlfriends here and there. No one serious." Mouth twisted in mild distaste as though it was barely worth rehashing.

"Oh?" The word came out thick and choked, unconvincing. "Which was the longest?" This perverse desire to strike at one's own heart. To hear more. To scratch at this newly acquired wound to see how much one could stand.

"The longest? Um. This girl named Callie."

The name instantly and forever scrawled on a one-woman hit list. Was she white? Black? Asian? Hispanic? Native American? Why on earth would it matter? She couldn't even work out whether she wanted him to have a "thing" for Asian girls or to never have looked at anyone nonwhite before her. All the options felt unbearable.

"Short for California?" A feeble joke for this enfeebling moment.

"Ha. No. Callista, would you believe. I think one of her parents was Greek."

Now that her breathing had been wrestled under control, she had energy to spare to parse every word. Why didn't he know for sure whether one of her parents was Greek? Surely that implied a casual entanglement rather than the passionate one she dreaded? Hope tiptoed back in.

"How long were you together?"

He frowned, trying to remember.

"I think about two years?" A question, as if Marlo could supply a different, more accurate, answer. "She was kind of sad and lost. I think I felt sorry for her more than anything. She'd lost a brother to cancer a few years before I met her, and she was pretty messed up."

Marlo swallowed, tried to modulate her tone to ultracasual. "Do you keep in touch?"

He gave her one of his endearing *Are you shitting me?* faces.

"Ah. No. I don't even think about her anymore." *Anymore.* "Since I met you I haven't thought about anyone else, not even for a second."

He changed the subject, perhaps embarrassed at laying all his cards on the table, but a relieved bird sang on its little perch inside Marlo's heart. There was nothing to worry about, after all.

24

There were picnics and cookouts and, as the days deepened into fall, harvest celebrations and bonfires that threaded smoke signals into the cooling evenings. Birthday parties for the few children left on the ranch, whose milestones were always greeted with the seriousness and pomp of a royal visit. There were the usual weekly potlucks and the occasional group meeting (still no decision on who would be the new newsperson) and a flurry of action as the solstice drew near, to pickle, preserve, and store the year's bounty for the long winter ahead. A steady schedule of hosting and attending dinner parties and book discussions. Animals were born and died (one relief: no more bald eagles among the fallen) and measures were taken for the coming cold: ensuring every dwelling, both human and beastly, was properly winterized; checking on the integrity of the greenhouse; shaking out and airing the comforters and down jackets; stocking up on antifreeze and snow chains. They attended a ranch bar mitzvah and a vow renewal and a Day of the Dead celebration, all of which were treated as secular cultural events rather than religious ones. Then it was a straight stretch until the new year, which afforded an opportunity to begin nesting in Marlo's hobbit house, because Wolf's new house was only half-built. And all the while the wall grew higher, stone by stone.

Kenneth's mysterious workforce reappeared from time to time, shipping in materials and laboring at the property's far reaches until the wan sun dipped below the horizon. The wall even straddled the river and the two creeks that bisected the property, although it didn't restrict their flow—the stone was fashioned in thick arches above the water, and Marlo had heard there were plans to install grated gates into the arches like in medieval times, she supposed as a measure of extra security. All other construction and repair projects had been put on hold. The skeleton of Wolf's future abode haunted its bleak concrete slab, a sad armature of beams and scaffolding and rebar, girdled by a moat of icy mud. But Wolf didn't seem to mind. Whenever Marlo tried to talk to others about the wall, even Wolf, she was met with obfuscation or blankness. In the end, she didn't have the energy to maintain a one-woman protest when no one else seemed to think there was anything wrong. There was no trap tightening, she consoled herself. How could there be, if everyone she loved failed to feel its grip?

At the same time, and in the same peacekeeping spirit, she made another decision: to cease discussing the possibility of Wolf and her leaving the ranch. She told herself she'd take it up again down the road, but the truth was that Wolf's arguments had begun to stick. Staying on the ranch was their only hope, he would insist. He'd gently remind her how good she had always had it here, how kind and egalitarian everyone on the ranch was, in contrast to the Disaster, where life was miserable for a vast swath of people, and the levers of power were controlled by kleptocrats and sociopaths. He would concede that yes, giant walls were bad in principle, but, "In this case, I think of it more as liberation. You can't imagine how amazing it is to be free of the psychopaths and corporatist craven assholes and sycophants and bad opinion-havers out there."

"But what about the regular people out there, having to live with the psychopaths and corporatists and the rest?" Marlo would counter, not entirely with innocent motives. "Those blameless victims of late-stage capitalism. Don't you feel bad for them?"

That was the only reliable crack in his zealotry. She could tell being accused of an empathy deficit ran counter to his idea of himself. But in the end, tribalism trumped all else. As long as some of them were safe, that was better than no one being safe, he declared. Marlo certainly didn't need any extra tuition in *that* philosophy. She'd grown up listening to self-righteously selfish lectures like that her whole life.

The furthest he'd go was to acknowledge occasionally that the ranch had its problems. He urged her to think about how miraculous it was, how in building this community the ranchers had largely eliminated the key ills of society: patriarchy, racism, misogyny, homophobia, rampant inequality. Wasn't it extraordinary, the chance to live in such a world? These were all difficult things to argue against, and in truth Marlo no longer felt the burning desire to leave that she had before Wolf came along.

Just before Christmas, four new ranchers arrived: Kerry and Jenny, the lesbian couple from New York, and two people Marlo had never heard of before, Darsh and Carrie Patel. Darsh was an old friend of Kenneth (pre-vetted, which was always useful for fast-tracking a new recruit), a Silicon Valley refugee who'd been a rising star at Tesla and was an expert on new-gen batteries. In a short, terse pitch at a hastily arranged November meeting, Kenneth assured the ranchers that Darsh would be an invaluable addition to the community: not only was he fabulously wealthy and looking to invest almost all his net worth into the ranch, but his wife Carrie was an oncologist, which would add another vital medical expert to their ranks. The couple had no children, which made some faces in the audience fall—there had been an agreement that young couples with young children would be prioritized going forward—but Kenneth felt the other skills they brought to the table more than compensated for their multigenerational lack.

She knew Kenneth had always been keen to find a better way to store and distribute solar, to cut off their remaining reliance on the public power grid. What better way to effect that, than to invite some solar tech genius to come and stay? She would have liked to talk with him about the new arrivals, but Kenneth continued to engage her in only the bare minimum of communication whenever their paths crossed, and she knew he couldn't even stand to look at Wolf. On the occasions when she did see him, though, he looked happier, less worried, as if some last puzzle piece had finally been located.

Darsh and Carrie moved into a temporary home, a two-bedroom split-level house recently vacated when one of the ranchers had to fly to Houston to nurse a sick relative. The blueprints were already being drawn up for their permanent lodgings, a decidedly more grandiose pile a half mile from the Commons, set in a clearing surrounded by birch trees that Marlo had always loved. Construction was due to start in the bitter throes of January. When Marlo was browsing in the library one day, she decided to take a look at the blueprints, which were always put on display for several months when a new building was in the works. Every rancher had a right to lodge objections or make suggestions, and these would be discussed at the meetings. In all her time there, she'd never heard of a rancher being denied permission to build something— the worst that might happen would be a requirement that someone add another exit or adjust sight lines if there were privacy issues. There was a second set of blueprints displayed next to the ones describing the Patels' future home. They were marked "Hospital." Marlo studied them with interest. Later, when she mentioned them to her father, he confirmed what she had already gleaned.

"Yes, we're building an ambitious new medical building. It's going to be very exciting. Quite state-of-the-art, really, for our Little House on the Prairie community here."

"*We're* building? Who's we, Dad? I thought these things were supposed to be put to a vote."

"Oh, it will be, honey, of course. These are just the initial plans. A sketch, if you will. It's on the agenda for whenever we hold the next meeting, actually."

"So what's the deal, exactly?"

"The idea is that it greatly increases our ability to treat the residents in-house, without having to rely on the outside hospital system. Of course there's no way we can reproduce a full-scale hospital, but the

241

hope is to install enough equipment to handle most, uh, situations. So an operating theater, an X-ray suite with a CT scanner, mammogram machine, chemotherapy supplies. That kind of thing. We've already got the means to carry out a lot of simple functions: vaccinations, vitamin boosters, even childbirth, should it ever come to that again. Carrie is going to advise us on what she thinks we need for a basic setup. Of course we'll still need to buy supplies and drugs. But we're trying to develop a high-tech storage system that means we could stockpile medical supplies for a long time. At least that's what Darsh says might be possible. Brilliant young man and woman. What a gift to the ranch."

"Wow, that's incredible. Sounds expensive."

He chuckled. "Naturally. That part isn't really the problem."

"What is the problem, then?"

"The usual." He sighed and stretched his right leg in front of him, rubbed the thigh ruefully. "Not enough trained medical professionals to staff it. Although Carrie's arrival will help alleviate that. Still, we can't expect her to bear the entire burden of ministering to one hundred aging people."

"We could train people. Especially ones who already have some scientific background. Wasn't Brett a vet at some point? Or am I just thinking that because it rhymes?"

They both laughed.

"That's the idea. Train up some of the ranchers to assist Carrie, until we can recruit some more doctors and specialists."

"Is there a particular reason this is happening now?"

"What do you mean? I'd say this has been in the works for a long time actually, love. Since you were a little girl. These things take time."

"Of course. It just all feels kind of . . . reactionary, I guess."

He reached over to stroke her hair and deliver one of his soothing smiles.

"Well, there's plenty to react *to*, if we're going to be totally honest. You know what's happening out there. If anything, this is overdue."

"Sure," said Marlo chirpily, answering his reassuring smile with one of her own. "Better to be safe than sorry."

She said it without thinking, but the creaky aphorism sounded suddenly ominous to her ears, as if after all there had only ever been a binary choice between safety and regret.

25

She blinked, took a moment to try to orient herself. The light was slanting in through the sheer curtain in such a way that she could tell it was still early, before seven. The sun had only recently risen—even the cheeping of the birds in the trees outside sounded sleepy, not yet in full voice. She closed her eyes again, stretched out the full length of her body beneath the sheet, then turned her head from side to side. When she opened her eyes again her unfocused gaze landed on her side-table drawer, half-open. Inside, among the books and reading glasses and bottle of ibuprofen and other ephemera of the sleep-adjacent world, something bright and white caught her eye. She flopped a lazy arm out from under the sheet, rummaged in the drawer, and pulled it out. It was a white feather. She'd almost forgotten where it came from, and then it came crashing back, the portentous events of last spring, before she'd even known Wolf existed. A year had passed since she had found the dead bald eagles; an entire year and the world hadn't gone up in flames or sunk beneath the waves. That was something.

There was a weight gently pressing on her calf, and when she looked down the length of her body, chin tucked into the fold of the sheet, she saw that Wolf was already up and half-dressed, his left hand the source of the weight. He wasn't looking at her but his phone, and there was an intensity to the way he stared at the screen that caused a familiar anxiety to crest up through her throat. She sat up too abruptly and tiny discs of light danced in front of her eyes. The sheet fell away, and Wolf reflexively looked over, but it wasn't her nakedness that preoccupied him. Not this time. His eyes drilled into hers, and he gave a tiny, almost imperceptible shake of his head.

"What is it?" she asked, her voice thick and unwieldy.

"I got a message from a friend. It's starting."

He opened his mouth to fill her in, but she shook her hair across her face, held up an admonishing hand. "You know what? On second thought, I need coffee before I deal with, well, whatever is happening in there." She gestured in disgust at the phone, as though it were the instigator of the crisis rather than the neutral instrument of its message.

She brandished the white feather in his face to demonstrate she was surrendering, then threw off the sheet and bounded out of bed and out of the room before Wolf could furnish any more details. She knew it was childish, this desire to delay bad news, but even an extra few minutes of ignorance felt worth negotiating.

As she padded around the kitchen topless, making coffee, she heard Wolf enter the kitchen, scrape one of the barstools back. She glanced briefly at him, sitting and waiting for her in silence, and she felt the agitation that coursed beneath the silence like an underground river. The silence continued as she poured the water in, lined the little plastic well with a paper filter, scooped the coffee grounds in, and hit the button. It stretched on as she got two mugs down from the cabinet, poured a dribble of milk in each, and stood with her butt pressed against the bench, arms crossed over her breasts, waiting for the coffee to start its drip, drip, drip. If there had been a clock on the wall, it would have ticked into the silence. But there was no clock, just their breathing and the labors of the coffee maker. Finally, after what might have been a million years, the jug was full. She poured the coffee into the mugs and placed one in front of Wolf. She stood on the other side of the bar holding her mug in front of her belly like a shield. What she really would have liked was to be separated from the news that lay on his tongue, waiting. She sighed, took a sip of coffee.

"So tell me."

His mouth pulled into a grim asymmetrical grin, then he took in a dose of air through his nostrils.

"So there's been a huge die-off in crops from California to Mexico. Completely gone, like literally the whole breadbasket of the country, both countries. Some blight killed them all virtually overnight."

"Oh, my god. What kind of blight?"

"No one really knows. They're trying to work it out. And it's not just North America. Parts of Europe and the Middle East are reporting the same thing."

She came around to his side of the bar, leaned her head on his shoulder while she stared down at the screen displaying the *New York Times* banner headline.

WORLD FOOD SUPPLY THREATENED

There were always things like this—scares, small signals of a slow-moving doom—but this time the alarm bells were clanging loudly.

"How is that even possible?"

"They're all the same seed stock, that's how." He spoke fast, the words tumbling out. He was eager to share the knowledge he'd been stockpiling. "GMO, man. Some disease or I-don't-know-what got into them and wiped it all out. They're genetically identical, so no chance that any of the crops would survive it."

"What about the regular non-GMO crops, though? They're OK, surely?"

Wolf shook his head. "There are problems there too. There's so little biodiversity now, something like this was bound to happen sooner or later. And that's not all that's happening. There's a huge algae bloom in several reservoirs in the Northern Hemisphere. Water sources for hundreds of thousands of people completely contaminated. There are already riots in some places. Panic buying. Supermarket shelves wiped clean. It's probably an overreaction, but . . ."

"Fuck."

"The *Times* is saying this is going to have severe effects on the global food supply. There's a real chance of widespread famine sometime this year. And not just in the usual places."

"Fuck."

"I know."

There didn't seem much more to say after that, so they sat in silence side by side, holding hands as they finished their coffee. It occurred to Marlo that this might be the last batch of coffee beans they'd ever drink. But it didn't help to think like that.

They couldn't stop holding hands, all through the remainder of that day and even into the emergency meeting the following day. In their fledgling relationship they'd never really been hand-holders. Marlo had always disliked the inevitable sweating and slipping of palms. They'd always been more inclined to sling arms around one another or subconsciously maneuver so that other parts of their bodies brushed together: thighs, shoulders, knees. But this situation seemed to demand a more committed engagement of the flesh. Holding hands felt like solidarity in a way that an arm flung around a waist never could. She noticed, looking around at the residents assembled for the meeting, that several other people were doing the same thing, clasping hands together with family members or even other ranchers to whom they weren't related—but they all were related really, weren't they? A crisis in the outside world threw that into relief.

"Well." Carlton stood at the podium, waiting for the room's attention to redirect his way. While he waited he transferred his weight gently from leg to leg, as though unable to commit to a stance. The room finally quieted down as the community came to the realization that the meeting was about to start. People elbowed and nudged and shushed one another, especially the delinquent ranchers who insisted on finishing whatever they were talking about. "Thanks for coming, everyone. I was talked into chairing this meeting, since we still haven't appointed a newsperson, which I can't say I'm completely happy about. I guess it's not an exaggeration to say that the eleventh hour has finally arrived."

The eleventh hour. Wolf, staring in transfixion at Carlton, squeezed Marlo's hand. He didn't have to say anything; she was certain the whole room could feel the solemn power of those words. It reverberated through their bodies.

"By now you're all aware of the events of the last few days out in the Disaster. Obviously it's very distressing, what's happening, but it's important that we all stay calm and concentrate on what we can do to safeguard the ranch."

A murmur of what sounded like agreement rippled around the room.

"The usual internet, uh, guidelines, are relaxed, so that everyone who wishes to can keep informed about the situation. Kenneth wanted me to update everyone on the agriculture situation at home. Our crops haven't been affected, which is a great relief obviously, and our water table is fine. We conducted some tests this morning. Kenneth will of course keep everyone apprised of any changes there. For the foreseeable future we'll be monitoring soil health, crops, and water every day. Oh, and one more thing I've been told to convey: security around the property is going to be upped for the time being, just in case things get, well, hairy out there. There's a volunteer sheet in the kitchen. We'd appreciate as many sign-ups as possible for the patrols. Let's see, what else?" He frowned down at his notes while the audience rumbled and muttered. "Oh, yes. So there was some debate about whether we'd still hold the spring picnic next week, but the consensus among the planning committee was that it should and will go ahead. So that's it from me. See you all at the picnic!"

His smile dissolved as soon as he stepped off the stage. Marlo and Wolf stayed for a little while after the meeting, and they weren't the only ones. Dozens of people milled around the Commons in a state of mass nervous excitement, discussing the crop devastation in high-pitched voices. Crises in the outside world always seemed to galvanize the ranchers, to perpetuate their innate belief that when the chips were down it was them against the rest of the world. The doomed world, to which they somehow didn't believe they belonged.

After a while Marlo couldn't stand it anymore and dragged Wolf away from a passionate discussion whose participants were speculating about which country's governments would collapse first (the conventional wisdom was that already-unstable regimes in North Africa, the Middle East, Southeast Asia, and Eastern Europe would crumble before the marginally more stable Americas and Western Europe). The intellectual detachment that characterized the fragments of conversation she overheard struck Marlo as lacking in compassion, and she and Wolf nearly got into a fight about it on the way home. He swore up and down that he was just as distressed about the events as she was, but that he had different ways of processing it. She wasn't sure she believed him, but, having no desire to add interpersonal fractures to geopolitical ones, she let it drop.

On the way back to her house, they visited the site for Wolf's new house, which had been developing rapidly since work on raising the wall had now been mostly finished. Kenneth had finally, grudgingly, allowed his workforce to be diverted from the supposedly crucial work of fortifying the ranch to projects of lesser importance. (Marlo couldn't imagine a project of lesser importance in Kenneth's eyes than building a new house for Wolf, whom he still considered illegitimate, an interloper—nevertheless, he had signed off on shifting a small labor force to complete the construction.)

She loved the delight Wolf found in watching the house take shape. Some of it was the sheer, primal pleasure of watching the creation of something beautiful out of nothing, of course, but there was more to it than that. He would never admit it, but there was a proprietorial thrill to ownership. His former self would have despised the notion, and Marlo was discreet enough not to remind him of that. Wolf had insisted on using every cent of the paltry amount of money his father had left in his will (most of it siphoned off to pay down his debts, anyway) to build the house, but they both knew the contribution was symbolic. The bulk of the budget—a considerable sum—had been put up by Marlo's parents. They stood for a while, watching the laborers hammering and plastering and shifting stones.

"Weird to think that one day that'll be our bedroom," said Wolf, watching a worker hammer in a window frame, the man's head appearing for a moment in the center of the frame as though he were posing for a portrait. Marlo turned to look at Wolf.

"*Our* bedroom?"

He dropped her hand—they had continued being joined in this way—in favor of pressing his arm around her shoulder, drawing her closer into his orbit.

"I want you to move in here with me when it's finished. What do you say?"

Marlo smiled. He looked so like a child waiting to see if his favorite pals would come to his birthday party.

"Well, sure. I'd love to. Thank you."

She dropped into a mocking curtsy, and he laughed, picked her up, and swung her around in triumph. A couple of the workers glanced over and then immediately looked away without changing expression. Marlo couldn't recall ever having seen one of Kenneth's army ever look fazed by anything. She wondered what would happen to them now. Did they worry about the blights sweeping their world? Or did catastrophic events fail to really shift the needle in their daily existence, which for most of them had always been difficult and limited by their economic circumstances? Perhaps this was finally the leveling of the playing field, when even the rich would be forced to suffer the consequences of a planet rebelling against the travesties perpetrated against it. It made her feel sad, that this might be what it took for egalitarianism to really take hold: the redistribution of devastation.

"We should raise a motion at the next meeting, to admit these workers and their families into the ranch," said Marlo impulsively. "Waive the fee. It seems unfair that they've helped build this place, and now we're leaving them at the mercies of the Disaster."

"That's a great idea," said Wolf. He looked into her face admiringly. "I love that you're always thinking about other people."

"I doubt it would ever pass, though," she said with glum certainty. "You may have noticed it's not exactly diverse around here."

Wolf looked confused. "Are you kidding? There are probably more races and orientations represented here than in my whole Los Angeles neighborhood. It's like a goddamn poster for diversity!"

Marlo sighed. "Ugh, no, I don't mean racially or anything like that. I mean socioeconomically. Everyone on the ranch is here because they have the money to be here."

"Well, except me."

"That's different."

"Is it?" He sounded a little wounded. "I'm just as unworthy as any other random out there."

"That's not true. You've earned your place here a million times over. And my parents paying for you to be here, how is that functionally any different from the fact that they've bankrolled me since day one, just for the happy accident of being their daughter? That's my whole point. It's an elite system that only rewards the already advantaged."

"I guess." He didn't sound convinced, but she could tell he was trying to be upbeat so as not to let anything ruin the magic of watching his house grow out of the earth, this everyday miracle with his name on it. "Hey!" He grabbed her hand again with a new, rabid eagerness. "Want to get married?"

She laughed, infected by his sudden ebullience. "What?"

"I mean it. Why not?"

Marlo thought for a moment. She shrugged. "No reason, I guess. Apart from the possible imminent demise of the planet."

"But don't you see, that's exactly why we should do it!"

"Fiddling-while-Rome-burns kind of thing?"

"Yes, fiddling. More fiddling!" He swung her around again, and she squealed loud enough to raise the heads of the workers and some nearby grazing cows alike. He put her down, and she smoothed her hair, shaking her head and trying not to laugh.

"You're an idiot, you know that?"

"Yes." He fell mock somber. "I am aware of this. Marry me anyway? But let's keep this whole thing modern. Don't make me get down in this mud."

"OK, OK." She raised her arms in surrender. "Let's do it."

They agreed to wait a few days before telling her parents. There was something unseemly about announcing happy news so soon after a global disaster, Marlo explained to Wolf, although they both knew she was just stalling. She wasn't sure what she was waiting for. She was filled with a strange, churning mix of euphoria and anxiety that felt like stage fright.

A series of texts arrived from Alex and Ben. The general reaction to the unraveling of the globe's food security was shock and panic, as far as Marlo could tell from the news, but the emotional weather was very different in Alex and Ben's world. She should have known. They weren't triumphant, exactly, but there was a calm, get-to-work pragmatism to their tone that suggested they had been expecting something like this for a long time. It chastened Marlo. Not only had her friends accurately predicted what was coming, but they had been actively preparing for it, and not by sealing themselves off from the world like the ranchers had.

This is it, they wrote her, *the tipping point.*

Riots quickly followed the panic buying and the empty supermarket shelves. Barricades had gone up in downtown Portland and other cities around the country, as if the government were preparing for some kind of confrontation.

Gee, wonder what they're scared of? Alex had written. *They've only had decades and history's greatest single accumulation of wealth to do something about all this.*

Are you guys safe? Marlo wrote fretfully once she'd read all their dispatches.

Of course, came Alex's answer. *If anything, Portland is better situated than most places to withstand a food shortage, for a while anyway. All those urban farms and vertical gardens and artisanal small-batch kids had the right idea, who'da thought? But things are going to start getting really bad.*

So what are you going to do? Marlo responded.

Everything we can. There are a bunch of collectives around the country who've been warning about this shit for years, and we've got plans underway already to replant on a vast scale, with non-GMO seeds this time. But it's going to take time obviously. There are other actions in the meantime. How are things there?

Marlo sketched for them a quick overview of the situation—the emergency meeting, the accelerated plans for ranch autonomy. She didn't mention her and Wolf's decision to marry. She worried her friends would be scathing, or find her frivolous. Alex and Ben didn't make any comment on the ranch's preparations. The next message was simply:

It's past time, Marlo, our dear friend—we need you out here.

Marlo wrote something and then deleted it. She stared at the screen, waiting for her friends' next words to appear.

Now or never, baby. Which brings me to the favor we want to ask you . . .

❧

After she had signed off, she went to find Wolf. She didn't intend to tell him everything, but she needed to get some of it out into the open. He was predictably appalled when she mentioned that Alex and Ben wanted her to leave the ranch and join them in the fight.

"Are you shitting me? They want you to go and join them now that the meltdown has started in earnest? Why on earth would you do that?"

Marlo shut her eyes for a moment, tried to channel the defiant moral certainty of her friends.

"Because it's cowardly to stay in here, inside the bubble, when I could be trying to help out there."

"Cowardly. That's what they said?"

"I happen to agree with them."

"They're lunatics, Marlo. They've got a death wish."

"You're wrong about them. They want you to come out as well."

"Wow, I'm so flattered. My big chance to be cannon fodder when World War Three breaks out."

"We can't just stay here forever."

"Why not? That's exactly what I want to do. I want to marry you, and then I want to live on this ranch forever."

"Even if the world outside is burning?"

"Especially then."

"And you think we'll be spared in here?"

"Listen, I've been trying to tell you this since I met you. There's nothing out in the Disaster for me. Less than nothing."

"Well, I think there's something out there for me."

"What, exactly?"

"I don't know. Call it a purpose. A meaning."

"Don't you see? Alex and Ben are just trying to seduce you into leaving like they did. What exactly is it they think you're going to be able to do? Why do they need you? I mean, you're amazing and everything and who wouldn't want you on their team, but it's not like one extra person can make any difference to this failed cause."

"Let's just say they think I have something valuable to bring."

She couldn't look at him when she said this—especially given the clandestine visits she'd been paying to the mausoleum over the last few weeks.

"Please, Marlo." She could hear the change of tack in his tone. "I'm not trying to talk you out of it on some intellectual level. This is just pure selfishness. I don't want you to leave. I need you. More than your friends do. More than the Disaster does."

How could she argue with that?

It was Wolf's idea to announce their engagement at the picnic, and Marlo had no objections. The spring tradition had always been a time of celebration on the ranch, a communal triumph at having outlasted winter's trials. Although the particular winter just behind them had been as mild as a lamb, full of disconcertingly balmy afternoons and snow that didn't stick. The two of them had taken to calling the engagement their *betrothal,* a way to make peace with taking seriously an institution that neither of them had really believed in before now. They bandied around the words *fiancé* and *affianced* as sly quips, to reassure each other they understood the absurdity of swapping vows within a gated community while storm clouds gathered outside. But even the worsening news from the Disaster wasn't entirely capable of tamping down the giddy joy Marlo felt at the idea of marrying Wolf. *It's just a formality,* she chastised herself. A piece of paper symbolizing a hopelessly anachronistic institution historically used to shore up alliances and consolidate wealth. Marriage no more defined love than net worth defined a person's value. So why did she feel a new and solemn devotion to him? Social conditioning, reason suggested. *Oh, shut up,* she told reason.

Even wrapped in her happiness, Marlo couldn't help noticing that the prevailing mood at the picnic struck a somber note. The sky was clear, but there was a gusty breeze that disarranged hairdos and snatched napkins off tables. Pollen counts were out of control—several allergic ranchers were felled before the day even began, retreating indoors with bottles of antihistamines. Nature felt out of kilter, as it had for weeks and months now. Acrid scents were carried to them on the breeze, like fires burning far away. The few children fretted and spoiled their outfits. Marlo's father complained of aching joints but declared he wouldn't miss the fun, even if it was more subdued in tone this year. Marlo thought of agrarian times, when the solstice festivals and harvest celebrations signified not just a changing of seasons or a chance to indulge, but the future fortunes of the community. A good crop could boost spirits, a bad one spell ruin. Entire societies once lived and died at the pleasure of droughts and monsoons. Perhaps they were returning to that time. Perhaps it wouldn't be so bad.

It was a tradition of sorts, after dessert had been devoured and the adults had reached the mellow-but-garrulous stage of intoxication, for someone to tap a glass and get the group's attention. Sometimes the person would raise a toast, or propose going around the tables declaring what they were thankful for, in an echo of the Thanksgiving rituals at the other end of the season. Sometimes there would be impromptu roasts of some hapless rancher (never mean-spirited, and only directed at those who could take it), or recitals of jokes or stories. Even songs, if someone had brought a guitar and enough of the ranchers felt in good voice. Occasionally there would be an announcement.

This year, Wolf stood up amid the wreckage of dessert scattered across wooden tables branded with wine-glass rings, rapped a fork against his glass to get the group's attention. It took a while. Marlo locked her hands tightly between her knees. She was too nervous to look at him or anyone else, so she concentrated on an ant making its patient, laborious way along the table in search of sustenance or building material. How overwhelmed it must feel, presented with such plenty. She and Wolf hadn't discussed how they would break the news, so she was gratified when he announced it in what she considered just the right way. Simple and heartfelt. Nondramatic.

"Some news." He called out once the chatter had simmered down and most eyes were directed his way. "Marlo and I have decided to get married."

The tables erupted with cheers and applause. Marlo looked up finally, faced the tidal wave of smiles with shy delight. Gratified to provide the source of such uncomplicated joy. Wolf felt it too: he leaned down to her and said with a laugh, "We should get married more often." She nodded wildly, unable to speak. The mood had turned in an instant from serious to jubilant. Marlo thought she understood: it was hard-wired, this bias to believe in signs suggesting that everything might be OK, after all, rather than those that suggested things were slipping, and fast. A wedding perpetuated the notion, however illusory, of normality. Her parents, seated down the end of the same table, were both crying. Marlo rose and walked as if in a trance to accept their happiness and congratulations. All along the way, people stretched out their hands to touch her clothes, as though she were a saint passing.

She enveloped herself in her father's embrace first, then her mother's, then somehow, with awkward clashings of elbows and chins, both of them.

"Finally, some good news," her mother said, brushing away tears.

"And Wolf," beamed her father, stretching out his arms to include his future son-in-law, who was hovering shyly just out of reach. They clapped each other on the shoulders in that awkward way of men, then mutually abandoned the protocols for a hug instead. "So looking forward to having you as part of the family, son."

"Thanks." It might have sounded gruff to a stranger, but Marlo could tell Wolf was choked up and didn't trust himself to say anything more profound. The rest of the evening was a blur of hugging and hand-shaking and shoulder-slapping and demands for more information. (Marlo and Wolf shrugged happily, not having any further information to offer.) Someone dragged a case of champagne out of the cellar, and a bathtub was filled with ice. The celebration went on into the night. At one point Marlo looked up at the sky, the mesh of stars, and felt like nothing was real. She sensed Wolf by her side constantly, yet he seemed more an idea than a corporeal presence.

Several times over the course of that surreal night she searched for Kenneth, anxious to see how he had reacted to the announcement. Part of her thought this would be an end to it, his unrequited yearning, that they could start again on a fresh landscape as friends and coconspirators. Now that she was staying on the ranch, especially as someone else's wife, he had to come to his senses, surely. Maybe he could finally find someone else to love. But Kenneth was nowhere to be seen.

26

"This is weird."

Marlo padded over to Wolf, slid her arms down his bare chest, and looked over his shoulder at the screen.

"Oh, god, what now?"

"Someone broke into this seed bank in Svalbard, Norway, yesterday and stole everything. Cleared it out. And then the same thing happened with the UK seed banks. Overnight raids. They don't know if it was coordinated. Some people are saying it's a terrorist attack."

Marlo stared at the screen. She could see her own blurred face and his reflected there, distorted and worn looking. Wolf craned his neck to look up at her.

"I guess I'd vaguely heard that there were seed vaults. Countries have them as a kind of insurance, right? But why would anyone break into one?"

Marlo struggled to keep her voice calm. "Either to replenish a destroyed seed stock or for leverage."

His face was quizzical; he wondered how she knew all this stuff. "What kind of leverage?"

She straightened up, kept her hands clamped down on his shoulders as she stared out the window, thinking.

"Hmm? Oh. Well, to use for extortion, I guess. Force a desperate government to fork over a ton of cash to get the seeds back."

"Seriously?" He sounded incredulous and not at all perturbed. She had to remind herself that he hadn't grown up around doomsday preppers, hadn't had it hammered into him what the true stakes were.

"I don't know. Just guessing." Better not to alarm him. Things were going bad fast enough now that it was necessary to ration some of the dire news. "Coffee?"

"Sure. Thanks, baby."

He beamed over his shoulder at her, and she saw that he'd already navigated away from the page and was reading something else. A new strain of affection pulsed through her as she gazed at him, so vulnerable and innocent-looking. The perilous task of loving someone, how it threw into stark relief your inability to protect them.

❦

In the weeks that followed the picnic a new solemnity dawned. When they showered together the morning after the announcement, Marlo found herself turning suddenly shy, soaping her breasts and between her legs with her back half-turned to him. Shaving his face under the jet he remarked, "I love this shower." He stuck his tongue into his cheek to create a smoother surface, ran the blade across his skin while he looked around admiringly, at the Spanish-tiled walls and the huge shower head that created the effect of standing beneath a waterfall and the round window through which they could see the branches of the maple tree nodding. As always these days, Marlo made an effort to scrutinize her familiar surroundings intently, trying to see it all through his eyes.

"Mmm," she said.

"You should have seen the bathroom at my parents' place. In Hollywood."

"What was it like?" She pictured palm trees against a blazing sky, stark white letters spelling out a message of hope against the hill. This was new, him volunteering information about his family life. Wolf stuck his face under the water. When he emerged from the deluge, he opened his eyes again and said quietly, "It was unspeakable. One of those cheap, nasty molded plastic shower units, like they make for trailers. Mildew caked in all the cracks. Bugs occasionally, especially after Mom left. Like a horror movie. The whole house was like that, more or less. Like, the kind of house a location scout in Hollywood would set-dress to depict a low-income family whose father was a secret drug dealer. Funny that."

"I'm sorry." Those shopworn words so inadequate.

"It was OK when I was a kid. I mean, it wasn't, but you don't notice things like that so much when you're a kid. Whatever your predicament is, you kind of accept it as immutable fact, right? Like, I just accepted not having siblings as the normal state of affairs, even though all my friends had them. But being an only child, I was kind of a weird loner."

"I wouldn't know anything about that," she teased. He smiled, but he wasn't even looking at her, immersed in the reel playing in his head.

"Did I tell you about the time a cricket got into the bathroom?" He didn't look for an answer, because of course he hadn't told her about the cricket. Their relationship so far had been lived almost entirely in the present and future tense. The few times he had alluded to events from his past had only added to her sense of unease about how little she really knew him.

"There was a torn wire screen that my dad was always promising to fix, and these louvered glass windows, and it must have flown in through the gap. It took up residence in the shower stall. And I kind of befriended it." He laughed ostentatiously so she'd know he knew it was foolish. "I tried to set it free at first, but I'd balance it on my finger and try to encourage it to fly out the window and it would just sit there. Looking at me with its buggy little cricket eyes. So I just let it stay in the shower. I'd look for it every morning, to make sure it had survived the night."

"What happened to it?" she asked, inexplicably anxious. "It didn't die, did it?"

He shrugged and returned to the present moment, bright-eyed but with something harder in his gaze. "One day it just wasn't there anymore."

"Oh. I'm sorry."

For reasons she didn't quite understand, his story made her feel bereft. Guilty, too, somehow. She yearned to run into the fields and find him a new replacement cricket. As if such things could be replaced. Her childhood had been so different, any moments of solitude orchestrated at her own behest. Whenever she had wanted company there had been dozens of people to talk to, both fellow kids (Alex and Ben had always felt like a better version of siblings to her) and the kinds of adults who treated children like autonomous beings whose utterances and desires were considered as valid as their own. She had run wild and free, a proper childhood.

That evening they took a bottle of wine out to the garden, lay with their bodies pressed together on the grass, taking turns drinking and kissing. The sky turned from silver to lavender.

"The parade begins," said Wolf. He still found it fascinating, the nightly dance, with its strict codes of succession, and Marlo had begun to see the wonder of it too. First the mosquitoes and tiny bugs, then as evening swept over the world the swallows would enter, darting and swooping after their prey, their bodies stamping neat black *W*s against the sky, then when the swallows departed the bats would arrive, skittering and chirping. Skinny tongues of lightning flickered every now and then in the blueberry sky.

"You're so beautiful," he murmured, nuzzling his face into her hair, masking himself in her. "I can't even stand it."

Her entire body seemed to swell as she sucked in air. They were incandescent under the moonlight. As Marlo stroked Wolf's warm arm, she marveled at her luck: she had always been resigned to the idea that she would need to go questing to find love, and instead it had come to find her. Remember this, Marlo thought, remember that this was the beginning.

27

She had so few cultural guidelines to draw on when it came to marriage. Womanhood, a largely unexamined state in her life prior to this moment, suddenly demanded further scrutiny. Would its mysteries suddenly be revealed when she publicly fused her life to another's? Would she be required to sacrifice some portion of her autonomy? Some days it felt ridiculous, this planning a wedding, like the war brides and grooms who desperately gambled that love might outlast catastrophe. Every married couple on the ranch had passed into that state decades ago: their certificates were artifacts from a different time.

Some of the older ranchers still nurtured sentimental notions about the institution, solemnly marking anniversaries and displaying photographs in their hallways that depicted only vaguely recognizable couples: the women billowing in white tulle, the men straitjacketed into stovepipe pants and tuxedo shirts. The hippie types had eschewed marriage back in the 1960s and '70s as an outdated hazard, a leftover of the patriarchy. Anyone younger than middle-aged tended to be agnostic on the question. Kenneth, for instance, had shrugged the only time Marlo had asked him if he intended to ever get married again. "Not if I can help it," he had growled, but his bright eyes gave her to understand he'd reconsider under the right circumstances. Alex and Ben of course famously despised marriage as a bourgeois distraction. She understood in principle that marriage—or more specifically, the wedding that preceded a marriage—was a big deal out in the Disaster. Although marginally aware of the wedding-industrial complex, she hadn't grown up in its shadow, so its intensity came as something of a shock.

🌿

In those weeks leading up to the wedding, she looked at dresses, so many dresses, and imagined she smelled the briny sea on the wind, although they were more than a hundred miles from the ocean. The dresses were all for her mother, really. Her own interest was feigned, but she feigned it for tender reasons. In secret she had already decided on a simple green gown that she planned to have delivered, sight unseen, from a department store on the other side of the country. But that had been before the food crisis and the sickening stock market correction out in the Disaster. Even if the department stores were still shipping, it seemed frivolous and wrong to care about something like a dress. She knew she could borrow something from one of the ranchers: many of the women had closets full of mothballed expensive gowns from their previous lives.

But she went along with it because she could see the planning brought her mother an unexpected joy, or if not unexpected, at least secretly longed for. If her mother was using the wedding as a coping mechanism, a way to keep anxiety about the state of the world at bay, who could really blame her? The news from outside was a garbage fire of bad signs, and getting worse. Easier all around to reimpose a news blackout. Instead, mother and daughter huddled over magazines and web pages and endless cups of Earl Grey tea and earnest discussions of napkin border design, consulting on the details of the day, and it filled Marlo with a doting love—ironically, a maternal kind of love—to see her mother so animated by the prospect of a wedding.

"And here I'd always thought you were the model of a modern feminist," Marlo teased.

"I think I'm allowed to be excited about my only daughter's wedding," Maya said without rancor. She stroked Marlo's hair absentmindedly as she bookmarked a page. An ersatz bride swamped by a strapless white confection; a woman drowning in frothed cream. Marlo's eyes widened. The enthusiasm was contagious, though. If anything, Carlton was even more excited than his wife about the upcoming nuptials. He had an endearing habit of rubbing his palms together when he was anticipating something pleasant. *You're going to invent fire if you keep rubbing your hands together like that, Dad,* Marlo admonished him affectionately. But it warmed her heart that the news had smoothed some of the worry lines away.

All the while, Wolf stood off to the side, diplomatically staying out of this hallowed space. He fretted about whether to buy a ring, but that was where Marlo drew the line. No gems paid for with the blood of modern-day slaves. She'd read the articles. One of the ranchers, Michael, a jeweler in his previous life, offered to make them a set of identical white-gold bands, simple and unadorned. This, Marlo would agree to. She imagined them being forged in a furnace and hammered on an anvil as sparks danced, although she guessed that wasn't how it worked these days. But in this stormy, bewitched season anything felt possible.

One day when she was walking near the front gates, she stopped to watch a fleet of rancher vehicles—trucks and larger SUVs—returning to the ranch, their back seats and beds loaded to the brim with boxes and crates. She stopped to watch them drive by, unsettled in some way she couldn't name by the urgency with which the drivers rocketed through the gates and down the drive, kicking up nebulae of dust. The last car in was driven by Jamal, an affable former geneticist who had lately become fast friends with Wolf. Marlo flagged him down, and he swiveled his head at the movement. She thought he looked reluctant as he slowed and wound the window down.

"Hey, kiddo," he said, glancing once in the rearview mirror, then squinting up at her. "What you up to?"

"Not much. Just out for a walk. Where have you guys all come from? And what's all this stuff?" Marlo made a cave for her eyes and peered through the tinted windows of his car. Jamal glanced toward the back seat, as though only noticing the pileup of goods blocking his rear vision for the first time.

"Oh, this. Just a supply run. Stocking up on bulk provisions. Stuff we might not be able to get later."

"You mean later in the year?" She was being deliberately obtuse, but Jamal didn't blink. She wished he would say something to help banish the feeling of dread the caravan of black cars had woken in her. The ranchers rarely did supply runs in groups: it was usually one or two cars at the most.

"More like insurance in case we need to get more self-sufficient." He had a soothing voice that when blended with the purr of his well-tuned engine created a kind of hypnotic white noise in her head.

"What's happening in town? How's the mood outside?"

Jamal ran a hand across his mouth. "Well." He seemed to deliberate for a few moments. Gnats wove a pattern in the air in front of Marlo's face. She swatted them away, and they returned almost instantaneously, infuriating in their dedication. The drumbeat of dread started up again under the ribs. She could see that beneath his tranquil exterior Jamal was shaken, and it frightened her. "There were a few things," he said carefully, not quite meeting her eye. "Some broken shop windows and a burned-out barn. Some of the stores were low on supplies."

"Oh," said Marlo. She stepped closer to the car to better hear him. He looked as though he had more to say. She rested her hand on the warm door panel, leaned in, and looked intently at Jamal's face. He hesitated for a moment.

"I don't know if I'm supposed to tell anyone just yet." Jamal blinked rapidly a few times, sorting through his thoughts. "But fuck it, everyone will find out soon, anyway. You've read about that new strain of bird flu they found recently?"

Marlo shook her head.

"Well, it turned up in a few locations around the world some months back. China, Russia, somewhere in South America, I think. And then reports came in about cases in Florida and Colorado and New York. Frankly, everyone thought it would kill a few people and then die down, like it has in the past."

"But it hasn't."

"Seems not. Apparently a few cases turned up last week in town. One person already dead, the others in pretty bad shape from what we could gather." He glanced up again at her face, gauging her reaction to see whether he should clam up, but Marlo kept her face blank: she knew that was the only way to get him to continue. "Most of the people in town are wearing those surgical masks. The people that are actually prepared to get out on the streets, that is. A lot of businesses were shut. It was like a ghost town. Pretty creepy."

"Are you guys all OK?"

"Oh, sure."

"Do you think it's going to spread? Is this the beginning of the pandemic they've been warning about?"

Jamal met her eye, gave a small but decisive shake of his head, and relief coursed through her. "It's probably just overreaction. You know how people get." He was one of those people who were born to reassure. He had a way with the horses, could calm down even the most skittish of them with a few words. She shot him a grateful, fragile smile, but he didn't return it, just squinted at a point behind her shoulder, his mouth twisting on something.

"There's something else, isn't there?"

"Well." He ran a hand through his wiry hair, cropped so neat on his well-shaped skull. "It was just that when we came out of the hardware store, someone had slashed the rear tires of my car." As if to reassure someone—Marlo? Himself?—he quickly added, "I mean, I'm sure it was just kids, just a prank. We got a new set put on quickly enough. No real harm. But it kind of weirded us out."

They looked at one another for a few moments, a span of time whose tempo felt guided by the low humming of the animal engine beneath the hood. Abruptly, Jamal gave a curt nod, as if they had come to a grim but satisfactory understanding. He saluted her solemnly, rolled up the window, and drove on.

As she cut through the sage grass on her way home, she passed Jane driving the mobile chicken coop to another location. She was a widowed social science professor who had taught Marlo through most of her school years. Now in her sixties, Jane—still Mrs. Kransky to Marlo—cut an austere but attractive figure, with her long neck and bobbed silver hair bright as a coin in the sunlight. She dressed more demurely than anyone Marlo had ever met—shirts buttoned to her neck, full skirts that grazed her ankles–but the effect was less ascetic than elegant. Even for this dirty outdoors work she wore a smocked white tunic over the top of her trousers. Jane (Marlo had to make an effort not to think of her as Mrs. Kransky) raised an unadorned hand in greeting, but they didn't speak, couldn't have been heard over the biodiesel roar of the engine. What a relief that the ranchers had several years ago perfected the distilling of biofuel, enough to run the farm machinery on indefinitely without ever having to rely on gas stations. She thought about those chickens coming home to roost out in the Disaster. Except that maybe there wouldn't be chickens anymore, once the next pandemic swept the world's poultry farms and pig factories, and the public realized that the last-resort antibiotics had failed long ago and there was nothing now standing between humanity and the next plague.

Some news had filtered through the bubble: there had been more rioting, but mostly restricted to the far-flung, below-the-fold destinations where riots had become a kind of grim recurring calendar appointment anyway. Some civil unrest in high-density cities and plenty of anger in areas that depended on agricultural subsidies. But mostly people appeared to be meeting the crisis by hunkering down. Waiting to see what came next. It had been a comfort previously, knowing that there weren't gangs of townsfolk gathering on their borders with shotguns. Yet. But if there really was a pandemic, and the world's food systems couldn't be saved from collapse, how long before the catastrophe's tide seeped into even their little utopia? It felt foolish, offensive even, to be planning a wedding under that cloud. As if reading her mind, an actual cloud crossed the sun at that moment, spilling a puddle of shade in her path. She shivered and hurried her stride.

❦

She received a text message over breakfast.

Can we speak soon if you have time?

A queer flutter in her chest. It was from Kenneth. They had barely spoken over the last few weeks, since Wolf had announced the engagement. Marlo would see him seething at the back of the room during community gatherings or studiously avoiding her eye while he worked in the fields. He hadn't offered congratulations or even acknowledgement, and she tried not to be stung by his shunning. She glanced up guiltily at Wolf, as if he might have gleaned the message telepathically, but of course he sat opposite her completely unperturbed, forking scrambled eggs into his mouth with his habitual dreamy morning detachment. He was one of those people to whom there was no point even trying to talk before 9:00 a.m.

Marlo dropped her phone into her lap, casually tapped back a response.

Sure, of course. Let me know when works for you.

A surge of gladness rushed in at hearing from him. The vain part of her was sure he wanted to talk about his feelings about her impending marriage, to openly declare his love finally and . . . what? Gallantly doff his hat to her paramour to demonstrate his acceptance that the better man had won, then ride off into the sunset? That fantasy didn't exactly jibe with the Kenneth she knew. More likely that he might try to dissuade her from the wedding with exhortations of it being too soon, or inappropriate when the world was falling apart. She began to bristle at the prospect of enduring a sanctimonious lecture, her initial pleasure at his message dissipating. If only he could accept Wolf into his life, maybe even embrace him someday—her imagination raced ahead to some gauzy future time when Kenneth would gruffly but with obvious pleasure accept the role of godfather to their first child. This vision, which wavered and dissolved as rapidly as it had come on, was so absurd she laughed aloud and wondered if she was coming down with something. If there was one thing she knew about Kenneth, it was that his unchangeable list of enemies ran deep. Oh, well. Perhaps they would find a more practical peace.

She agreed to meet Kenneth at the biodome the following day after lunch. She didn't see the point in telling Wolf about this meeting. It would only make him suspicious, and he would naturally assume Kenneth hoped to talk Marlo out of the wedding. She dressed carefully the next morning, singing softly at her own reflection. Skinny jeans, a loose white T-shirt, a little makeup so that her face was both fresh and radiant, hair straight and hanging loose over her shoulders. It was important to make the right impression: nothing sexy (that would be cruel), but just pretty enough that he might feel one last pang of regret at what could never be his (she was allowed the occasional narcissistic detour, surely).

As soon as she arrived at the biodome, she realized her ploy had worked all too well: the hungry, anguished way Kenneth looked at her, quickly up and down and then away, made her chastise herself for ever wanting to appear alluring to him. He radiated nervousness, thrusting his hands into his pockets and tugging them out as if he'd forgotten what to do with them when they weren't employed in some form of labor. It pulled at her heart to see him so miserable. She made a silent vow to be gentle with him, no matter what.

"Thanks for coming, Marl." Running his tongue over cracked lips.

"Of course," she said with a wide smile, already rehearsing her gracious response.

"There's something I need to tell you."

His face was an abject mask of discomfort, like he couldn't wait to get the confession over and done with. In that moment she guessed what he was here to tell her: that he was leaving the ranch to make his life somewhere else, with someone else. She prepared to permit herself a brief sentimental moment of regret and affection (how sad it would be to see him go, how much she would miss him, but also in the end how it was for the best for everyone) before the actual words he was saying filtered into her consciousness.

"Your parents bribed Wolf into coming here."

"What?" She blinked at him, her old friend whose face was burning and whose huge shoulders were tensed up under his checked shirt as if he were straining to keep his balance in a strong gust. The veins bulged blue and ropy in his arms. He didn't answer. "What are you talking about? Bribed him with what?"

Kenneth stared at her in consternation, and it took her a while to realize that he thought she understood and was just trying to make him say it aloud.

"No, really, I don't understand what you mean. What is it you think they bribed him with?"

"With you."

The greenhouse contracted around them. For a moment she thought she was dreaming this, as she had so often dreamed about walking through the biodome, its alien phosphorescence both familiar and haunting. A strange noise erupted from her chest—a strangled laugh of disbelief. Kenneth hung his head and then lifted it again, as though willing himself to go through with it.

"Me."

"I know it's hard to hear this. But no one else is going to tell you. Your folks desperately want you to stay and make a life here on the ranch. Give them some grandchildren. Start the next generation."

"So?"

A flicker of irritation broke through his hangdog expression then. He had never been tolerant of people willfully refusing to face facts. She used to find that endearing.

"You think it's some coincidence that this Wolf guy arrived just as you were thinking about leaving?" There was spite in his face now.

"You're out of your mind. You're saying my parents paid Wolf to, what? Seduce me so I'd want to stay on the ranch? Like some kind of . . . arranged marriage or something?"

He shrugged. "I'm not saying it was some big evil conspiracy."

"You must think I'm pretty dumb if you seriously think I'd believe that."

He looked at her sadly. "I don't think you're dumb at all. And you don't have to believe it."

"You're lying." But she wasn't so sure now. Hadn't in fact been sure as soon as Kenneth started talking. It engulfed her with shame, knowing that she could love someone as fiercely as she loved Wolf and yet so readily believe the worst of him. Kenneth shrugged again.

"I guess there's only one way to find out. Ask your boyfriend."

"I wouldn't insult him like that."

"Fine. Whatever story you have to tell yourself. As long as you're happy."

"Fuck you, Kenneth."

He looked at her as if she'd stabbed him, then shook his head slowly, like a warning. She didn't care. She felt wild and incandescent with rage. She felt she could shatter the glass around her, bury them both in a hailstorm of deadly shards.

"Oh, *wait*. Yeah, that's exactly what you always wanted, for me to fuck you. Is that what this is about?"

Kenneth took a step toward her and then stopped. Stepped back to where he had been. Afterward, long after the rage had simmered away, leaving behind only a sickening scum of loathing for everything and everyone around her, she wondered what he had been planning to do in that moment. Hit her? Kill her? Kiss her? Not that it mattered.

"I've got an idea," Kenneth said calmly, as if everything he was saying were entirely reasonable. "Why don't we go and ask him? Settle this."

"I don't think so."

"Suit yourself."

She knew then. That even if she refused him now, the day and the hour would come when she would need to confront Wolf about it, pray that he had a really good story and have Kenneth there to witness it. Why not now, then? A nauseating sense of the inevitability of this encounter fell over her mind like a smothering blanket. She looked deep into her old friend's faded blue eyes, rimmed with red as though he hadn't slept. Faded, washed out, washed up—just like Kenneth himself. So different from her beloved Wolf, whose eyes were the kind you could drown in. Which, actually, was probably only a good thing if you considered drowning romantic. Cast that thought away. She could feel her own eyes flashing as though she had lasers inside. She could tell Kenneth was a little scared of her. She was scared of herself. Maybe scared of what she might find, or be forced to find.

In the early days of the ranch, someone had instituted a weekly wellness session in a long wooden pavilion overlooking the foothills, for anyone who wanted to join. Yoga, meditation, drum circles; the therapies varied, and the sessions soon became irregular, but somehow the practice had survived the years. Especially during times of global strife, many ranchers found solace there, a chance to alleviate the stresses of modern life. Sometimes there were instructors leading the way, ranchers who had been yoga teachers or gym instructors or had simply adhered to mindful living in a previous life. Sometimes the pavilion had only two, three, or four occupants. Occasionally Marlo had been the only one, stretching in a parallelogram of sunlight like a cat.

She tried to reap the fruits of those years practicing silence and stillness now, as she and Kenneth embarked on the grim, silent drive in the golf cart back to her house. It had taken years, but she had become fairly adept at clearing her mind on demand, visualizing brushing away the chaos and ushering in serenity and emptiness. It took everything she had to summon that blankness in her mind now. Panic demanded to be let in. Who was she even angry at: Kenneth? Wolf? Her parents? The amorphous fury waited to be told where to deploy. She breathed deeply in and out through her nostrils. It didn't help.

As they rumbled along the road—both of Kenneth's hands gripping the wheel, although she'd never known him to drive any way but one-handed—she had a chance to scrutinize her surroundings. They passed the back of Jamal and his wife's home. A jade-green lawn, newly mowed, sloped gently down to the road. If you knew where to look it was plain to see, the subtle divot in the grass that traced a large rectangle. From an aerial perspective it might have looked like a crop circle, exciting potential evidence of aliens, but it really just meant a concrete bunker lay beneath there. A precaution, like the basement at her parents' house, where Wolf had hidden out. It was no good. Every thought threaded its way back to Wolf.

They arrived outside her house all too soon. Kenneth turned off the ignition and began to hoist his body out of the vehicle, but when he saw that Marlo hadn't moved, he shifted back into his seat. They sat together in silence for a moment, listening to the whirring of insects. Marlo's hands were folded in her lap like stilled doves.

"You know," she said in a dreamy tone, "when I was growing up, I used to think the bomb shelters were so exciting and romantic." She swiveled her head to look at him. "Isn't that crazy?"

He shook his head.

"I thought it would be so fun to live in one of them for a few weeks. Like camping. There was something about the candles and the canned food and the whole roughing-it thing . . . so different from our usual lives. Do you know what I mean? Of course you don't. You've only lived here as an adult. But for a kid, a sheltered, pampered little kid, let's face it, those bunkers and shelters were like a secret game. Now they just make me shiver."

"Marlo . . ."

"I'd rather kill myself than live underground like that. Hoarding life while the rest of humanity is dying horribly. Waiting for . . . what?"

Kenneth looked at her pleadingly. She knew he thought her cruel, to sit here with him like this outside her house, stringing along the moments he had to spend listening to her when he was so eager to get inside and destroy the one romantic relationship she had ever valued.

"Well, what are we waiting for?" she said, flashing him a smile bright like a knife. Kenneth almost fell in his keenness to get out of the car, although that may have just been a newfound desire to put a distance between the two of them. Funny how he wanted that now. It would have felt weird to knock on her own front door, so Marlo just opened it and walked in, calling ahead to Wolf as a kind of warning.

"Hey, baby," he called back.

"I have someone with me," Marlo announced as she arrived at the lounge room, where Wolf sat with his laptop open, thankfully dressed and engaged in nothing more compromising than staring at a screen. He looked up in anticipation, his face softening with affection, his mouth open to say something that would remain forever unspoken. Wolf's gaze moved from Marlo to Kenneth, who was standing behind her in the doorway, his chafed hands hanging at his sides, his face twisting in miniature spasms. Then Wolf looked back at Marlo, and there was something new in his face. He blinked rapidly, like a sputtering transmission. Then he collected himself, managed a thin smile.

"Kenneth. What a nice surprise."

He got to his feet, scraping back the chair with a jarring screech. Perhaps subconsciously needing to be on their level. Marlo, for all that she was an innocent party here, couldn't help feeling a Judas. *I'm sorry,* she mouthed to him, but he didn't seem to see her. It was as though she were no longer in the room: it was just the two of them now, the man who loved her and the man who hated the man who loved her. Wolf gave an almost irritated shake of his head. His dark hair flopped over his forehead, and Marlo had to resist reaching out a hand to push it back.

"What is this?" he asked, politely enough, but there was something behind the words, a warning directed at Kenneth. Marlo looked over at Kenneth, raised an eyebrow to indicate she wasn't about to come to his rescue. This was his bed, and he would be required to lie in it. She'd never seen him look nervous before. His left hand tapped out a tattoo against his thigh. He cleared his throat, and she winced; it sounded so loud in that suddenly silent room.

"Hey, so Marlo and I were just having a little talk. That night you first arrived at the ranch. We were just wondering, how is it you came to be here again?"

Wolf ran his tongue along his bottom teeth, looked from Kenneth's face to Marlo's and back again.

"What the hell is this about? Marlo? You know this story."

She frowned down at the worn Turkish rug, wondering where it had come from in the first place. She'd had it for as long as she could remember but had no idea as to its provenance. Strange. She couldn't bear to look at Wolf or to answer him. She wished he would just answer in some way that was both satisfactory to Kenneth and exculpatory, so they could all get on with their lives.

"Kind of weird that Marlo's parents made such a huge exception in letting you stay. A stranger. No money, no ties to the community."

"Why don't you just get whatever it is off your chest, Kenneth? What are you accusing me of, exactly?"

"I'm saying you had an agreement with Marlo's parents, to come and start a relationship with her. Get married, start a little family. You know, the plan that seems to be shaping up nicely."

"You're crazy, Kenneth."

"Yeah, that's what she said too. At first."

Wolf turned to Marlo pleadingly. "Marlo, babe? You don't believe this crap, do you? He's insane. He's always had a thing for you. Don't you see? He's just trying to turn us against each other!"

She swallowed. The situation was horrible, sickening, the kind of thing she'd tried to avoid her whole life. These tawdry soap opera scenes. But the moment seemed to require some contribution from her, so she said quietly in Wolf's direction:

"So that's not what happened?"

"No, of course not!" It should have heartened her to see that he appeared so genuinely outraged, a flush spreading across the sharp planes of his cheekbones. But something had begun to grow in her, a toxic seed Kenneth had planted. She felt caught in its thrall, obliged to see it through to harvest.

"You'd never been in touch with my parents before you arrived here?"

"No." But he hesitated just a second too long. That was when she knew.

"So if I were to interrogate my parents, they wouldn't corroborate Kenneth's theory, right? You know they hate lying to me. They always give in."

He stared, incredulous. "I can't believe you're actually going to believe this motherfucker's story." The heat of his righteous anger soothed her doubt a little.

"I'd just like to hear you say it's not true."

"Come on, Marlo, this is crazy . . ." But it was obvious now to everyone, that he hesitated to actually say it. To lie to her. She watched panic seep into his face. She turned away from him, almost crashed into Kenneth, who had positioned himself behind her like a protector.

"Get the fuck out of my way," she said low and dangerous, pushed past him and vaguely registered his face, frozen in shock, his mouth hanging open. Then she was out of the house, stumbling over a rock in the grass and almost going down, then inside her car where the keys luckily dangled in the ignition. She was peripherally aware of people shouting, of movement as someone approached the vehicle, but she refused to even look and see whether it was Kenneth or Wolf. At that moment they struck her as equally worthless. She spun the steering wheel breathlessly, turned up the volume on the music so that a throbbing beat filled the cabin, and with tires skidding on the pebble drive, headed to the home of her parents.

❧

The river was in full voice, swelled by recent rains. She sat on the pebbly bank, jeans rolled up to her knees, dangling her feet in the water. Their solid form wavered beneath the surface, pale and insubstantial like the ghosts of legs. The shock of the water, rarely warmed by the sun beneath the shade of this tree, so cold the breath caught in her throat. She'd chosen this part of the river because it was as far from the civilization of the ranch as one could get while still fenced in. The stone wall, which had gradually blurred into benign abstraction over the last few happy months, suddenly loomed concrete and sinister again.

She knew that sooner or later someone would track her down here. She was resigned to that. Even on a property this vast you couldn't stay lost forever. Who would it be? Kenneth, possibly. (He had looked genuinely scared as she had passed him in the house, as if he hadn't fully thought through the consequences of his little revenge fantasy.) Wolf, probably. Her mother and father, perhaps. Although their modus operandi suggested a more considered approach, their daughter's disappointment just another problem to be puzzled over and litigated until a satisfactory solution could be arrived at. It made her weary to think of it.

She flicked her toes at a curious silvery minnow that came boldly close to take an experimental nip at her foot. It darted away, flashing in a shaft of light, then almost instantly returned, hovering in the current close to her instep as if finding her proximity irresistible. Marlo sighed, fanned her hands out over her forehead, and pressed, savoring the momentary lightless oblivion to be found in her palms. She was upset her parents had told her everything right away rather than trying to deny it. Denial would surely have been galling, but their eager willingness to swamp her with the truth wasn't much better in the end. She suspected confronting them had offered a welcome salve for their guilty consciences. Everyone always wants to confess, she thought bitterly. There's an exquisite relief to finally getting it all off your chest. It's the ones being confessed *to* who suffer the most.

Everything Kenneth had said was true: her parents *had* invited Wolf there so he could be a potential mate for her. When he contacted them, distraught after the death of his father, they had felt bad for him, but that had been the end of the story. It was only after they decided to invite him to come and stay for a while that they saw the opportunities for a friendship with Marlo, their lonely daughter, the last of the line. (Naturally they didn't say it in those words.) At first their only thought was for the boy's welfare, they swore. Wolf's parents had been their dear friends once, after all. Offering him temporary shelter was the least they could do.

"At what point did you decide to offer up your daughter as a bonus introductory gift?" she had asked them, savage with hurt. That had made them blanch, but they had quickly recovered. It helped, she realized, to be so secure in the unassailable rightness of your own convictions.

"It wasn't like that, sweetheart. You must know that. We just saw Wolf as a potential friend, at first. We knew how much you missed Ben and Alex."

Marlo was startled to realize this was the first time she'd heard her parents mention Ben's and Alex's names since they had left the ranch. There was something almost creepy about how readily the residents had erased her friends. Yet it must have been something the two of them had discussed, that with Ben and Alex gone, their daughter was in danger of slipping into an acute, dangerous solitude. They had figured that Wolf might make up for the absence of her friends, and that perhaps in time he might even convince her to stay.

"So you told him this was your plan. Wolf. That he'd be a kind of friend-for-hire for your daughter?"

This was the question she'd been dreading asking them, and perhaps they'd dreaded it too, this shift from the general to the personal, because a swift uncomfortable look passed between them. Her father cleared his throat.

"Well, I wouldn't use those words exactly. But yes, it's fair to say we mentioned you to him. An incentive, if you will, to encourage him to leave his, uh, bad situation in LA, and perhaps start a new life here."

"An incentive." A horrible thought occurred to Marlo for the first time. "You didn't . . . send him pictures of me or anything like that, did you?"

They didn't look at each other this time, but she noticed their postures stiffen ever so subtly.

"Of course not, honey," Maya said smoothly, and it was like a dagger in Marlo's chest to know her mother was lying.

"You pimped me out. Like breeding stock."

They fell over one another to object strenuously, both of them rising and coming to her side of the table to engulf her in love, to assure her with words and gestures that she had never been anything but loved, that everything they had ever done—up to and including this admittedly dubious thing—had been driven purely by love. She submitted to their smothering concern, but she felt cold inside.

"And after all," her mother said in her best soothing tone when they had emerged from their familial huddle, "it's not like we made the two of you fall in love. You did that of your own accord, honey. It all worked out in the end."

That they really believed this made her feel a new sadness for them. She had excused herself and gone to the bathroom then, sat on the closed toilet lid for a few bleak, unthinking minutes and then taken her leave, assuring them that she was feeling better and would see them soon. She was sure they had believed her, were perhaps even congratulating themselves on how well it had gone, all things considered. The bridal magazines retrieved from the bottom drawer, plans for the future restarted, like a factory that had suffered a calamity but was now back in full production. Then she had ridden her bike out to the river.

Her features screwed up with shame to remember how fervently and eagerly she had believed in the fiction that Wolf had just "arrived" at the ranch, a mysterious stranger turning up on their doorstep on a rainy night. No pharaoh's daughter had ever been more eager to take in a stranded innocent than Marlo had been to nurture her Moses back to health.

There was a thick, fraying rope looped several times around the gargantuan oak bough that dipped toward the water. The rope hung still, unmoved by the breeze, the whole tableau stark and creepy as a gallows. A little shiver passed over her flesh. It was time. Wolf wasn't coming to find her. No cavalry would be cresting the hill. The riverbank was cold and sharp beneath her thighs, now stippled with goose bumps. The light slanting through the leaves felt chilly, unfriendly all of a sudden. She scrambled to her feet, brushed away the tiny pebbles embedded in her palms. She slipped a little in her espadrilles as she climbed the bank to the grass. Retrieving her phone from her bike basket, she typed a quick message to Ben and Alex.

OK, I'll do it.

It felt like one of the river stones had lodged in her chest as she righted the bike and pedaled slowly back home.

28

When she woke she couldn't work out at first why her jaw was so sore. Then she realized it was aching from grinding her teeth through the night. The bed felt huge and empty without him in it, the sheets adhering in patches to her clammy skin. She pulled on a sweatshirt, went to the kitchen and started coffee, cut up the fruit as though it was just a normal day. She performed a few sun salutations to get the blood flowing properly into her brain. Scrolled through the music collection and chose a Leonard Cohen album. When the coffee was ready, she sipped at it, wincing at the sudden bitterness. She pushed the plate of fruit away, her stomach roiling.

Since the confrontations of yesterday she had been cycling through stages of anger and disappointment: first at Kenneth, then her parents, then Wolf, then herself. But as the other injuries lessened, her self-contempt blossomed. The whole situation stemmed, after all, from her own naivete, her foolish willingness to interpret the world through the prism of her own fantasies. She had longed for a purpose to justify her continued existence on the ranch; she had longed for love, secretly perhaps even desired rescue. And Wolf's arrival had so neatly provided the answer to those lacks. She got up suddenly, turned the music off with an irritated shiver. What was she doing listening to music from her parents' era, anyway? It suddenly occurred to her that she had borrowed her entire worldview, had ceded her autonomy, in favor of convenience. Need a philosophy? Here's one ready-packaged for you! Is it time for a boyfriend? Let your parents pick one for you! She spoke three foreign languages—two of them passably well—and yet knew next to nothing about the world outside these walls. Perhaps if she'd ever experienced life in the Disaster she might have been equipped with the tools to deal with more personal kinds of disaster.

There was a persistent itch under her skin that compelled her to get up and walk around, although she couldn't think for the life of her how to start this day. She drifted through the rooms of her house like the ghost of her former self. When she got to the front room, she pushed aside the gauzy curtain and stared out the window, but nothing moved out there. No returning soldier limped along the path. An intuition told her that Wolf had already left. She felt a new absence. It loomed in the blank chalk of the sky, in the drooping leaves of the chestnut. The ominous stillness before a calamity. Of course he had left, no doubt ashamed of the role he had played in her humiliation. She felt a quick hot rush of longing for him, picturing him back in the all-black ensemble in which he'd first appeared, ragged backpack hoisted over one shoulder, disobedient hair tufting in all directions, sticking his thumb out by the side of the lonely highway.

She was so caught up in this romantic, tragic vision that it took her a while to register the fact that the actual, corporeal Wolf was even now approaching her front door. He was on foot as she'd imagined, walking slowly with his chin tilted toward his chest and eyes on the ground, like he was searching for something. Marlo quickly stepped away from the porthole window. The choice before her was jarring. Within moments she would be required to either hide or speak with him. Instinctively she smoothed her hair, moved to the nearest mirror to check her face.

Every nerve and fiber of her being tensed, waiting for his knock at the door. But nothing happened as the seconds and minutes dripped by. She leaned over cautiously to see whether he'd chickened out and was walking away, but the path was empty. He must have been just standing there outside her door. Finally she couldn't stand the tension anymore and went and opened the door to him, stood there with hip jutted out. He looked up, and she almost laughed, his face was so pitiful.

"Hi," he mouthed.

"Hi." She didn't think it through, just put her arms around him and hugged him. She could feel the gratitude for this unexpected kindness vibrating through him. His hands clenched her lower back so tightly she would later find little grape-shaped bruises tattooed on her spine. "OK, that's enough," she protested finally with a short laugh, when it became apparent Wolf had no intention of honoring the socially sanctioned time frame for hugs. "Do you want to come in?"

She turned briskly, without waiting for a response, and strode down the hallway. The kitchen felt like the most neutral zone in which to perform the required vivisection, but she felt tired at the thought of it. He followed her there, and they stood facing one another across the endless terrain of her expensive tiled floors. She didn't offer him anything. Her only strong conviction at that moment was this: the time for refreshments was behind them. Wolf appeared to be waiting for her to speak first, so finally she crossed her arms and said, "So." That syllable seemed to shake him out of whatever torpor he was stuck in, because he gave a little shake of his head and retreated to one of the stools, letting his hands hang between his bent knees.

"So I'm not here to say sorry. I realize that would just be insulting. But I thought I should tell you some things before you make your final judgment on the whole saga. Get the story straight."

She shrugged as though it was immaterial to her either way, but part of her was curious, how his story would line up with what her parents had told her. She came and joined him at the bench, hugged her arms around her torso.

"There are some, uh, details I didn't tell you about my dad dying." He looked under his eyelashes at her and she nodded to signal he should go on. "I saw him spiraling into this dark place, you know, not just the weed-growing and dealing but the paranoia, the depression. I was desperate, and there was no one around to help."

"So you contacted my parents? Complete strangers?"

"Yeah, like I said, I was kind of running out of sensible options. So I wrote to them, pleading Dad's case, asking if they'd consider allowing me and Dad to move to the ranch, even though it was against protocol. I didn't tell them what was going on, but I hinted at the fact that Dad was unraveling and that I needed to get him to a safe place, kind of tried to play on their sympathy, any sense of loyalty and friendship they still had."

"And they turned you down?"

"Yeah. I mean, they were nice about it, explained the rules of the ranch and said that if it were up to the two of them, we'd be warmly welcomed, but that the rest of the community would never allow it. And it wouldn't be fair. All that crap."

"OK."

"Then after Dad died I wrote to them again. I wanted to let them know my father was dead . . . I said it was a car accident. It was a dick move. I knew it would make them feel bad, but I was all kinds of messed up, and I wanted them to feel bad too. I didn't expect anything more to come out of it. But they wrote back saying they felt terrible about it and then out of the blue they offered for me to come and live with them on a trial basis. I couldn't believe it . . . after all that had happened, holding out on my dad, and then changing their minds now that he was gone. I have to admit I kind of hated them for that. I asked why they'd changed their minds. They said they had a proposal for me. They said there was one condition of joining the ranch, which was that I provided some companionship for their daughter. They used that word, *companionship*. They said that you'd been lonely since your friends had left the ranch and that they worried about you not having any friends your own age.

"I know, I should have told them to fuck off, that I wasn't some kind of friend-for-hire, or more like fuckboy-for-hire." She tried to swallow down a smile, to hold on to her ebbing resentment for a while longer. "But I swear I didn't know that then. I figured you were some kind of spoiled brat, some sheltered kid who wouldn't know anything about life."

"Thank god that didn't turn out to be the case." They smiled wanly at one another.

"I didn't even write back to your parents. The whole thing just seemed so ludicrous. But then I ended up basically on the run in California, and I panicked. The ranch suddenly seemed like, I don't know, a desperate last resort. I didn't know what it was going to be like. I figured I'd come along, lay low for a while here, siphon as much out of your folks as I could, and then split. I figured they owed me, for what happened to my dad, and I'd just stay for the minimum amount of time until I could get my shit together. I fully expected that everyone at the ranch was going to be called, I don't know, Leaf or Waterfall, and that you'd be making your own peanut butter and having drum circles. But then I got here, and, well, you know the rest. I never expected to like you as much as I did. Or the ranch itself. Or your parents. Like, I wanted to hate them, but instead I ended up loving them like they were my own parents. Like the parents I never had."

As he spoke, something dawned on her. "So you're saying Mom and Dad weren't actually expecting you that night you turned up?"

"No. Definitely not. I think they were as shocked as everyone else in the end. I'm sure they never thought I'd actually come. You should go easy on them."

"Hmm." Marlo shot him a cynical look. "They sure leapt into action pretty quickly to cover up that they knew you. They *sure were* enthusiastic about paying for you to stay around."

Wolf looked abashed.

"Anyway, I didn't want you to find out that way. I told you Kenneth was a jerk."

"Oh, so Kenneth's the jerk? And you were of course planning to tell me about this . . . this arrangement you had with my parents?"

"Of course, sooner or later." He looked wounded she'd even think otherwise. "I felt so guilty about it once I met you, and we, well, got together. I fell in love with you, and that's when I knew I was fucked. That one day you'd find out and never want to see me again. And I totally get it. I'd feel the same way. The thing is, after I left LA, I had days where I was suicidal. I would have done anything, agreed to anything. It was so wrong of me, but I never really intended to honor the agreement with your folks. I was just a cynical asshole."

"So I guess that makes everything alright, then."

"No, no, of course not. I'm just trying to tell you the truth. There's something else too."

"Oh, great."

"Not to do with you. To do with something I did, before I got here."

"What is it? You may as well tell me. It's not like it matters now."

He looked around the room in a panic of uncertainty, perhaps still debating whether there was anything left to keep back, or to barter. Or to salvage. Then, with a long whistling sigh, he plunged in.

"You know that time I told you that I thought I killed somebody?"

"Um, yeah. It was kind of hard to forget."

"Well. I passed it off as a joke at the time, but I was serious. When I was trying to run away from the police, I . . . I hit someone. With my car. And then I left."

She swallowed, tried to get her voice right. "Who did you hit? Did they die?"

"The thing is, I don't know. I just felt the thump and saw something, at least I think I saw something, a black shape limping away. I was so scared and I was a little bit high and paranoid . . . My dad had just been killed by the cops for dealing drugs, for fuck's sake, and I just kept driving. I never saw anything about it on the news. I looked for weeks afterward. And the car . . . Well, it was such a shitbox that I couldn't even tell whether the dents in the fender and the front panels were from that night or some other time. The car was all rusted up, and maybe there were a few little streaks that could have been blood or not, it was just so hard to tell. I put it through the car wash three times to be sure. God, Marlo." He cradled his forehead in his hands. "I have nightmares all the time."

"Maybe it was just a deer."

"That's what I tried to tell myself. But the thing is, I knew that corner. There was a guy, a homeless dude, who was always hanging around near that corner. I'd seen him staggering around before, close to the road. He was always pretty out of it, mountain man hair, pants held up with string, the whole bit. But that's where it happened. Right near there."

"But you don't know that it was him. Or even anyone at all."

"No. I don't know for sure." But she could tell he was sure in his heart. That the possibility had eroded his ability to be happy, had carved those shadows beneath his eyes. In the end it was this certainty, and the burden it must have been to carry around, that finally enabled her to let him back in. She had to forgive someone, and she chose him. She reached over impulsively and slicked a lock of his hair to the side. He didn't react, slumped inside his cage of misery.

"I've never told anyone that."

"I'm so sorry, Wolf. If it helps, I don't believe you killed anybody." She continued stroking his hair, then his shoulder, his leg, letting her affection for him flow back through her veins. It was like a limb being released finally from a cast, the blessed relief of a return to feeling. "I think you were just in a distressed state, and it made you think you saw something you didn't. Kind of like a mirage. A manifestation. Because you felt so guilty about everything."

For a moment, she regretted the words. Wasn't this letting him—and herself—off the hook a little too easily? Absolving him from the potential crime of hitting someone, or something, with his car, could be construed as a blanket forgiveness for everything he had done. Maybe she was allowing herself to be deceived, yet again. To let her own comfort and peace of mind override doing what she knew was right, no matter how uncomfortable it might be. All the more reason to try to make amends now. She had stayed on the ranch too long, and she was ready this time.

"I don't deserve this," he said, grasping her free hand and smothering it with kisses. "Don't deserve you."

"Well, that's the thing."

His eyes shot up to study her face.

"What?"

"I'm leaving."

His sharp Adam's apple bobbed in his throat. "Leaving me?"

"Leaving here."

She was surprised to read the shock on his face. So he hadn't guessed that this might be one of the possible outcomes of Kenneth's little confrontation. Perhaps he'd expected to be banished himself. Or there would be a blowup and then a reconciliation, harmony restored. Strange to not really know each other at all, in the end.

"But you can't," he protested, eyes wide and imploring, as he grappled with a child's logic: *if I don't want something to happen, how can it be so?* She laughed with closed mouth, as if the statement wasn't worthy of a spoken response. He tried another tack. "I just mean with everything that's happening out there. You'd rather hazard the Disaster than stay here with me?"

She sighed in irritation. "This might be a news flash, my love, but not everything is about you."

That arrow found its mark. His eyes went bright with hurt.

"I never said it was."

"Listen," she said, more softly now. "I wanted to leave long before you arrived. And now that all this has happened, I want to leave again.

It's not personal." She instantly regretted saying that, when all he wanted was for it to be personal. "I just mean I need to get out of here. See the world. I've been living in this bubble for far too long."

"See the world," he repeated in a voice thick with bitterness. "Be sure to send a postcard. Maybe of some burning tire fires?"

"Very funny. Easy for you to dismiss something you've always taken for granted."

"Touché, babe," he said with a small grin, and she could see this lover's banter was already making him feel better. If only it were working that way on her, instead of settling like iron in her soul as she knew she'd have to leave all this behind. Later she'd wonder if it was this sentimental moment of weakness that guided her onto his lap and her mouth onto his and a few minutes later into urgent gyrations with clothes peeled half-off against the kitchen bench, her legs wrapped around his torso and her lower vertebrae grating against the marble edge as he pushed himself into her with a force that felt both tender and scouring. A mortification of the flesh. Afterward they stayed in that awkward position for a moment, panting and sweating with garments hanging and bunched around extremities, like some kind of ragged beasts, then they both burst into wordless laughter at the fact that something so absurd could also feel right and true.

She had always prided herself on being able to ruthlessly divorce sex from decision-making, so it couldn't have just been their coital reunion that drove her when they were sitting together later cross-legged on the lounge room floor, glasses of wine in hand, to ask whether he'd like to leave with her. Where had the words come from? Perhaps she subconsciously aimed to test where his loyalties lay.

"Really? You really want to be with me after everything?"

She took a deep draught of wine, the kind she knew would leave feathery stains around her mouth. It didn't seem important.

"Well, I think marriage is kind of off the table now. And kids. But that was all kind of a silly idea, anyway. More for Mom and Dad's sake than anything." It turned out she couldn't resist a final little dig at his pride. She needed him to know how much he had wounded her. No matter how much she still desired him, the rift between them wasn't going to be magically healed by one roll around the Turkish carpet. It would take time, maybe years. Sobering to think they might not have that long.

"Yeah, I deserve that." He glared into his glass.

"But if you want to help us out there, an extra body certainly wouldn't go astray."

His eyes narrowed. "Wait. Who's us?" Although surely he had already guessed.

"Alex and Ben. I'm going out to join them. Get involved."

"Ah." He sat for a while, forefinger circumnavigating the rim of his glass as he grappled with this new and surely undesirable turn of events. "I see. The fearless ass-kicking activists."

She grinned, flashed him a cheeky peace sign. He smiled, but the expression was devoid of joy. She slumped across the floor and grabbed at his ankle. "It'll be fine, Wolfie. They know what they're doing. And you won't be just a warm body. Well, you will, but you'll be *my* warm body. I want you there. You're my guy." Her voice cracked on the last word.

"Well, I guess I don't have a choice, then."

"Damn straight."

He pulled her into his chest, squeezed her arm solemnly, and they lapsed into silence, locked inside their separate thoughts, together but walled off.

🍃

Later. Hot limbs tangled in clammy sheets. The sting of morning light through the curtains they'd forgotten to close. She sat up on one elbow, squinted into his face, and took up their conversation where they'd left off the previous night.

"Oh, there's one condition. You have to help me with something before we leave."

"Uh-oh." He grimaced and rubbed his face, groggy with sleep. "Is this where you go all Bonnie and Clyde on me?"

"What? No. I just need you to help me, uh, take something."

An eyebrow shot up. He was fully awake now. "Steal something, you mean?"

She gave a lazy shrug to suggest the distinction was purely academic. She stretched her legs like a cat, pointed her arched feet toward the wall as if she might be able to reach, while pretending not to notice his hungry gaze on her body.

"So, do I get to know what it is that we're *taking*, my queen?"

"Nope. Not until we get it out of here."

He licked his lips, thinking, then his face lit up. "It's the mausoleum! Right? We're taking what's in there." When she nodded he looked pleased to have figured it out. Then he frowned. "But it's something that doesn't belong to you. Something valuable to the ranch."

"Bingo."

He ran a hand across his stubbled jaw. She'd always hated that sound, like fingernails on a blackboard.

"Fine, OK. I'll help. Tell me what you need."

❧

They decided to wait for a week. A barbecue was scheduled for the following weekend, and Marlo declared this occasion the perfect cover for their stealth departure. Barbecues were the most popular group occasions, and they could be reasonably assured that most of the residents would be happily occupied there. They agreed it was important to act normal in the interim, so they continued their assigned chores, and

Marlo scheduled dinner with her parents. It was easier to busy herself with preparations than to think about it as the last time she might see her parents for a long time, perhaps ever. Whenever the thought insisted on surfacing, she held it under until it stopped moving. She knew if she began to worry about her father's health, about the hole her leaving would blow in their lives, she might lose her nerve altogether.

On the night she dined for the last time with them, she went alone. They were extra solicitous of her, perhaps trying to atone for their role in luring Wolf to the ranch. It was clear from the moment she entered the house that what had happened would never be referred to again except obliquely and in carefully neutral, passive terms—"That time we had the trouble over Wolf" or "Your husband's unorthodox arrival at the ranch." That was their family tradition, to lay enough rhetorical bandages over the wounds that you eventually forgot what was under them.

Marlo had always hated saying goodbye but had been blessed by so rarely being in a position to have to say it. So it was a relief when she and Wolf decided together that she shouldn't forewarn her parents of her departure. They would never understand, would try to talk her out of it, would hijack her resolve with their consuming love. She hated it, but it had to be this way.

"I'll send them a message to explain everything as soon as we're far enough away from the ranch," Marlo had assured Wolf, although of course the assurance was more for her own sake. "I know they'll understand." *Understand* being code for *forgive*. Wolf had just nodded sympathetically, a little ruefully. She knew he'd miss her parents almost as much as she would, despite everything.

She made an excuse to leave early after her dinner with them. They were both in an ebullient mood—clearly thrilled that the schism in the family unit had been repaired, and so neatly!—and this oblivious joy threatened to upend her firm resolve. There was no point drawing it out.

"I'll see you soon," she called as she moved out of the sheltering light of the portico and into the darkness. Her parents were just silhouettes now, two waving blurs in the doorway. *We'll come back often,* she promised herself silently. But there were tears blurring her vision as she walked away.

❦

Even from so far away they could smell the flinty richness of a newly lit fire. A sustainably raised and humanely slaughtered local pig laid up in the walk-in fridge. Field mushrooms and rounds of Brie that would be swaddled in aluminum foil and shoved deep into the coals for the vegetarians. Someone had festooned the oaks with strings of tiny lights. After all the bad news, it was time for some innocent, uncomplicated pleasure.

Within Marlo, opposing desires grappled. The longing to stay, of course, to smooth over the wrinkled future before it even happened—it wasn't too late, after all, to abort the plan. They could turn up to the barbecue hand in hand, the wedding back on, join the revelry, and commit themselves to life in the community. No one but she and Wolf would ever have to know. (She was certain he was secretly pulling for this outcome.) But the other desire, grimmer though it was, burned stronger. To fling herself out of the only world she'd really known and exchange it for life in the Disaster, whatever kind of life that would be.

They spent the day packing the things they'd be taking with them—clothes, of course, toiletries, their computers and phones and gadgets, a few books. In contrast to the accelerating energy of the atmosphere building outside the walls—Marlo heard someone testing fireworks and high-pitched voices whooping from the nearby forest—the mood was subdued inside her house. There was a defeated slump to Wolf's back as he bent over the duffel splayed open on the bed. The pained smile he'd stretch his mouth into whenever she caught his eye. Knowing she was snatching away her boyfriend's nascent happiness in the only place he'd ever considered home was almost enough to make her reverse course. But then she reminded herself sternly of how he had colluded with her parents, and she zipped the feeling back up again. So they stalked through the hours mostly in silence, marinating in their separate misgivings.

The day conspired to be both lightning fast and interminable. By the time twilight was smearing the windows, it was almost a relief to have it upon them. From here on out it was all logistics, with no wiggle room for the disorder of emotion. After they had finished packing their things into the car, Marlo sent a short message to her parents, explaining that she had a migraine and would try to join the barbecue later on, but not to worry if she didn't show up early. She knew this wouldn't buy them much time, but even minutes counted now. She signed off with assurances that she loved them, hoping this wouldn't tip them off—she often signed off that way. The sense of her own good fortune fluttered again across her consciousness: Wolf, silently going about his undesired work, had never taken love and security for granted the way she had. Did that make it easier or harder when the time came for casting free? The blood thumped in her skull, but she felt strangely calm as she went about the business of leaving.

The fear ratcheted up as the riskiest moment grew closer. She hadn't fully initiated Wolf into her subterfuge, had just told him there was something they needed to take with them and that none of the other ranchers could know. She had brought along a duffel bag stuffed with clothes, but she didn't stop to explain what was inside to Wolf—she gathered from his queasy expression he assumed there were weapons. The first move was to disable the security camera pointed at the mausoleum. She was fairly sure no one monitored the footage, that it was used more as a deterrent at this stage, although who they thought it was deterring was a mystery. Did they really think thieves roamed these woods, waiting for their chance to pounce? Soon enough they'd know where the real danger had been lurking—but it was better not to take any chances.

Wolf stood guard alongside the marble entrance, spotlit by a single solar lamp that came on automatically when darkness fell. His demeanor a universe away from nonchalant, neck swiveling and dark eyes darting around the clearing, as Marlo shinnied up the trunk of the oak that leaned over the storage shed facing the mausoleum and unscrewed the camera from its mount. She imagined a blinking eye in some fluorescent room. They shot a look at one another, breath stilled, waiting for . . . what? Black-clad men to rush the clearing? Shouts as someone sent up the alarm that the security system had been breached? But nothing happened. Leaves rustled and whispered peevishly overhead. The poignant sound of happy faraway voices carried to them on the breeze.

"What now?" Wolf said under his breath. Beads of sweat stood out on his forehead.

"We go inside."

Funny how he had always been so obsessed with the contents of the mausoleum, but now that he stood at the threshold, its secrets moments away from being revealed, he looked as though he was going to throw up. Like he would have paid good money to be anywhere but here. Marlo squeezed his arm, as much for her own comfort as his.

"Keep an eye out," she said, dropping a kiss on the neat shell of his ear.

She walked briskly toward the decorative urn, crouched down and removed the lid, and, wrinkling her nose a little, plunged her arm inside. Wolf's eyes widened. He stared at her, all guarding duties abandoned, as she rummaged around inside. Finally she found it, slipped her arm out of the urn, and held the key up triumphantly, black ash sifting through her fingers and floating down around her like flakes of radioactive snow. The key was the backup part of gaining entrance: first she needed to punch in a code into the digital panel by the side of the door. When it glowed green she inserted the key into the old-fashioned lock and turned it, feeling somewhat absurd about the unnecessary drama of it, until she looked over her shoulder at Wolf, whose face glowed with wonder.

"Just a warning: we can't stay in here for long."

"Why?"

"You'll see. Here, put these on."

She unzipped the bag, pulled out gloves, hats, and two bulky coats with fur-lined hoods, and began to dress herself quickly. He hesitated for only a moment before pulling his own gear on. By the time they were done, they looked like two sumo wrestlers, and sweat was already beginning to prickle inside Marlo's collar. She gestured for him to follow, and they approached the mausoleum.

Marlo locked the heavy door behind them, and they stood for a moment in the entrance, letting their eyes adjust to the inky darkness. There was no adjusting to the cold, though, which swept across their exposed faces in an unholy wave. It was like entering a giant walk-in deep freeze. They huddled together for a moment. Even Marlo had rarely been inside the mausoleum. Not only had its contents never been her purview, as a kid she had been frightened of its inescapable associations with death and decay—in spite of its real purpose. Marlo removed a glove, pulled out her phone, and switched on the flashlight, trained it around the long, narrow room, which vibrated with a low electrical hum. The room was lined floor to ceiling with aluminum shelves, each stacked with narrow black boxes.

Wolf gazed around, uncomprehending. She squeezed his gloved hand.

"A freezer," he said after a while, his words frosting in the air. A thermometer on the wall read minus twenty degrees Celsius. His voice sounded strange, canned. There were no echoes in that place.

"Kind of."

His forehead furrowed: Marlo understood that he didn't want to be told what was in there but needed to guess it for himself. So she waited, buzzing with impatience, as he took in his surroundings, propped her phone on the edge of a shelf facing the ceiling so that its beam cast a more central light, rhythmically rubbing her gloved hands together.

"Treasure," he said softly, but it didn't seem to be a question, at least not one for her. "Jewelry?" She could see how he might think that: the black boxes resembled the kind that jewelers use to display precious pieces. "Samples of something?" Getting warmer, she wanted to say, but she bit her tongue.

"Something alive?" This time he turned to her for confirmation, and she smiled affirmation. "OK. Cells? Human tissue? Animal tissue?" She stuck her tongue out at this idea, and then he yelled so loudly that she jumped: "Seeds!"

"Well done, Wolfie."

He looked around, face suffused with wonder again. "A doomsday seed vault. Like the ones that got raided."

"Exactly. On a smaller scale, but still."

"So . . ." His face clouded with confusion again for a moment as he pondered what exactly they were doing there, inside this place of death packed to the rafters with the raw ingredients for life. Then she saw it break over his eyes. "You're stealing them for Alex and Ben. So they can take them out into the Disaster."

She nodded but had to correct him. "*We're* stealing them."

"Fuck, Marlo. This is a huge deal. This is the ranch's insurance."

"Yeah, well, I'm not exactly thrilled to be in this position either. But this is what's happening." She had a lecture all prepared, a screed to justify the morality of stealing one community's future to shore up another's. But it would have to wait. "There's still time for you to pull out."

A flash of hurt tightened his mouth. "I didn't say that. This is the right thing, I get it. I want to go with you."

"Well, I'm glad. Let's start packing these up and loading them into the car. Ben says they should be fine out of temp control for a few hours, but we still need to hustle. They're picking us up at eight in some refrigerated truck they found."

Marlo ducked outside for a moment to make sure there was no one around, then they began the laborious process of gathering the seed trays—balancing as many as they could at once in teetering piles in their arms—and transferring them to the car. They ended up having to do several runs before all the trays were moved, and by the end they were both lathered with sweat and light-headed.

In the most casual voice she could manage, Marlo told Wolf to go on ahead, she'd catch up with him. After ensuring he was out of sight, she pulled one final tray from its hiding place behind the generator, placed it at eye level on the middle shelf, and stood for a moment looking at it. Inside was a layer of seeds, just one each of the important varieties. Over the last few months, she'd been sneaking in and adding seeds to the hidden tray, knowing she'd be unable to explain it away if she were caught. But she needed to leave them something. It felt like an act of penance.

She wasn't sure why she didn't want Wolf to know. Perhaps because he'd think her weak. Perhaps because it was such a meager gift, in the end. Almost insulting to all the people she loved; people who had trusted her.

Finally, she locked the door of the mausoleum behind her and replaced the key in the urn.

"Whose ashes are they?" Wolf asked when she got back to the car.

Marlo laughed at his expression as he valiantly struggled against disgust.

"No one's. They're just bonfire ashes. It was someone's bright idea to make it look like an authentic urn. In case anyone came sniffing around. Never mind that it wouldn't have passed any kind of real scrutiny. Cremated ashes don't look anything like this."

"Right. And the generator is there to keep the place cold. I always wondered what it was powering."

Straightening up, she impulsively lunged toward him, kissed him long and hard on the mouth. Their teeth clashed together, and she tasted the metallic tang of blood welling on her lip.

"Come on."

They drove back to the house, and Marlo texted Alex and Ben to let them know they were ready.

"They're almost here," she informed Wolf, and while she had meant to simply convey practical information, her voice unexpectedly cracked a little on the *here*. He stroked her arm wordlessly. She knew he regretted leaving, but that it was different for him, the pangs of a home newly acquired and lost in a different register from the keener anguish of severing the deep roots that bound her to this place. Perhaps she would never see her home again. Perhaps she would die out in the Disaster.

She buttoned her coat up, the good pale pink cashmere one she had bought on an impulse that time in San Francisco. Who knew where they might be headed or where they would end up, but it felt important to dress for this unknown future. Alex and Ben would definitely laugh at her in her expensive designer coat, affectionately call her Princess. Anticipating this moment made her smile, made her feel genuinely excited for the first time about joining them.

They drove slowly with the headlights off to the far eastern border of the property, the furthest location from the night's festivities and their rendezvous point with Alex and Ben. They'd packed a ladder to scale the wall, and it jutted comically out the back window like the setup for a scene of slapstick, the impediment occasionally catching on tree branches as they drove along the dirt road. There would be few satisfactory explanations if anyone saw them. Ranchers rarely used this road as a thoroughfare, as it led nowhere particularly useful, so the surface hadn't been graded in a while. The car jolted and bucked over uneven parts worn away by rain or cattle hooves. It put Marlo's teeth on edge, but there was something exhilarating as well about riding through the darkness, alive to the night in ways that tended to shrivel under the usual illumination.

It was that time of the evening when vision starts playing tricks, so when the form appeared suddenly out of the grainy dark, she and Wolf yelped in unison, unsure at first whether it was an animal, a human, or a phantasm or some other trickery. The figure loomed on the road in front of them. Marlo slammed her foot on the brake, and they skidded to a halt, the chassis rocking gently as the car settled.

"Jesus."

"Who is it?" Marlo asked, having retrieved enough composure to be fairly certain that the shape looming there was human. She leaned forward, shaded her forehead with her hand.

"Three guesses."

The bitterness in Wolf's voice tipped her off, and in that moment she realized there was no one else it could have been: that familiar bulk, the way he stooped, trying to take up less room but resenting that it was expected.

"Kenneth. Fuck."

"Just keep driving. Straight through him."

She glanced at Wolf, appalled to see he wasn't even joking. A nerve in his jaw twitched.

"Don't be crazy. I'm going to talk to him. You stay here."

Wolf licked his lips and nodded tersely, understanding if not approving of the fact that there was no choice but for her to face him. It would have looked too suspicious to drive past. They both had the presence of mind to resist looking over their shoulders to the precious cargo in the back, covered in only the most cursory way by a couple of blankets, a subterfuge that wouldn't have stood up to even the most casual scrutiny. As she stepped out of the car, heart hammering but wearing an expression that feigned innocent surprise, she hoped fervently that Kenneth wouldn't insist on looking inside the car. But why would he? Only someone who suspected the motives of two people driving in a deserted part of the ranch for no apparent reason would insist on such a thing.

"Hey, Kenneth," she called out. "What's up?"

He watched her approach, his eyes cloaked by the gathering darkness.

"Not much. What's up with you? Headed somewhere?"

She didn't like the tone of his voice. Didn't like the intense, almost excited way Kenneth stared past her into the car. Didn't like anything about this scenario.

"Just out for a drive?" he pressed on, smiling nastily. Marlo stood in the road and contemplated her old friend. She had to admire his tenaciousness.

"That's right. Is there something I can do for you?"

Her tone must have thrown him a little, because he shifted his feet and gazed away from her, mouthing something, as if working out his to-do list.

"You're leaving, aren't you." It wasn't even a question in the end. Marlo hesitated for a moment, then nodded. It was a relief not to hide it anymore. A storm gathered at the center of Kenneth's face. "With him?" he spat out, gesturing with disgust toward the car and Wolf, waiting. "After all he did."

"You didn't exactly act like a hero yourself, Kenneth."

He made a guttural sound that could have meant anything. "Your parents will be devastated, I hope you realize that." Pulling the last, desperate card out of the pack.

Marlo bowed her head. "I know." She reached out and grasped his arm. She could feel the muscles bound up and tensed beneath his skin, his worst self itching to be set free. "Tell them I'm sorry, will you? Tell them I love them and I'll be back someday." She thought of the stolen seeds in the back of the car, and of her parents' faces when they found out what she had done. The impossibility of returning. Kenneth shook her hand off.

"I could stop you, you know."

She sensed rather than saw that he had a gun hidden somewhere in his clothes. She took a step back, stumbling a little on the dirt and stones, and Kenneth reached out a hand to steady her, then reconsidered, pulled it back tight against his side. She could hear something happening behind her, a car door opening perhaps, Wolf calling out something. She wasn't afraid anymore, though. A new, reckless feeling engulfed her. *I'm not going to die on this road tonight,* she thought. *That's not what's in store for me.* She had never believed in fate, but it seemed tangible at that moment, certain as the ground beneath her feet.

She stepped toward Kenneth again, reached up—she had to stand on tiptoe—and embraced him. He stiffened, and she felt the phallic menace of the cold metal beneath his jacket, but then his muscles unclenched and his whole body softened, as if he were finally giving in to something that had been tormenting him. For an infinitesimal moment he allowed himself to bury his nose in her hair, his rough cheek laid against her smooth one. She could feel him breathing her in, then he was letting her go, pushing her roughly away, back toward the car and the life she had chosen.

"Go," he said hoarsely. "I'll cover for you, but not for long."

She ran then, in spite of knowing it would look bad to run, threw herself back in the car and gunned the accelerator, not even really looking to see where Kenneth was, just knowing he would stay out of the way, his final gift to her. Wolf stared at her, opened his mouth to speak, and then thought better of it. She laughed, a wild, hyena-like sound that contained particles of everything that roiled in her: grief, relief, euphoria.

But she grew somber again as the wall came into clear view. When she cut the engine and stepped out of the car, several sounds settled into clarity: a barn owl hooting; some kind of fast-tempo music, muffled as it traveled across the acres; and the thrum of a large engine, growing closer on the other side of the wall. Marlo knew there were only dirt roads on that side as well, cow tracks really, and she indulged a fretful moment worrying that Alex and Ben might get bogged down or stuck in a ravine. But soon the engine was loud enough that she could tell they were close, so loud it seemed likely the ranchers miles away could hear it. A cheeky, outrageously loud yodel went up on the other side, and car doors slammed. Marlo rolled her eyes and shook her head, but her blood felt hotter and more energized already.

"Hey!" she called back recklessly. Wolf grabbed her sleeve, but she shrugged him off. "We're coming!"

She ran around to the back of the car, and together she and Wolf wrestled the ladder out of the back, leaned it against the wall, and she climbed up with the first of the seed boxes pressed into her rib cage. She laid it carefully on top of the stones and then peeked over, saw the pale ovoids of Alex's and Ben's faces grinning up at her. Alex blew her a kiss, and Marlo laughed again like she was drunk.

"Love the work you've done around the place," called Ben, gesturing with mock appreciation at the wall. "Real carceral."

"Yeah," said Marlo. "Help me with these, will you?"

Resting her belly on top of the wall with her feet curled around the top rung of the ladder—Wolf held it steady below—she began to pass the trays down. They formed a mini production line, Alex grabbing the trays and passing them to Ben to slide into the back of the van, whose sides were emblazoned with some kind of mural that looked to Marlo in the half-light to depict crudely painted marine creatures.

"Cool ride," she panted.

"We're fishmongers, guv'nor," Alex chirped in a bad Cockney accent. "Fancy some haddock?"

"Ha. You couldn't have found something more conspicuous?"

It seemed like an eternity before they had all the seeds and their meager belongings loaded. Finally they were scaling the wall themselves and landing, in Marlo's case, in the outstretched arms of her friends. They moved for a moment in a fierce, tight circle, a shuffling, swaying six-legged creature that grunted out incoherent, joyous sounds before spinning off into three separate entities again. Wolf stood off to the side, watching, a small smile coming and going, coming and going. Marlo drew him over, and Alex and Ben hugged him as well, with only a slightly lessened ardor, and she saw that this was the role in which he had been cast for most of his life, the person who waited patiently on the sidelines for the diluted affection to ripple out to him.

All at once, her fear of leaving the ranch disappeared. A burning need engulfed her, to make communion with the Disaster, every fallow field and ravaged coastline. To help hold whatever lines remained to be held.

"Ready to rock and roll?" asked Alex, her wide-set blue eyes glinting in the moonlight. Marlo and Wolf nodded with varying degrees of sincerity. "Man, have we got a lot to fill you in on!"

They piled into the van, and Ben got behind the wheel, grinning and swiveling his head to wink at the two of them in the back seat, pressing on the accelerator without releasing the hand brake, revving the engine so that it protested and screamed, and dust plumed up all around the car, cloaking them in a red cloud. Perhaps his final act of defiance toward the ranch and the virtuous insularity he had long ago rejected.

Then they were away, the van bouncing along the uneven ground as Ben drove, so fast that sometimes they'd be briefly airborne as he passed over a hump in the land, the headlights bobbing and careening across the landscape, illuminating ditches and craggy rocks and the ghoulish silhouettes of trees. They reached the front edge of the ranch and the beginning of the well-lit, mile-long birch-lined paved road that led from the ranch to the highway, but Ben didn't swerve onto the road as Marlo had assumed he would, instead continuing parallel to it, so that anyone glancing out of a gate or watchtower wouldn't necessarily see a car at all.

The birches flickered as they passed in and out of the light, like an old television on the blink, and Marlo was so distracted by the hypnotic feeling of being afloat inside the membrane of the calamitous world, inside an unfamiliar van with some of the people dearest and most familiar to her, on her way to some potentially disastrous, but at least chosen, destiny, that she didn't even think to take one last look back at her home. So that fell to Wolf instead. He rolled down the window, stuck his head out of it like a dog gulping down the breeze and craned his neck to gaze back at the receding edges of the ranch, keeping his gaze fixed all the way until the road ended and Ben swung the van onto the highway, and the last of the birches disappeared from sight, and there was nothing left to look at but the road ahead.

ACKNOWLEDGMENTS

To my wonderful agent, Maggie Riggs, a true champion for new voices, whose enthusiasm, insight, and generosity helped shepherd this story into the world. To my brilliant editor, Vivian Lee, and the whole Little A team, for helping effect the small miracle of turning a bunch of words into a book.

To the MacDowell Colony, where the seed of this story was first planted, and the Wellstone Center in the Redwoods, where it was given the space to grow. To Elizabeth Penney and Julia Weber, who provided editing, guidance, and valuable early insights.

To my parents, Robert and Lyndall, who brought us up in a big, warm house full of books, and my dazzling sisters, Megan, Tatia, and Peta, and my niece, Emily, whose long-distance love and support mean the world.

To the dear friends whose encouragement and advice provided various lights in the darkness: Jennifer Paull, Dominic Tierney, Jane Barratt, Glenn McCulloch, Mark Ellwood, Sharon Krum, Carrie Seim, Gary DeRose, Laureen Vonnegut, and many others.

To the literary community on Twitter, whose wit, wisdom, solidarity, and exemplary literary citizenship provide constant inspiration and ruinous distraction from writing.

And to my husband, Adam, whose unflagging love and support, not to mention genius with storytelling, have made me an infinitely better writer and person.

ABOUT THE AUTHOR

Photo © Adam McCulloch

Emma Sloley began her career as a features editor at *Harper's BAZAAR Australia*, where she worked for six years. In 2004, she and her husband made the move to New York. As a freelance travel writer in NYC, she has appeared in many US and international magazines, including *Travel + Leisure*, *Condé Nast Traveler*, and *New York* magazine. She has also published fiction, short fiction, and creative nonfiction in literary publications such as *Catapult*, *The Masters Review Anthology*, and *Yemassee Journal*. Her work has been twice nominated for a Pushcart Prize, and she has received a fellowship from the MacDowell Colony, where she wrote her debut novel, *Disaster's Children*. Today she divides her time between the United States, Mexico, and various airport lounges. Visit her at www.emmasloley.com.